image comics presents

CHEW

created by John Layman & Rob Guillory

written & lettered by

John Layman

drawn & colored by

Rob Guillory

Color Assists by Taylor Wells

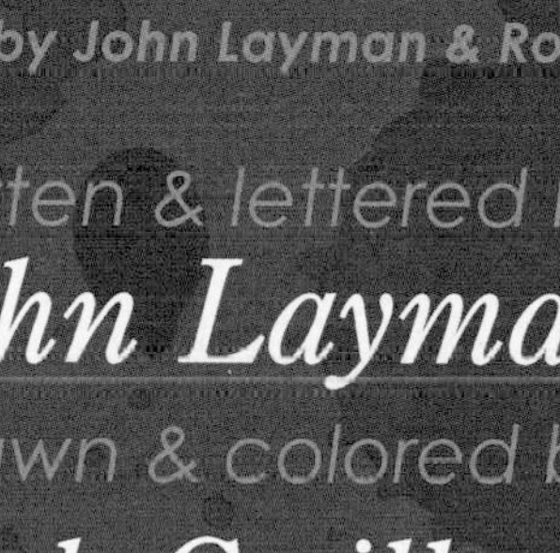

IMAGE COMICS, INC.

Robert Kirkman - chief operating officer
Erik Larsen - chief financial officer
Todd McFarlane - president
Marc Silvestri - chief executive officer
Jim Valentino - vice-president

Eric Stephenson - publisher
Todd Martinez - sales & licensing coordinator
Jennifer de Guzman - pr & marketing director
Branwyn Bigglestone - accounts manager
Emily Miller - accounting assistant
Jamie Parreno - marketing assistant
Jenna Savage - administrative assistant
Sarah deLaine - events coordinator
Kevin Yuen - digital rights coordinator
Jonathan Chan - production manager
Drew Gill - art director
Monica Garcia - production artist
Vincent Kukua - production artist
Jana Cook - production artist

www.imagecomics.com

CHEW, VOL. 6: SPACE CAKES. First printing. December 2012. Published by Image Comics, Inc. Office of publication: 2134 Allston Way, 2nd Floor, Berkeley, CA 94704. Copyright © 2012 John Layman. Originally published in single magazine form as CHEW #26-30, and CHEW: SECRET AGENT POYO #1, by Image Comics. All rights reserved. CHEW™, its logos, and all character likenesses herein are trademarks of John Layman, unless expressly indicated. Image Comics® and its logos are registered trademarks and copyright of Image Comics, Inc. All rights reserved. No part of this publication may be reproduced or transmitted, in any form or by any means (except for short excerpts for review purposes) without the express written permission of John Layman or Image Comics, Inc. All names, characters, events, and locales in this publication, except for satirical purposes, are entirely fictional, and any resemblance to actual persons (living or dead) or entities or events or places is coincidental or for satirical purposes. Printed in the U.S.A. For information regarding the CPSIA on this printed material call: 203-595-3636 and provide reference # RICH – 463229

For international licensing inquiries, write to: foreignlicensing@imagecomics.com   ISBN: 978-1-60706-621-7

Chapter 1

BUONGIOVANNI, U.
"POULET"
MIXED MEDIA.
2013.

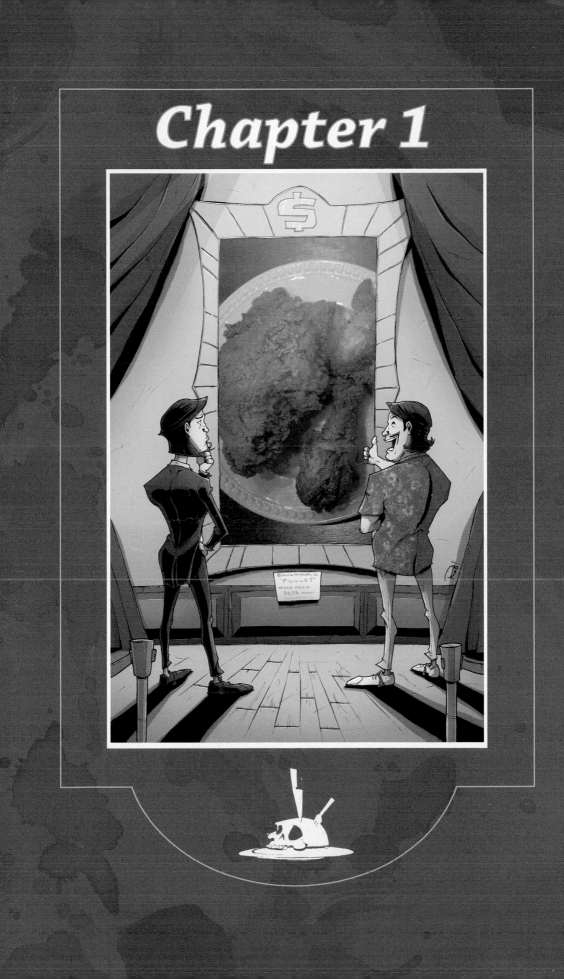

Dedications:

JOHN: *To Toni, with apologies.*

ROB: *For Layman, who took a chance.*

Thanks:

Taylor Wells, *for the coloring assists.*
Tom B. Long, *for the logo.*
Comicbookfonts.com, **for the fonts.**

And More Thanks:

*Rich Amtower, Gabriel Bautista, Jen Cassidy, Charlie Chu,
Joe Eisma, Andrew Elder, Tony Fleecs, Michele Foschini,
Chris Giarrusso, Matt Hawkins, Zach Howard, Rich Johnston,
Brandine Jerwa, Robert Kirkman, Erik Larsen, Emi Lenox,
Rob Liefeld, Jim Mahfood, John McCrea, Todd McFarlane,
Ryan Ottley, Tony Parker, Allen Passalaqua, Tammy Peterson,
Nick Pitarra, Felipe Sobreiro, Alex Sollazzo, Tyler Shainline,
Marc Silvestri, Ben Templesmith and Jim Valentino. Plus the
Image gang of Branwyn, Jonathan, Drew, Sarah, Todd and eric.
And, as always, Kim Peterson and April Hanks.*

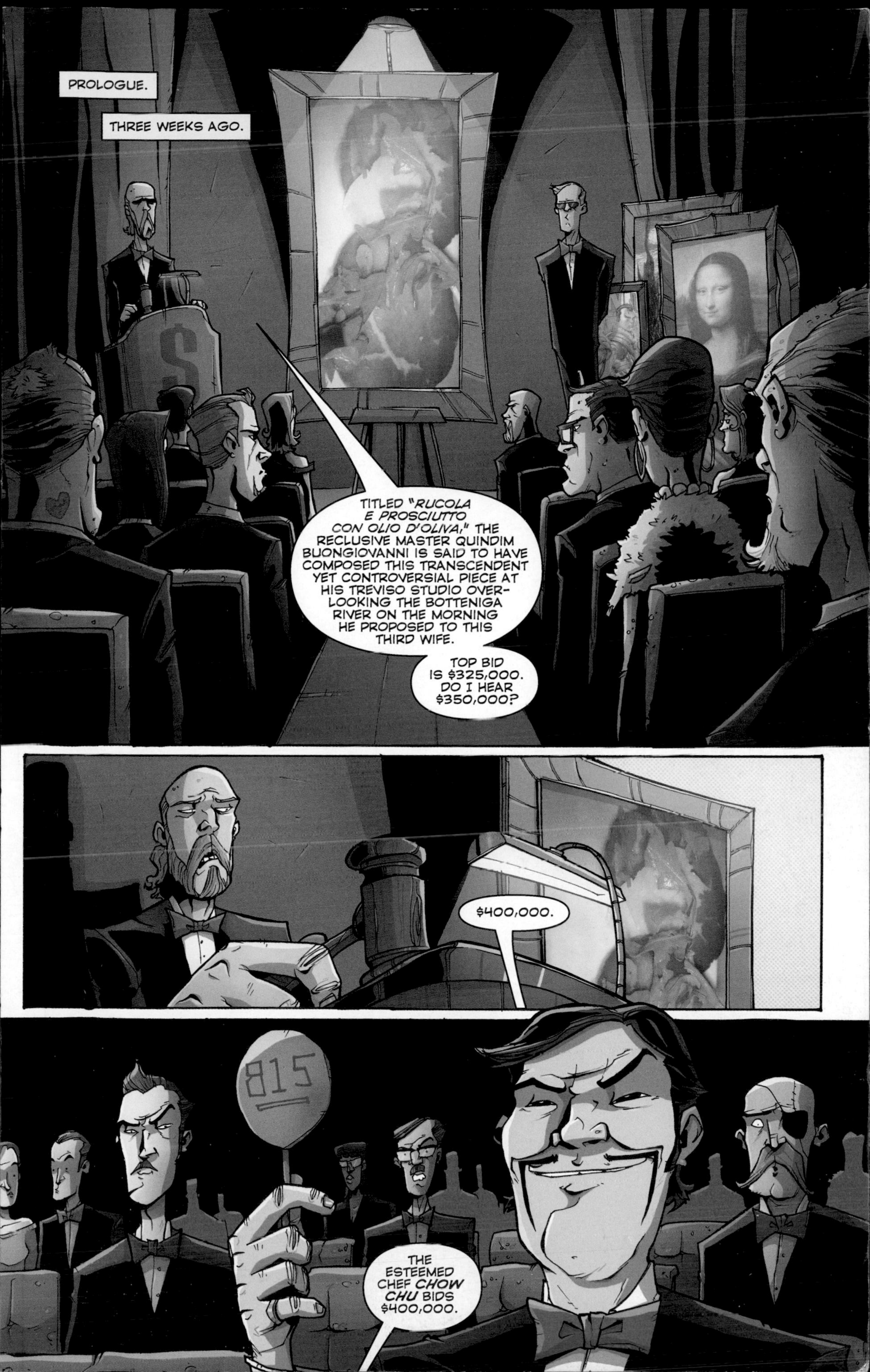
PROLOGUE.
THREE WEEKS AGO.
TITLED "RUCOLA E PROSCIUTTO CON OLIO D'OLIVA," THE RECLUSIVE MASTER QUINDIM BUONGIOVANNI IS SAID TO HAVE COMPOSED THIS TRANSCENDENT YET CONTROVERSIAL PIECE AT HIS TREVISO STUDIO OVER-LOOKING THE BOTTENIGA RIVER ON THE MORNING HE PROPOSED TO THIS THIRD WIFE.
TOP BID IS $325,000. DO I HEAR $350,000?
$400,000.
815
THE ESTEEMED CHEF CHOW CHU BIDS $400,000.

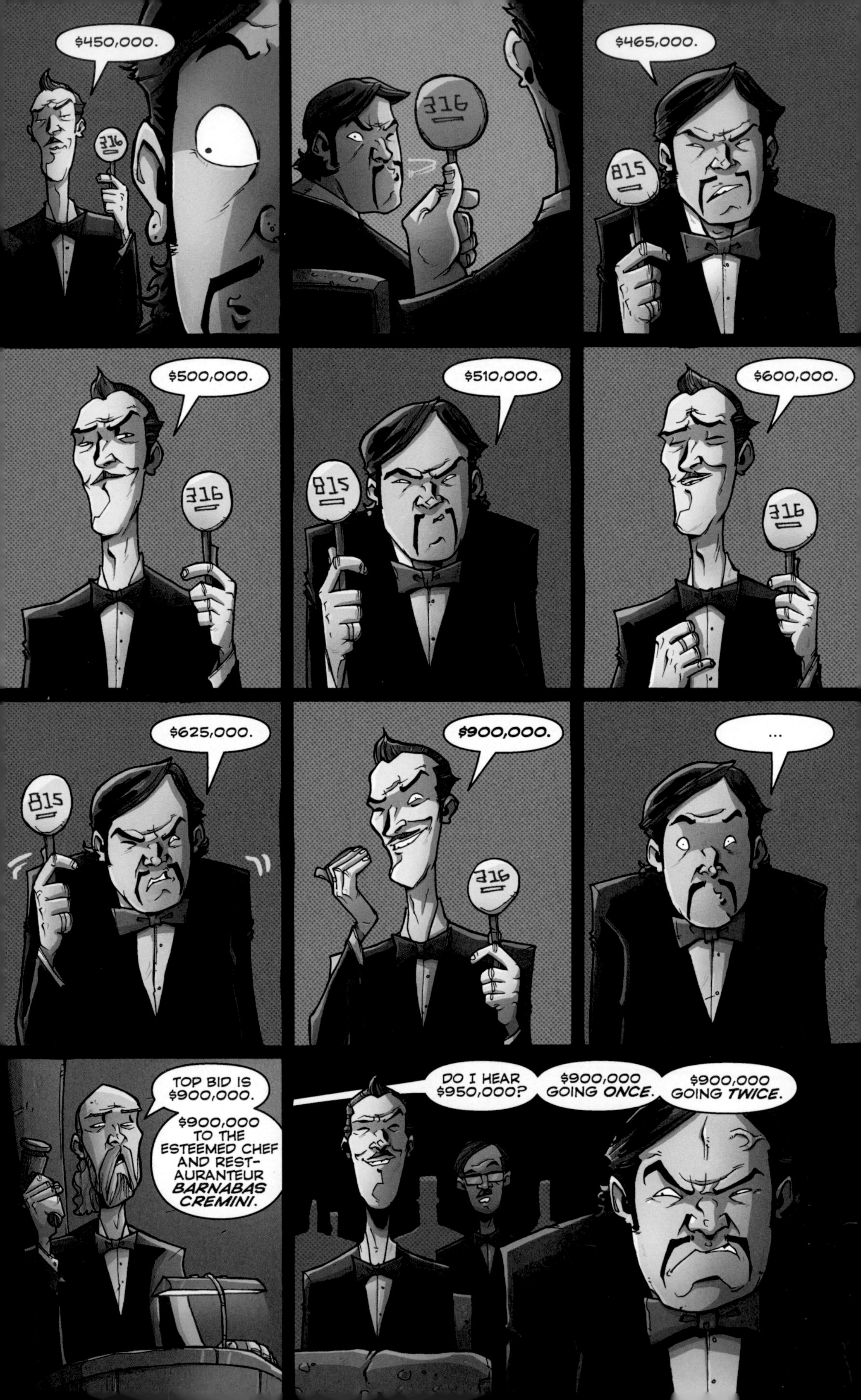

$450,000.
$465,000.
$500,000.
$510,000.
$600,000.
$625,000.
$900,000.
...
TOP BID IS $900,000.
$900,000 TO THE ESTEEMED CHEF AND REST-AURANTEUR BARNABAS CREMINI.
DO I HEAR $950,000?
$900,000 GOING ONCE.
$900,000 GOING TWICE.

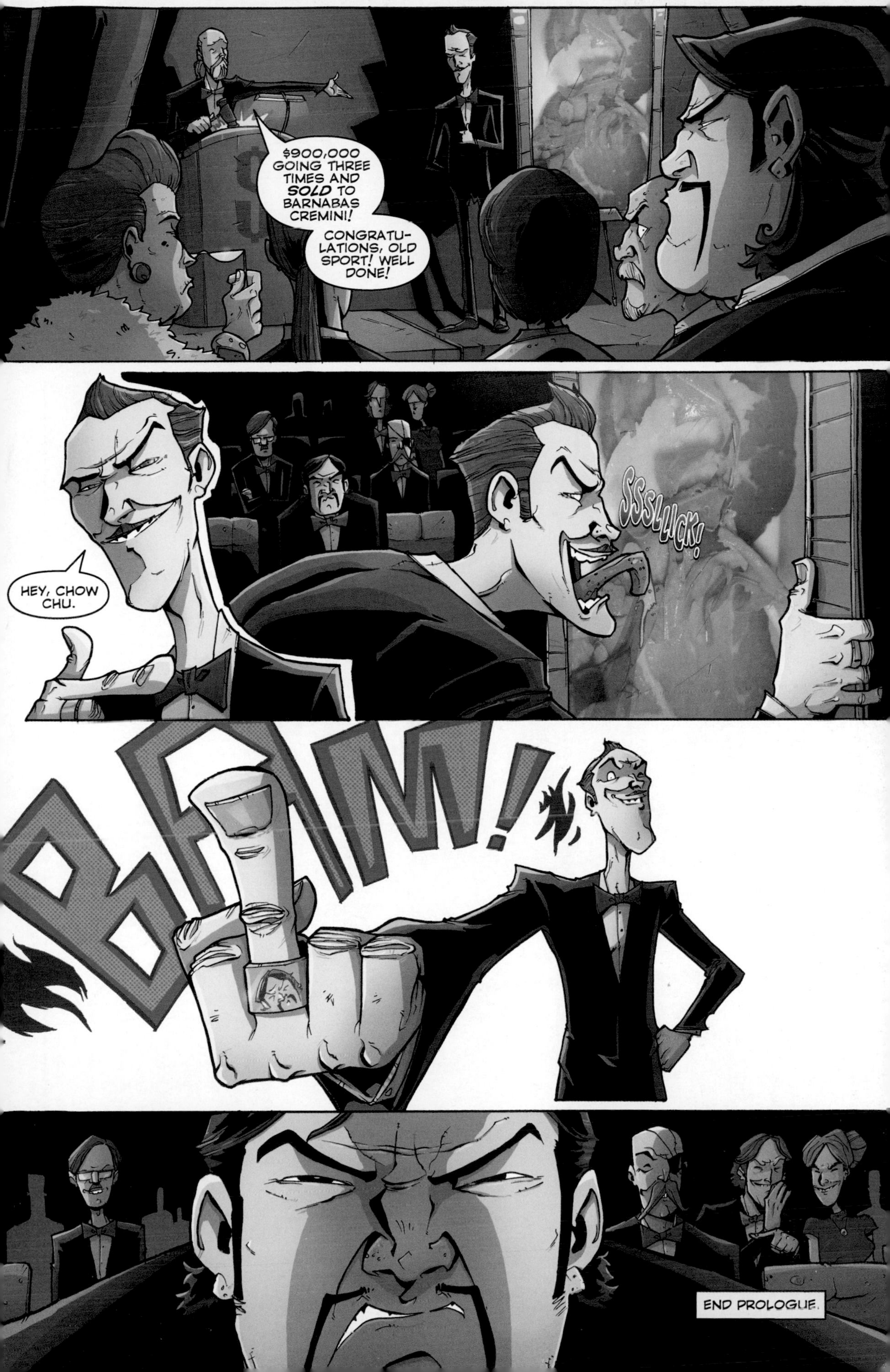
$900,000 GOING THREE TIMES AND SOLD TO BARNABAS CREMINI!
CONGRATULATIONS, OLD SPORT! WELL DONE!
HEY, CHOW CHU.
SSSLUCK!
BAM!
END PROLOGUE.

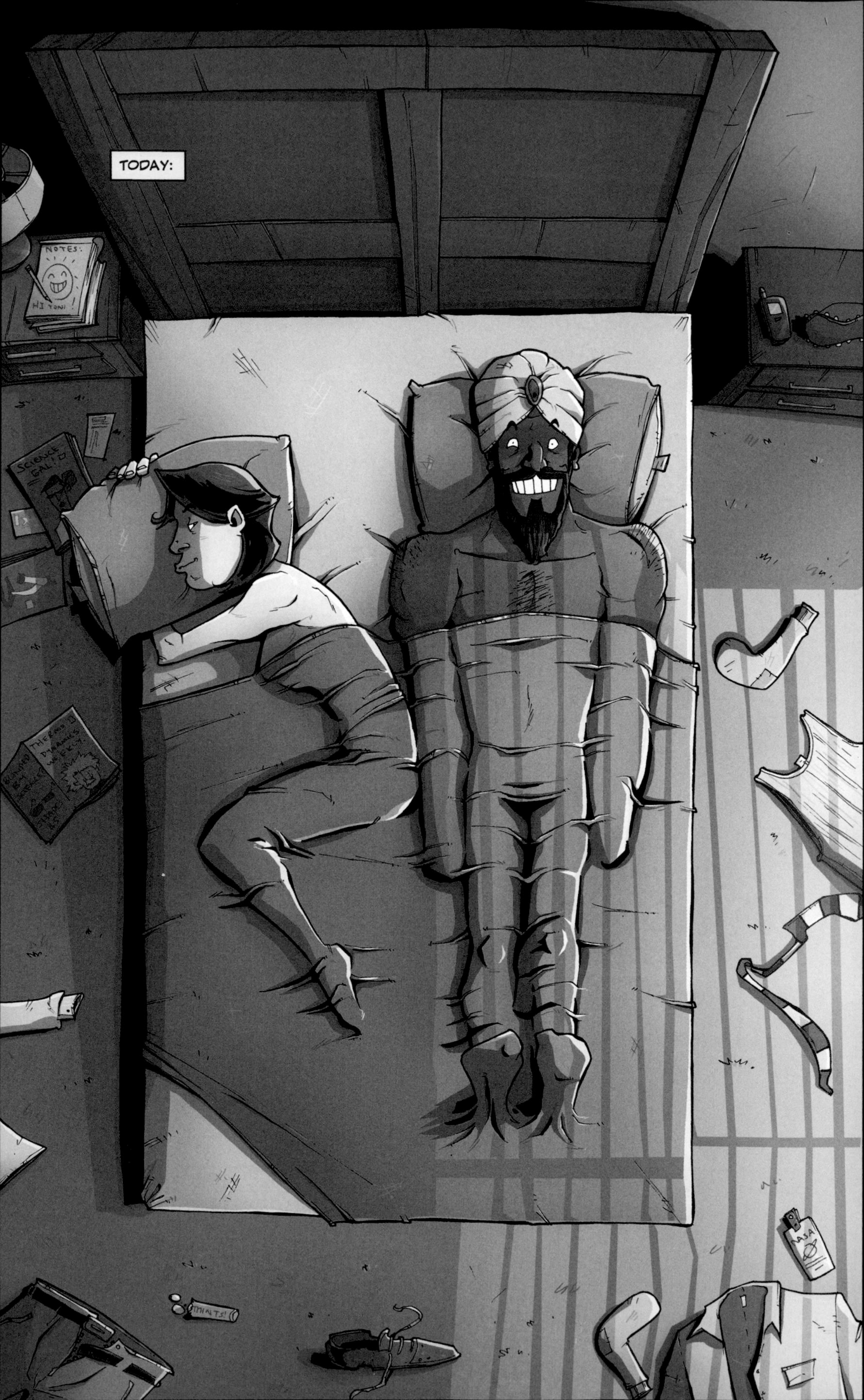
TODAY:
NOTES:
HI TONI
SCIENCE GAL!
THERMO DYNAMICS WEEKLY
MINTS!
NASA

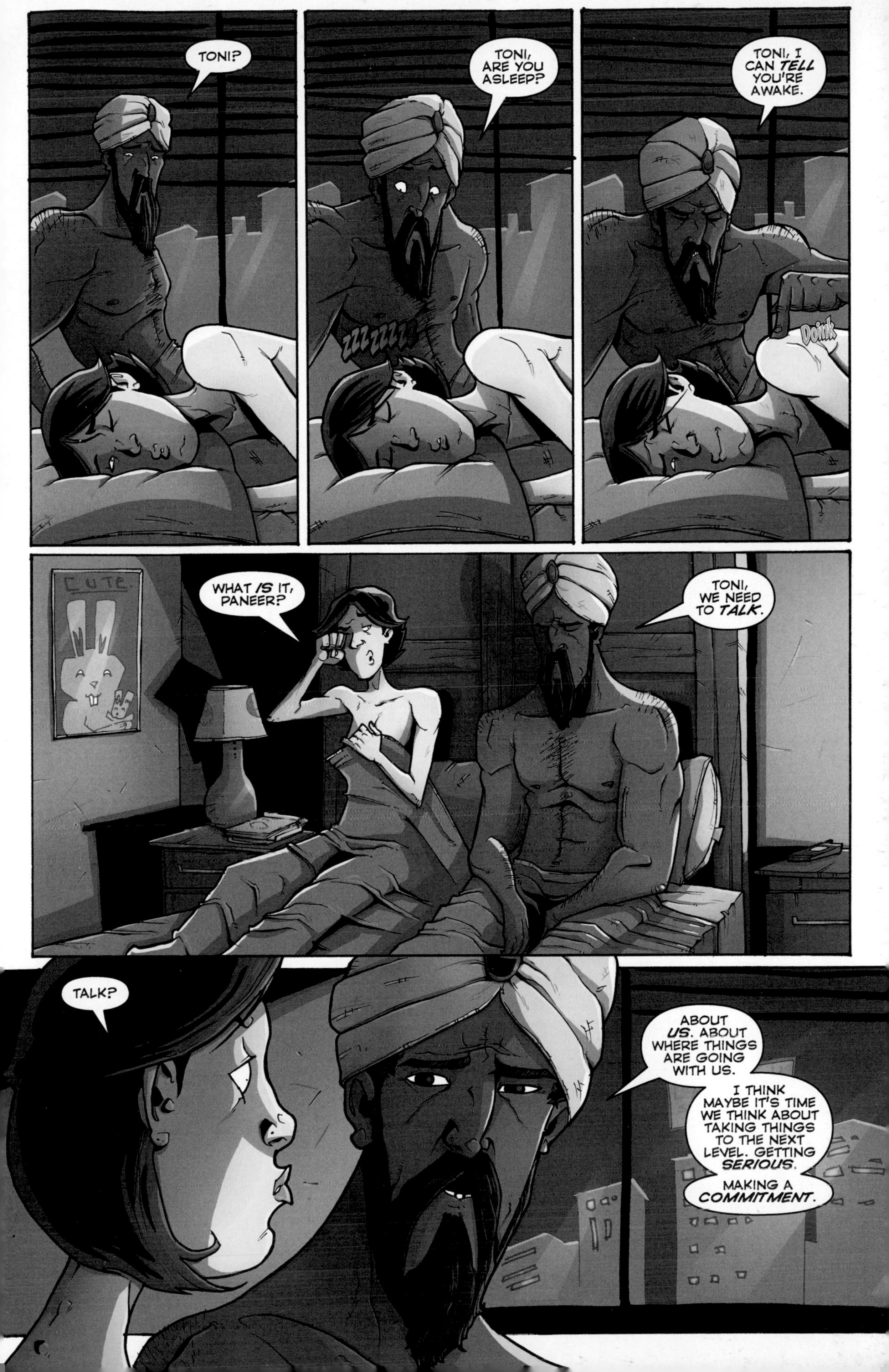
TONI?
TONI, ARE YOU ASLEEP?
ZZZZZZZ
TONI, I CAN TELL YOU'RE AWAKE.
Doink
WHAT IS IT, PANEER?
TONI, WE NEED TO TALK.
CUTE
TALK?
ABOUT US. ABOUT WHERE THINGS ARE GOING WITH US.
I THINK MAYBE IT'S TIME WE THINK ABOUT TAKING THINGS TO THE NEXT LEVEL. GETTING SERIOUS.
MAKING A COMMITMENT.

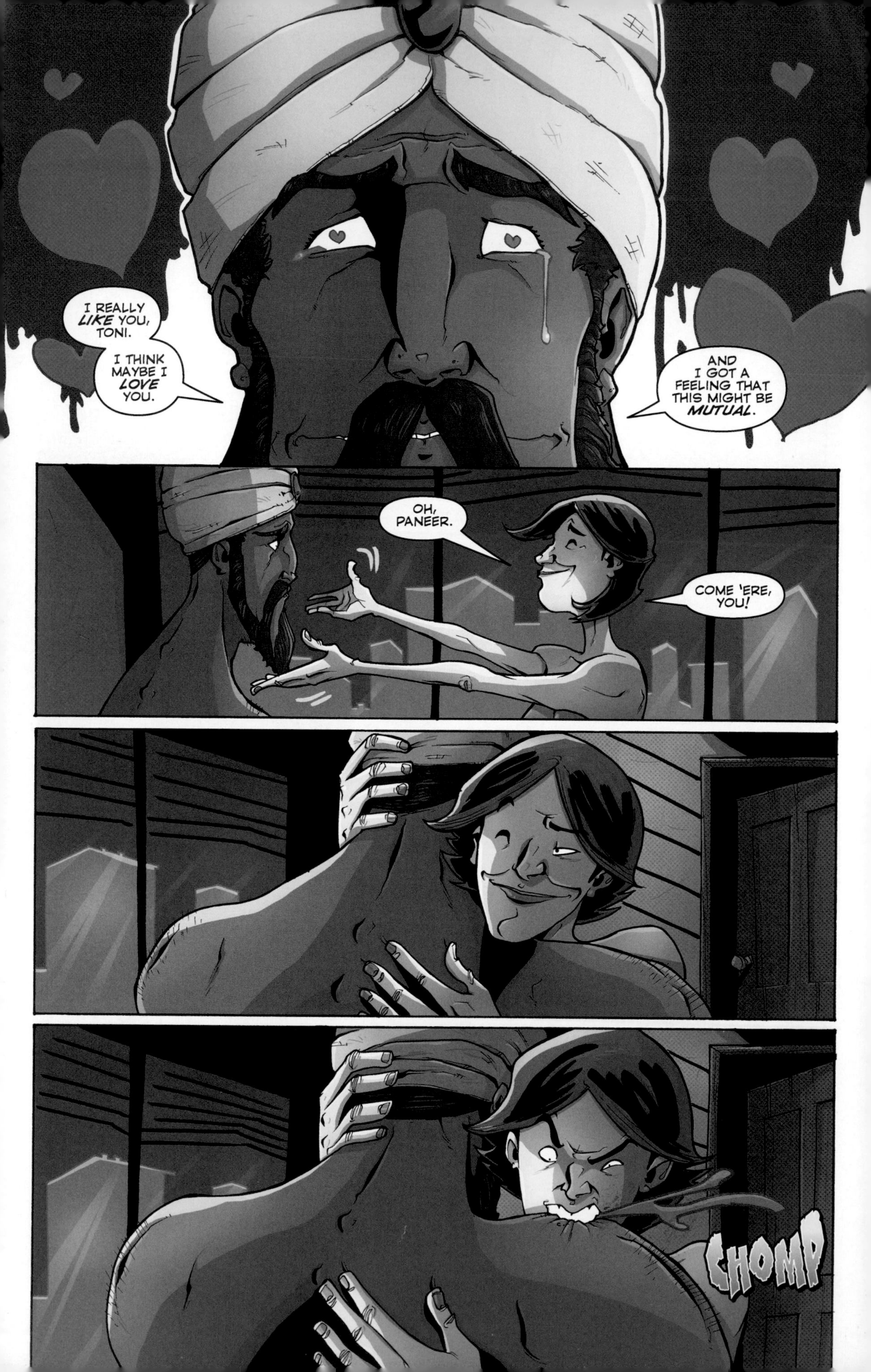
I REALLY LIKE YOU, TONI.
I THINK MAYBE I LOVE YOU.
AND I GOT A FEELING THAT THIS MIGHT BE MUTUAL.
OH, PANEER.
COME 'ERE, YOU!
CHOMP

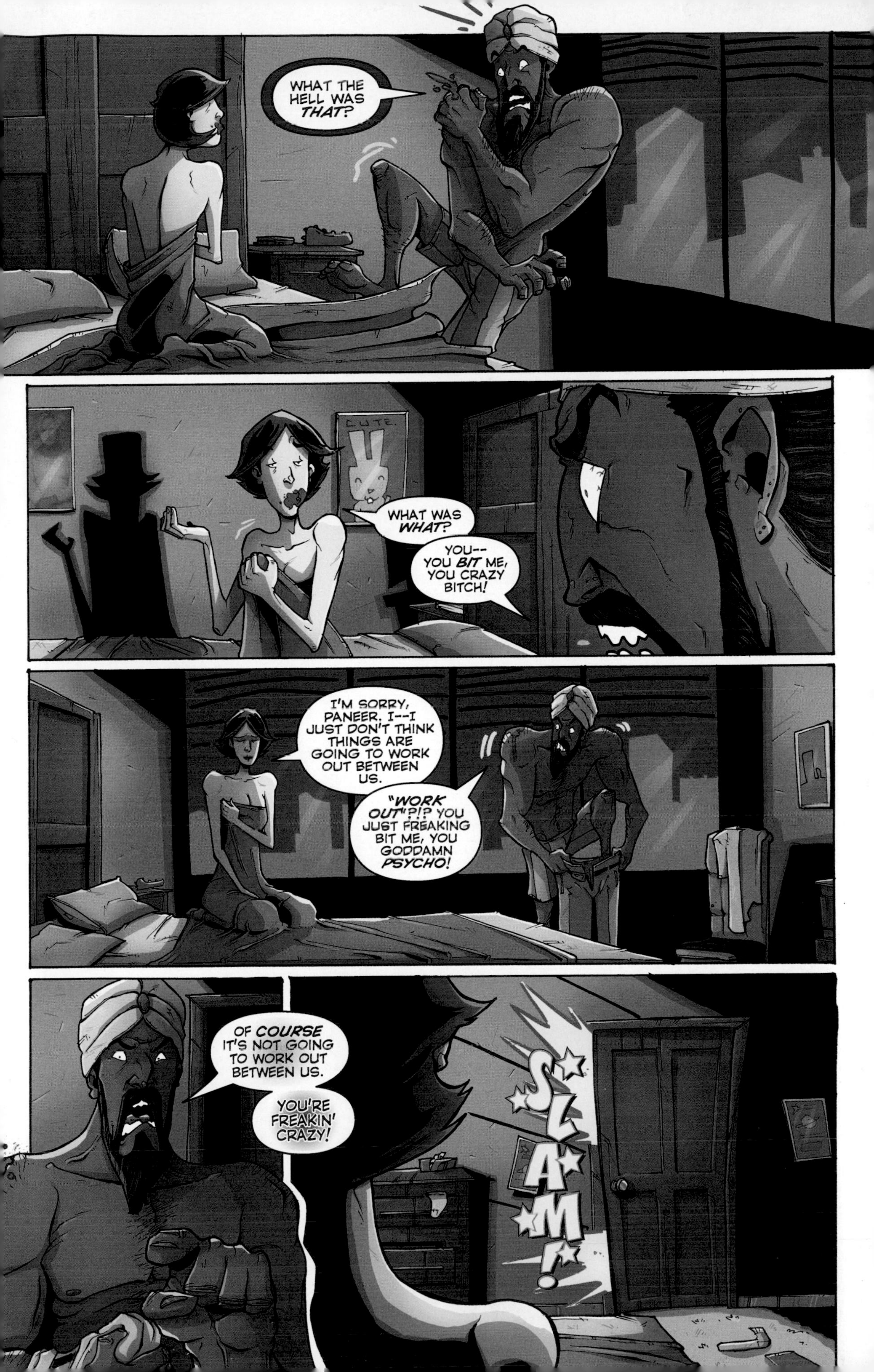
WHAT THE HELL WAS *THAT*?
WHAT WAS *WHAT*?
YOU-- YOU *BIT* ME, YOU CRAZY BITCH!
CUTE
I'M SORRY, PANEER. I--I JUST DON'T THINK THINGS ARE GOING TO WORK OUT BETWEEN US.
"*WORK OUT*"?!? YOU JUST FREAKING BIT ME, YOU GODDAMN *PSYCHO*!
OF *COURSE* IT'S NOT GOING TO WORK OUT BETWEEN US.
YOU'RE FREAKIN' CRAZY!
SLAM!

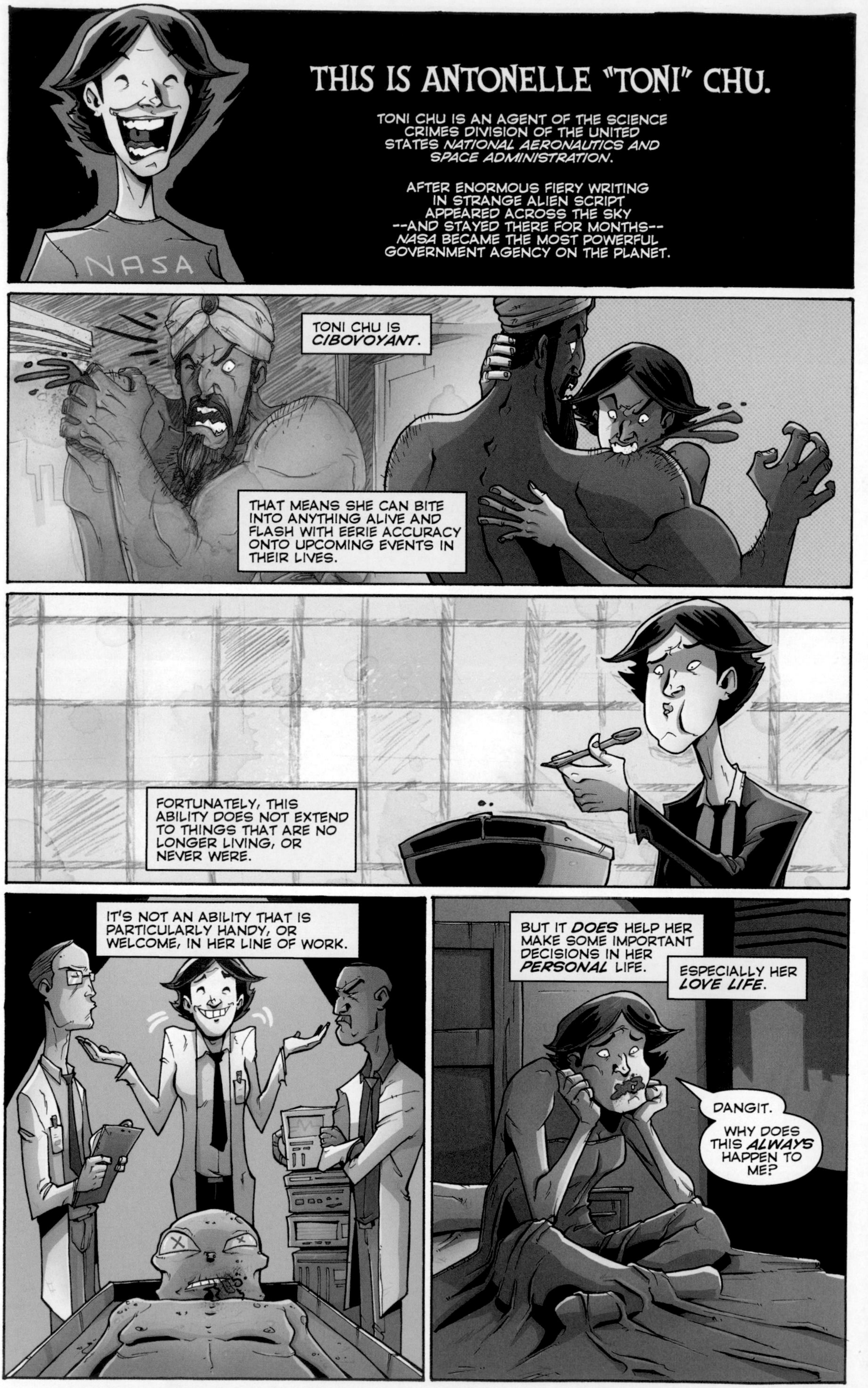
NASA
THIS IS ANTONELLE "TONI" CHU.
TONI CHU IS AN AGENT OF THE SCIENCE CRIMES DIVISION OF THE UNITED STATES *NATIONAL AERONAUTICS AND SPACE ADMINISTRATION*.
AFTER ENORMOUS FIERY WRITING IN STRANGE ALIEN SCRIPT APPEARED ACROSS THE SKY --AND STAYED THERE FOR MONTHS-- *NASA* BECAME THE MOST POWERFUL GOVERNMENT AGENCY ON THE PLANET.
TONI CHU IS ***CIBOVOYANT***.
THAT MEANS SHE CAN BITE INTO ANYTHING ALIVE AND FLASH WITH EERIE ACCURACY ONTO UPCOMING EVENTS IN THEIR LIVES.
FORTUNATELY, THIS ABILITY DOES NOT EXTEND TO THINGS THAT ARE NO LONGER LIVING, OR NEVER WERE.
IT'S NOT AN ABILITY THAT IS PARTICULARLY HANDY, OR WELCOME, IN HER LINE OF WORK.
BUT IT ***DOES*** HELP HER MAKE SOME IMPORTANT DECISIONS IN HER ***PERSONAL*** LIFE.
ESPECIALLY HER ***LOVE LIFE***.
DANGIT.
WHY DOES THIS ***ALWAYS*** HAPPEN TO ME?

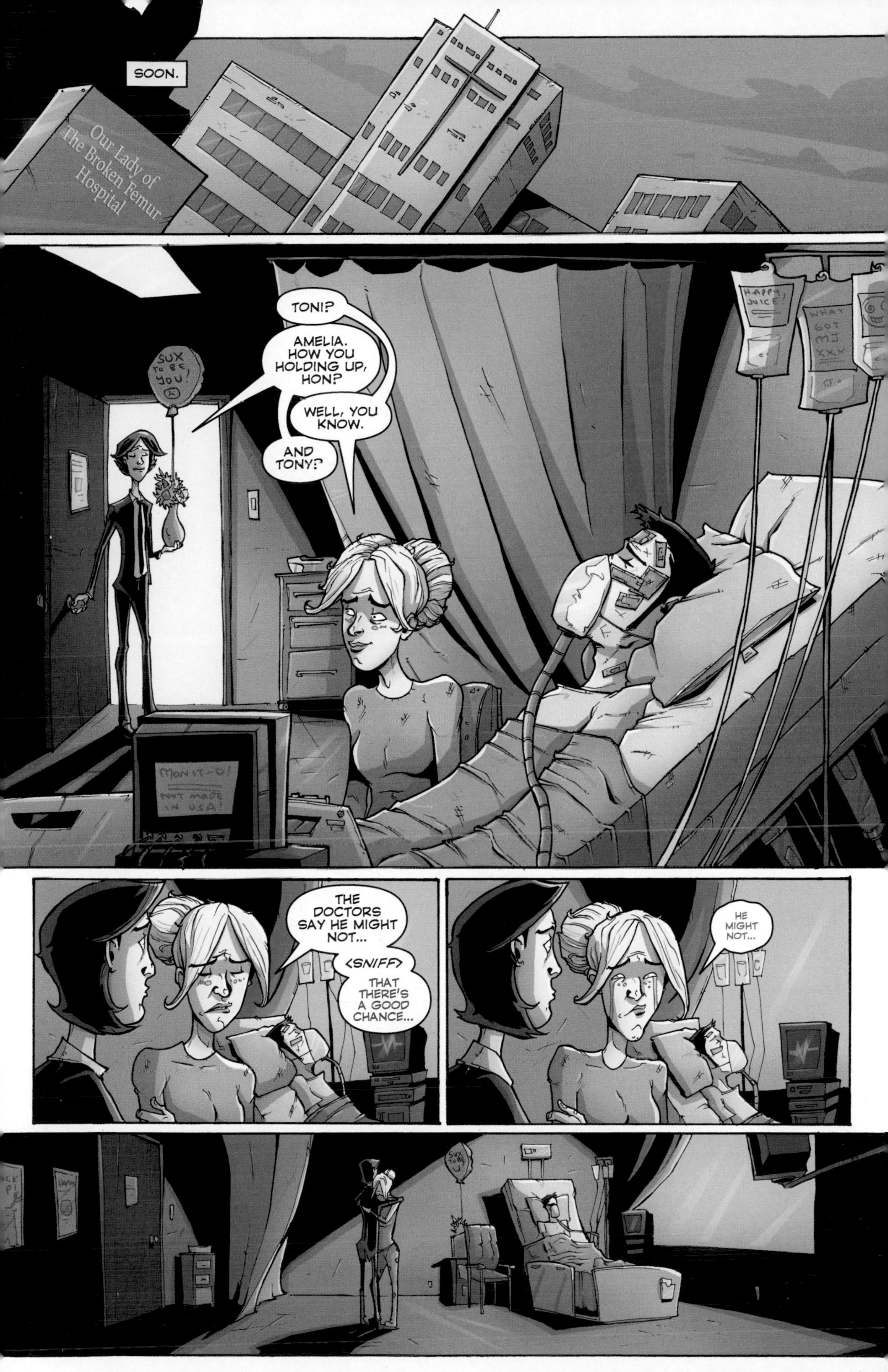
SOON.
Our Lady of The Broken Femur Hospital
TONI?
AMELIA. HOW YOU HOLDING UP, HON?
WELL, YOU KNOW.
AND TONY?
SUX TO BE YOU!
HAPPY JUICE!
WHAT GOT MJ. XXX
MON-IT-O! NOT MADE IN USA!
THE DOCTORS SAY HE MIGHT NOT...
<SNIFF>
THAT THERE'S A GOOD CHANCE...
HE MIGHT NOT...

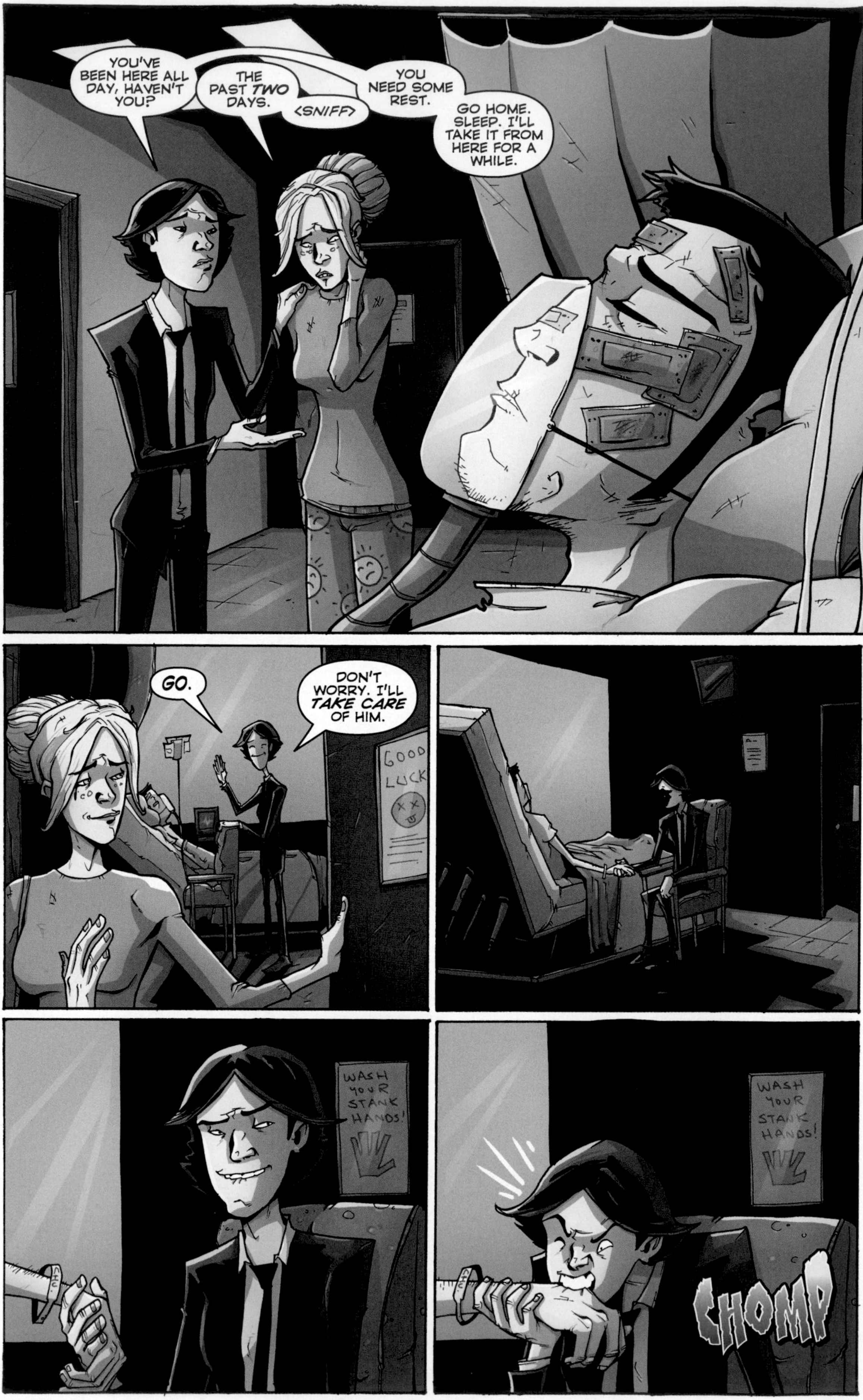
YOU'VE BEEN HERE ALL DAY, HAVEN'T YOU?
THE PAST *TWO* DAYS.
<*SNIFF*>
YOU NEED SOME REST.
GO HOME. SLEEP. I'LL TAKE IT FROM HERE FOR A WHILE.
GO.
DON'T WORRY. I'LL *TAKE CARE* OF HIM.
GOOD LUCK
WASH YOUR STANK HANDS!
WASH YOUR STANK HANDS!
CHOMP

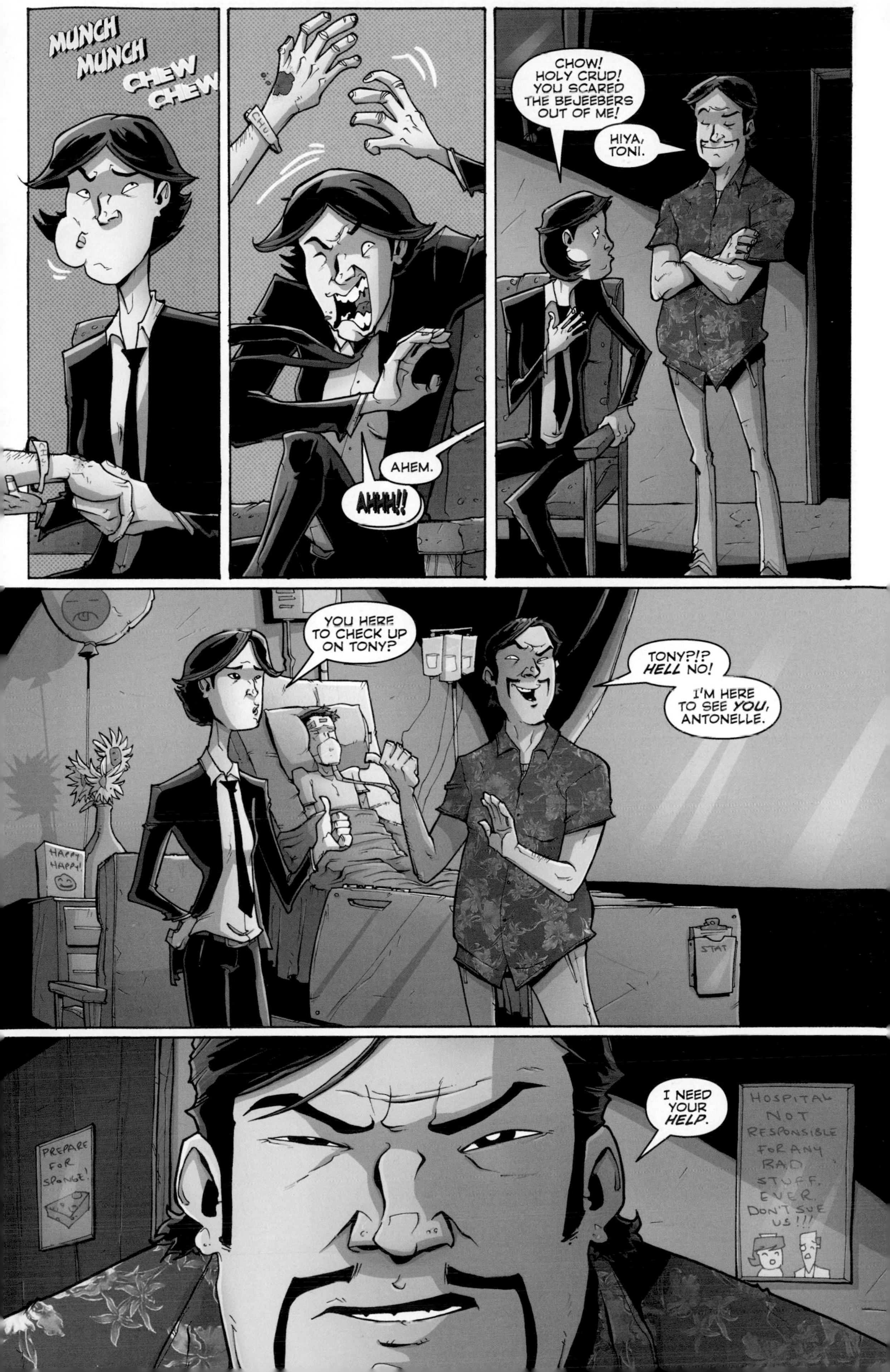
MUNCH
MUNCH
CHEW
CHEW
AHEM.
AHHH!!
CHOW! HOLY CRUD! YOU SCARED THE BEJEEBERS OUT OF ME!
HIYA, TONI.
YOU HERE TO CHECK UP ON TONY?
TONY?!? HELL NO!
I'M HERE TO SEE YOU, ANTONELLE.
HAPPY HAPPY!
STAT
PREPARE FOR SPONGE!
I NEED YOUR HELP.
HOSPITAL NOT RESPONSIBLE FOR ANY RAD STUFF. EVER. DON'T SUE US!!!

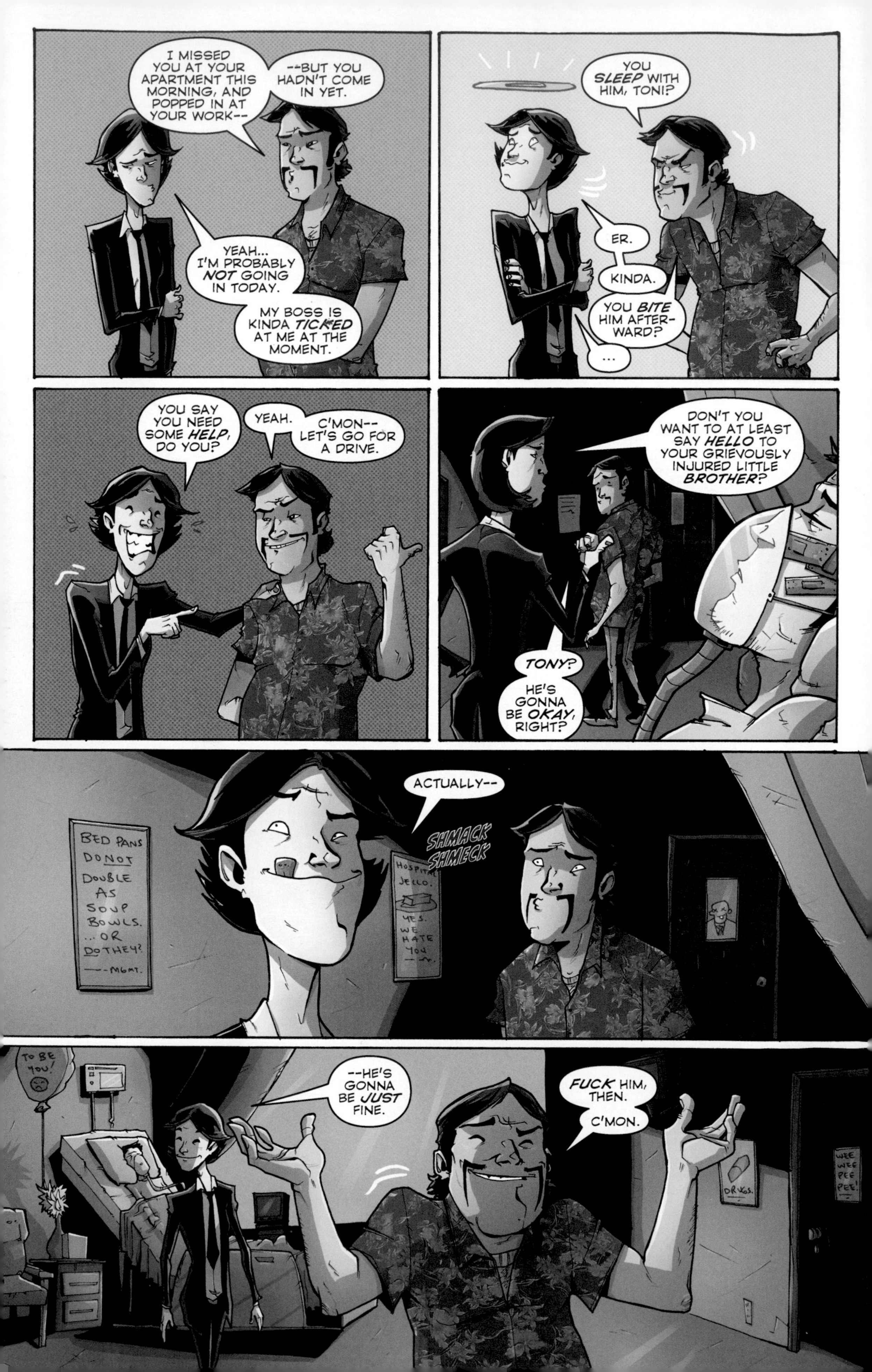
I MISSED YOU AT YOUR APARTMENT THIS MORNING, AND POPPED IN AT YOUR WORK--
--BUT YOU HADN'T COME IN YET.
YEAH... I'M PROBABLY NOT GOING IN TODAY.
MY BOSS IS KINDA TICKED AT ME AT THE MOMENT.
YOU SLEEP WITH HIM, TONI?
ER.
KINDA.
YOU BITE HIM AFTER-WARD?
...
YOU SAY YOU NEED SOME HELP, DO YOU?
YEAH.
C'MON-- LET'S GO FOR A DRIVE.
DON'T YOU WANT TO AT LEAST SAY HELLO TO YOUR GRIEVOUSLY INJURED LITTLE BROTHER?
TONY?
HE'S GONNA BE OKAY, RIGHT?
ACTUALLY--
SHMACK SHMECK
BED PANS DO NOT DOUBLE AS SOUP BOWLS. ...OR DO THEY? --MGMT.
HOSPITAL JELLO. YES. WE HATE YOU
TO BE YOU!
--HE'S GONNA BE JUST FINE.
FUCK HIM, THEN.
C'MON.
DRUGS.
WEE WEE PEE PEE!

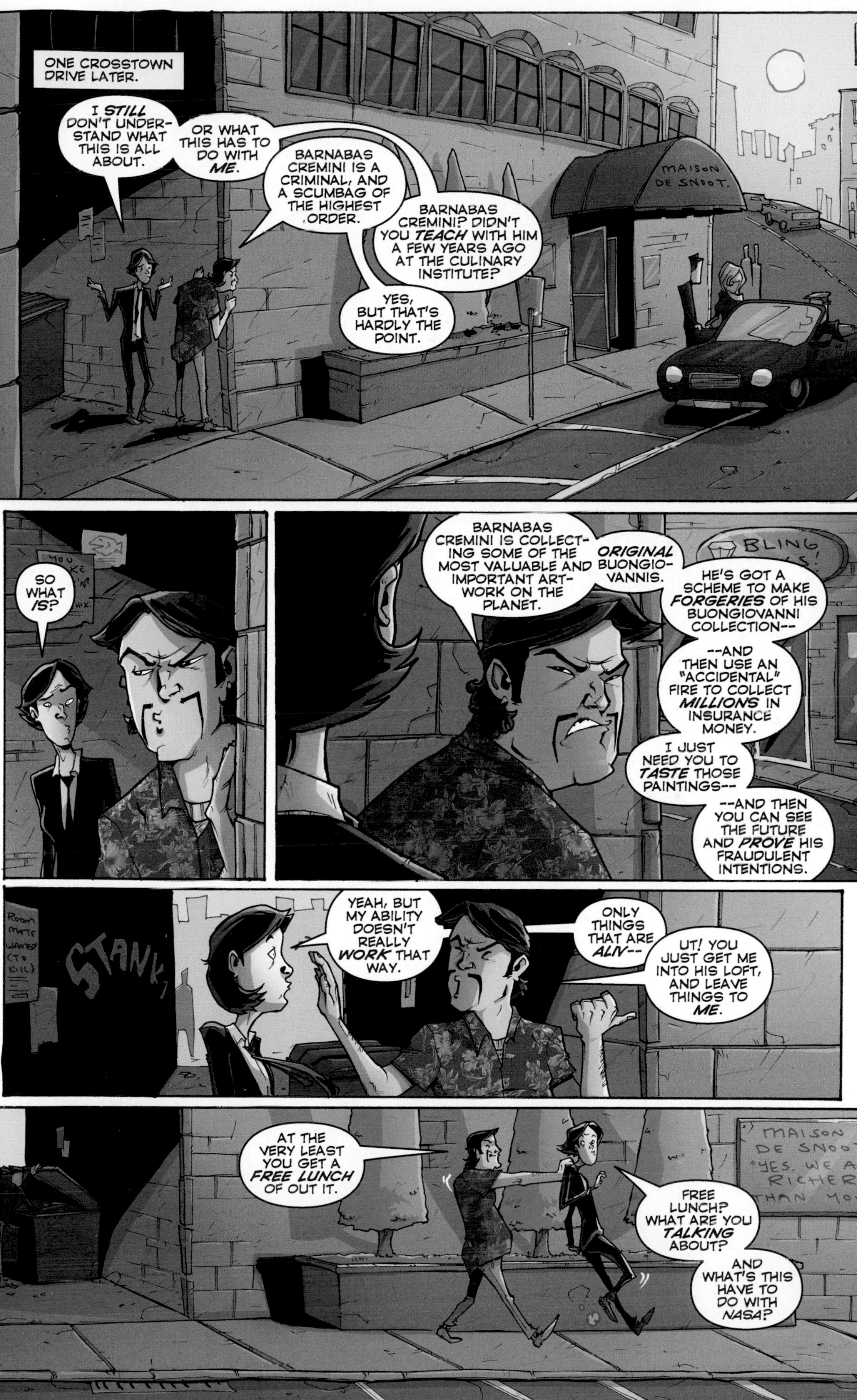
ONE CROSSTOWN DRIVE LATER.
I STILL DON'T UNDERSTAND WHAT THIS IS ALL ABOUT.
OR WHAT THIS HAS TO DO WITH ME.
BARNABAS CREMINI IS A CRIMINAL, AND A SCUMBAG OF THE HIGHEST ORDER.
BARNABAS CREMINI? DIDN'T YOU TEACH WITH HIM A FEW YEARS AGO AT THE CULINARY INSTITUTE?
YES, BUT THAT'S HARDLY THE POINT.
MAISON DE SNOOT.
SO WHAT IS?
BARNABAS CREMINI IS COLLECTING SOME OF THE MOST VALUABLE AND IMPORTANT ARTWORK ON THE PLANET.
ORIGINAL BUONGIOVANNIS.
HE'S GOT A SCHEME TO MAKE FORGERIES OF HIS BUONGIOVANNI COLLECTION--
--AND THEN USE AN "ACCIDENTAL" FIRE TO COLLECT MILLIONS IN INSURANCE MONEY.
I JUST NEED YOU TO TASTE THOSE PAINTINGS--
--AND THEN YOU CAN SEE THE FUTURE AND PROVE HIS FRAUDULENT INTENTIONS.
ROOM MATE WANTED (TO KILL)
STANK
YEAH, BUT MY ABILITY DOESN'T REALLY WORK THAT WAY.
ONLY THINGS THAT ARE ALIV--
UT! YOU JUST GET ME INTO HIS LOFT, AND LEAVE THINGS TO ME.
AT THE VERY LEAST YOU GET A FREE LUNCH OF OUT IT.
MAISON DE SNOOT "YES, WE ARE RICHER THAN YOU."
FREE LUNCH? WHAT ARE YOU TALKING ABOUT?
AND WHAT'S THIS HAVE TO DO WITH NASA?

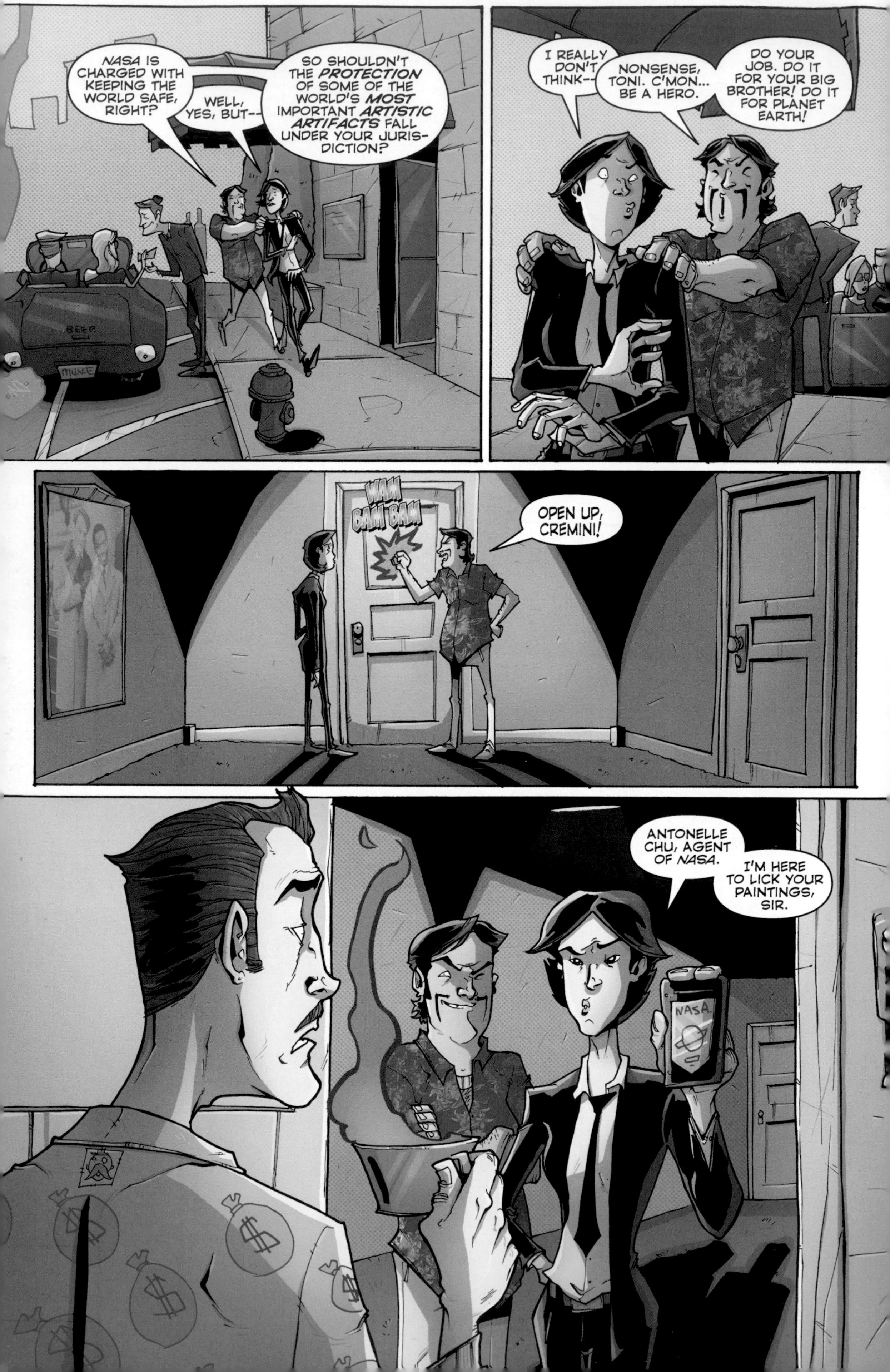
NASA IS CHARGED WITH KEEPING THE WORLD SAFE, RIGHT?
WELL, YES, BUT--
SO SHOULDN'T THE PROTECTION OF SOME OF THE WORLD'S MOST IMPORTANT ARTISTIC ARTIFACTS FALL UNDER YOUR JURISDICTION?
I REALLY DON'T THINK--
NONSENSE, TONI. C'MON... BE A HERO.
DO YOUR JOB. DO IT FOR YOUR BIG BROTHER! DO IT FOR PLANET EARTH!
WAM BAM BAM
OPEN UP, CREMINI!
ANTONELLE CHU, AGENT OF NASA.
I'M HERE TO LICK YOUR PAINTINGS, SIR.
NASA

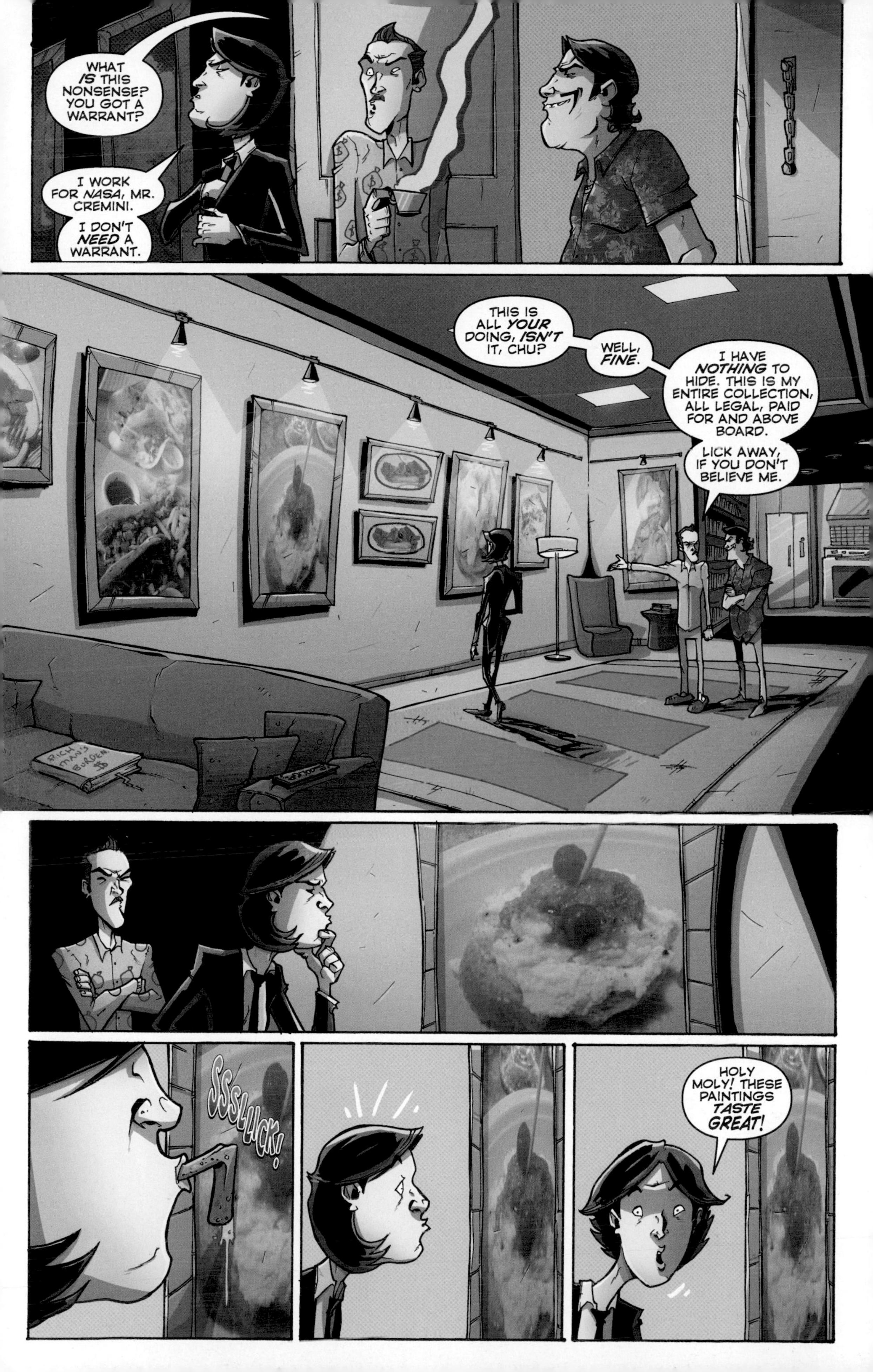
WHAT *IS* THIS NONSENSE? YOU GOT A WARRANT?
I WORK FOR *NASA*, MR. CREMINI.
I DON'T *NEED* A WARRANT.
THIS IS ALL *YOUR* DOING, *ISN'T* IT, CHU?
WELL, *FINE*.
I HAVE *NOTHING* TO HIDE. THIS IS MY ENTIRE COLLECTION, ALL LEGAL, PAID FOR AND ABOVE BOARD.
LICK AWAY, IF YOU DON'T BELIEVE ME.
RICH MAN'S BURDEN
SSSLUCK!
HOLY MOLY! THESE PAINTINGS *TASTE GREAT!*

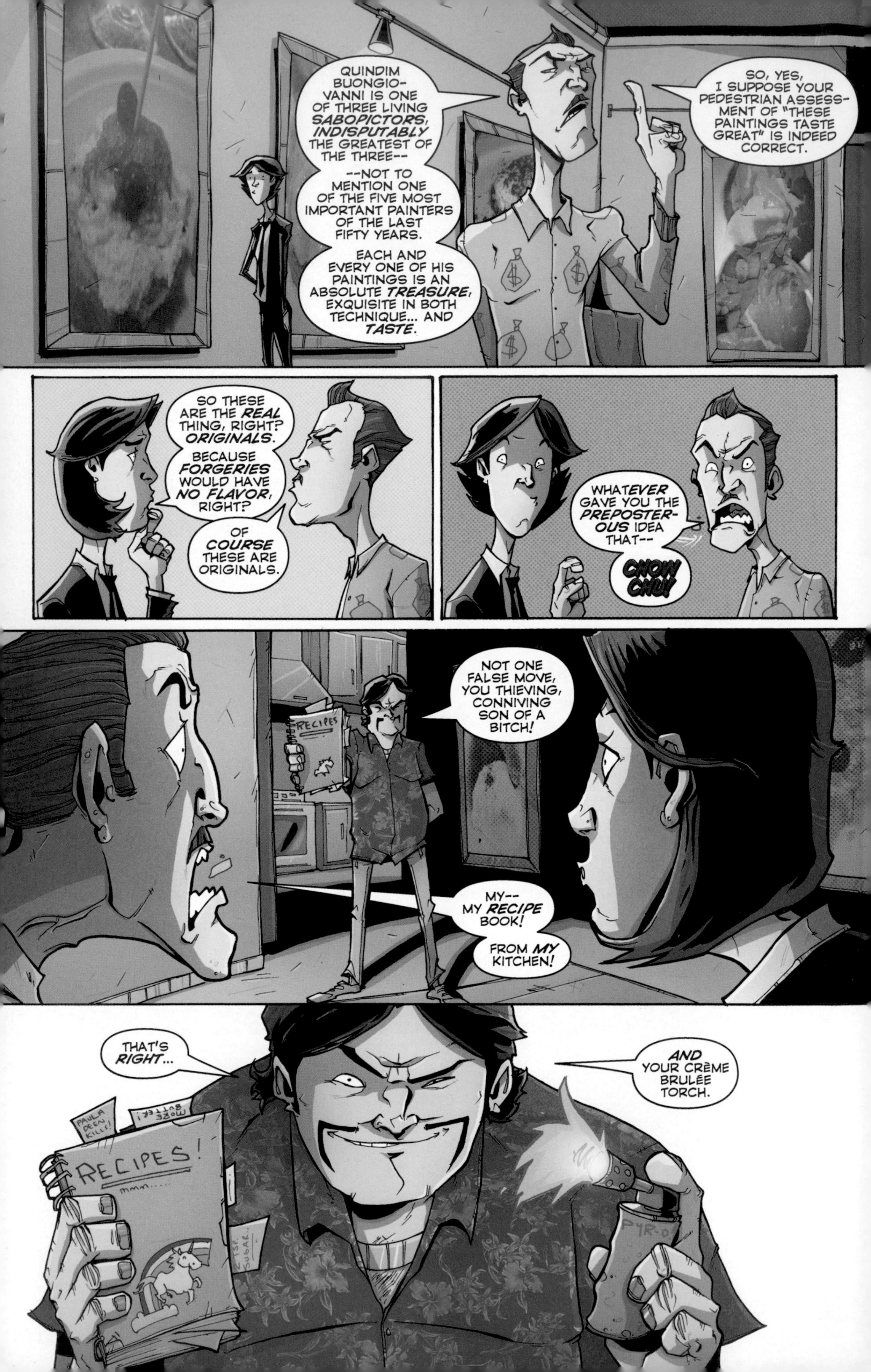
QUINDIM BUONGIO-VANNI IS ONE OF THREE LIVING SABOPICTORS, INDISPUTABLY THE GREATEST OF THE THREE--
--NOT TO MENTION ONE OF THE FIVE MOST IMPORTANT PAINTERS OF THE LAST FIFTY YEARS.
EACH AND EVERY ONE OF HIS PAINTINGS IS AN ABSOLUTE TREASURE; EXQUISITE IN BOTH TECHNIQUE... AND TASTE.
SO, YES, I SUPPOSE YOUR PEDESTRIAN ASSESS-MENT OF "THESE PAINTINGS TASTE GREAT" IS INDEED CORRECT.
SO THESE ARE THE REAL THING, RIGHT? ORIGINALS.
BECAUSE FORGERIES WOULD HAVE NO FLAVOR, RIGHT?
OF COURSE THESE ARE ORIGINALS.
WHATEVER GAVE YOU THE PREPOSTER-OUS IDEA THAT--
CHOW CHU!
NOT ONE FALSE MOVE, YOU THIEVING, CONNIVING SON OF A BITCH!
RECIPES
MY-- MY RECIPE BOOK!
FROM MY KITCHEN!
THAT'S RIGHT...
AND YOUR CRÈME BRULÉE TORCH.
PAULA DEEN KILLS!
MORE BUTTER!
RECIPES!
mmm.....
2 TSP. SUGAR..
PYR-O

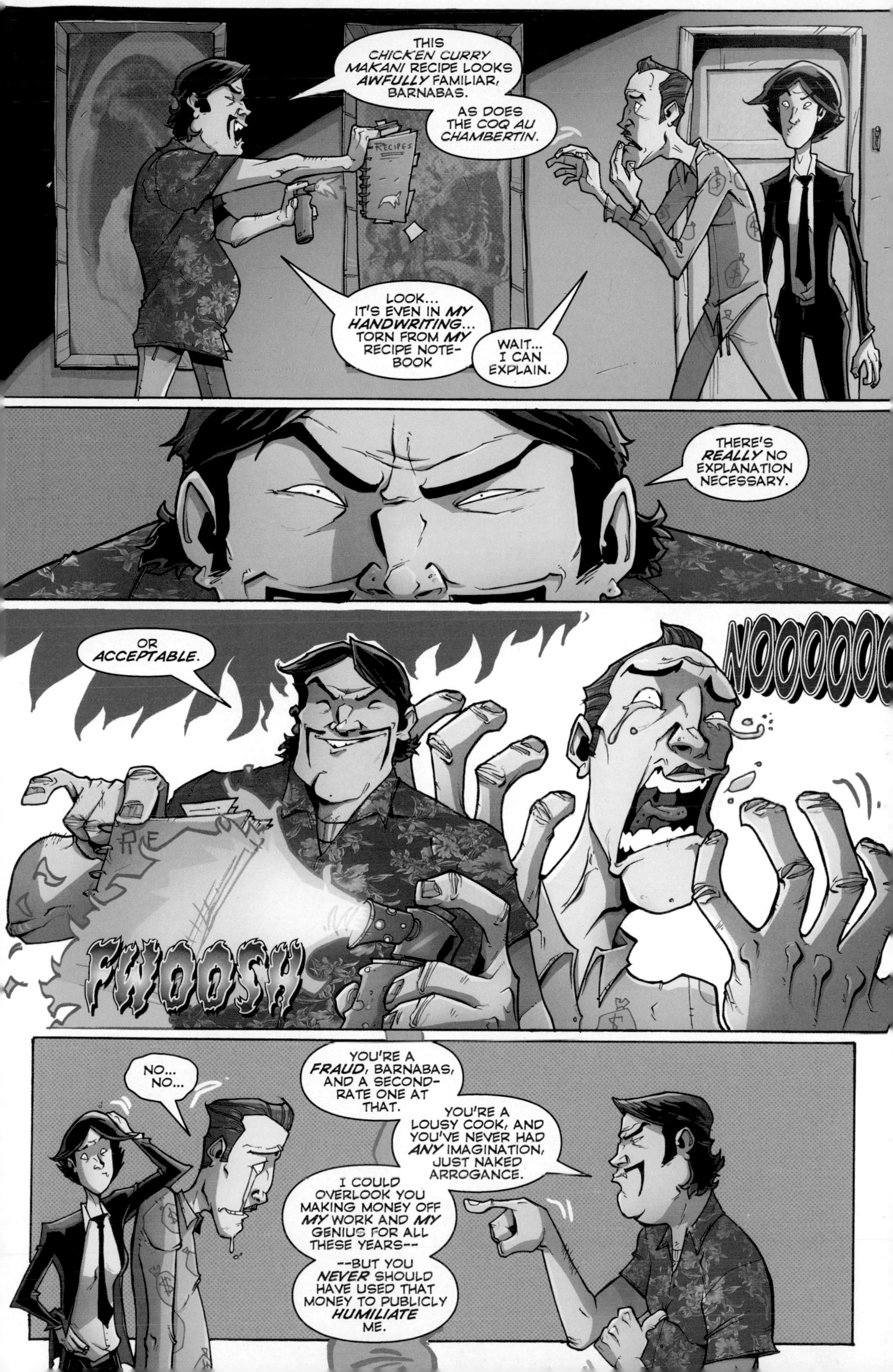
THIS CHICKEN CURRY MAKANI RECIPE LOOKS AWFULLY FAMILIAR, BARNABAS.
AS DOES THE COQ AU CHAMBERTIN.
RECIPES
LOOK... IT'S EVEN IN MY HANDWRITING... TORN FROM MY RECIPE NOTE-BOOK
WAIT... I CAN EXPLAIN.
THERE'S REALLY NO EXPLANATION NECESSARY.
OR ACCEPTABLE.
NOOOOOO
FWOOSH
NO... NO...
YOU'RE A FRAUD, BARNABAS, AND A SECOND-RATE ONE AT THAT.
YOU'RE A LOUSY COOK, AND YOU'VE NEVER HAD ANY IMAGINATION, JUST NAKED ARROGANCE.
I COULD OVERLOOK YOU MAKING MONEY OFF MY WORK AND MY GENIUS FOR ALL THESE YEARS--
--BUT YOU NEVER SHOULD HAVE USED THAT MONEY TO PUBLICLY HUMILIATE ME.

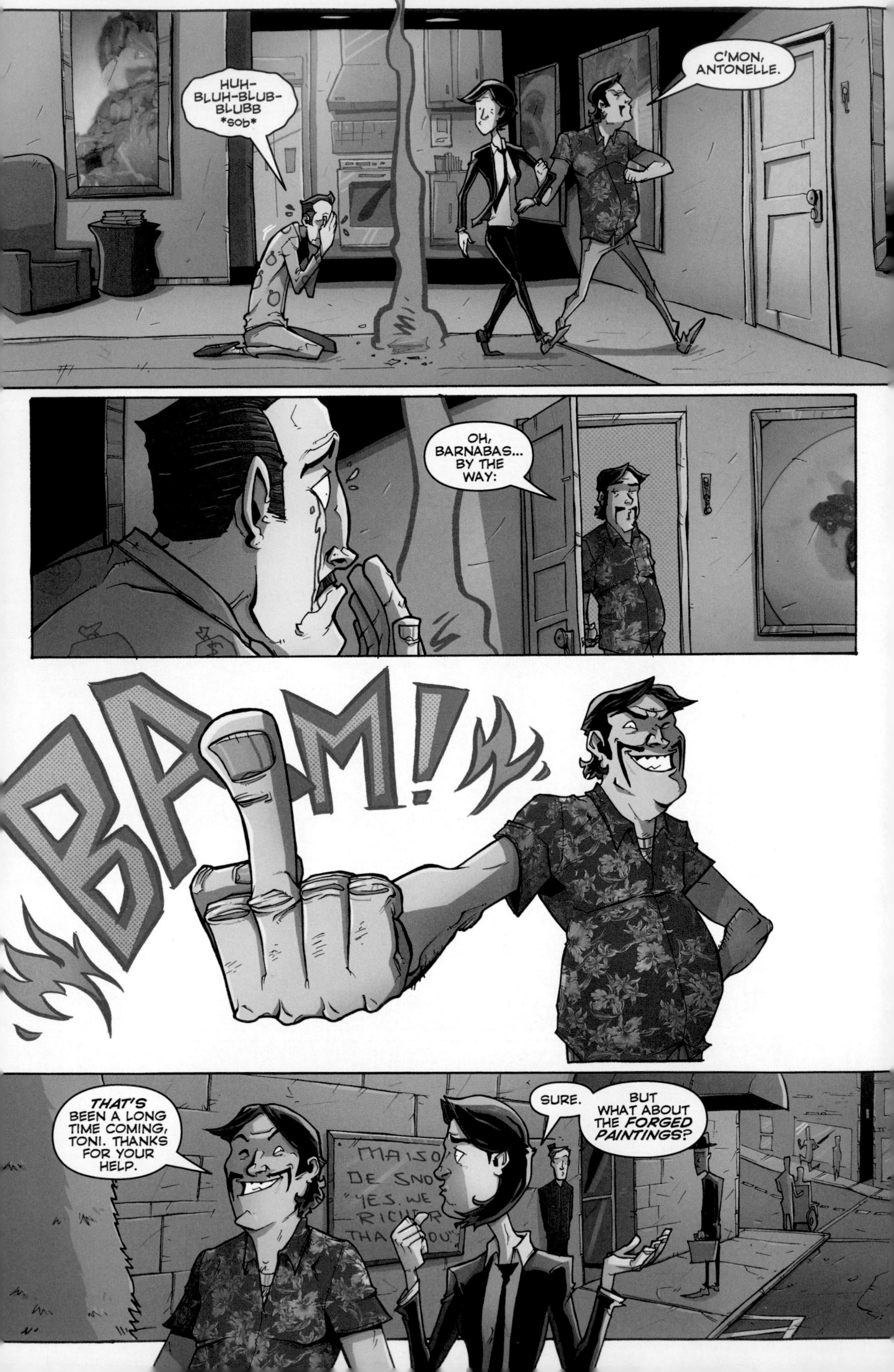
HUH-BLUH-BLUB-BLUBB *sob*
C'MON, ANTONELLE.
OH, BARNABAS... BY THE WAY:
BAM!
THAT'S BEEN A LONG TIME COMING, TONI. THANKS FOR YOUR HELP.
SURE.
BUT WHAT ABOUT THE FORGED PAINTINGS?

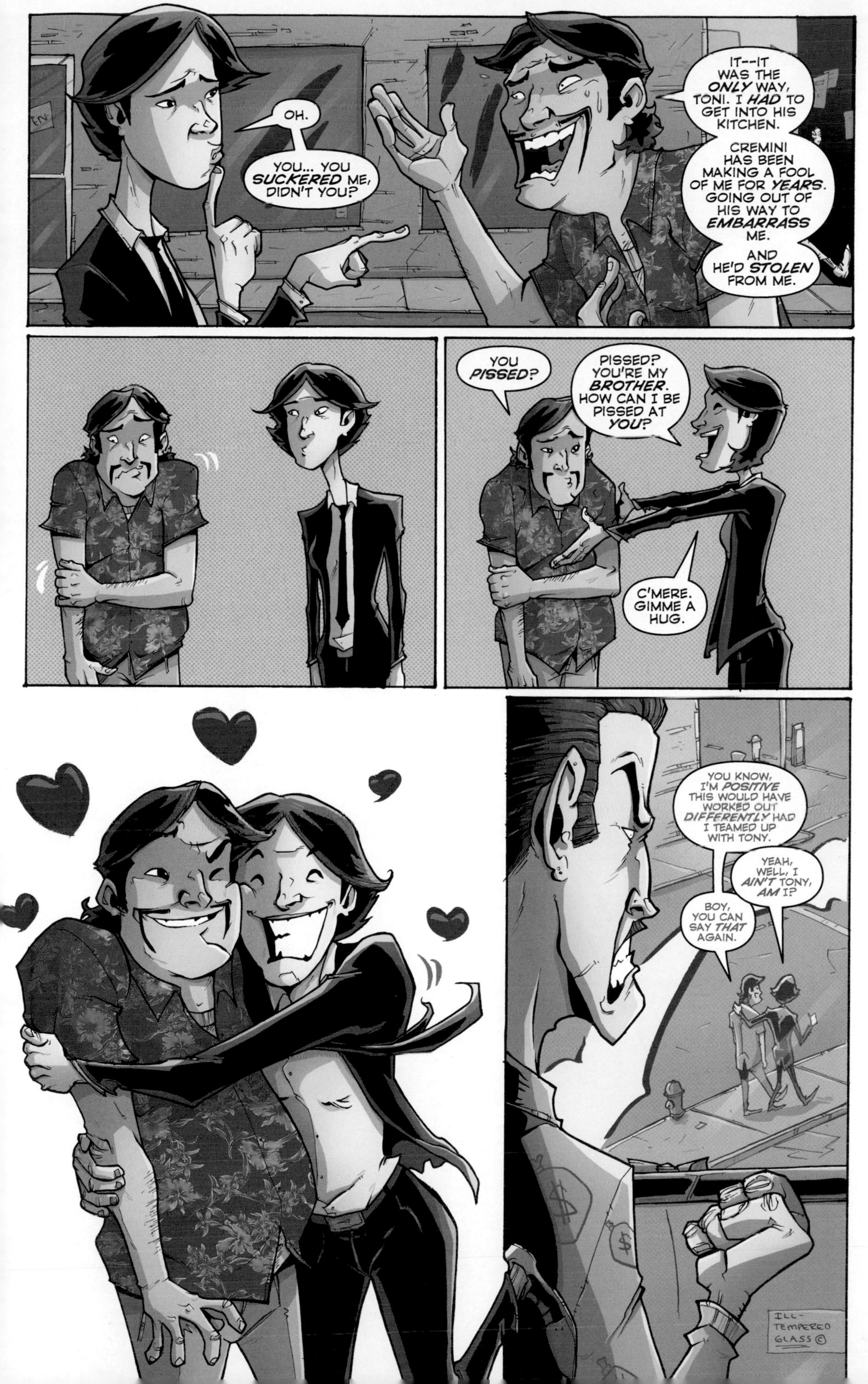
OH.
YOU... YOU SUCKERED ME, DIDN'T YOU?
IT--IT WAS THE ONLY WAY, TONI. I HAD TO GET INTO HIS KITCHEN.
CREMINI HAS BEEN MAKING A FOOL OF ME FOR YEARS. GOING OUT OF HIS WAY TO EMBARRASS ME.
AND HE'D STOLEN FROM ME.
YOU PISSED?
PISSED? YOU'RE MY BROTHER. HOW CAN I BE PISSED AT YOU?
C'MERE. GIMME A HUG.
YOU KNOW, I'M POSITIVE THIS WOULD HAVE WORKED OUT DIFFERENTLY HAD I TEAMED UP WITH TONY.
YEAH, WELL, I AIN'T TONY, AM I?
BOY, YOU CAN SAY THAT AGAIN.
ILL-TEMPERED GLASS ©

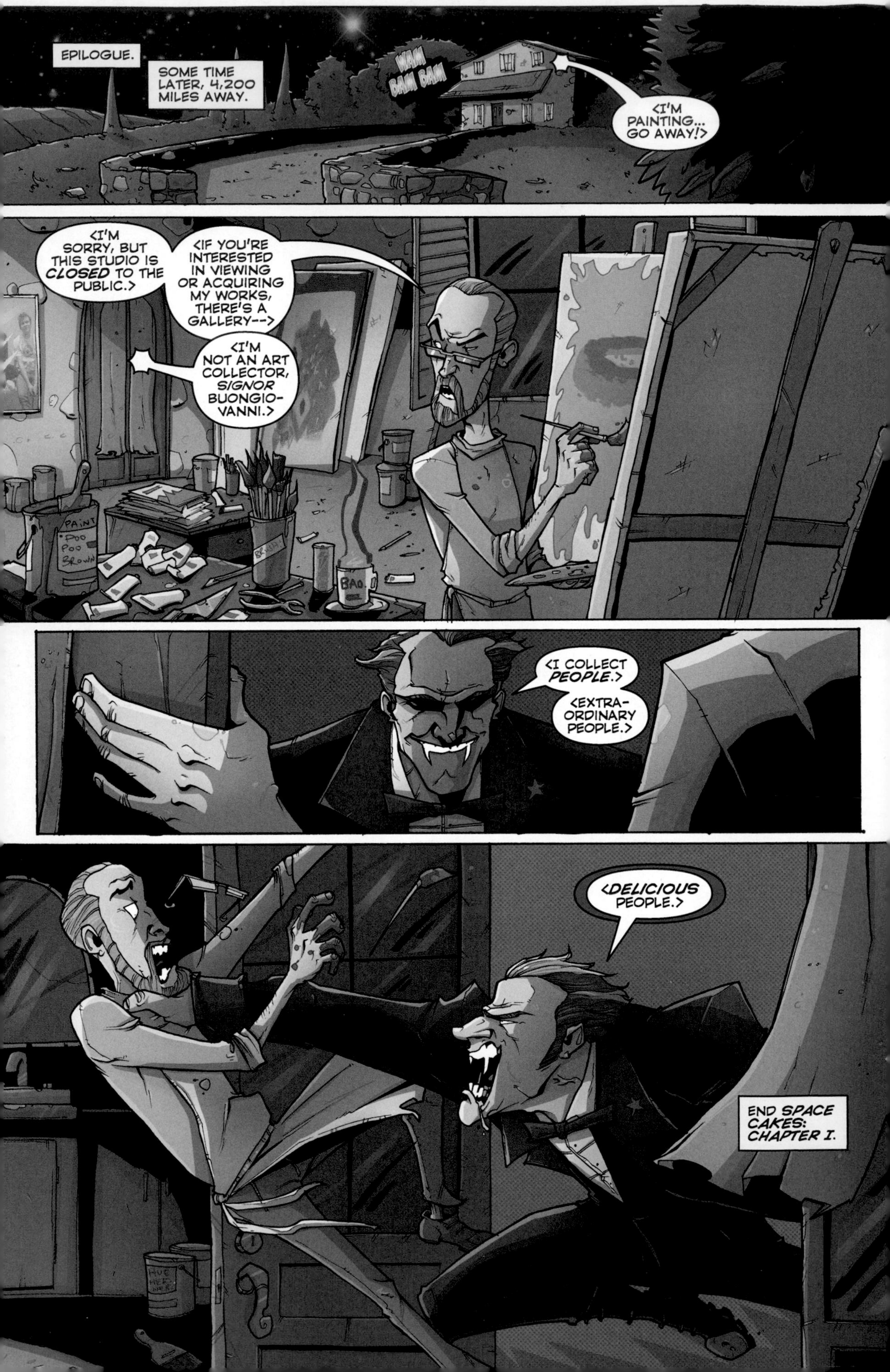
EPILOGUE.
SOME TIME LATER, 4,200 MILES AWAY.
WAM BAM BAM
<I'M PAINTING... GO AWAY!>
<I'M SORRY, BUT THIS STUDIO IS *CLOSED* TO THE PUBLIC.>
<IF YOU'RE INTERESTED IN VIEWING OR ACQUIRING MY WORKS, THERE'S A GALLERY-->
<I'M NOT AN ART COLLECTOR, *SIGNOR* BUONGIO-VANNI.>
PAINT POO POO BROWN
BAQ.
<I COLLECT *PEOPLE*.>
<EXTRA-ORDINARY PEOPLE.>
<*DELICIOUS* PEOPLE.>
END *SPACE CAKES: CHAPTER I*.

Chapter 2

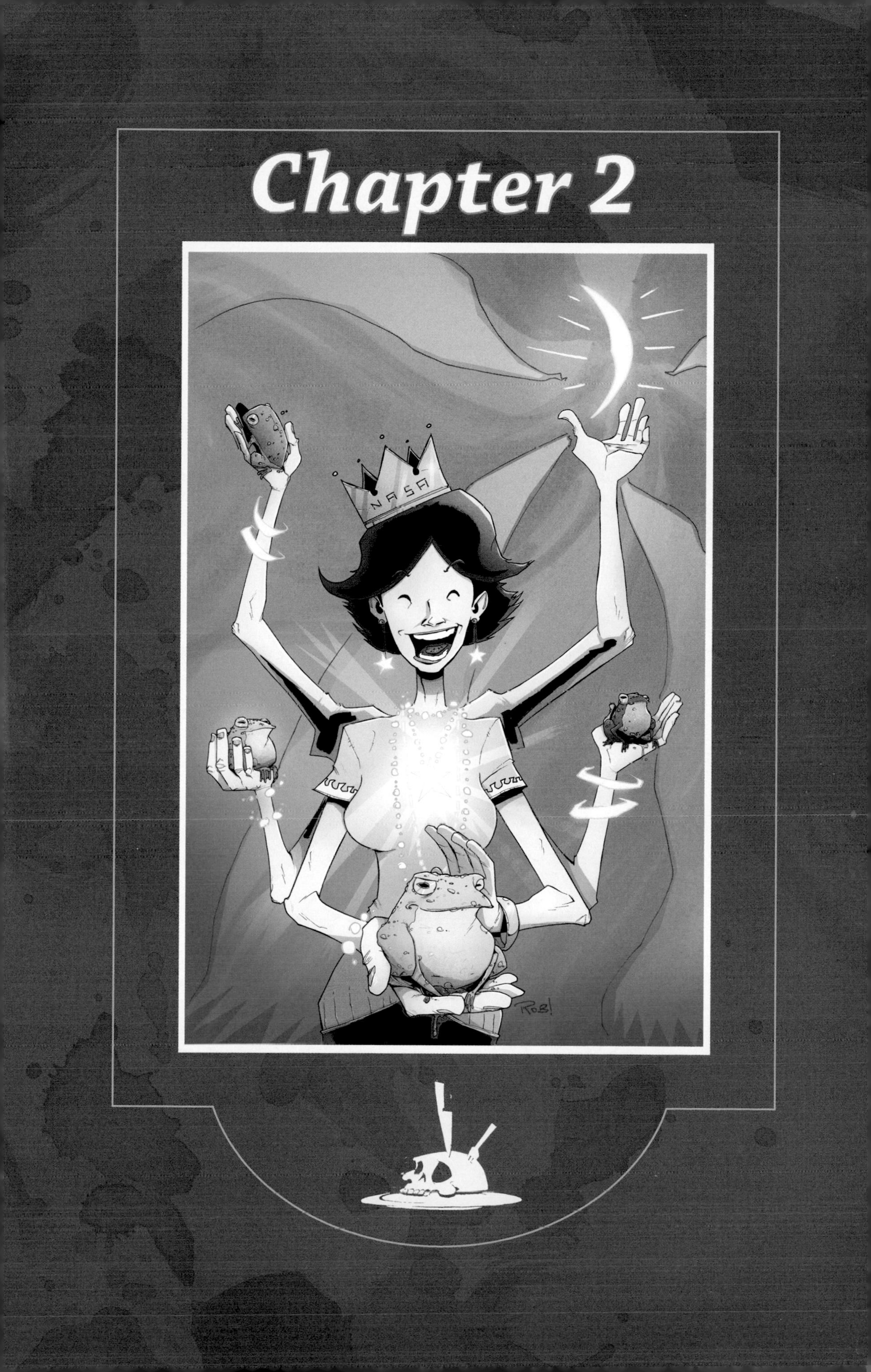

NASA
ROB!

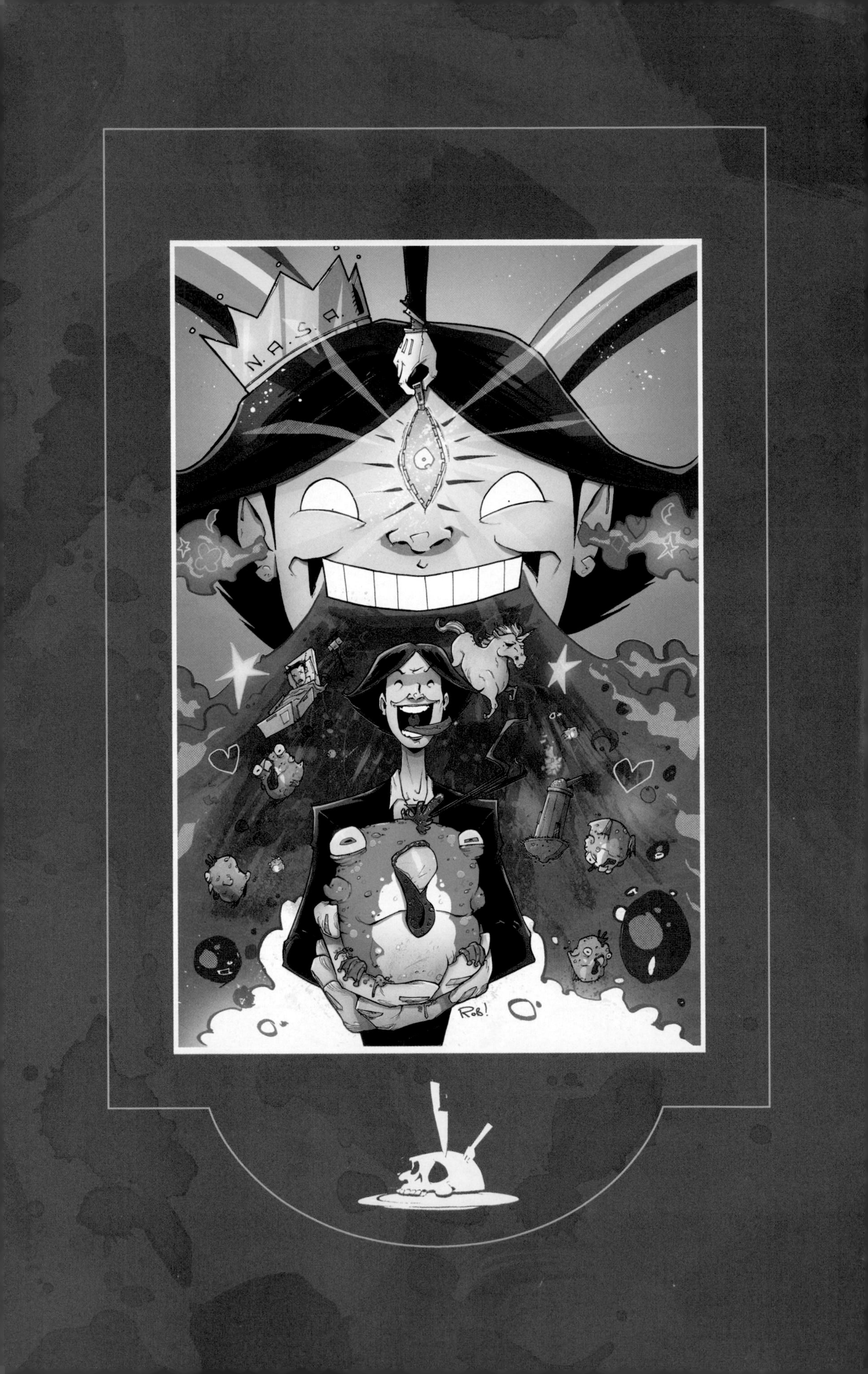
N.A.S.A.
ROB!

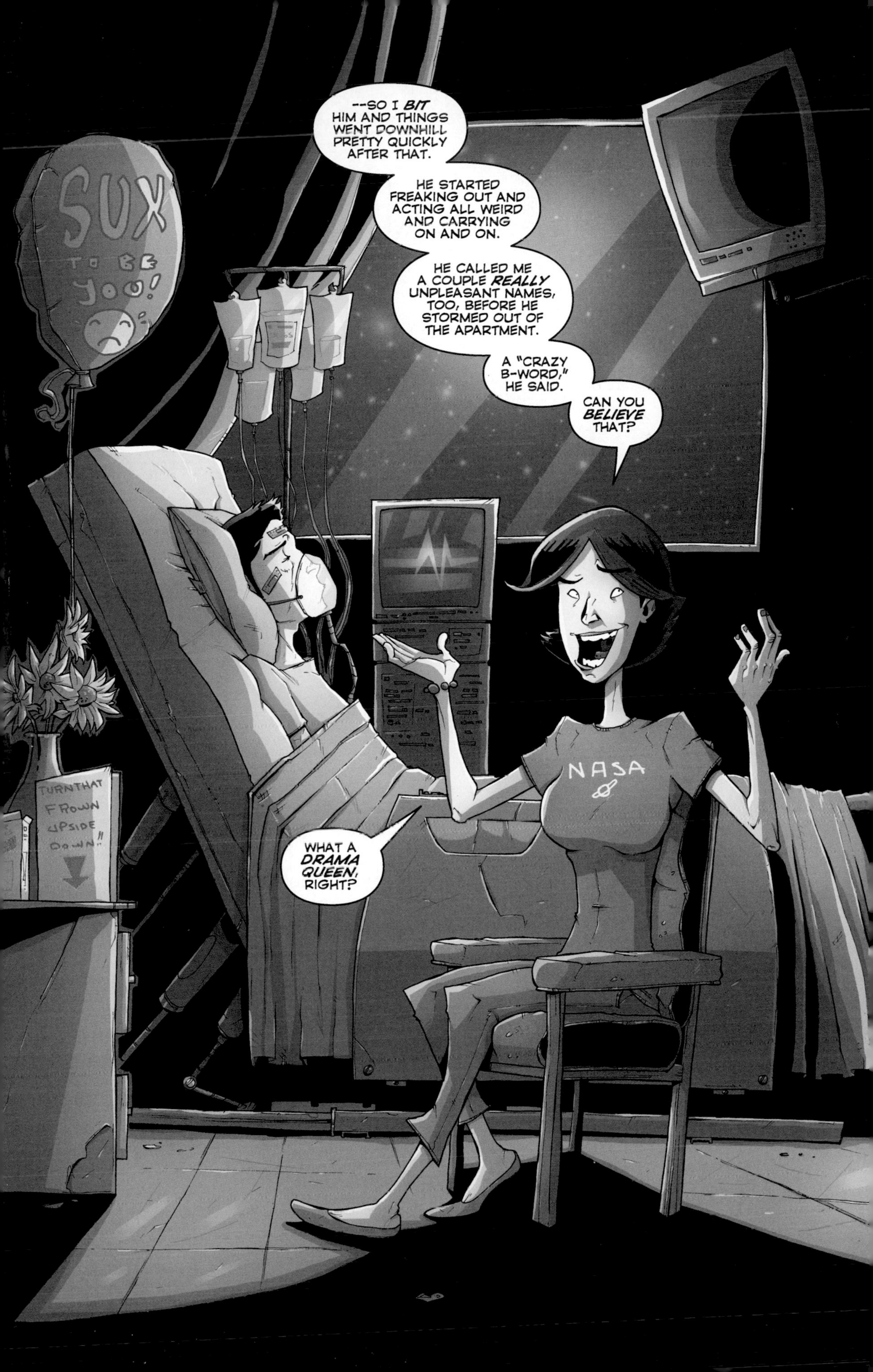
SUX TO BE YOU!
--SO I BIT HIM AND THINGS WENT DOWNHILL PRETTY QUICKLY AFTER THAT.
HE STARTED FREAKING OUT AND ACTING ALL WEIRD AND CARRYING ON AND ON.
HE CALLED ME A COUPLE REALLY UNPLEASANT NAMES, TOO, BEFORE HE STORMED OUT OF THE APARTMENT.
A "CRAZY B-WORD," HE SAID.
CAN YOU BELIEVE THAT?
NASA
TURN THAT FROWN UPSIDE DOWN!!
WHAT A DRAMA QUEEN, RIGHT?

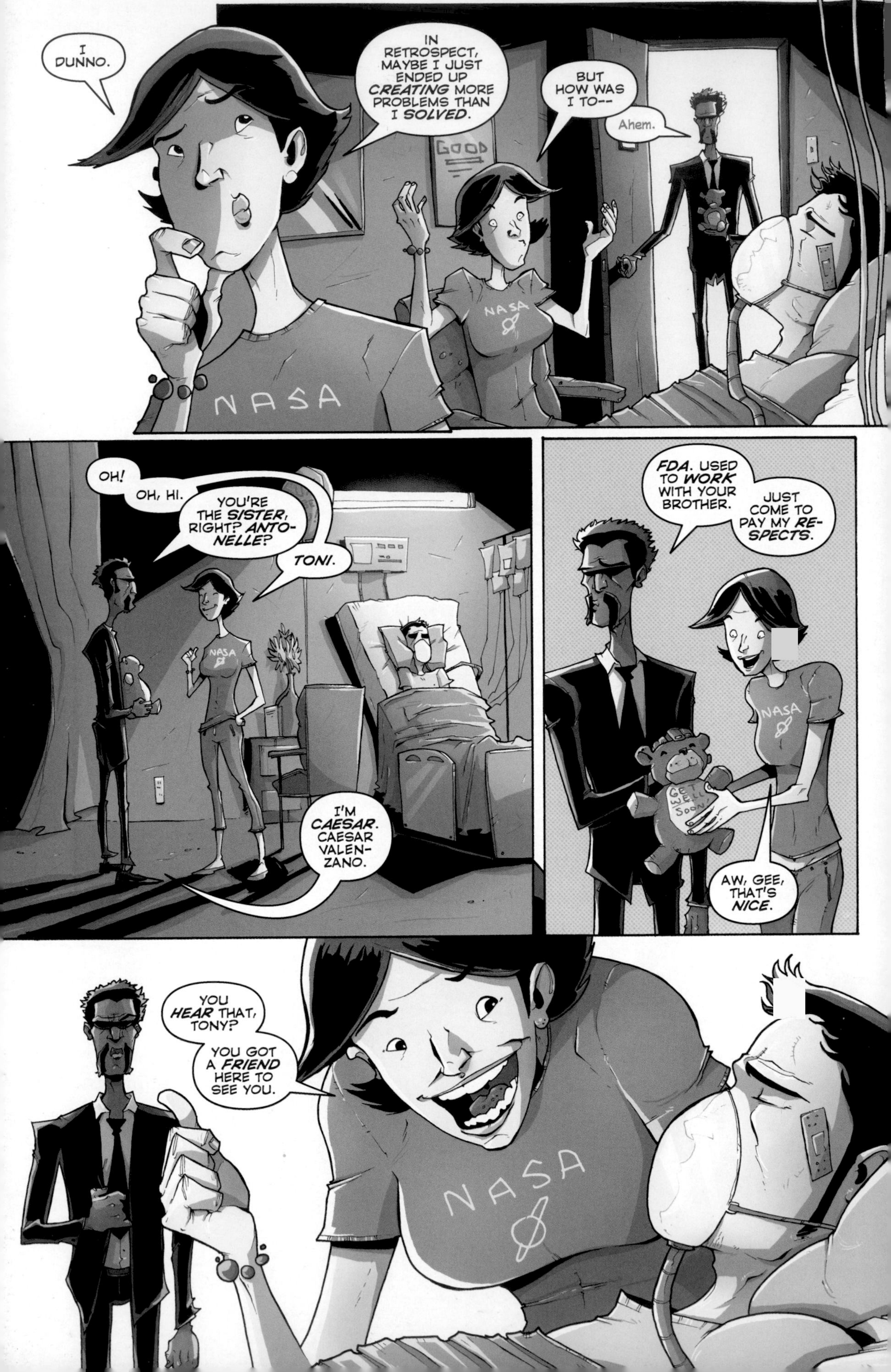
I DUNNO.
IN RETROSPECT, MAYBE I JUST ENDED UP CREATING MORE PROBLEMS THAN I SOLVED.
BUT HOW WAS I TO--
Ahem.
GOOD
OH!
OH, HI.
YOU'RE THE SISTER, RIGHT? ANTONELLE?
TONI.
I'M CAESAR. CAESAR VALENZANO.
FDA. USED TO WORK WITH YOUR BROTHER.
JUST COME TO PAY MY RESPECTS.
GET WELL SOON
AW, GEE, THAT'S NICE.
YOU HEAR THAT, TONY?
YOU GOT A FRIEND HERE TO SEE YOU.

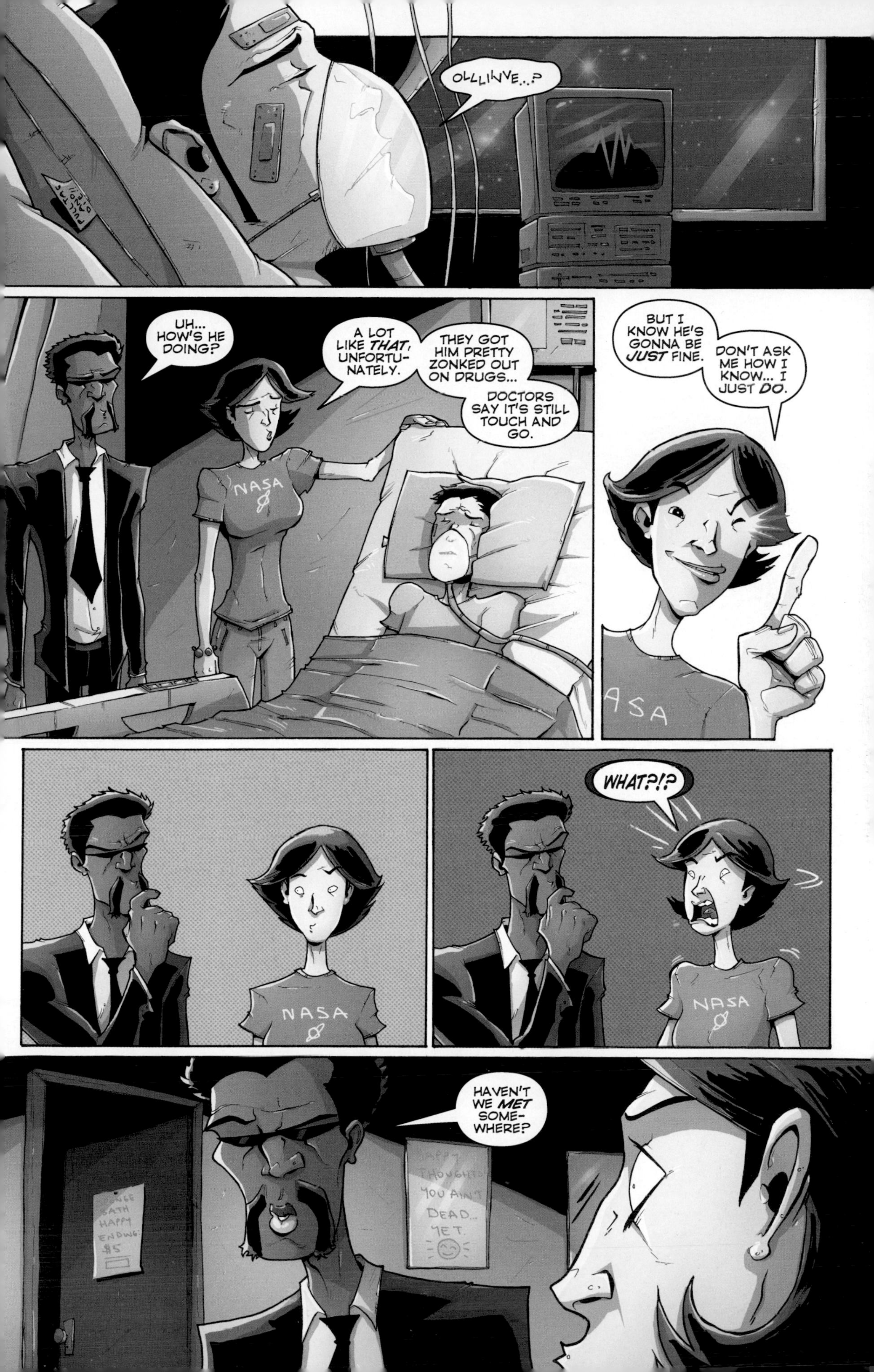
OLLLIIIVVVE...?
UH... HOW'S HE DOING?
A LOT LIKE *THAT*, UNFORTU-NATELY.
THEY GOT HIM PRETTY ZONKED OUT ON DRUGS...
DOCTORS SAY IT'S STILL TOUCH AND GO.
BUT I KNOW HE'S GONNA BE *JUST* FINE.
DON'T ASK ME HOW I KNOW... I JUST *DO*.
NASA
NASA
NASA
NASA
WHAT?!?
HAVEN'T WE *MET* SOME-WHERE?
HAPPY THOUGHTS! YOU AIN'T DEAD... YET.

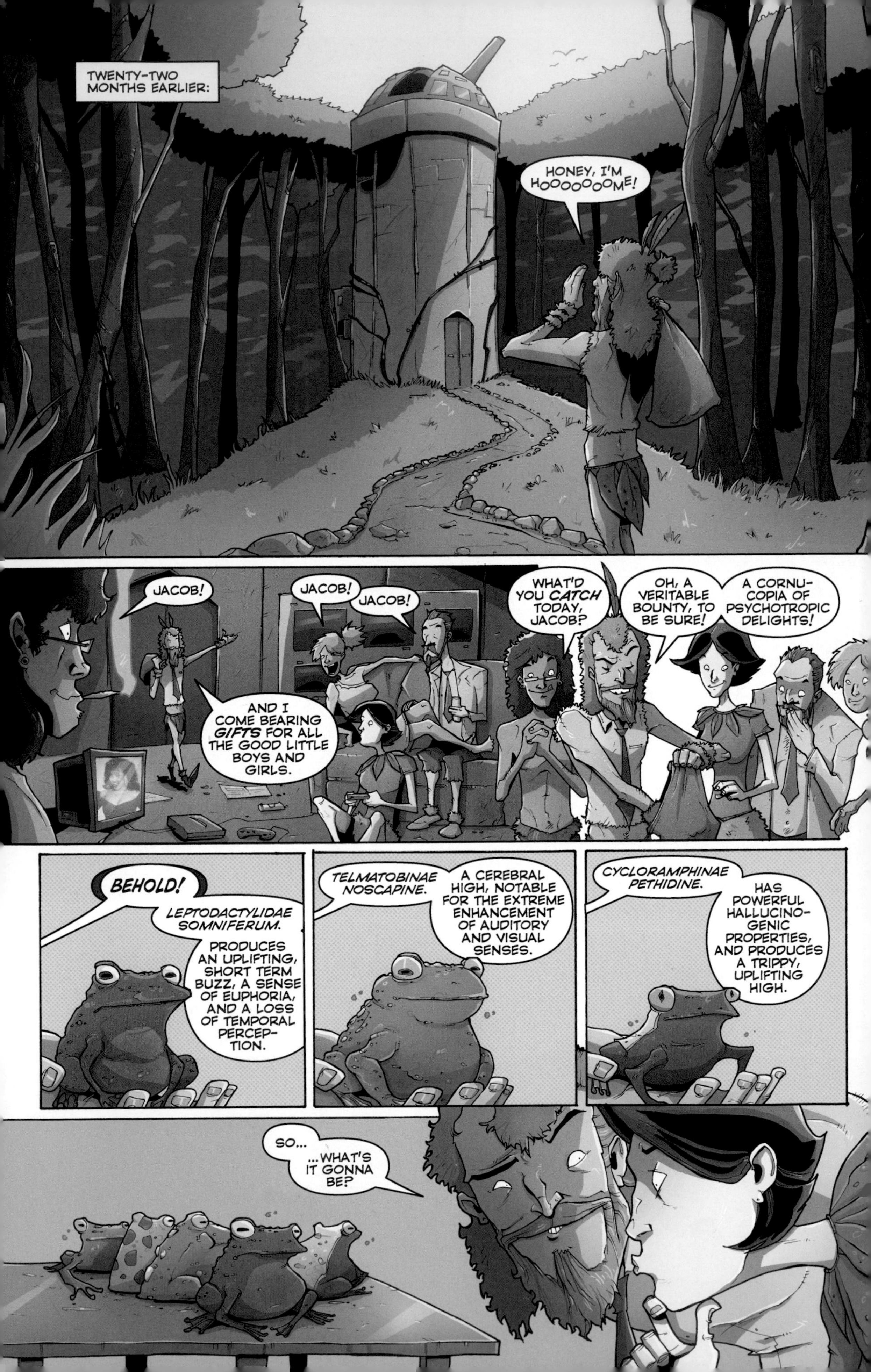
TWENTY-TWO MONTHS EARLIER:
HONEY, I'M HOOOOOOOME!
JACOB!
JACOB!
JACOB!
AND I COME BEARING GIFTS FOR ALL THE GOOD LITTLE BOYS AND GIRLS.
WHAT'D YOU CATCH TODAY, JACOB?
OH, A VERITABLE BOUNTY, TO BE SURE!
A CORNUCOPIA OF PSYCHOTROPIC DELIGHTS!
BEHOLD!
LEPTODACTYLIDAE SOMNIFERUM.
PRODUCES AN UPLIFTING, SHORT TERM BUZZ, A SENSE OF EUPHORIA, AND A LOSS OF TEMPORAL PERCEPTION.
TELMATOBINAE NOSCAPINE.
A CEREBRAL HIGH, NOTABLE FOR THE EXTREME ENHANCEMENT OF AUDITORY AND VISUAL SENSES.
CYCLORAMPHINAE PETHIDINE.
HAS POWERFUL HALLUCINOGENIC PROPERTIES, AND PRODUCES A TRIPPY, UPLIFTING HIGH.
SO...
...WHAT'S IT GONNA BE?

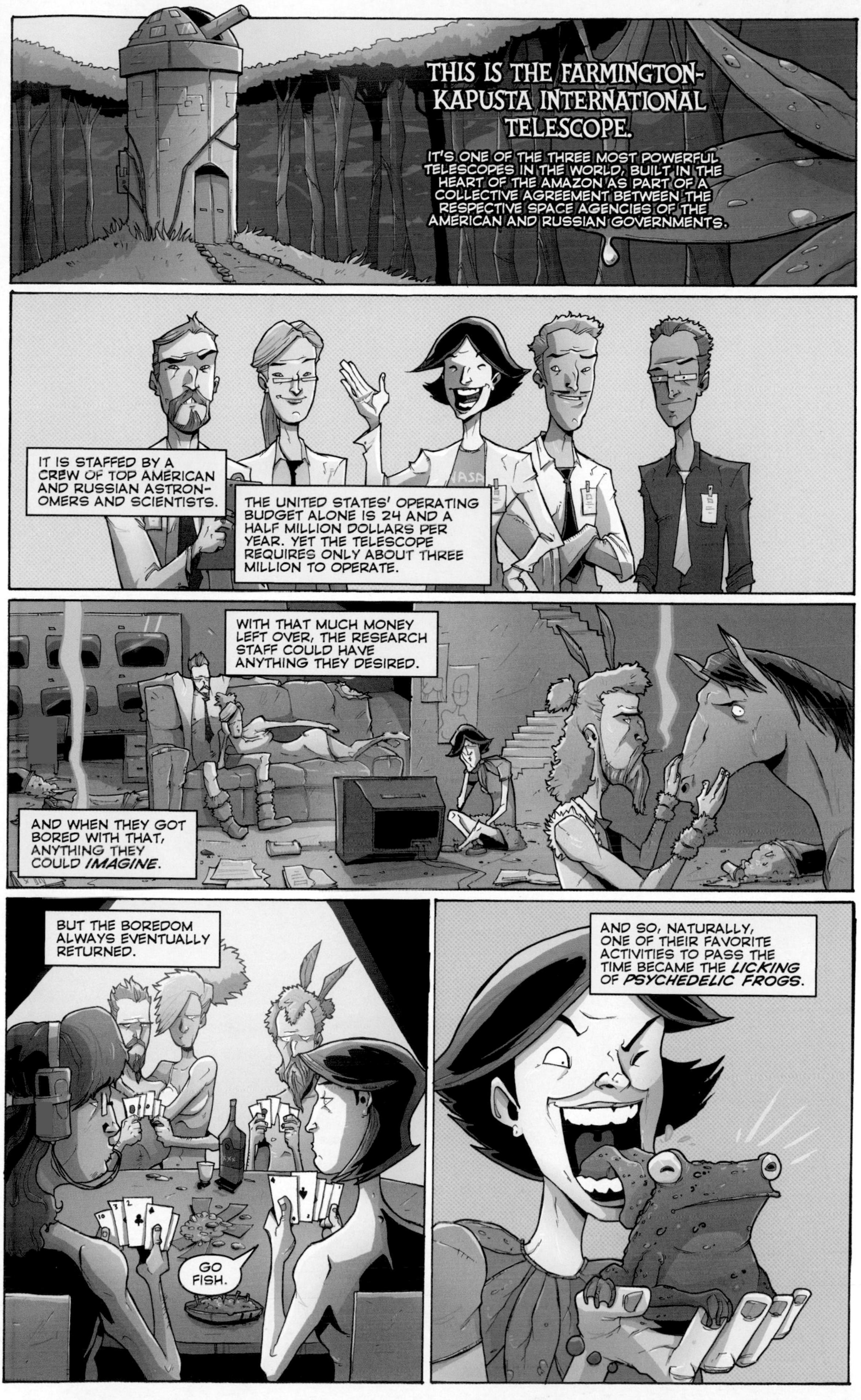
THIS IS THE FARMINGTON-KAPUSTA INTERNATIONAL TELESCOPE.
IT'S ONE OF THE THREE MOST POWERFUL TELESCOPES IN THE WORLD, BUILT IN THE HEART OF THE AMAZON AS PART OF A COLLECTIVE AGREEMENT BETWEEN THE RESPECTIVE SPACE AGENCIES OF THE AMERICAN AND RUSSIAN GOVERNMENTS.
IT IS STAFFED BY A CREW OF TOP AMERICAN AND RUSSIAN ASTRONOMERS AND SCIENTISTS.
THE UNITED STATES' OPERATING BUDGET ALONE IS 24 AND A HALF MILLION DOLLARS PER YEAR. YET THE TELESCOPE REQUIRES ONLY ABOUT THREE MILLION TO OPERATE.
NASA
WITH THAT MUCH MONEY LEFT OVER, THE RESEARCH STAFF COULD HAVE ANYTHING THEY DESIRED.
AND WHEN THEY GOT BORED WITH THAT, ANYTHING THEY COULD *IMAGINE*.
BUT THE BOREDOM ALWAYS EVENTUALLY RETURNED.
GO FISH.
AND SO, NATURALLY, ONE OF THEIR FAVORITE ACTIVITIES TO PASS THE TIME BECAME THE *LICKING* OF *PSYCHEDELIC FROGS*.

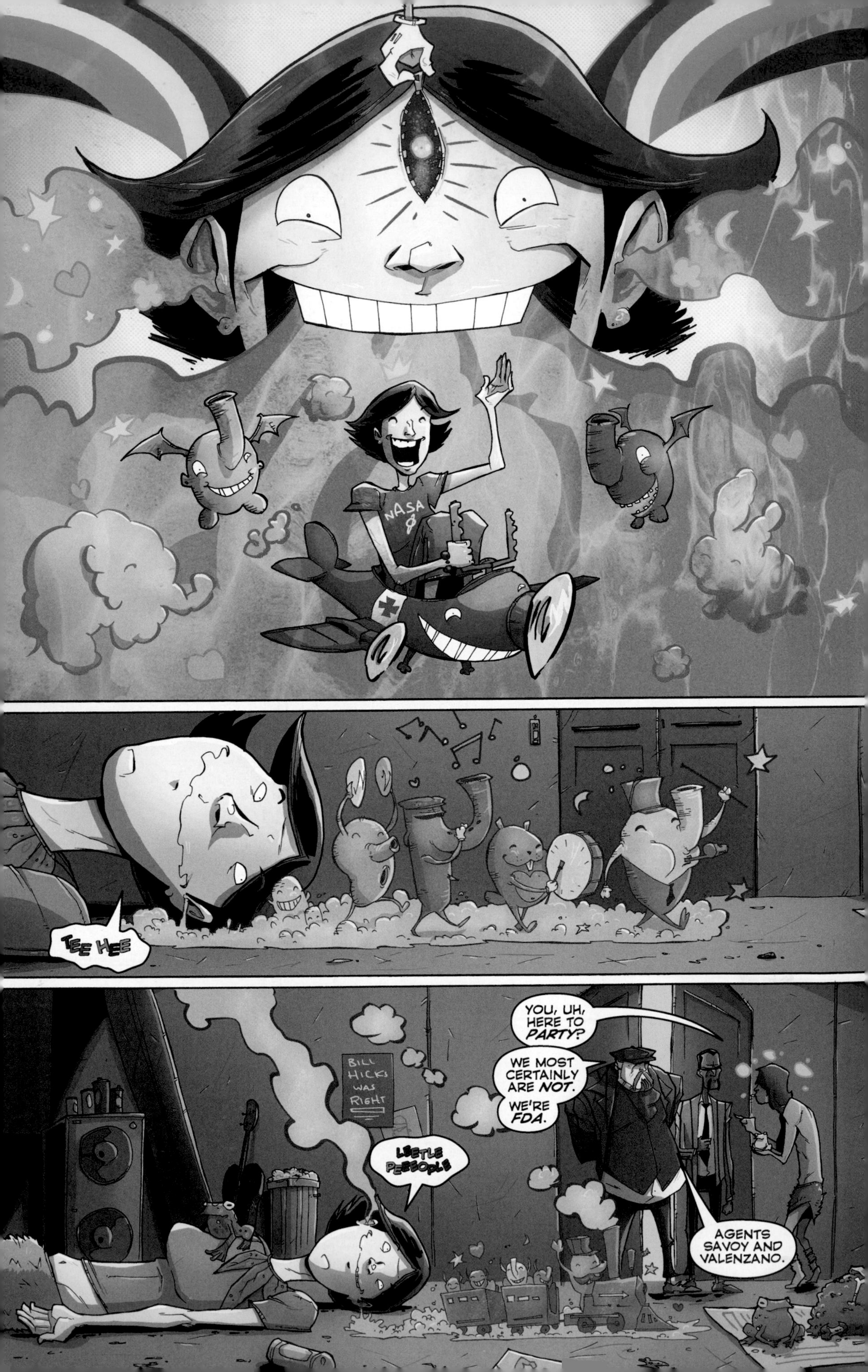

NASA
TEE HEE
BILL HICKS WAS RIGHT
LEETLE PEEEOPLE
YOU, UH, HERE TO PARTY?
WE MOST CERTAINLY ARE NOT.
WE'RE FDA.
AGENTS SAVOY AND VALENZANO.

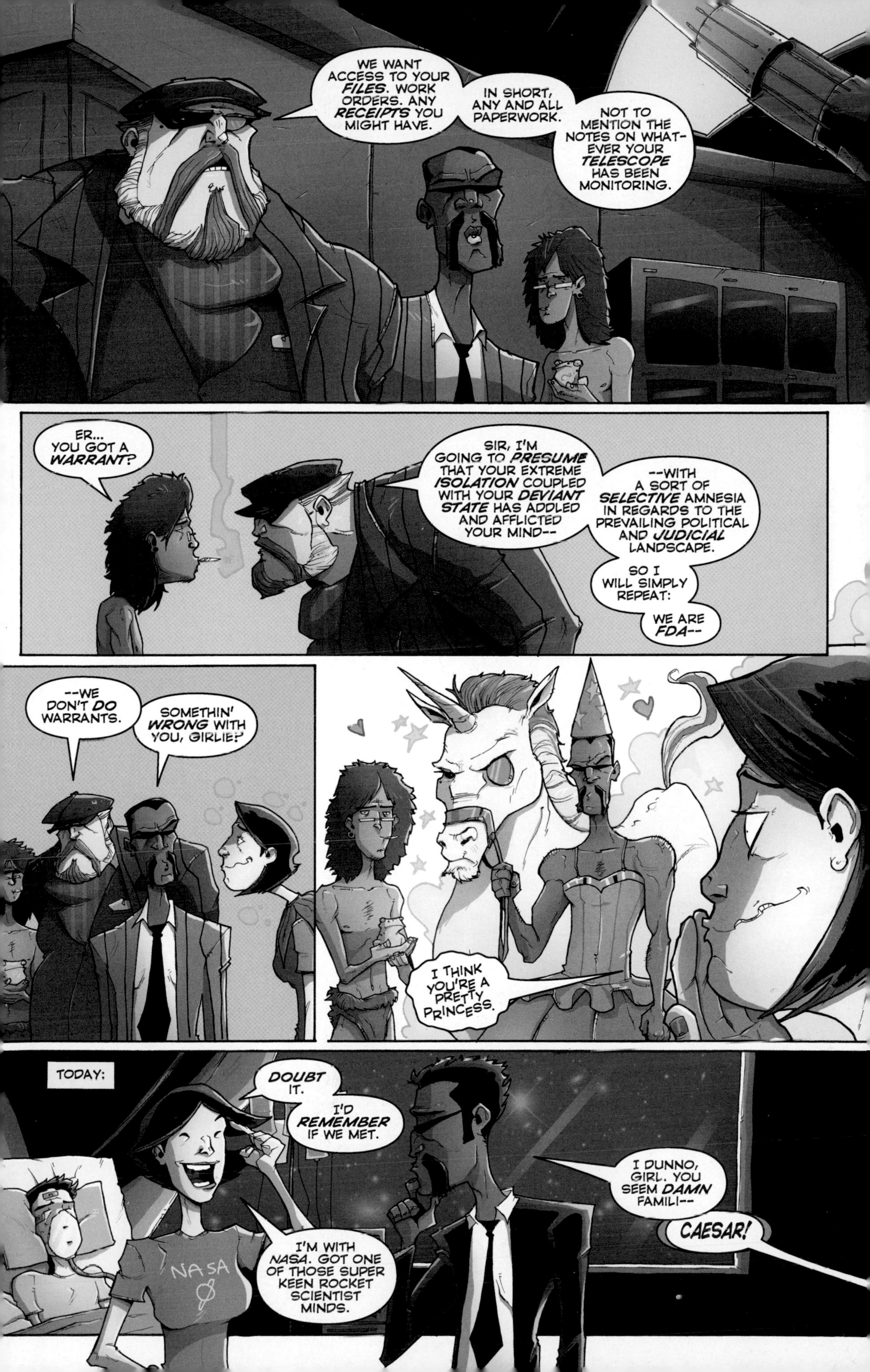
WE WANT ACCESS TO YOUR FILES. WORK ORDERS. ANY RECEIPTS YOU MIGHT HAVE.
IN SHORT, ANY AND ALL PAPERWORK.
NOT TO MENTION THE NOTES ON WHATEVER YOUR TELESCOPE HAS BEEN MONITORING.
ER... YOU GOT A WARRANT?
SIR, I'M GOING TO PRESUME THAT YOUR EXTREME ISOLATION COUPLED WITH YOUR DEVIANT STATE HAS ADDLED AND AFFLICTED YOUR MIND--
--WITH A SORT OF SELECTIVE AMNESIA IN REGARDS TO THE PREVAILING POLITICAL AND JUDICIAL LANDSCAPE.
SO I WILL SIMPLY REPEAT:
WE ARE FDA--
--WE DON'T DO WARRANTS.
SOMETHIN' WRONG WITH YOU, GIRLIE?
I THINK YOU'RE A PRETTY PRINCESS.
TODAY:
DOUBT IT.
I'D REMEMBER IF WE MET.
I DUNNO, GIRL. YOU SEEM DAMN FAMILI--
I'M WITH NASA. GOT ONE OF THOSE SUPER KEEN ROCKET SCIENTIST MINDS.
CAESAR!
NASA

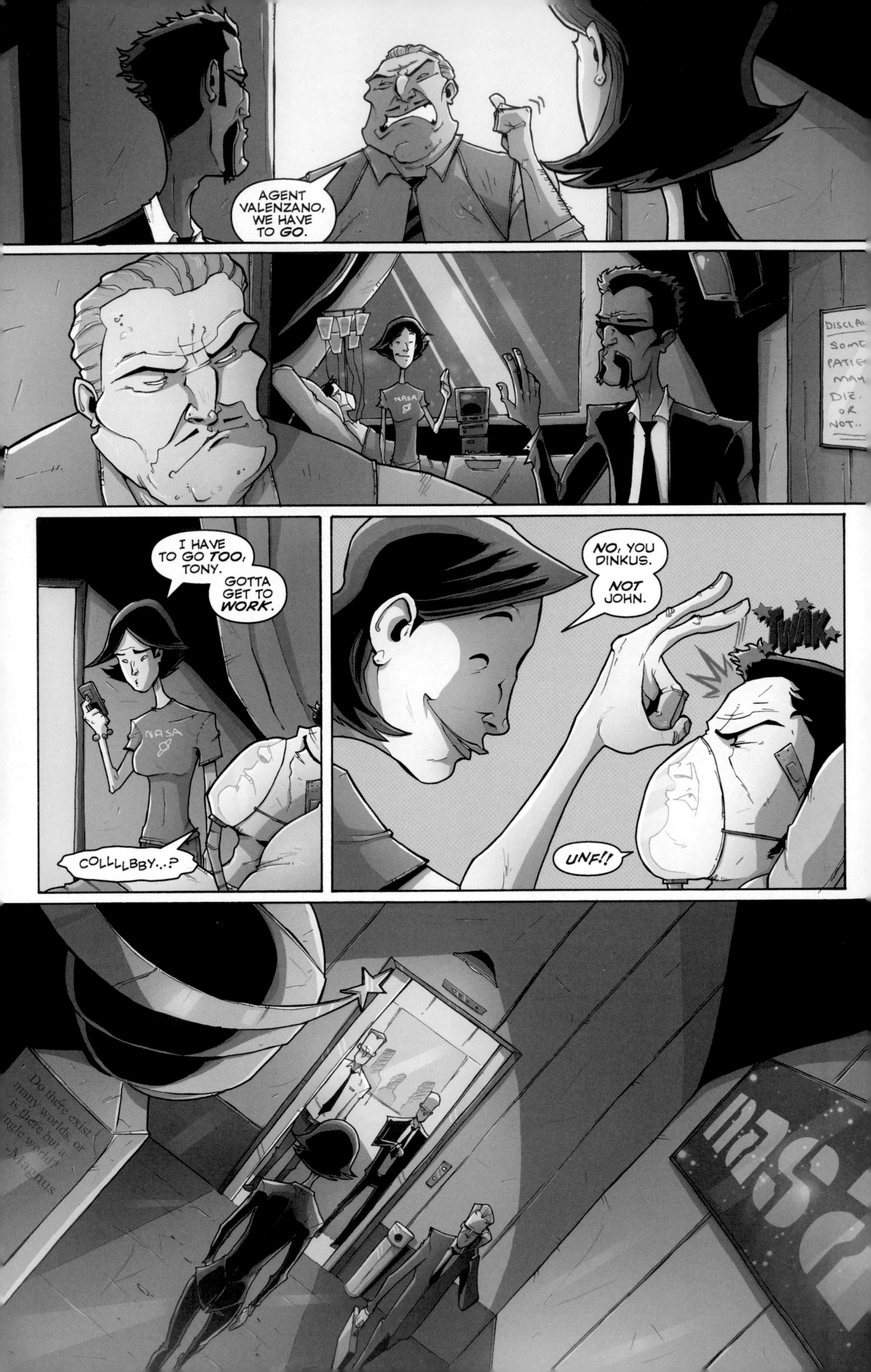
AGENT VALENZANO, WE HAVE TO GO.
I HAVE TO GO TOO, TONY.
GOTTA GET TO WORK.
COLLLLLBBY...?
NO, YOU DINKUS.
NOT JOHN.
TWAK
UNF!!
Do there exist many worlds, or is there but a
-Magnus

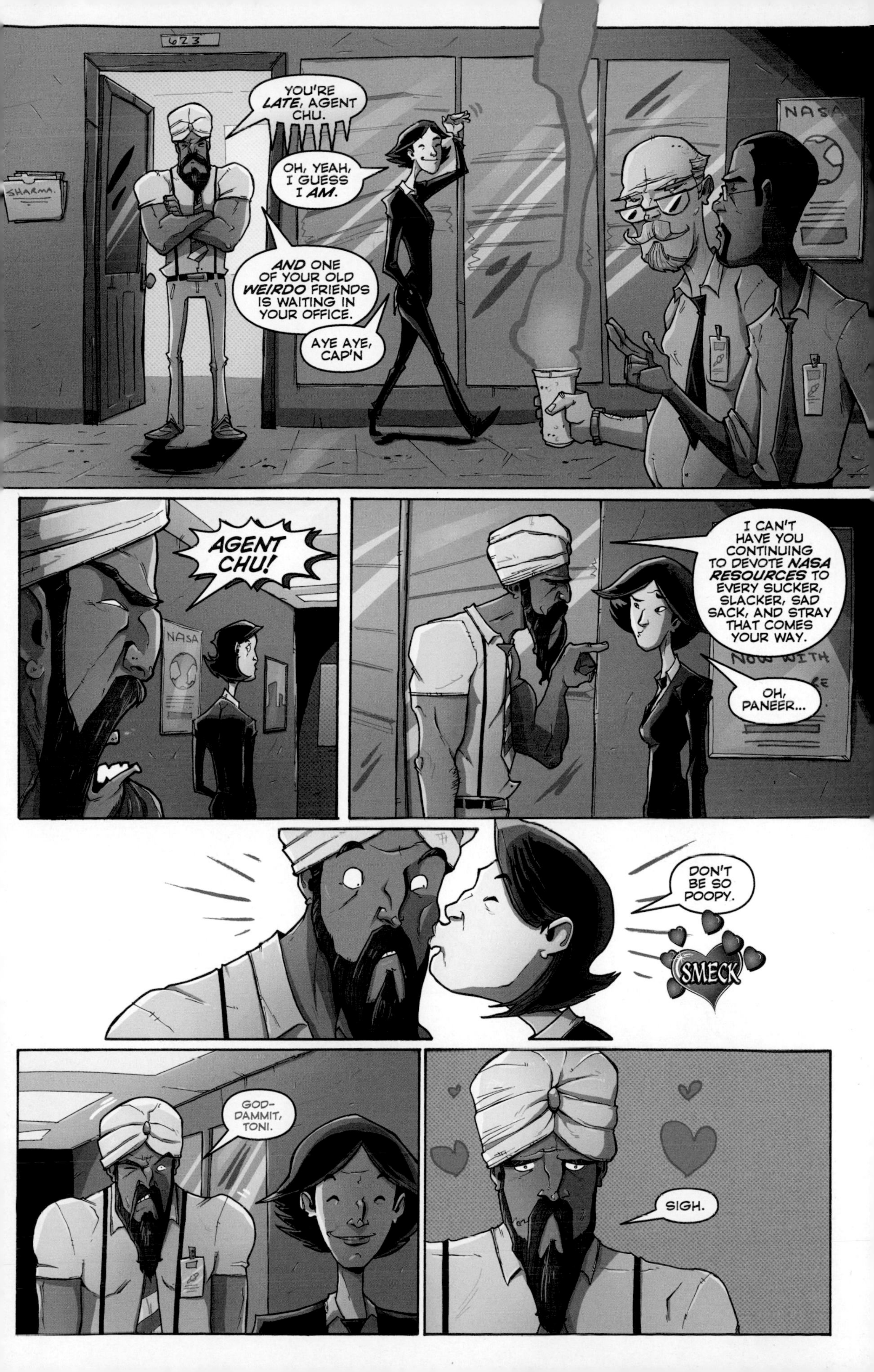
623
SHARMA.
YOU'RE LATE, AGENT CHU.
OH, YEAH, I GUESS I AM.
AND ONE OF YOUR OLD WEIRDO FRIENDS IS WAITING IN YOUR OFFICE.
AYE AYE, CAP'N
NASA
AGENT CHU!
NASA
I CAN'T HAVE YOU CONTINUING TO DEVOTE NASA RESOURCES TO EVERY SUCKER, SLACKER, SAD SACK, AND STRAY THAT COMES YOUR WAY.
OH, PANEER...
DON'T BE SO POOPY.
SMECK
GOD-DAMMIT, TONI.
SIGH.

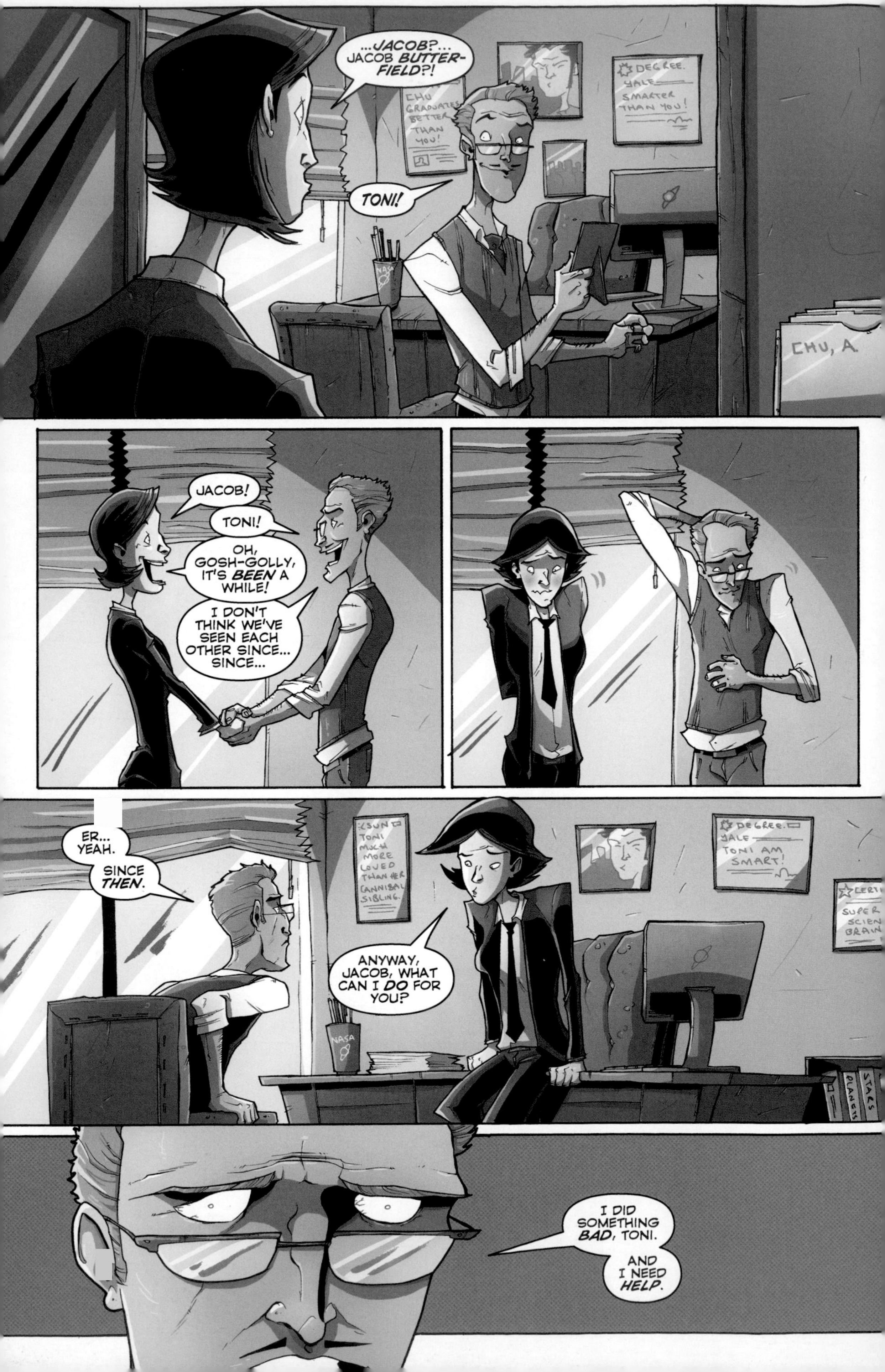

...JACOB?... JACOB BUTTERFIELD?!
TONI!
CHU GRADUATES BETTER THAN YOU!
DEGREE. YALE SMARTER THAN YOU!
NASA
CHU, A.
JACOB!
TONI!
OH, GOSH-GOLLY, IT'S BEEN A WHILE!
I DON'T THINK WE'VE SEEN EACH OTHER SINCE... SINCE...
ER... YEAH.
SINCE THEN.
SUN TONI MUCH MORE LOVED THAN HER CANNIBAL SIBLING.
DEGREE. YALE TONI AM SMART!
ANYWAY, JACOB, WHAT CAN I DO FOR YOU?
PLANETS
STARS
I DID SOMETHING BAD, TONI.
AND I NEED HELP.

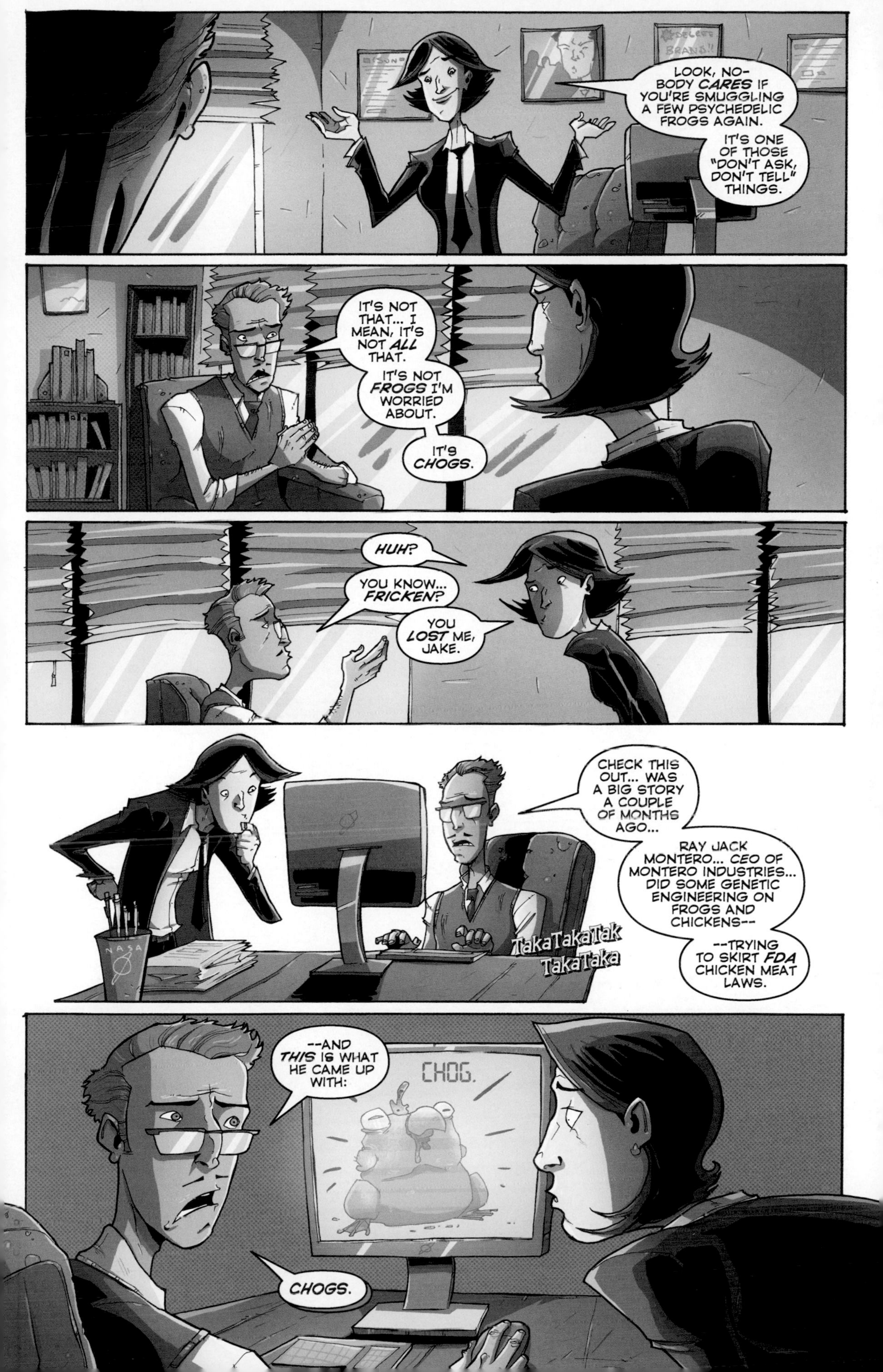
LOOK, NO-BODY CARES IF YOU'RE SMUGGLING A FEW PSYCHEDELIC FROGS AGAIN.
IT'S ONE OF THOSE "DON'T ASK, DON'T TELL" THINGS.
IT'S NOT THAT... I MEAN, IT'S NOT ALL THAT.
IT'S NOT FROGS I'M WORRIED ABOUT.
IT'S CHOGS.
HUH?
YOU KNOW... FRICKEN?
YOU LOST ME, JAKE.
CHECK THIS OUT... WAS A BIG STORY A COUPLE OF MONTHS AGO...
RAY JACK MONTERO... CEO OF MONTERO INDUSTRIES... DID SOME GENETIC ENGINEERING ON FROGS AND CHICKENS--
--TRYING TO SKIRT FDA CHICKEN MEAT LAWS.
NASA
TakaTakaTak
TakaTaka
--AND THIS IS WHAT HE CAME UP WITH:
CHOG.
CHOGS.

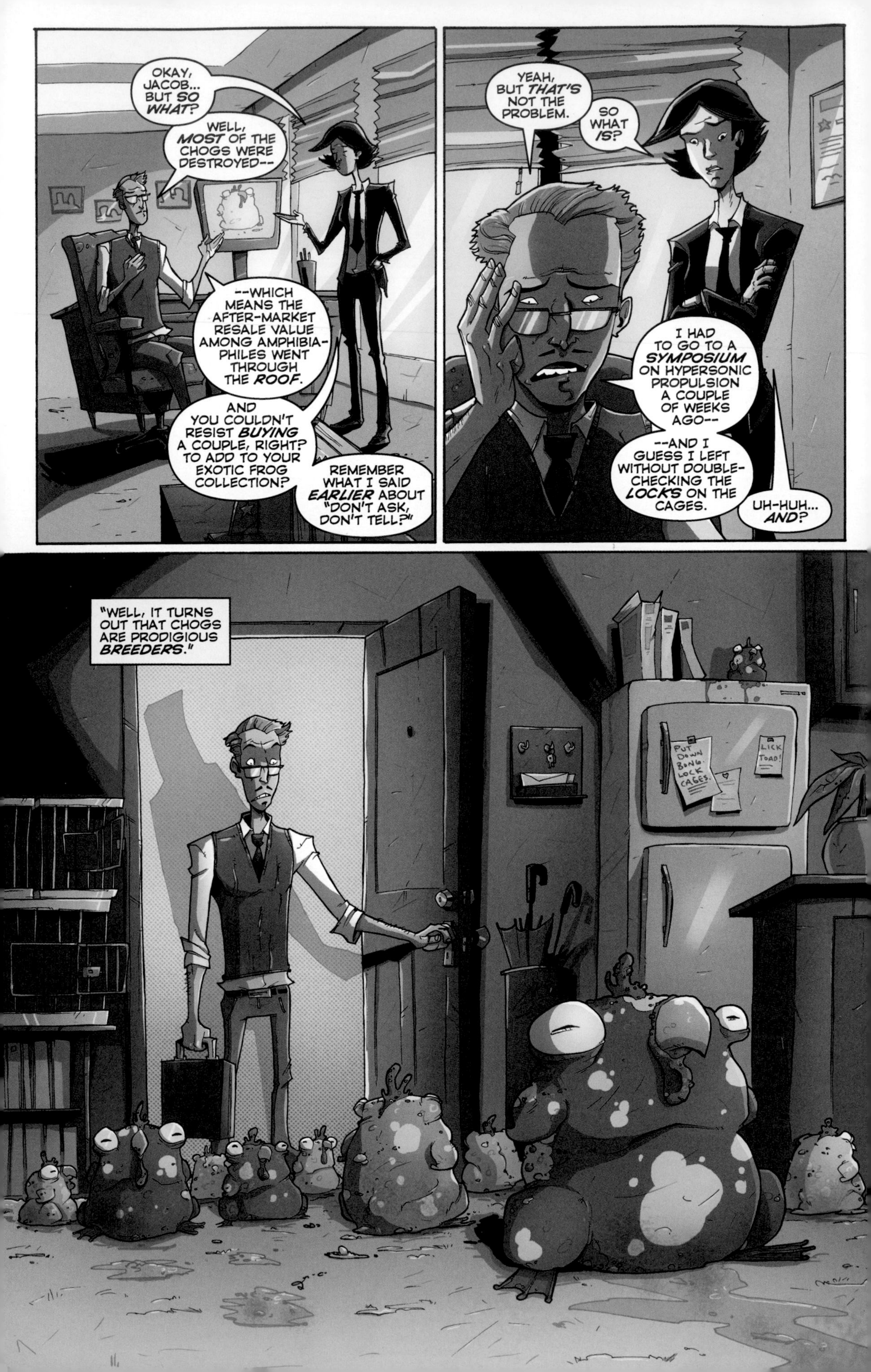
OKAY, JACOB... BUT SO WHAT?
WELL, MOST OF THE CHOGS WERE DESTROYED--
--WHICH MEANS THE AFTER-MARKET RESALE VALUE AMONG AMPHIBIA-PHILES WENT THROUGH THE ROOF.
AND YOU COULDN'T RESIST BUYING A COUPLE, RIGHT? TO ADD TO YOUR EXOTIC FROG COLLECTION?
REMEMBER WHAT I SAID EARLIER ABOUT "DON'T ASK, DON'T TELL?"
YEAH, BUT THAT'S NOT THE PROBLEM.
SO WHAT IS?
I HAD TO GO TO A SYMPOSIUM ON HYPERSONIC PROPULSION A COUPLE OF WEEKS AGO--
--AND I GUESS I LEFT WITHOUT DOUBLE-CHECKING THE LOCKS ON THE CAGES.
UH-HUH... AND?
"WELL, IT TURNS OUT THAT CHOGS ARE PRODIGIOUS BREEDERS."
PUT DOWN BONG. LOCK CAGES.
LICK TOAD!

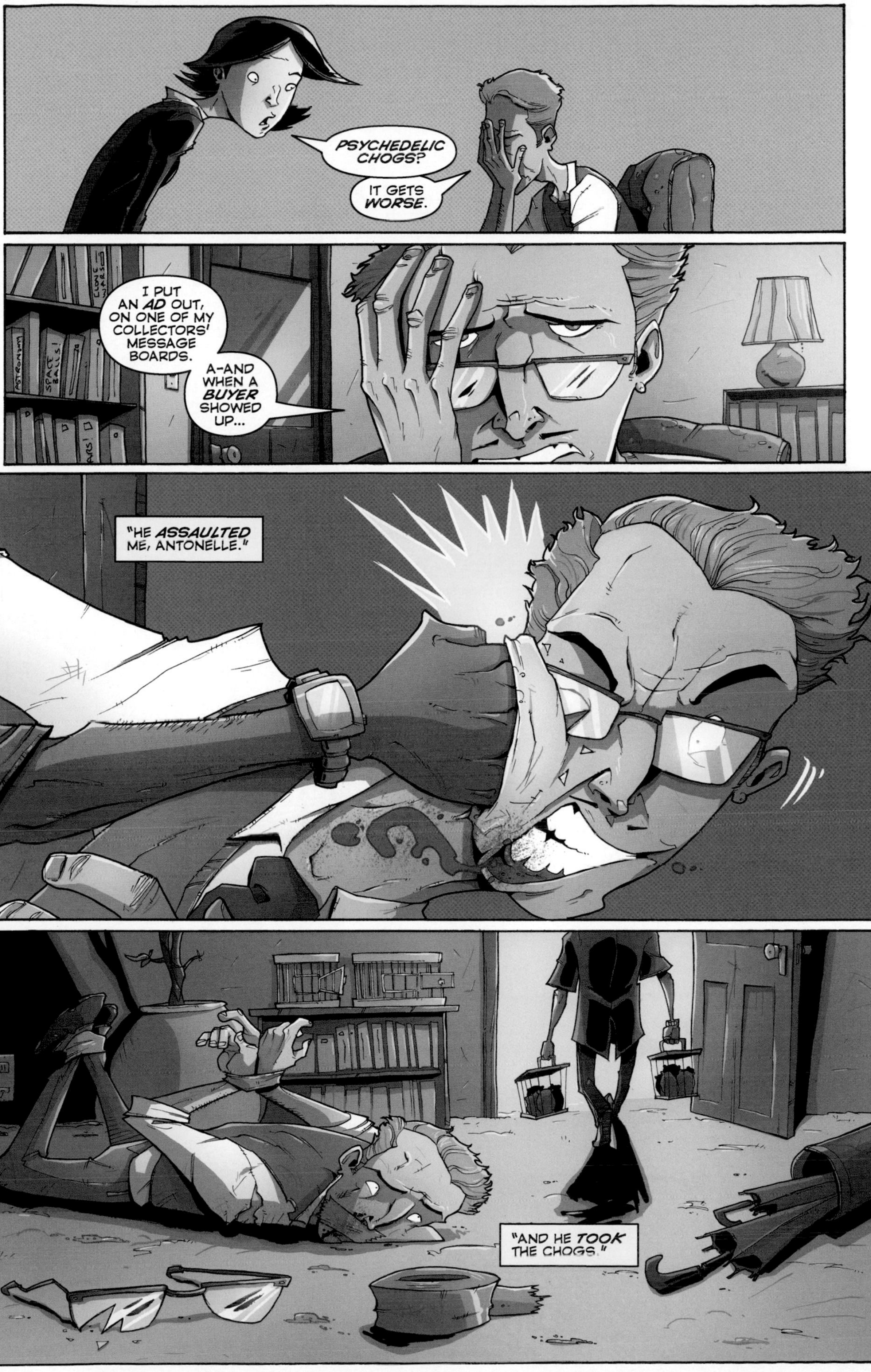

PSYCHEDELIC CHOGS?
IT GETS WORSE.
I PUT AN AD OUT, ON ONE OF MY COLLECTORS' MESSAGE BOARDS.
A-AND WHEN A BUYER SHOWED UP...
"HE ASSAULTED ME, ANTONELLE."
"AND HE TOOK THE CHOGS."

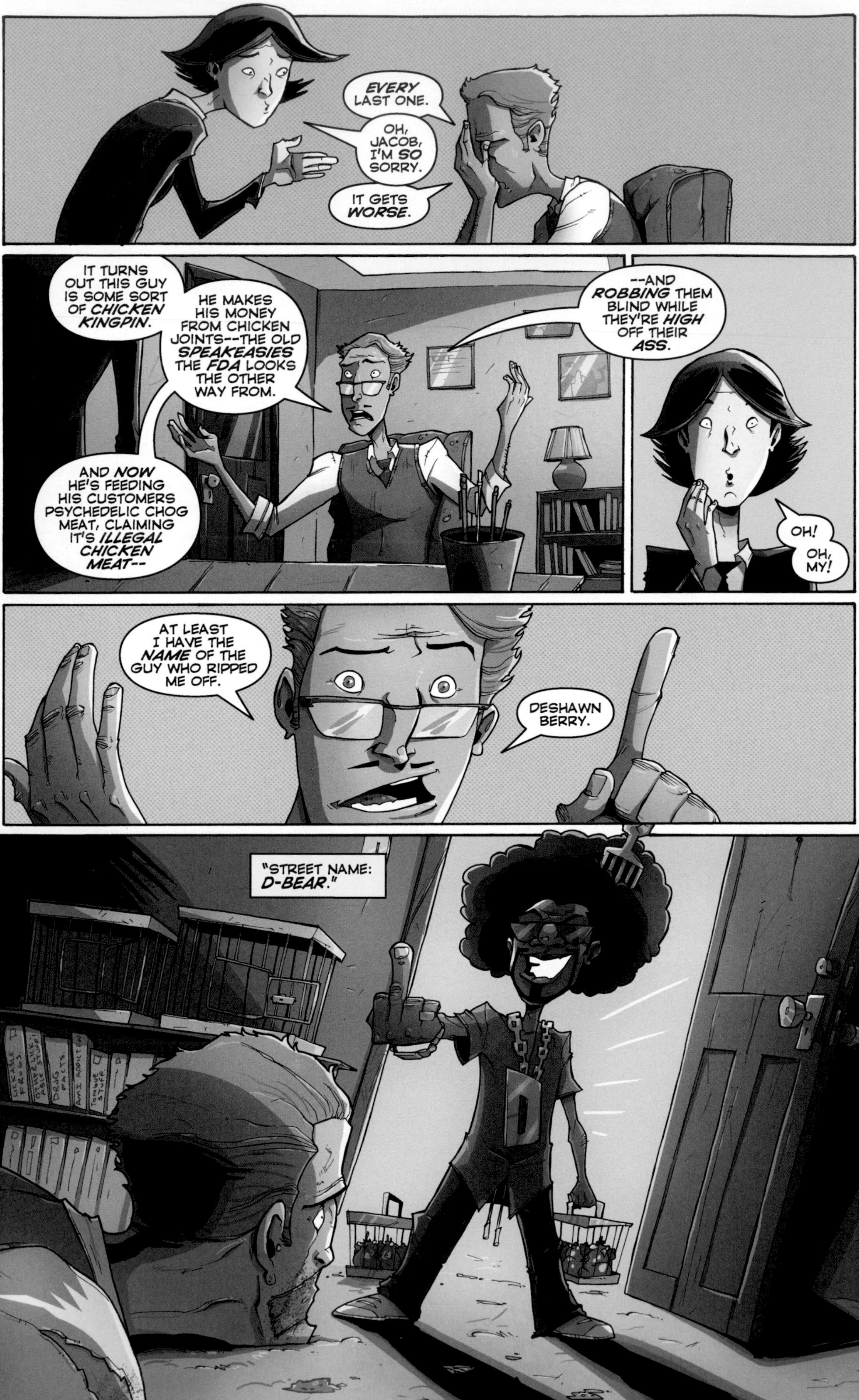
EVERY LAST ONE.
OH, JACOB, I'M SO SORRY.
IT GETS WORSE.
IT TURNS OUT THIS GUY IS SOME SORT OF CHICKEN KINGPIN.
HE MAKES HIS MONEY FROM CHICKEN JOINTS--THE OLD SPEAKEASIES THE FDA LOOKS THE OTHER WAY FROM.
AND NOW HE'S FEEDING HIS CUSTOMERS PSYCHEDELIC CHOG MEAT, CLAIMING IT'S ILLEGAL CHICKEN MEAT--
--AND ROBBING THEM BLIND WHILE THEY'RE HIGH OFF THEIR ASS.
OH! OH, MY!
AT LEAST I HAVE THE NAME OF THE GUY WHO RIPPED ME OFF.
DESHAWN BERRY.
"STREET NAME: D-BEAR."

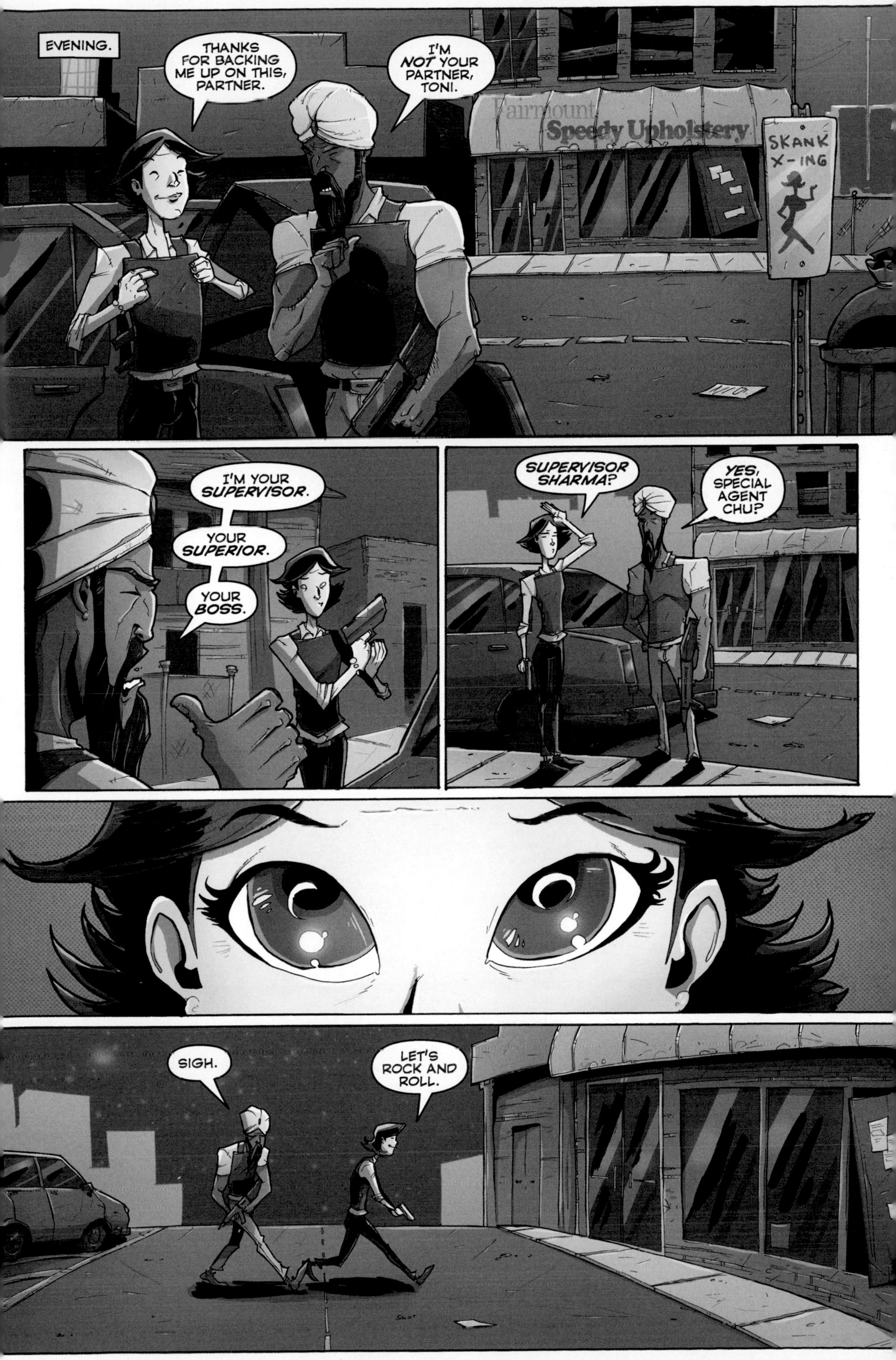
EVENING.
THANKS FOR BACKING ME UP ON THIS, PARTNER.
I'M NOT YOUR PARTNER, TONI.
Fairmount
Speedy Upholstery
SKANK X-ING
I'M YOUR SUPERVISOR.
YOUR SUPERIOR.
YOUR BOSS.
SUPERVISOR SHARMA?
YES, SPECIAL AGENT CHU?
SIGH.
LET'S ROCK AND ROLL.

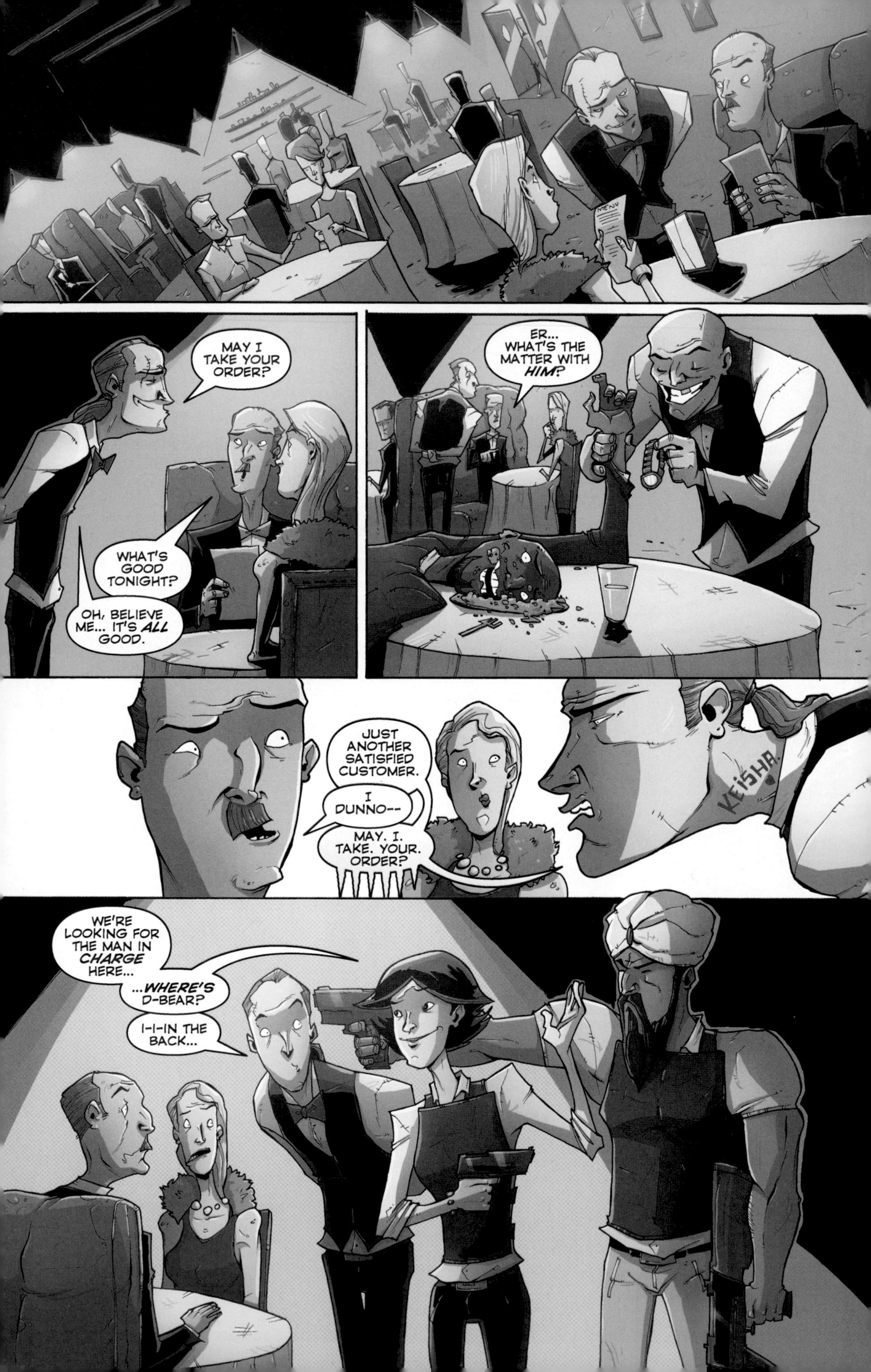

MENU
MAY I TAKE YOUR ORDER?
WHAT'S GOOD TONIGHT?
OH, BELIEVE ME... IT'S ALL GOOD.
ER... WHAT'S THE MATTER WITH HIM?
JUST ANOTHER SATISFIED CUSTOMER.
I DUNNO--
MAY. I. TAKE. YOUR. ORDER?
KEISHA
WE'RE LOOKING FOR THE MAN IN CHARGE HERE...
...WHERE'S D-BEAR?
I-I-IN THE BACK...

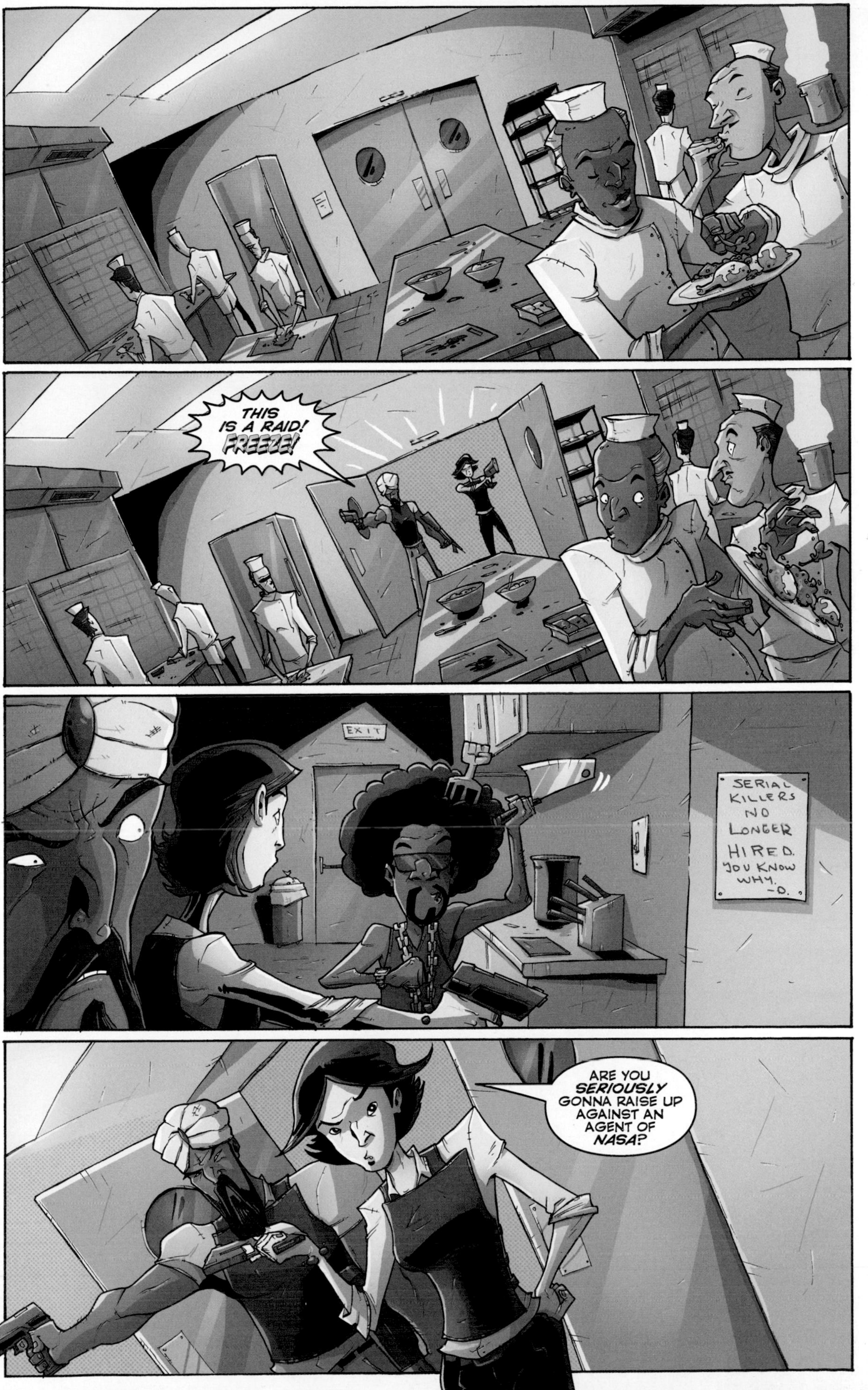
THIS IS A RAID! FREEZE!
EXIT
SERIAL KILLERS NO LONGER HIRED. YOU KNOW WHY. -O.
ARE YOU SERIOUSLY GONNA RAISE UP AGAINST AN AGENT OF NASA?

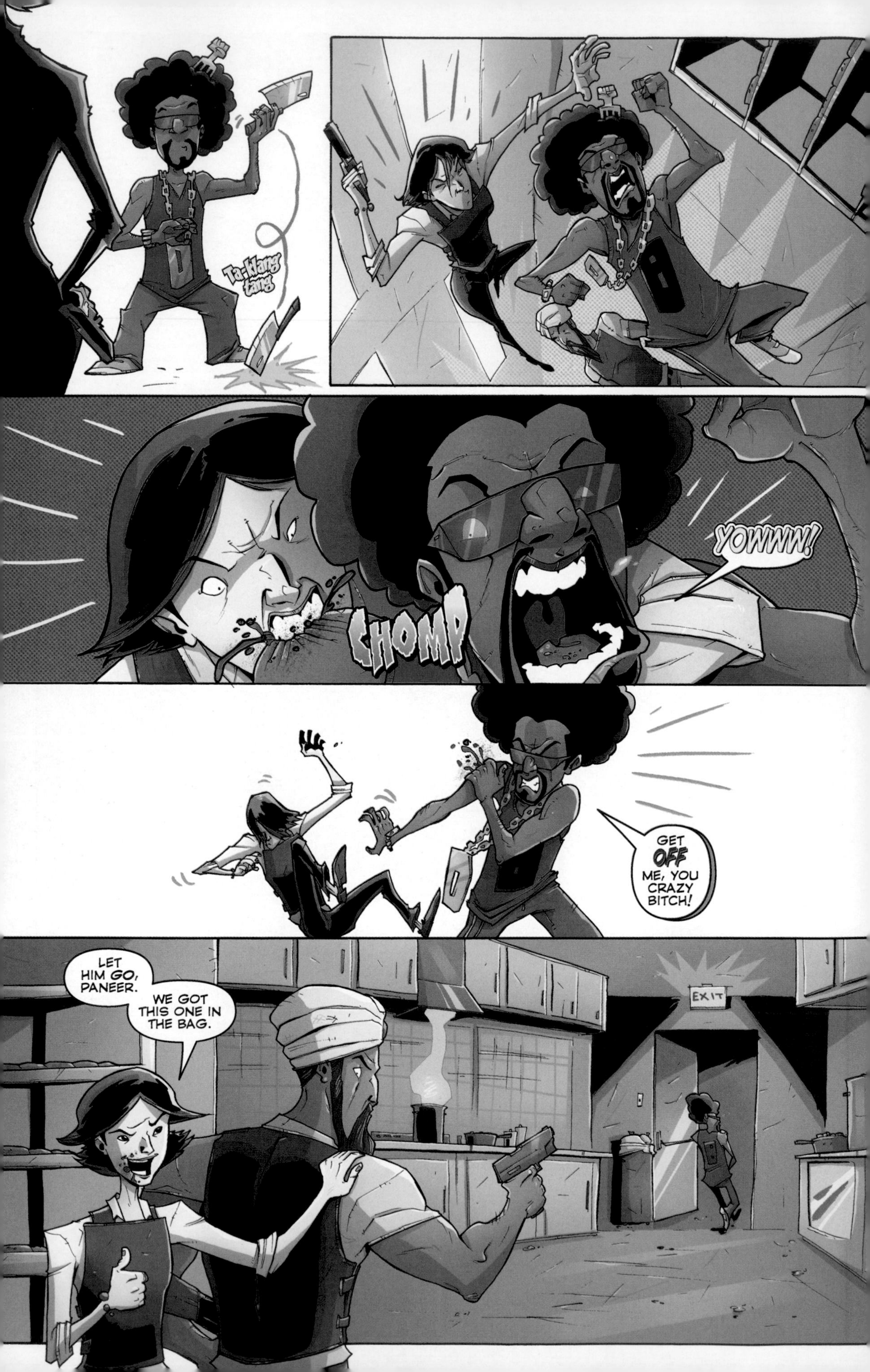

Ta-klang tang
YOWWW!
CHOMP
GET OFF ME, YOU CRAZY BITCH!
LET HIM GO, PANEER.
WE GOT THIS ONE IN THE BAG.
EXIT

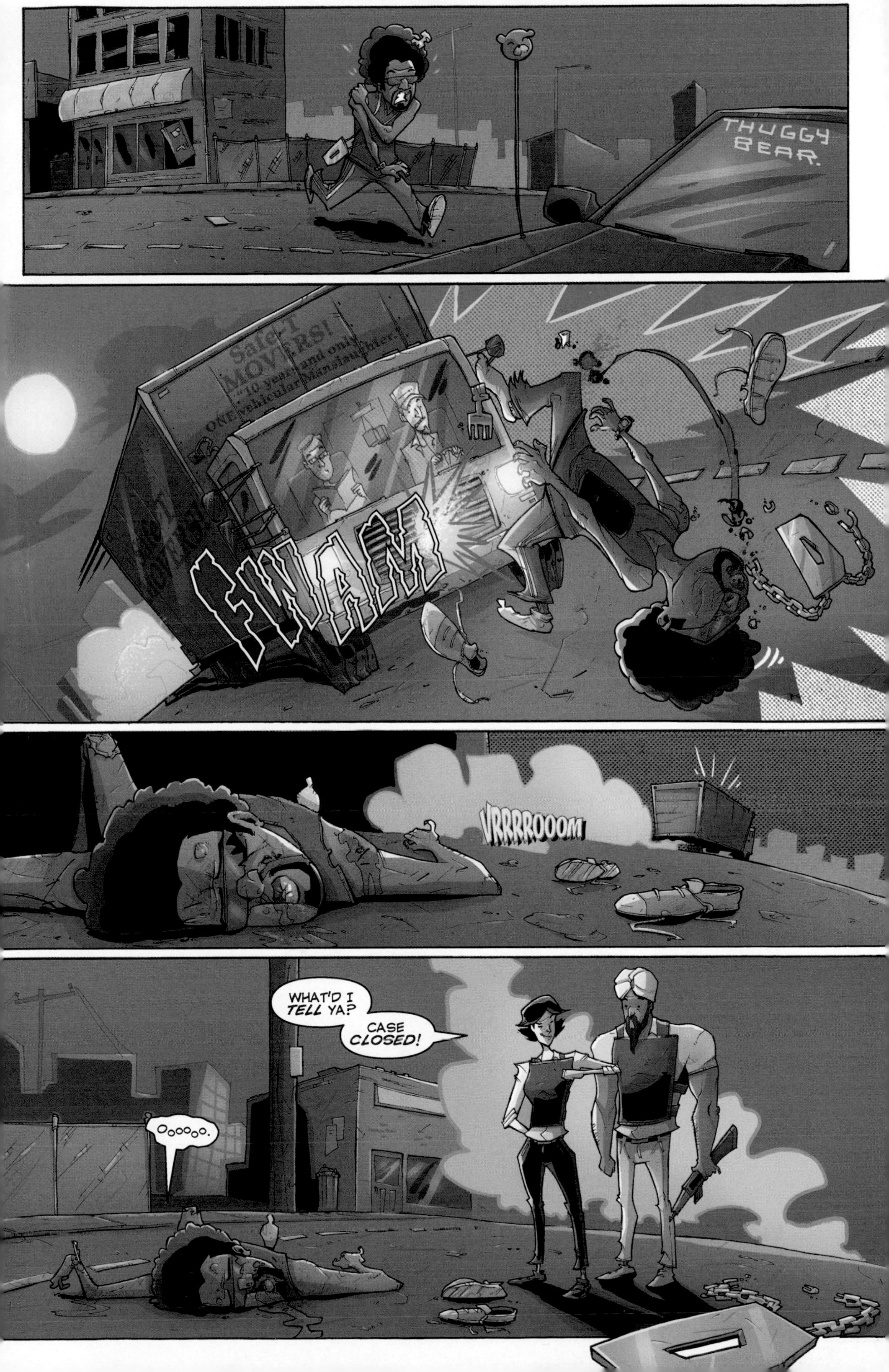
THUGGY BEAR.
Safe-T MOVERS!
"10 years and only ONE vehicular Manslaughter."
FWAM
VRRRROOOM
WHAT'D I TELL YA? CASE CLOSED!
Oooooo.

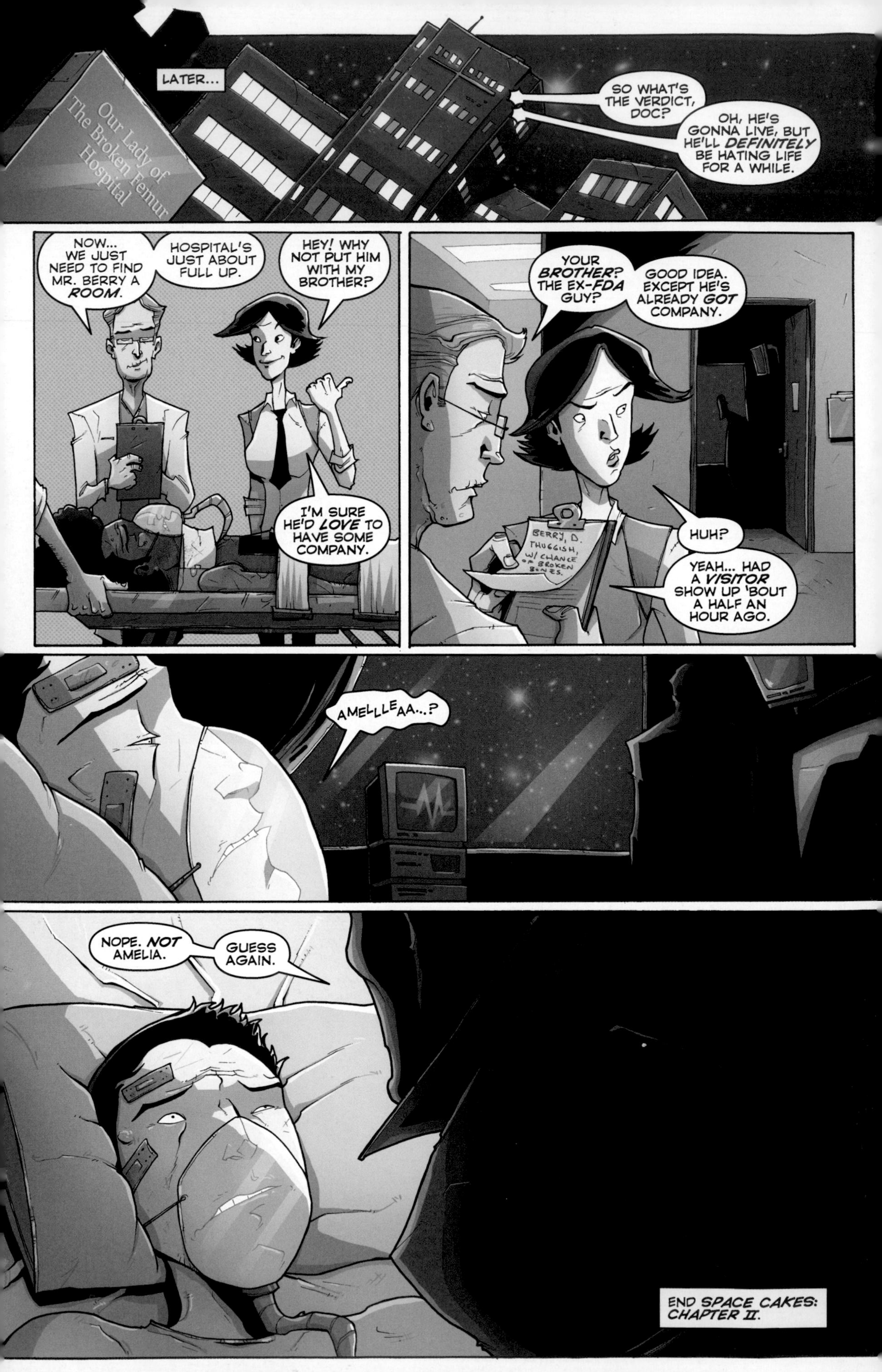
LATER...
Our Lady of The Broken Femur Hospital
SO WHAT'S THE VERDICT, DOC?
OH, HE'S GONNA LIVE, BUT HE'LL DEFINITELY BE HATING LIFE FOR A WHILE.
NOW... WE JUST NEED TO FIND MR. BERRY A ROOM.
HOSPITAL'S JUST ABOUT FULL UP.
HEY! WHY NOT PUT HIM WITH MY BROTHER?
I'M SURE HE'D LOVE TO HAVE SOME COMPANY.
YOUR BROTHER? THE EX-FDA GUY?
GOOD IDEA. EXCEPT HE'S ALREADY GOT COMPANY.
BERRY, D. THUGGISH, W/ CHANCE OF BROKEN BONES.
HUH?
YEAH... HAD A VISITOR SHOW UP 'BOUT A HALF AN HOUR AGO.
AMELLLEAA...?
NOPE. NOT AMELIA.
GUESS AGAIN.
END SPACE CAKES: CHAPTER II.

Interlude

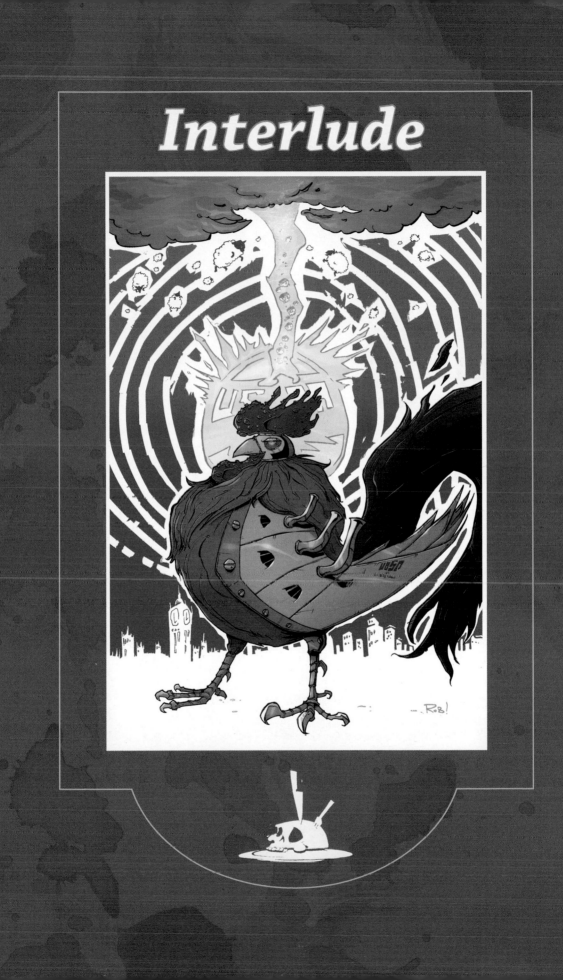

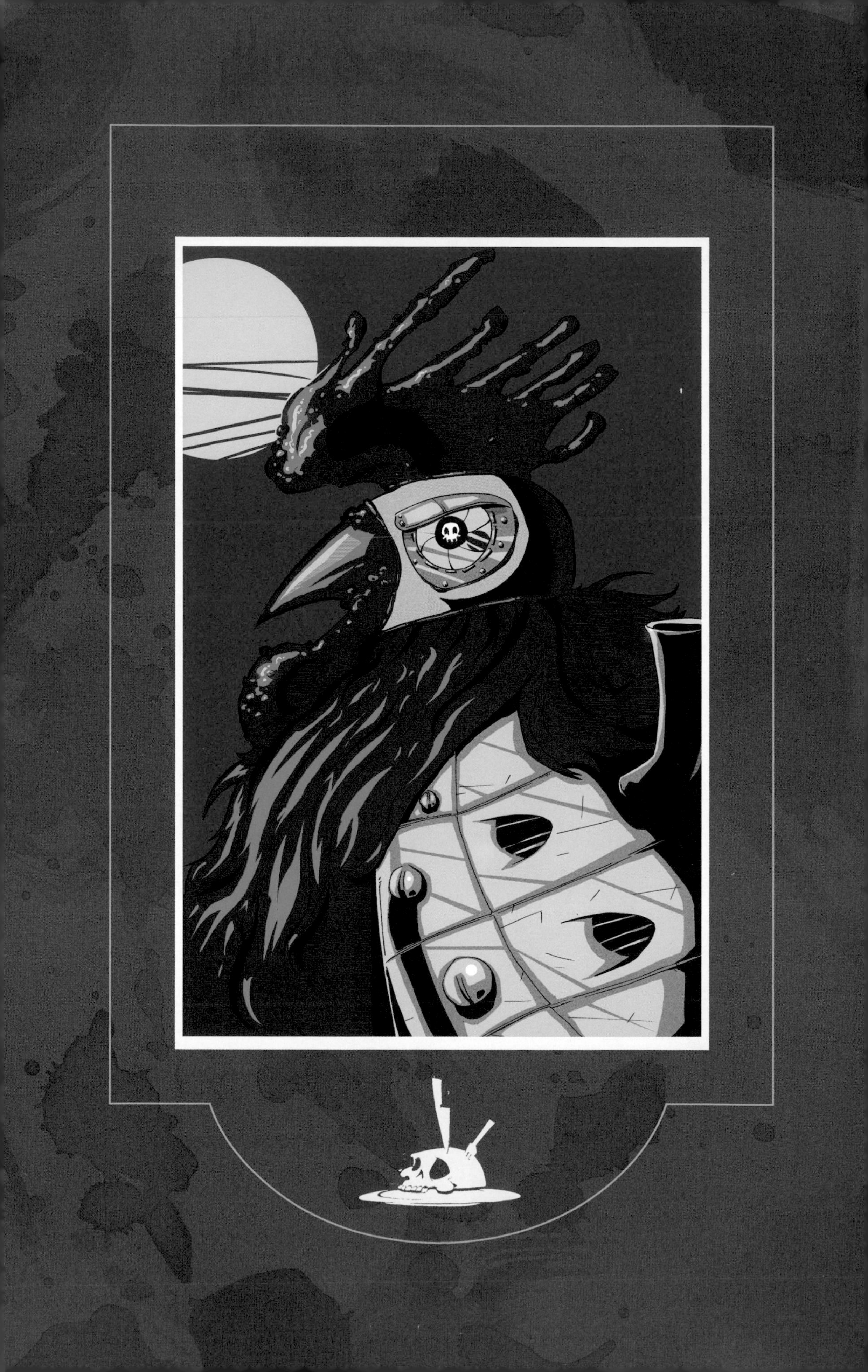

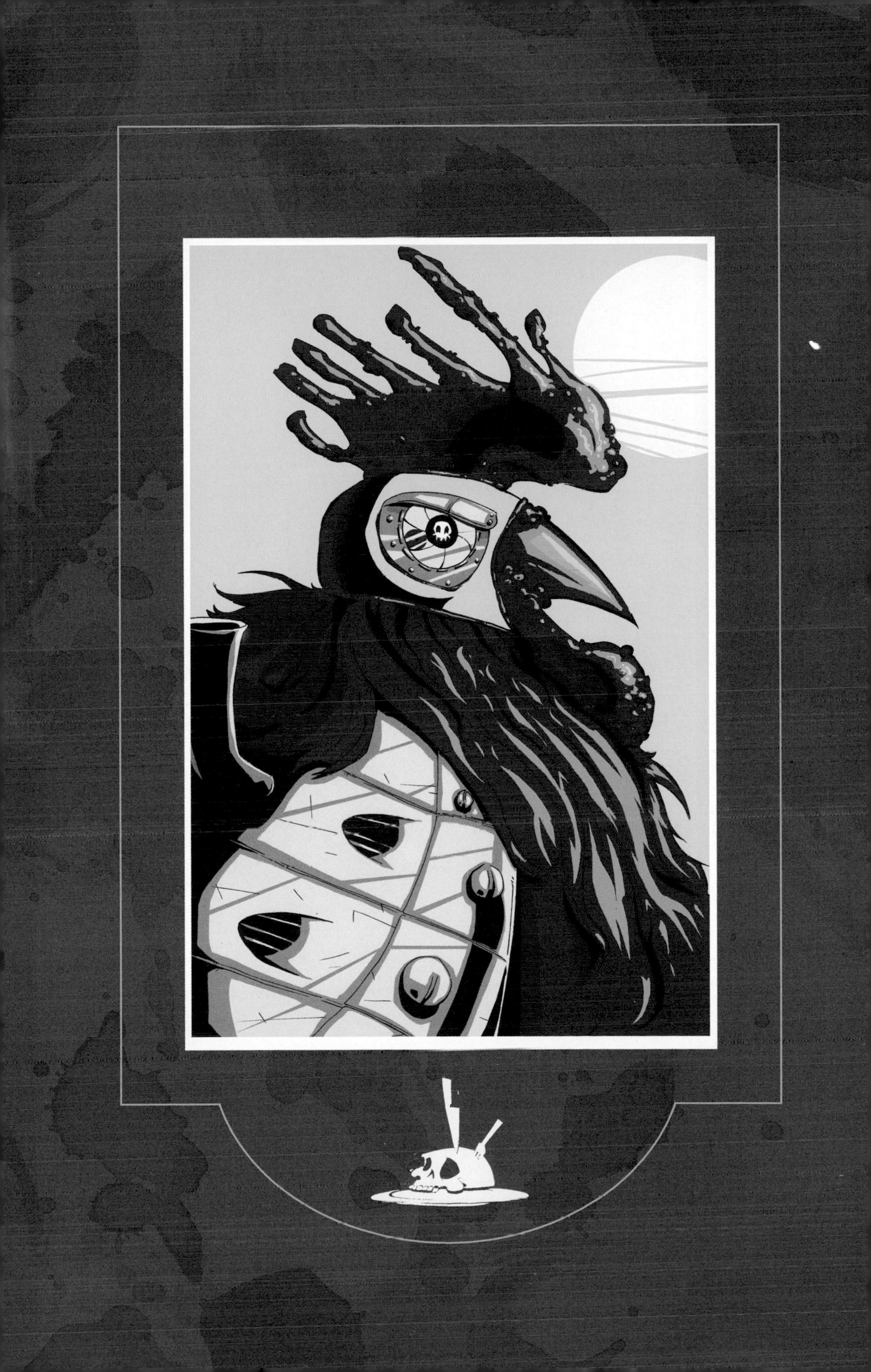

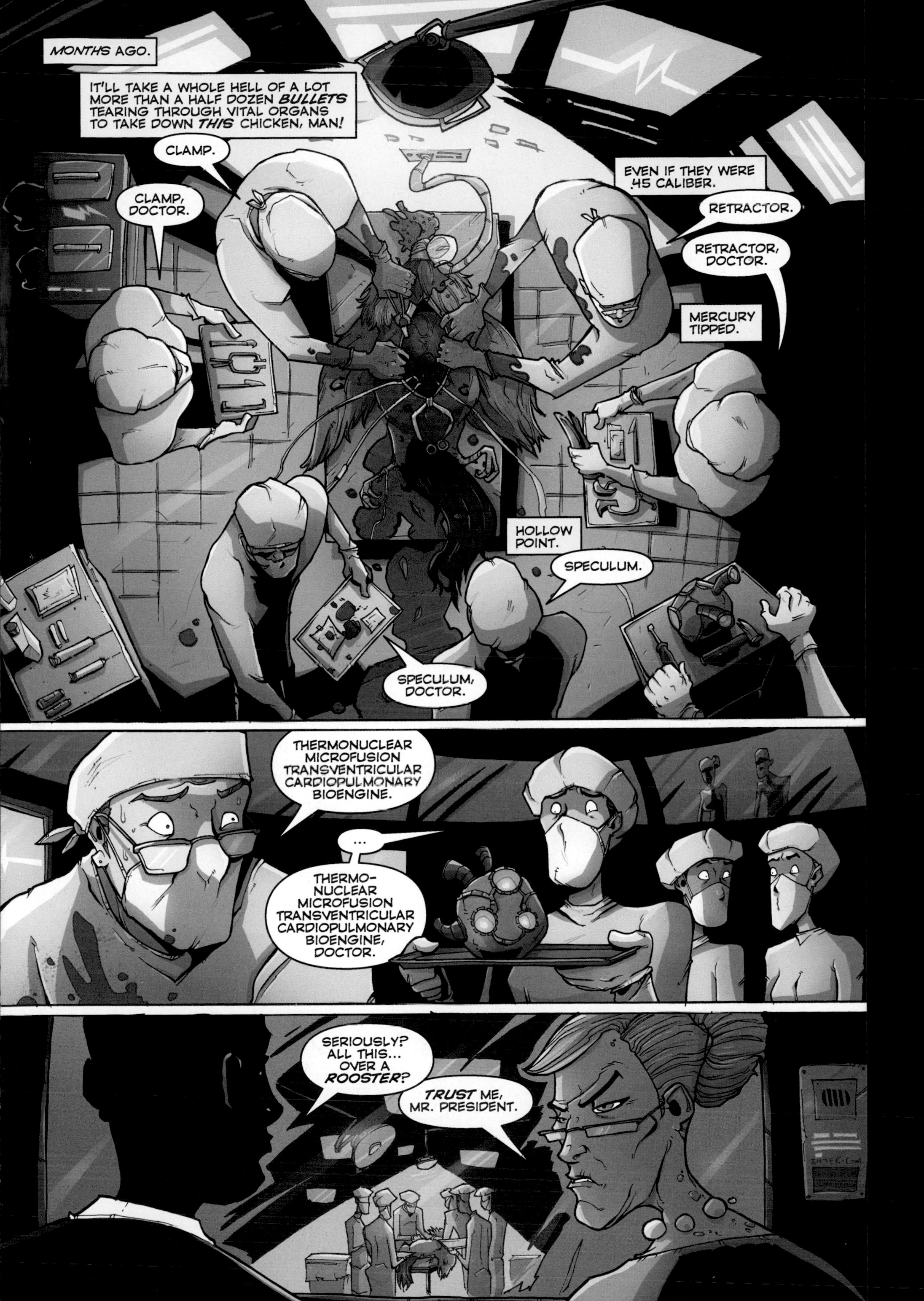
MONTHS AGO.
IT'LL TAKE A WHOLE HELL OF A LOT MORE THAN A HALF DOZEN BULLETS TEARING THROUGH VITAL ORGANS TO TAKE DOWN THIS CHICKEN, MAN!
CLAMP.
CLAMP, DOCTOR.
EVEN IF THEY WERE .45 CALIBER.
RETRACTOR.
RETRACTOR, DOCTOR.
MERCURY TIPPED.
HOLLOW POINT.
SPECULUM.
SPECULUM, DOCTOR.
THERMONUCLEAR MICROFUSION TRANSVENTRICULAR CARDIOPULMONARY BIOENGINE.
...
THERMO-NUCLEAR MICROFUSION TRANSVENTRICULAR CARDIOPULMONARY BIOENGINE, DOCTOR.
SERIOUSLY? ALL THIS... OVER A ROOSTER?
TRUST ME, MR. PRESIDENT.

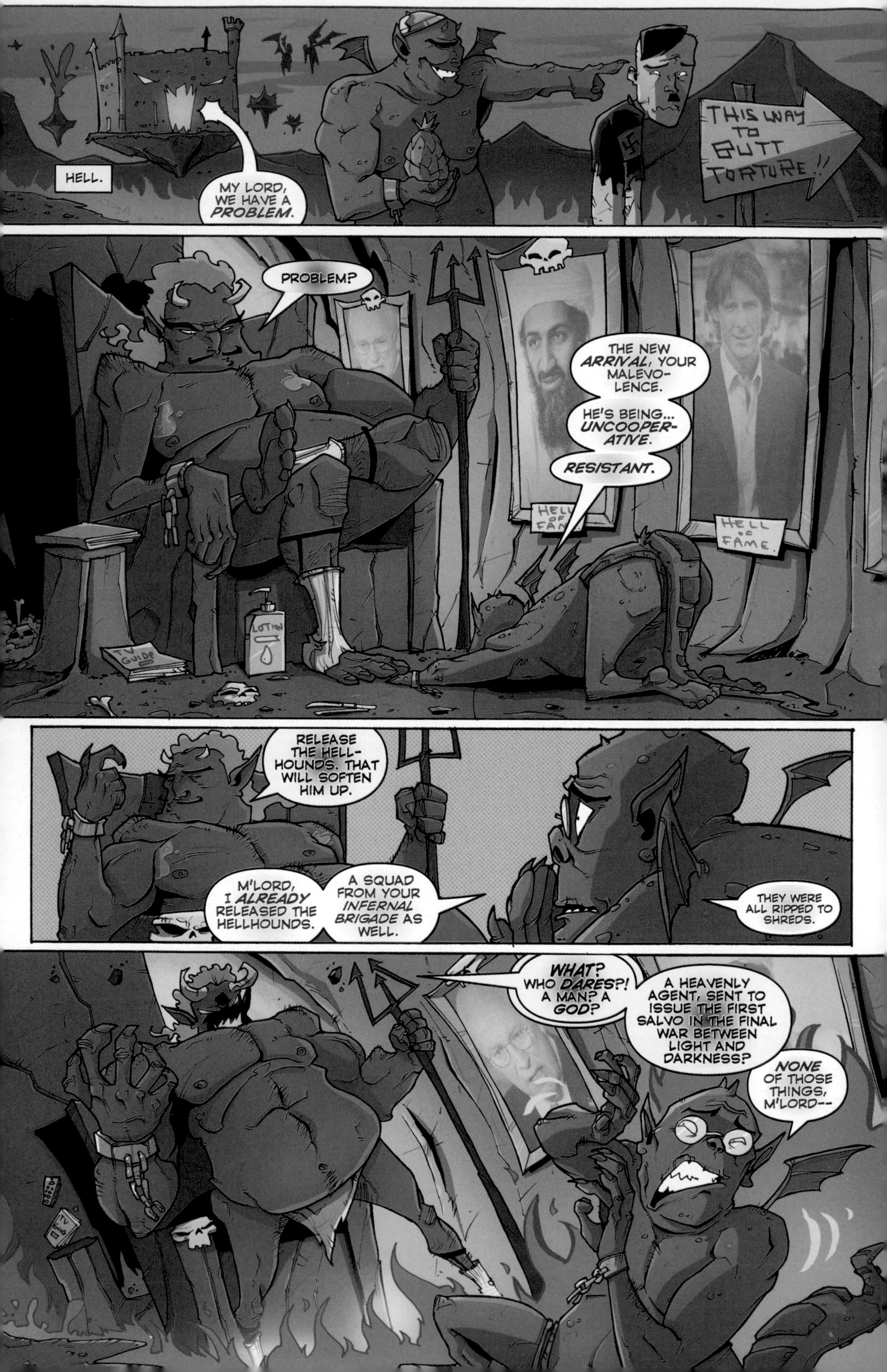

HELL.
MY LORD, WE HAVE A PROBLEM.
THIS WAY TO BUTT TORTURE!!
PROBLEM?
THE NEW ARRIVAL, YOUR MALEVO-LENCE.
HE'S BEING... UNCOOPER-ATIVE.
RESISTANT.
HELL OF FAME
HELL OF FAME.
LOTION
TV GUIDE
RELEASE THE HELL-HOUNDS. THAT WILL SOFTEN HIM UP.
M'LORD, I ALREADY RELEASED THE HELLHOUNDS.
A SQUAD FROM YOUR INFERNAL BRIGADE AS WELL.
THEY WERE ALL RIPPED TO SHREDS.
WHAT? WHO DARES?! A MAN? A GOD?
A HEAVENLY AGENT, SENT TO ISSUE THE FIRST SALVO IN THE FINAL WAR BETWEEN LIGHT AND DARKNESS?
NONE OF THOSE THINGS, M'LORD--

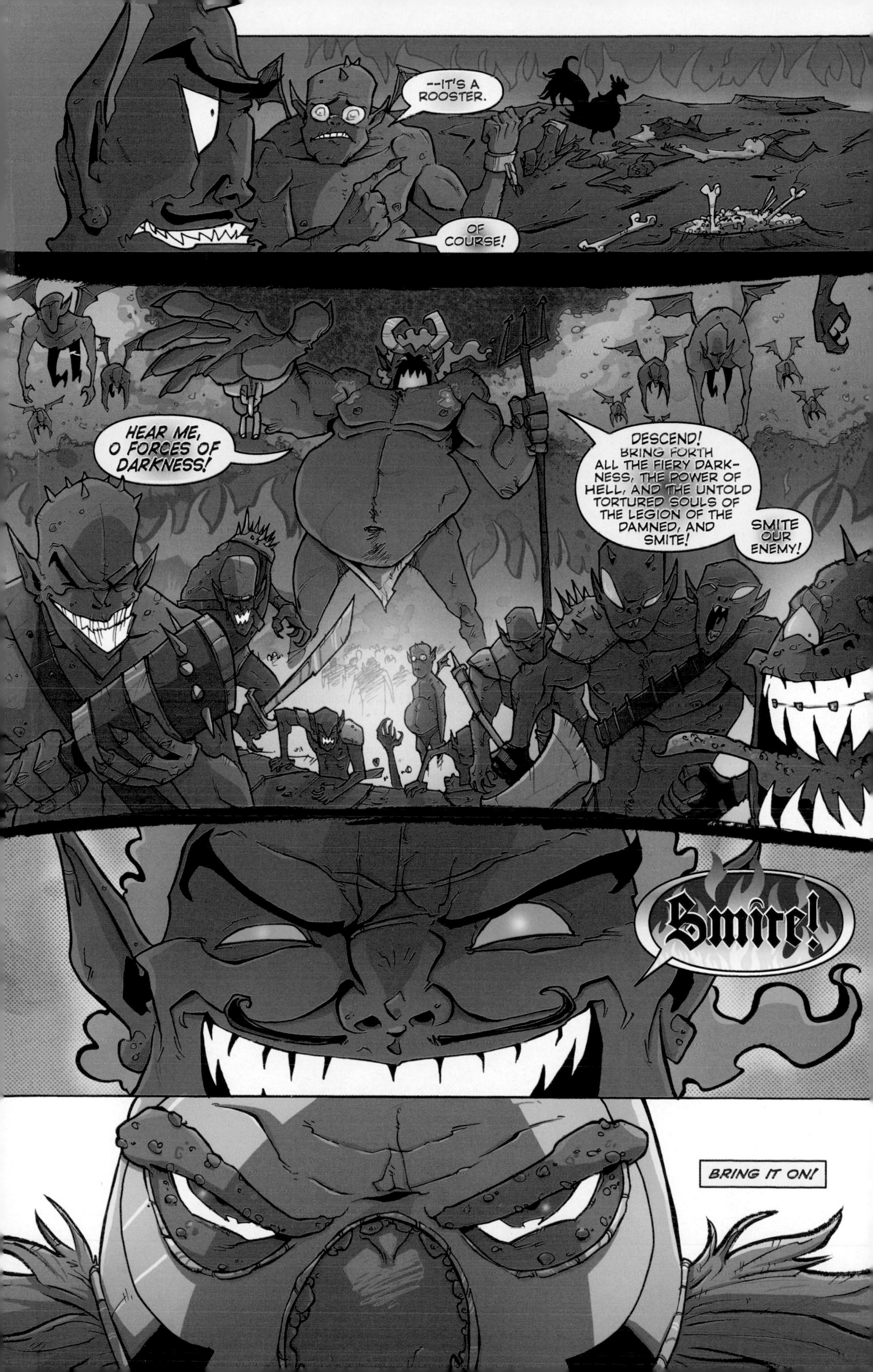
--IT'S A ROOSTER.
OF COURSE!
HEAR ME, O FORCES OF DARKNESS!
DESCEND! BRING FORTH ALL THE FIERY DARKNESS, THE POWER OF HELL, AND THE UNTOLD TORTURED SOULS OF THE LEGION OF THE DAMNED, AND SMITE!
SMITE OUR ENEMY!
Smite!
BRING IT ON!

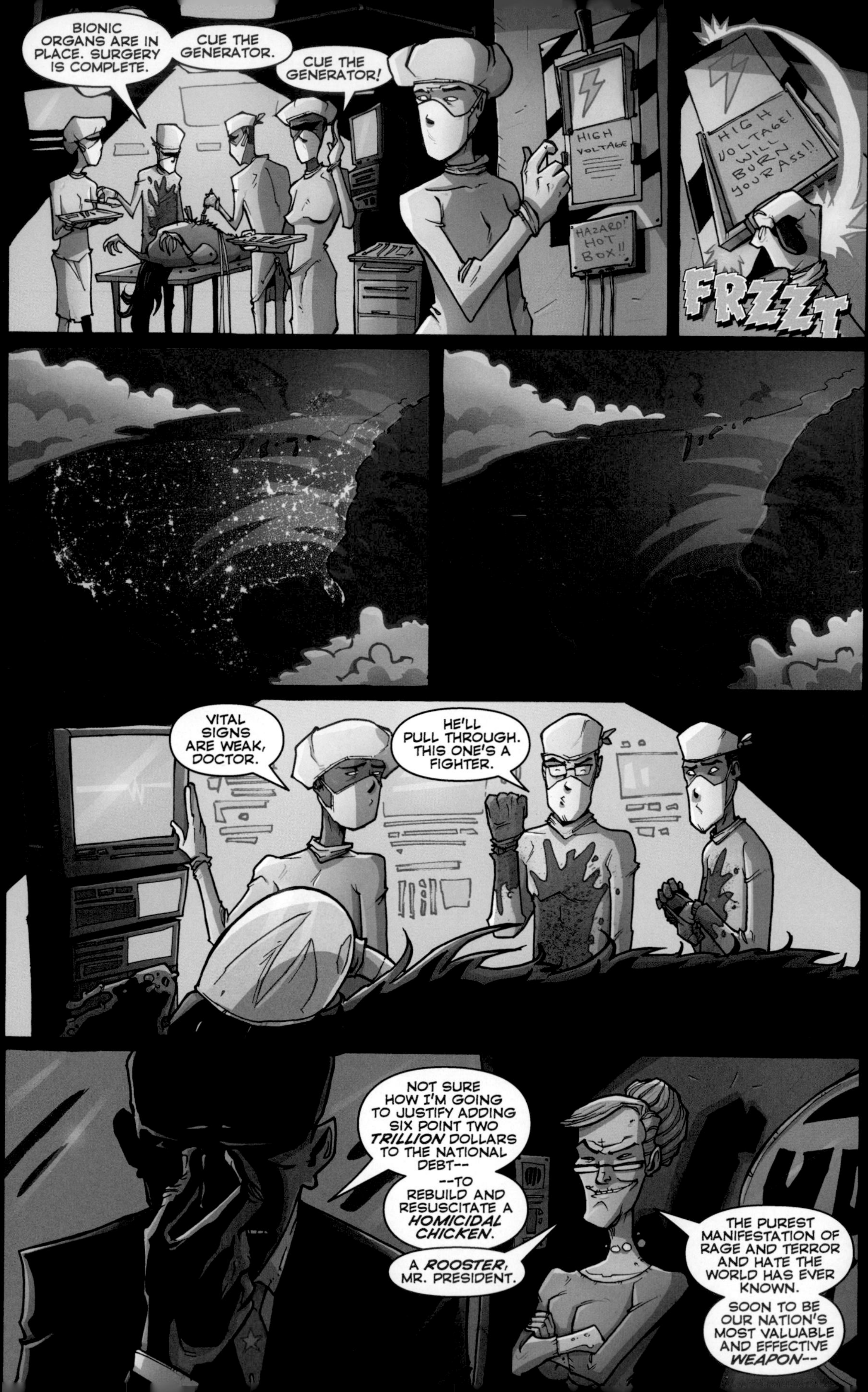
BIONIC ORGANS ARE IN PLACE. SURGERY IS COMPLETE.
CUE THE GENERATOR.
CUE THE GENERATOR!
HIGH VOLTAGE
HAZARD! HOT BOX!!
HIGH VOLTAGE! WILL BURN YOUR ASS!!
FRZZZT
VITAL SIGNS ARE WEAK, DOCTOR.
HE'LL PULL THROUGH. THIS ONE'S A FIGHTER.
NOT SURE HOW I'M GOING TO JUSTIFY ADDING SIX POINT TWO TRILLION DOLLARS TO THE NATIONAL DEBT--
--TO REBUILD AND RESUSCITATE A HOMICIDAL CHICKEN.
A ROOSTER, MR. PRESIDENT.
THE PUREST MANIFESTATION OF RAGE AND TERROR AND HATE THE WORLD HAS EVER KNOWN.
SOON TO BE OUR NATION'S MOST VALUABLE AND EFFECTIVE WEAPON--

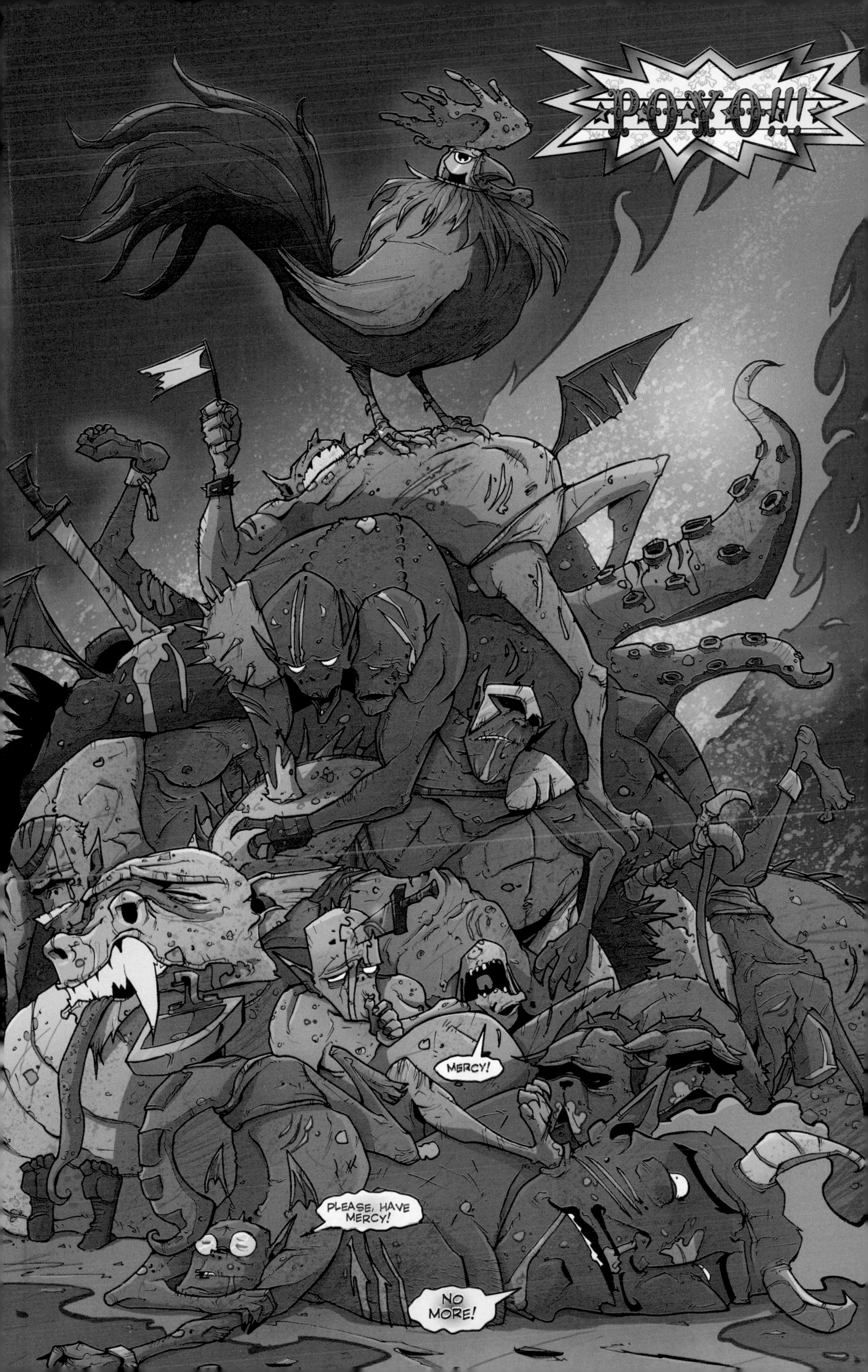
POYO!!!
MERCY!
PLEASE, HAVE MERCY!
NO MORE!

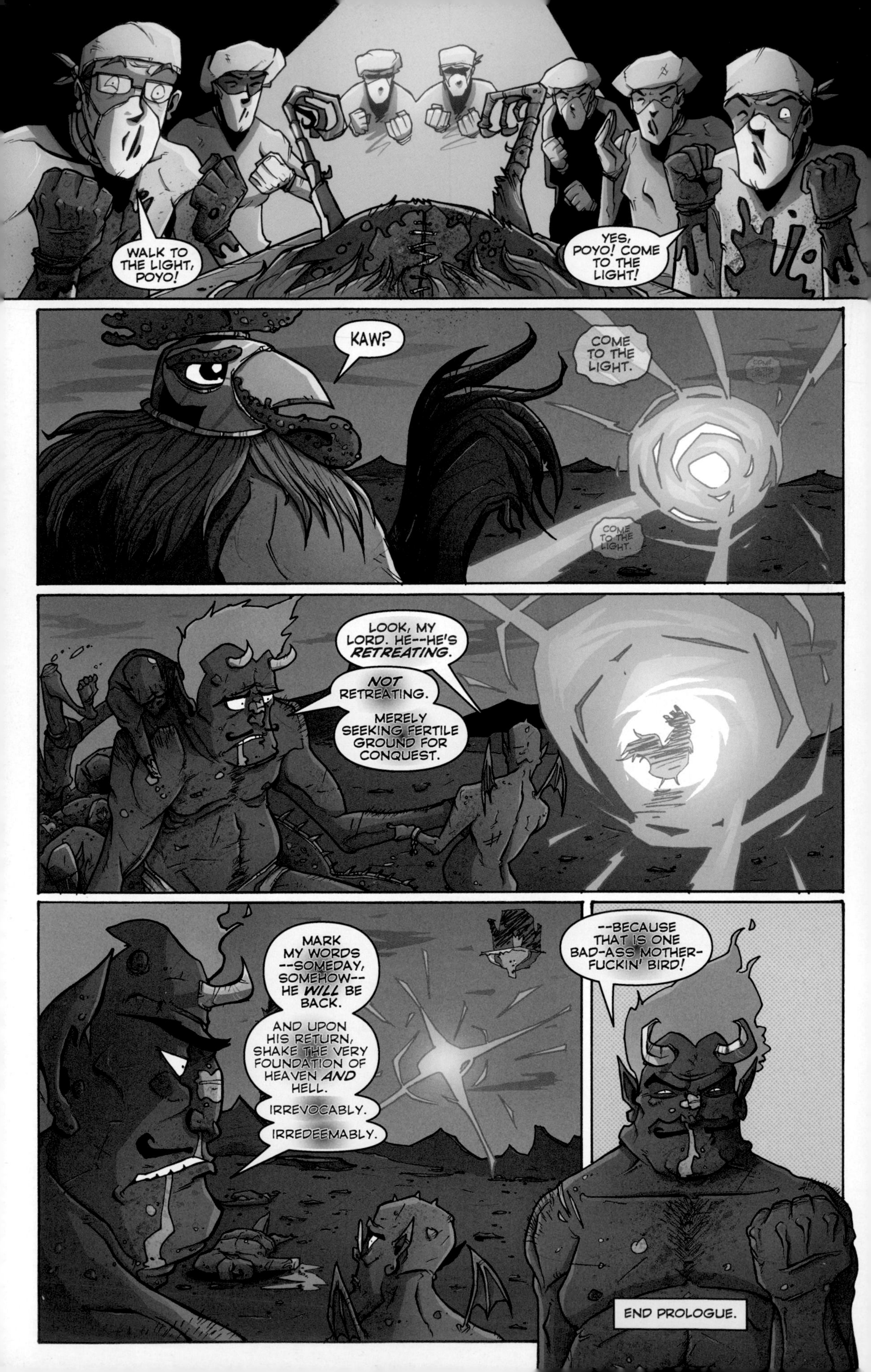
WALK TO THE LIGHT, POYO!
YES, POYO! COME TO THE LIGHT!
KAW?
COME TO THE LIGHT.
COME TO THE LIGHT.
LOOK, MY LORD. HE--HE'S *RETREATING*.
NOT RETREATING.
MERELY SEEKING FERTILE GROUND FOR CONQUEST.
MARK MY WORDS --SOMEDAY, SOMEHOW-- HE *WILL* BE BACK.
AND UPON HIS RETURN, SHAKE THE VERY FOUNDATION OF HEAVEN *AND* HELL.
IRREVOCABLY.
IRREDEEMABLY.
--BECAUSE THAT IS ONE BAD-ASS MOTHER-FUCKIN' BIRD!
END PROLOGUE.

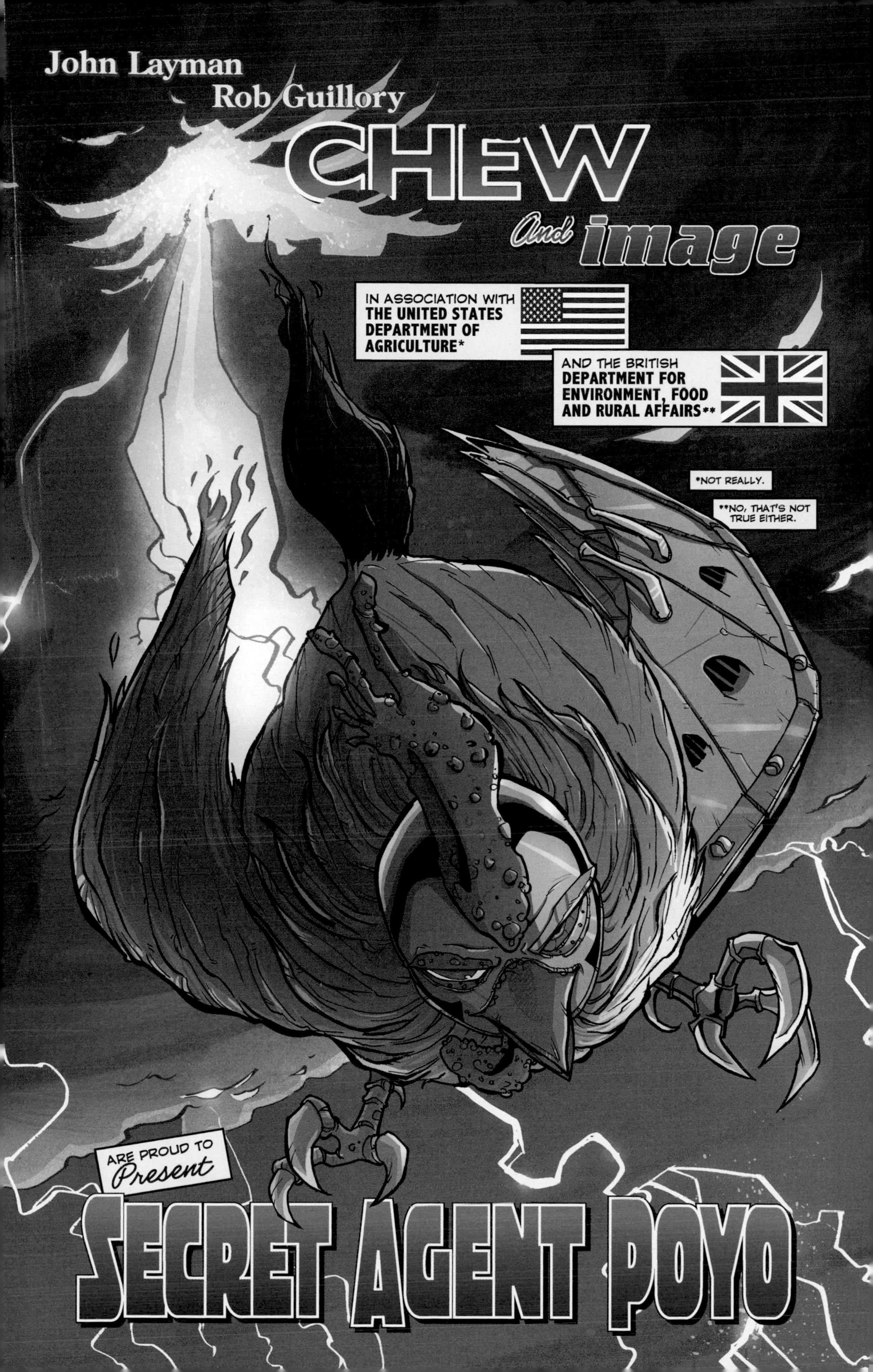
John Layman
Rob Guillory
CHEW
And image
IN ASSOCIATION WITH THE UNITED STATES DEPARTMENT OF AGRICULTURE*
AND THE BRITISH DEPARTMENT FOR ENVIRONMENT, FOOD AND RURAL AFFAIRS**
*NOT REALLY.
**NO, THAT'S NOT TRUE EITHER.
ARE PROUD TO Present
SECRET AGENT POYO

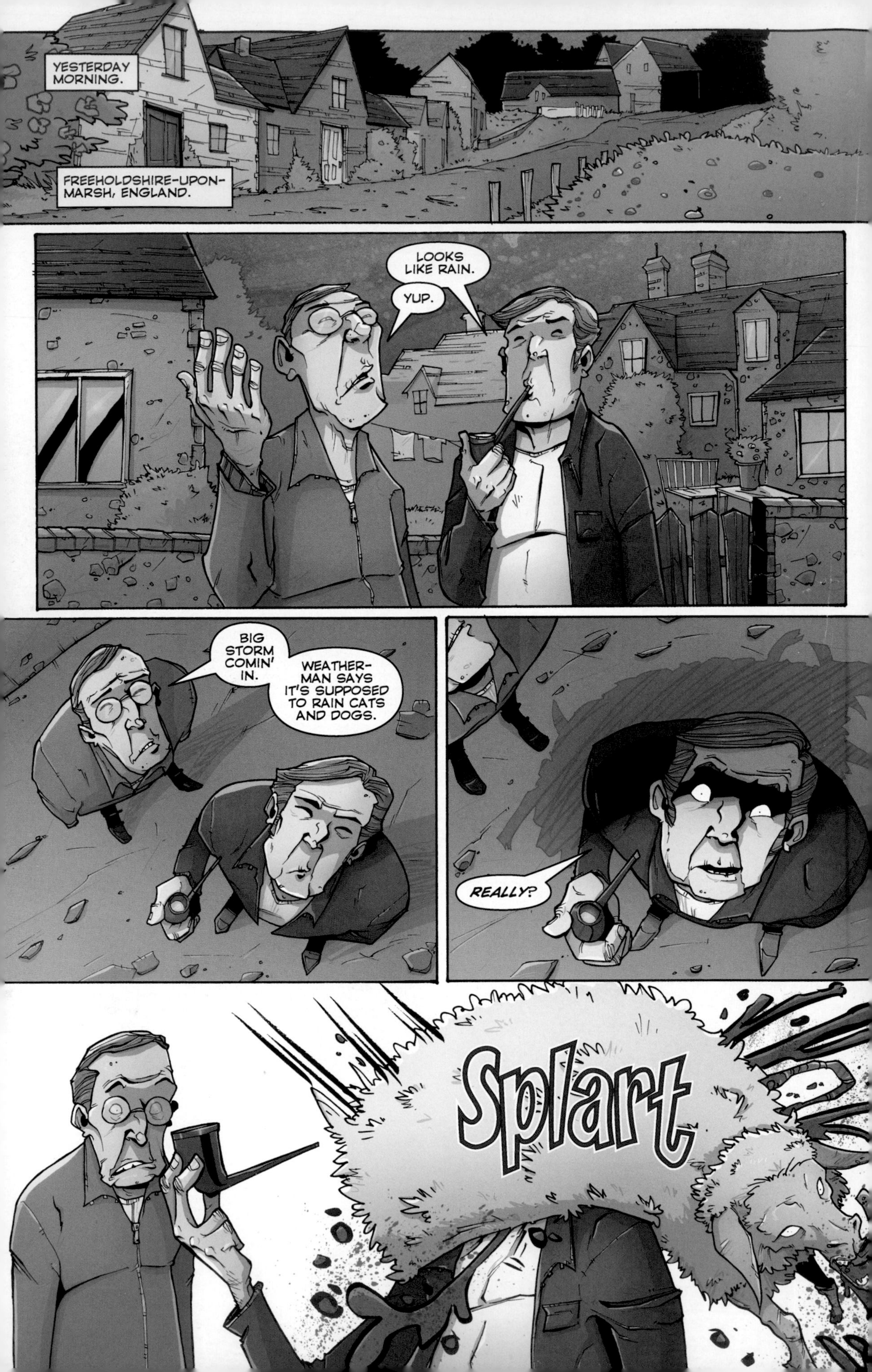
YESTERDAY MORNING.
FREEHOLDSHIRE-UPON-MARSH, ENGLAND.
LOOKS LIKE RAIN.
YUP.
BIG STORM COMIN' IN.
WEATHER-MAN SAYS IT'S SUPPOSED TO RAIN CATS AND DOGS.
REALLY?
Splart

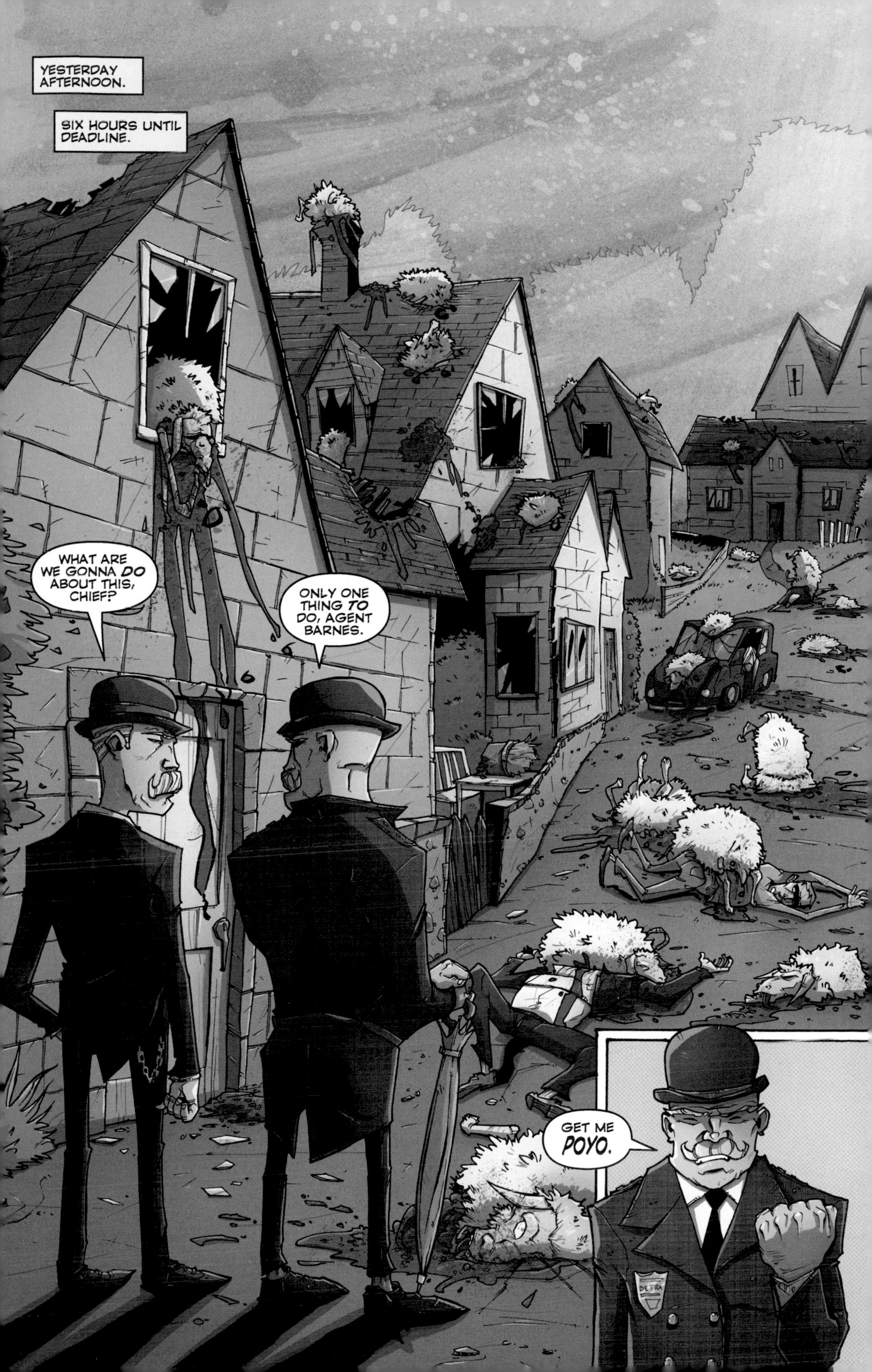
YESTERDAY AFTERNOON.
SIX HOURS UNTIL DEADLINE.
WHAT ARE WE GONNA DO ABOUT THIS, CHIEF?
ONLY ONE THING TO DO, AGENT BARNES.
GET ME POYO.
DEFRA

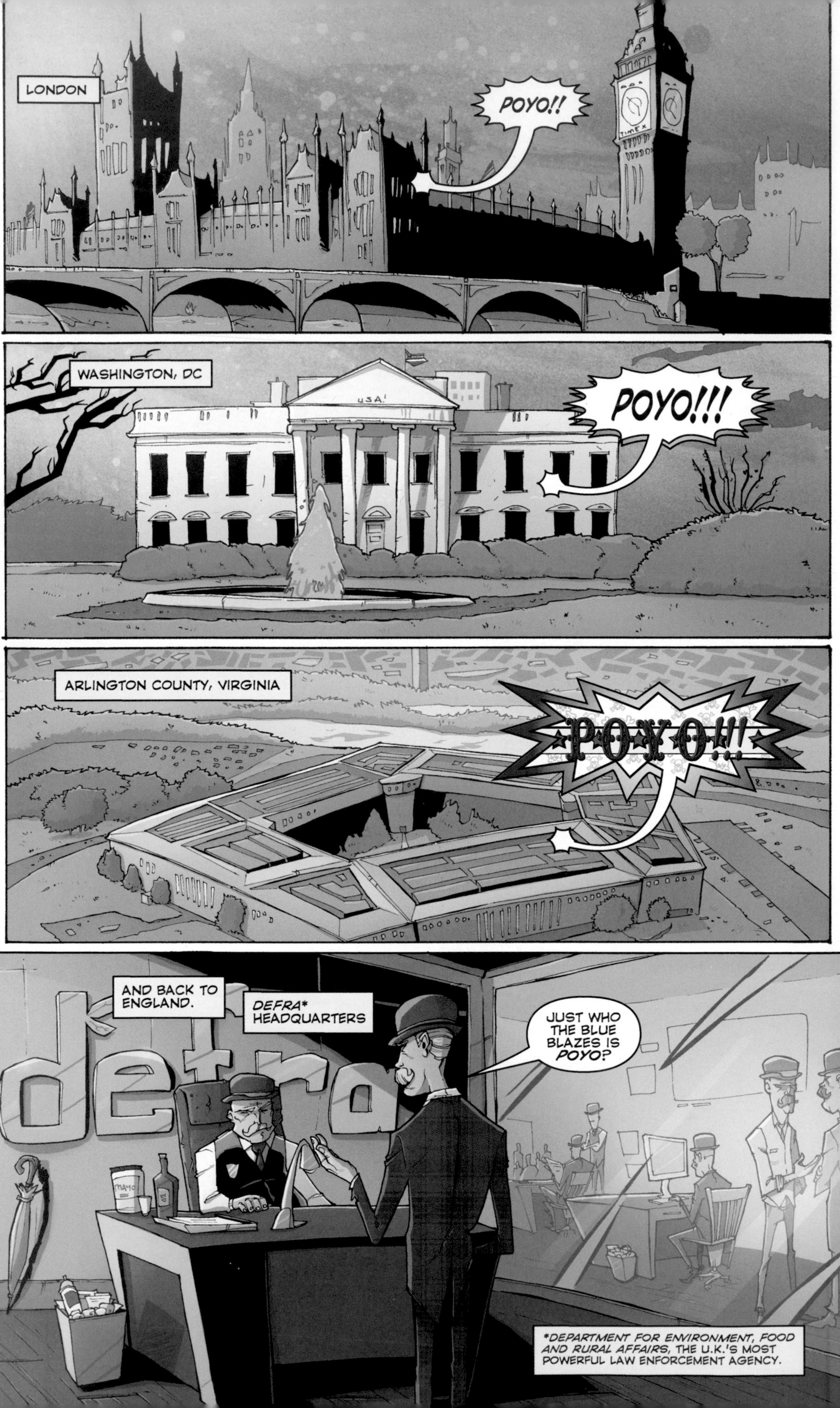
LONDON
POYO!!
WASHINGTON, DC
U.S.A!
POYO!!!
ARLINGTON COUNTY, VIRGINIA
POYO!!!
AND BACK TO ENGLAND.
DEFRA* HEADQUARTERS
JUST WHO THE BLUE BLAZES IS POYO?
*DEPARTMENT FOR ENVIRONMENT, FOOD AND RURAL AFFAIRS, THE U.K.'S MOST POWERFUL LAW ENFORCEMENT AGENCY.

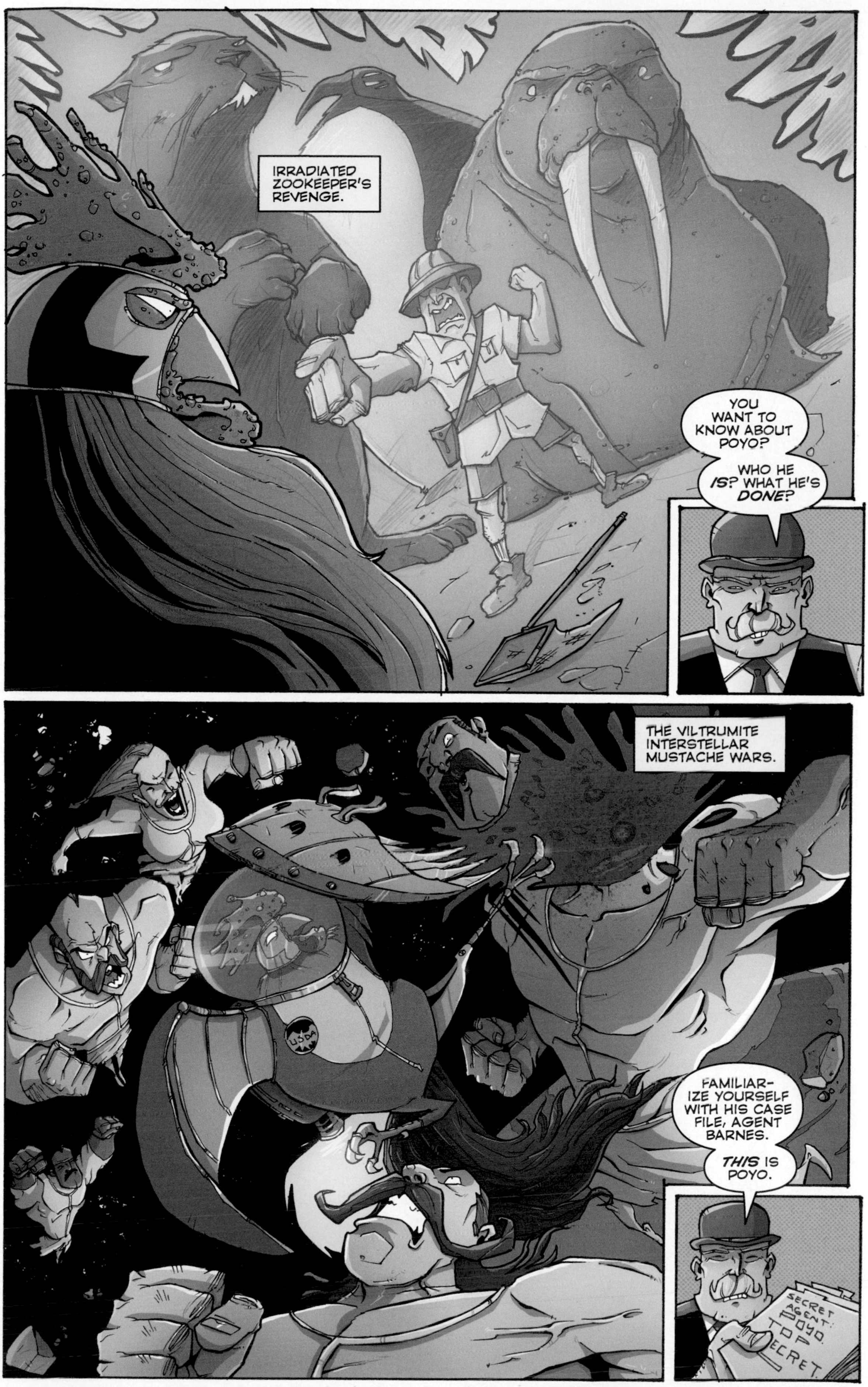
IRRADIATED ZOOKEEPER'S REVENGE.
YOU WANT TO KNOW ABOUT POYO?
WHO HE *IS*? WHAT HE'S *DONE*?
THE VILTRUMITE INTERSTELLAR MUSTACHE WARS.
USDA
FAMILIAR-IZE YOURSELF WITH HIS CASE FILE, AGENT BARNES.
THIS IS POYO.
SECRET AGENT: POYO. TOP SECRET.

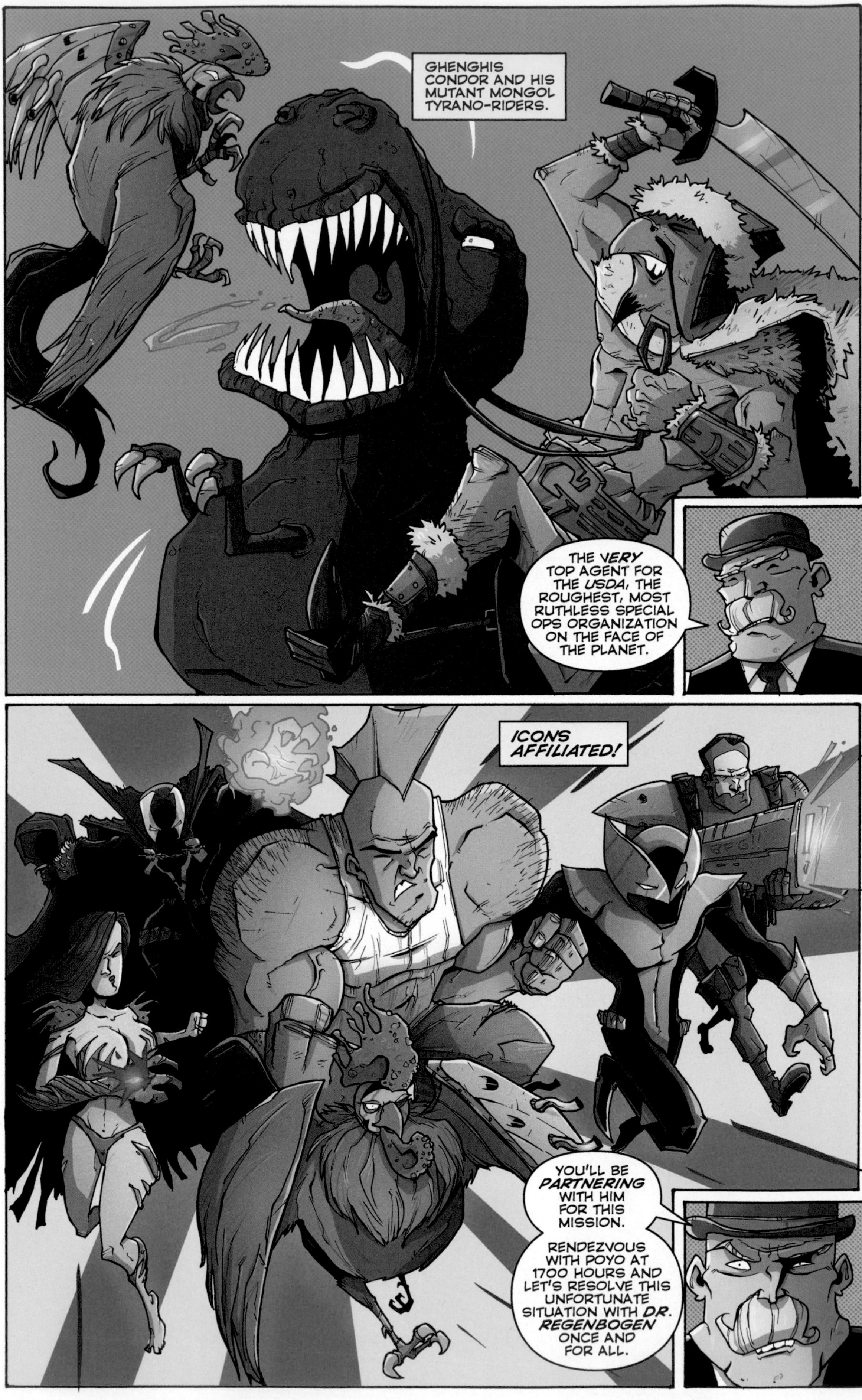
GHENGHIS CONDOR AND HIS MUTANT MONGOL TYRANO-RIDERS.
THE VERY TOP AGENT FOR THE USDA, THE ROUGHEST, MOST RUTHLESS SPECIAL OPS ORGANIZATION ON THE FACE OF THE PLANET.
ICONS AFFILIATED!
YOU'LL BE PARTNERING WITH HIM FOR THIS MISSION.
RENDEZVOUS WITH POYO AT 1700 HOURS AND LET'S RESOLVE THIS UNFORTUNATE SITUATION WITH DR. REGENBOGEN ONCE AND FOR ALL.

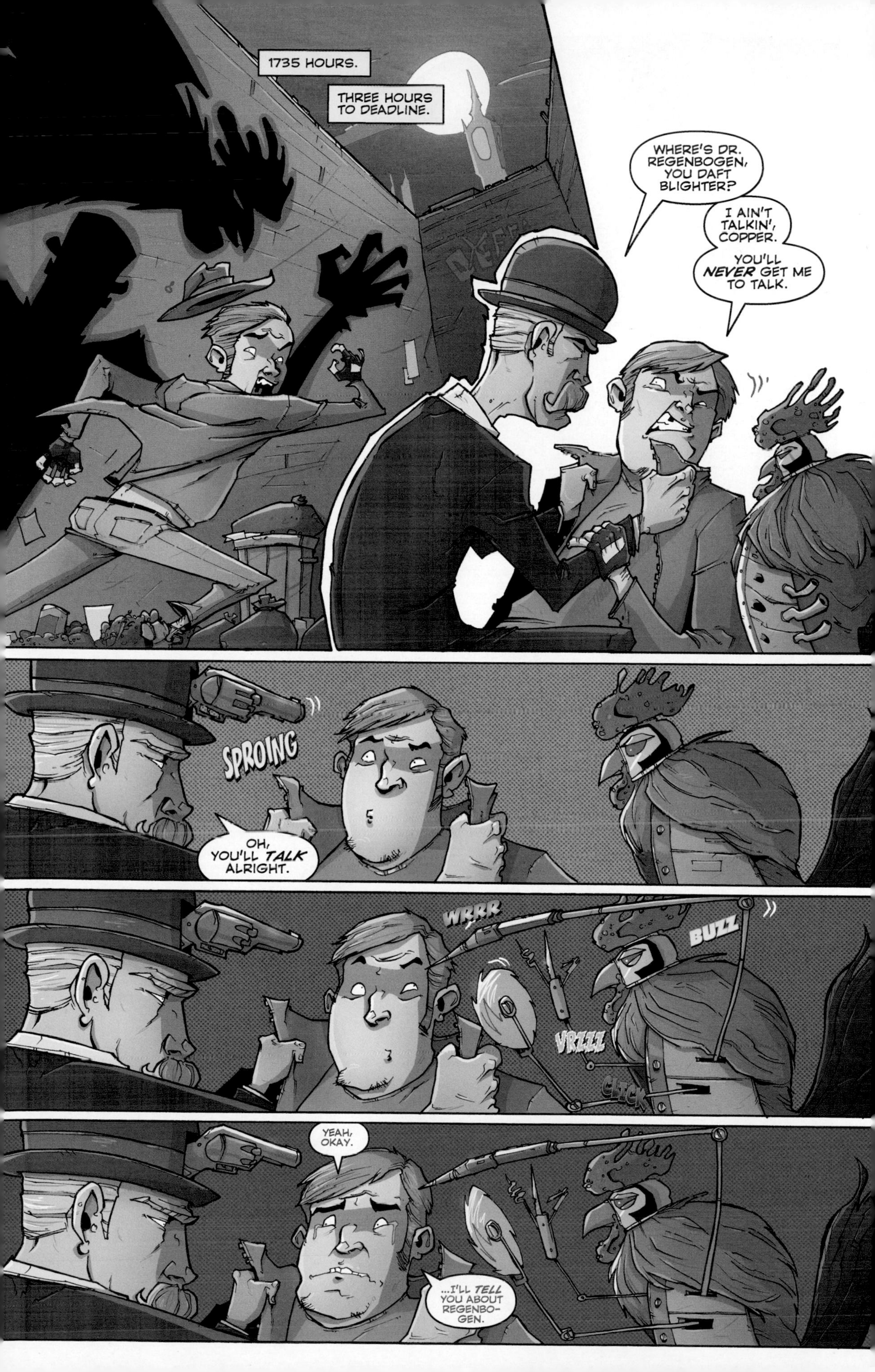
1735 HOURS.
THREE HOURS TO DEADLINE.
WHERE'S DR. REGENBOGEN, YOU DAFT BLIGHTER?
I AIN'T TALKIN', COPPER.
YOU'LL NEVER GET ME TO TALK.
SPROING
OH, YOU'LL TALK ALRIGHT.
WRRR
BUZZ
VRZZZ
CLICK
YEAH, OKAY.
...I'LL TELL YOU ABOUT REGENBO-GEN.

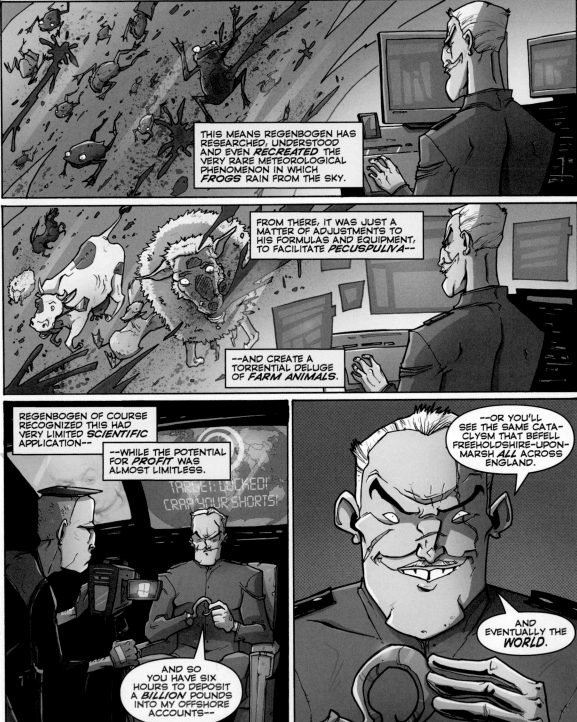

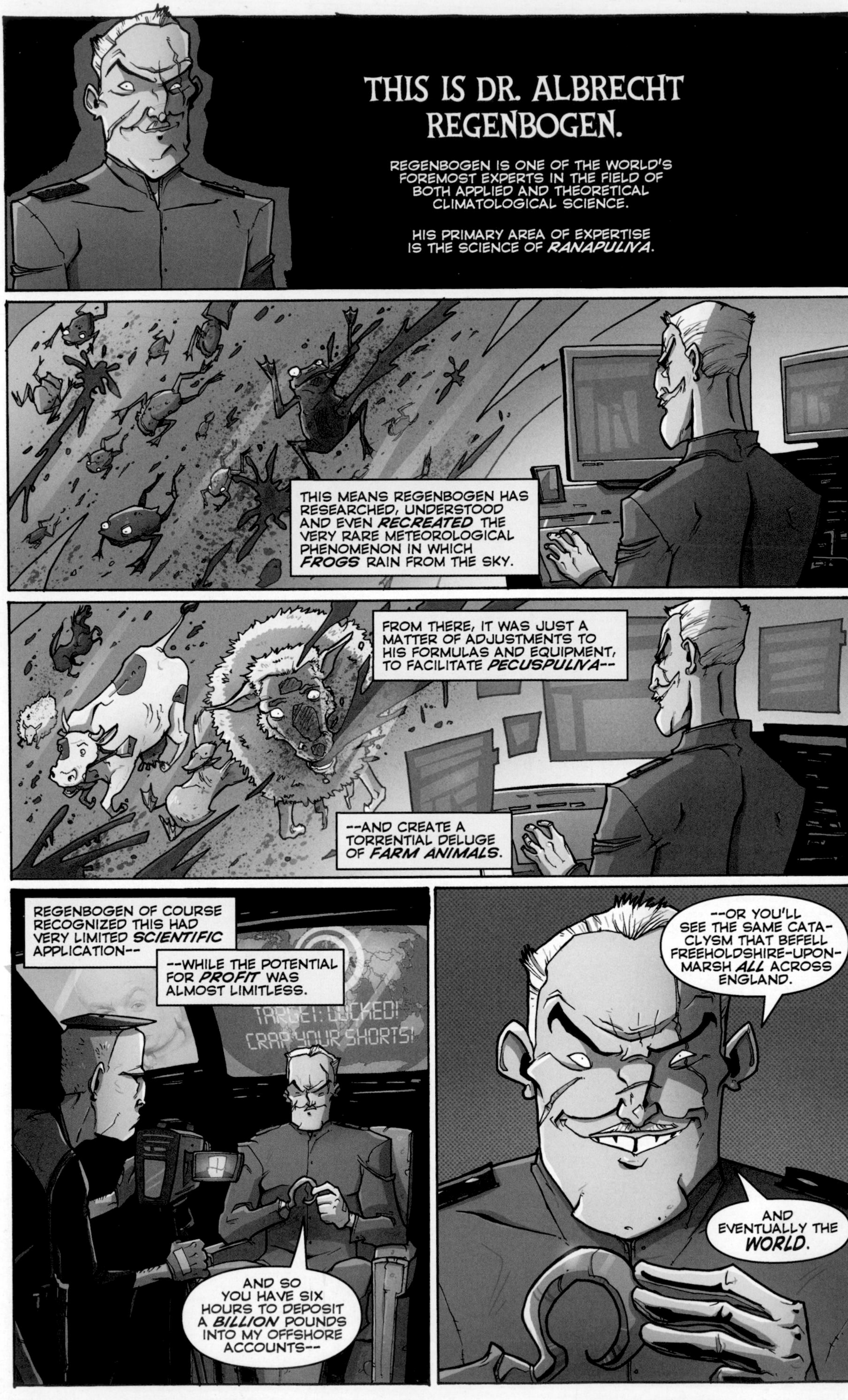

THIS IS DR. ALBRECHT REGENBOGEN.

REGENBOGEN IS ONE OF THE WORLD'S FOREMOST EXPERTS IN THE FIELD OF BOTH APPLIED AND THEORETICAL CLIMATOLOGICAL SCIENCE.

HIS PRIMARY AREA OF EXPERTISE IS THE SCIENCE OF *RANAPULIVA*.

THIS MEANS REGENBOGEN HAS RESEARCHED, UNDERSTOOD AND EVEN *RECREATED* THE VERY RARE METEOROLOGICAL PHENOMENON IN WHICH *FROGS* RAIN FROM THE SKY.

FROM THERE, IT WAS JUST A MATTER OF ADJUSTMENTS TO HIS FORMULAS AND EQUIPMENT, TO FACILITATE *PECUSPULIVA*--

--AND CREATE A TORRENTIAL DELUGE OF *FARM ANIMALS*.

REGENBOGEN OF COURSE RECOGNIZED THIS HAD VERY LIMITED *SCIENTIFIC* APPLICATION--

--WHILE THE POTENTIAL FOR *PROFIT* WAS ALMOST LIMITLESS.

TARGET LOCKED! CRAP YOUR SHORTS!

AND SO YOU HAVE SIX HOURS TO DEPOSIT A *BILLION* POUNDS INTO MY OFFSHORE ACCOUNTS--

--OR YOU'LL SEE THE SAME CATA-CLYSM THAT BEFELL FREEHOLDSHIRE-UPON-MARSH *ALL* ACROSS ENGLAND.

AND EVENTUALLY THE *WORLD*.

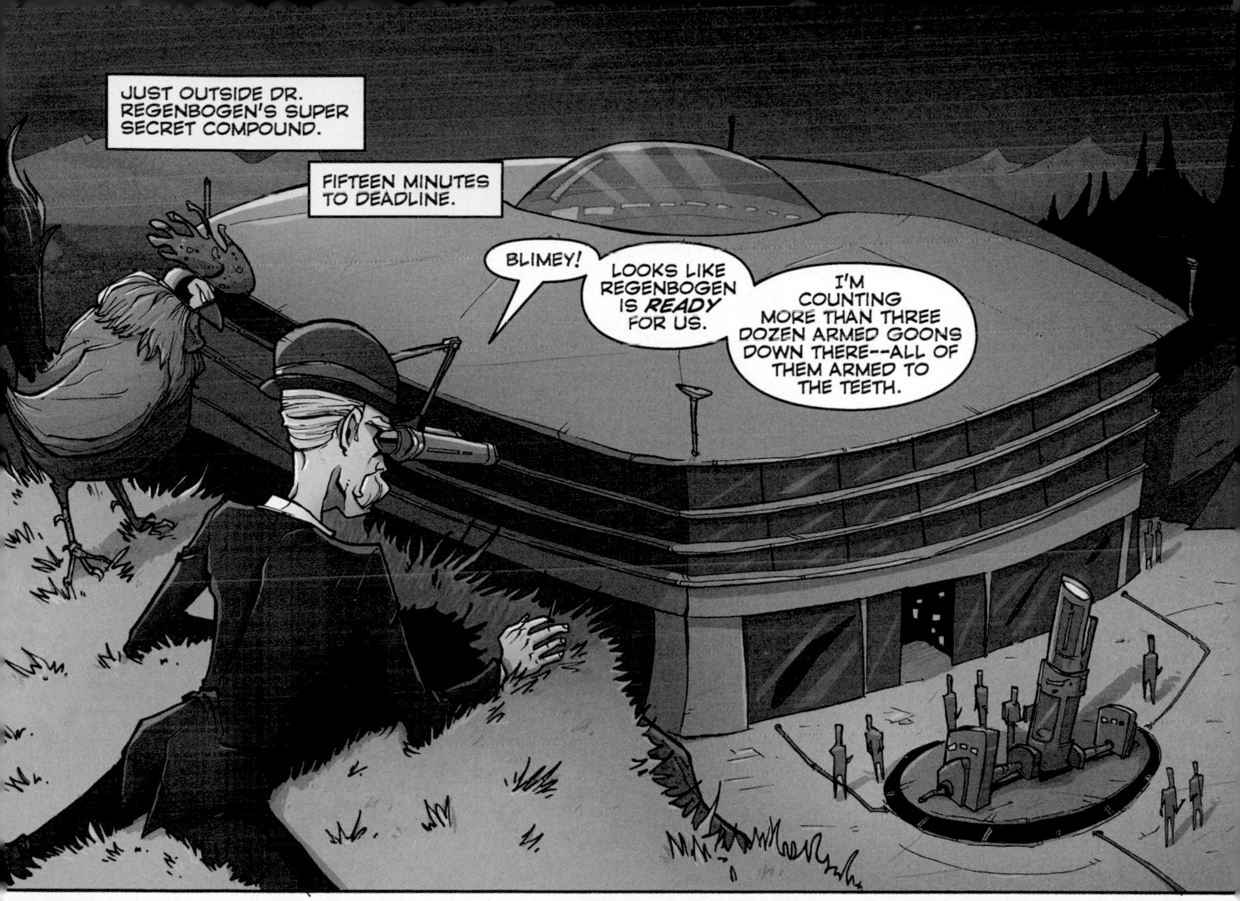
JUST OUTSIDE DR. REGENBOGEN'S SUPER SECRET COMPOUND.
FIFTEEN MINUTES TO DEADLINE.
BLIMEY!
LOOKS LIKE REGENBOGEN IS *READY* FOR US.
I'M COUNTING MORE THAN THREE DOZEN ARMED GOONS DOWN THERE--ALL OF THEM ARMED TO THE TEETH.

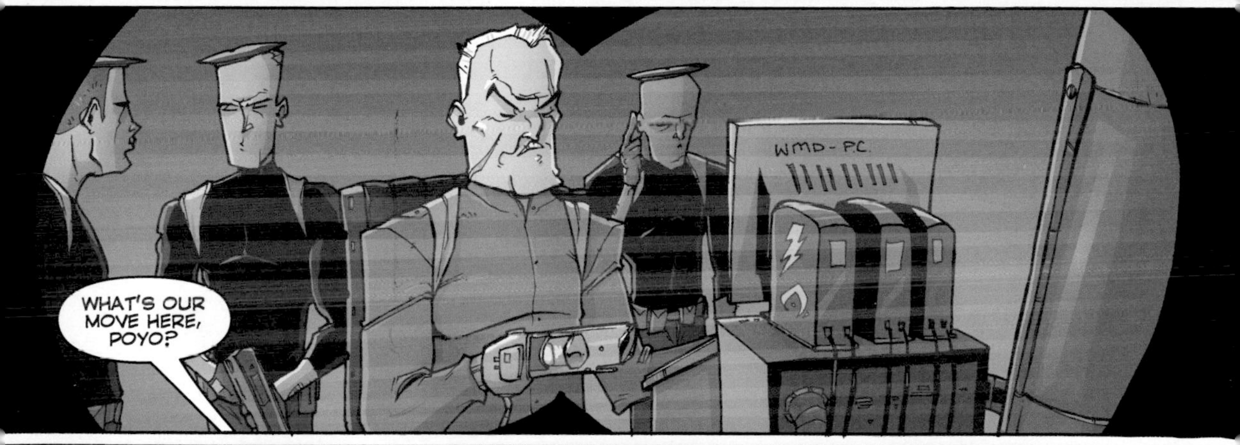
WMD-PC
WHAT'S OUR MOVE HERE, POYO?

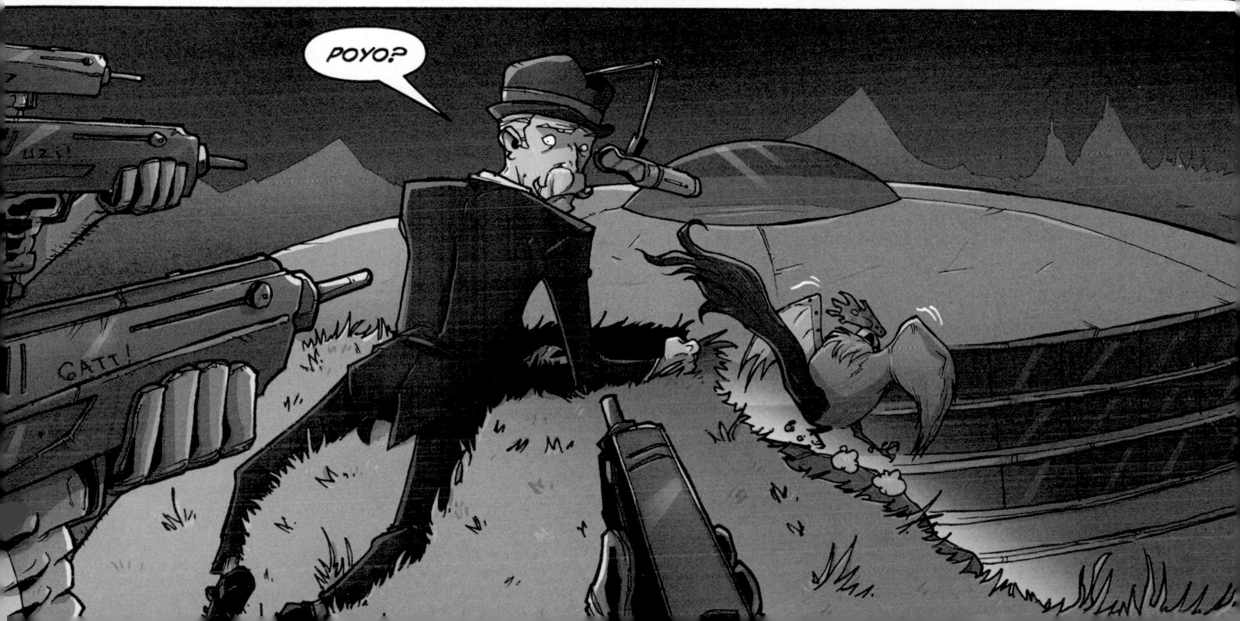
POYO?

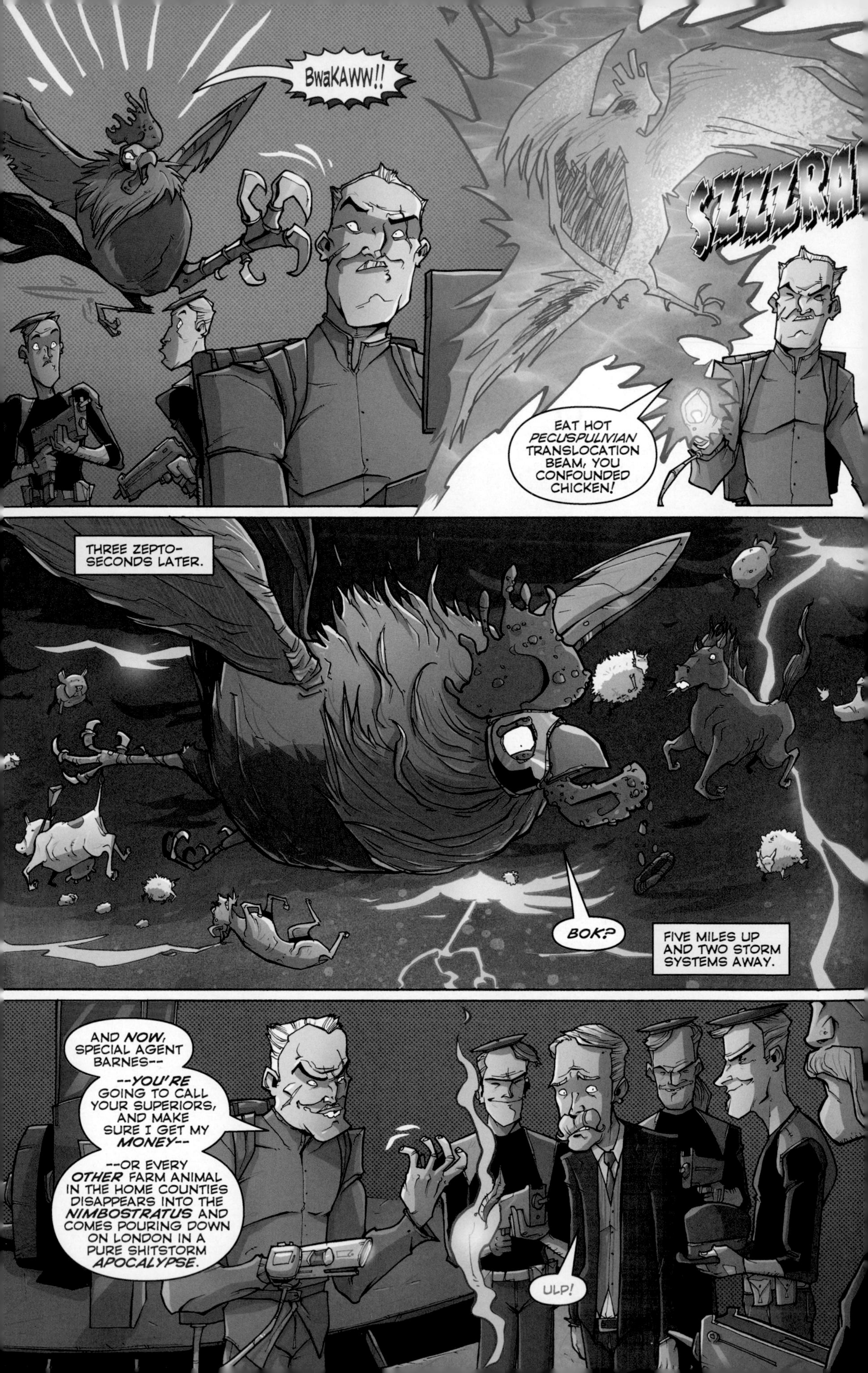
BwaKAWW!!
SZZZRA
EAT HOT *PECUSPULVIAN* TRANSLOCATION BEAM, YOU CONFOUNDED CHICKEN!
THREE ZEPTO-SECONDS LATER.
BOK?
FIVE MILES UP AND TWO STORM SYSTEMS AWAY.
AND ***NOW***, SPECIAL AGENT BARNES--
--***YOU'RE*** GOING TO CALL YOUR SUPERIORS, AND MAKE SURE I GET MY ***MONEY***--
--OR EVERY ***OTHER*** FARM ANIMAL IN THE HOME COUNTIES DISAPPEARS INTO THE ***NIMBOSTRATUS*** AND COMES POURING DOWN ON LONDON IN A PURE SHITSTORM ***APOCALYPSE***.
ULP!

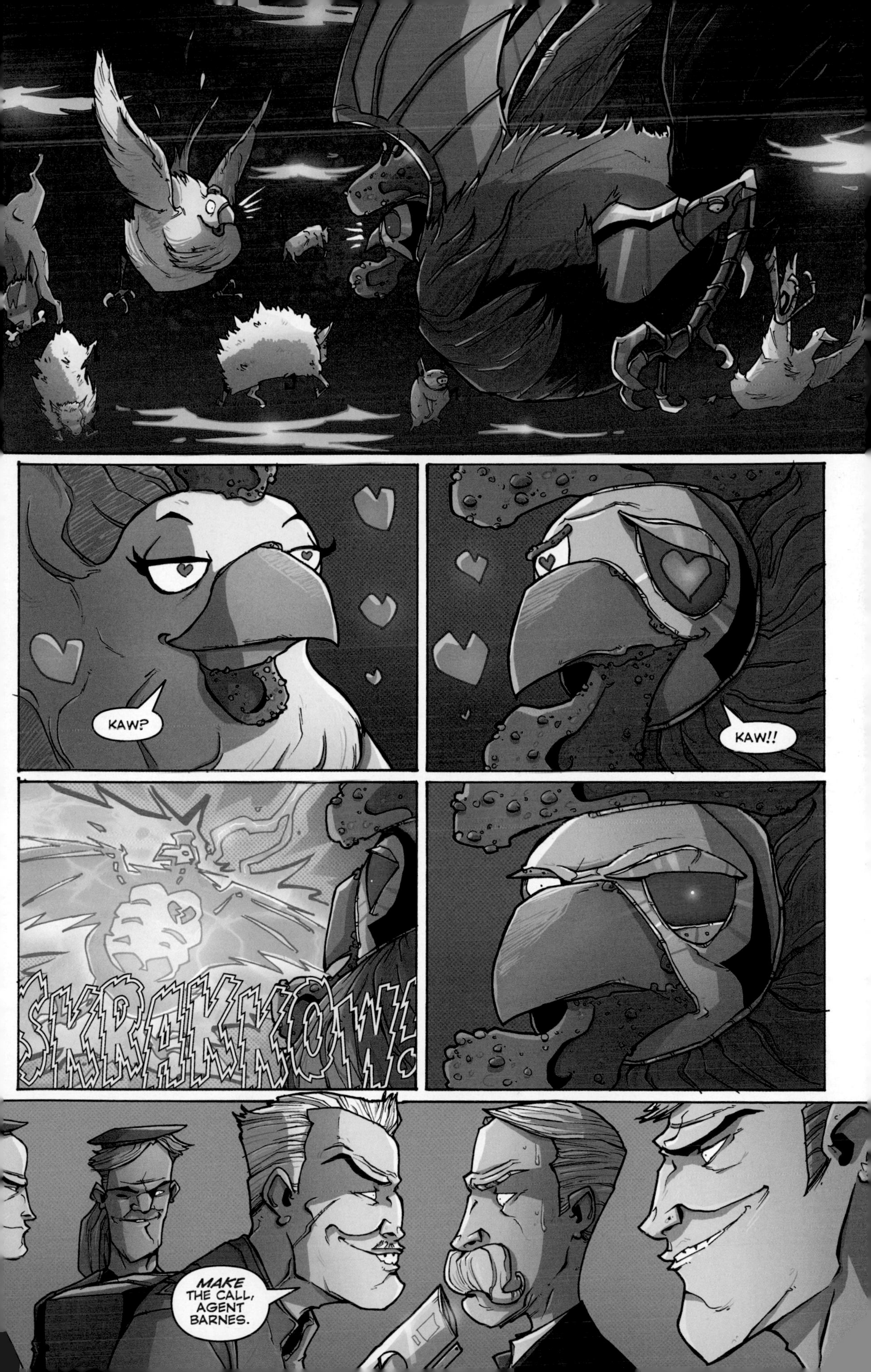
KAW?
KAW!!
SKRAKKOW!
MAKE THE CALL, AGENT BARNES.

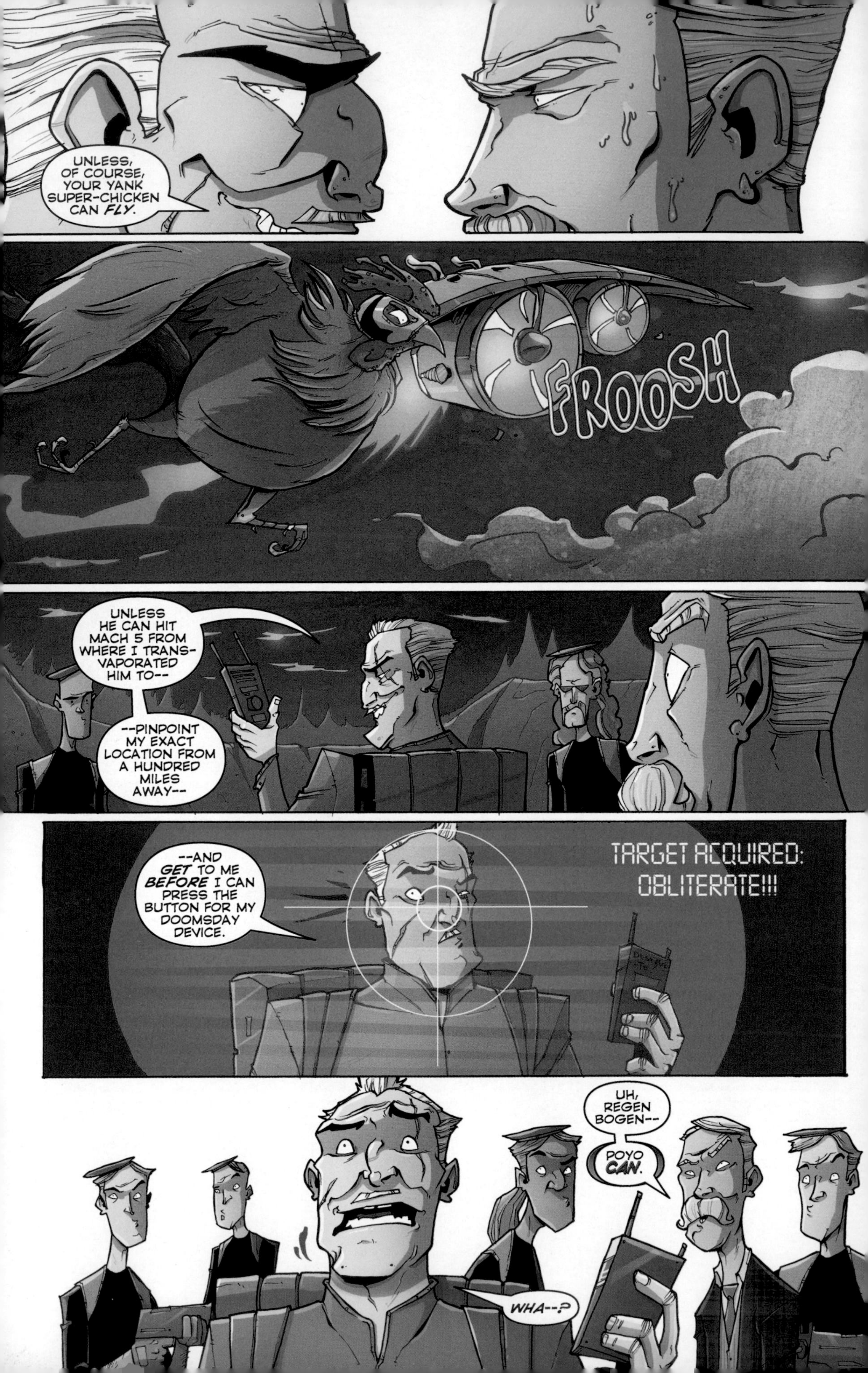

UNLESS, OF COURSE, YOUR YANK SUPER-CHICKEN CAN *FLY*.
FROOSH
UNLESS HE CAN HIT MACH 5 FROM WHERE I TRANS-VAPORATED HIM TO--
--PINPOINT MY EXACT LOCATION FROM A HUNDRED MILES AWAY--
--AND *GET* TO ME *BEFORE* I CAN PRESS THE BUTTON FOR MY DOOMSDAY DEVICE.
TARGET ACQUIRED: OBLITERATE!!!
UH, REGEN BOGEN--
POYO *CAN*.
WHA--?

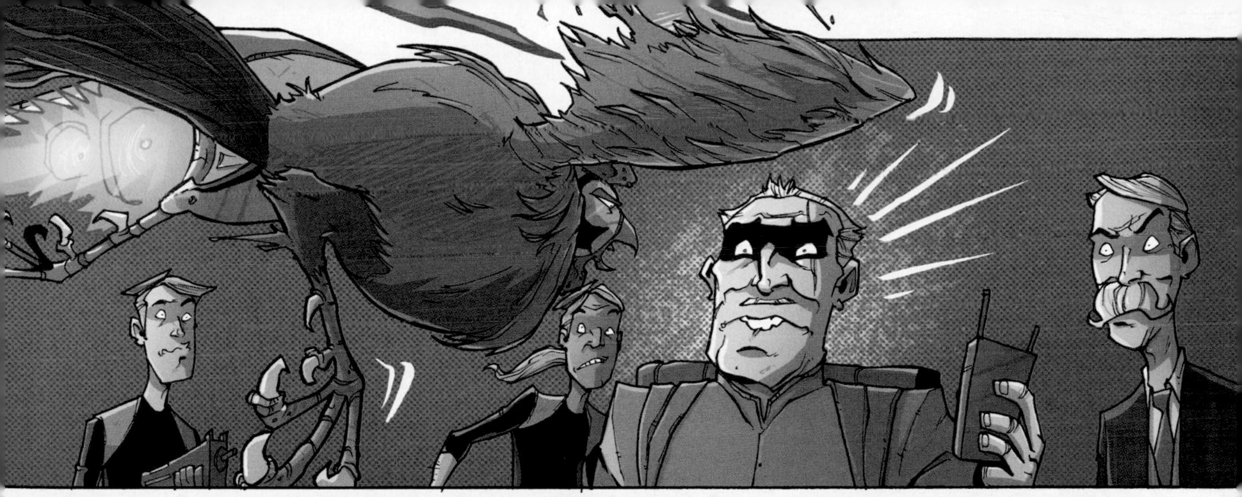

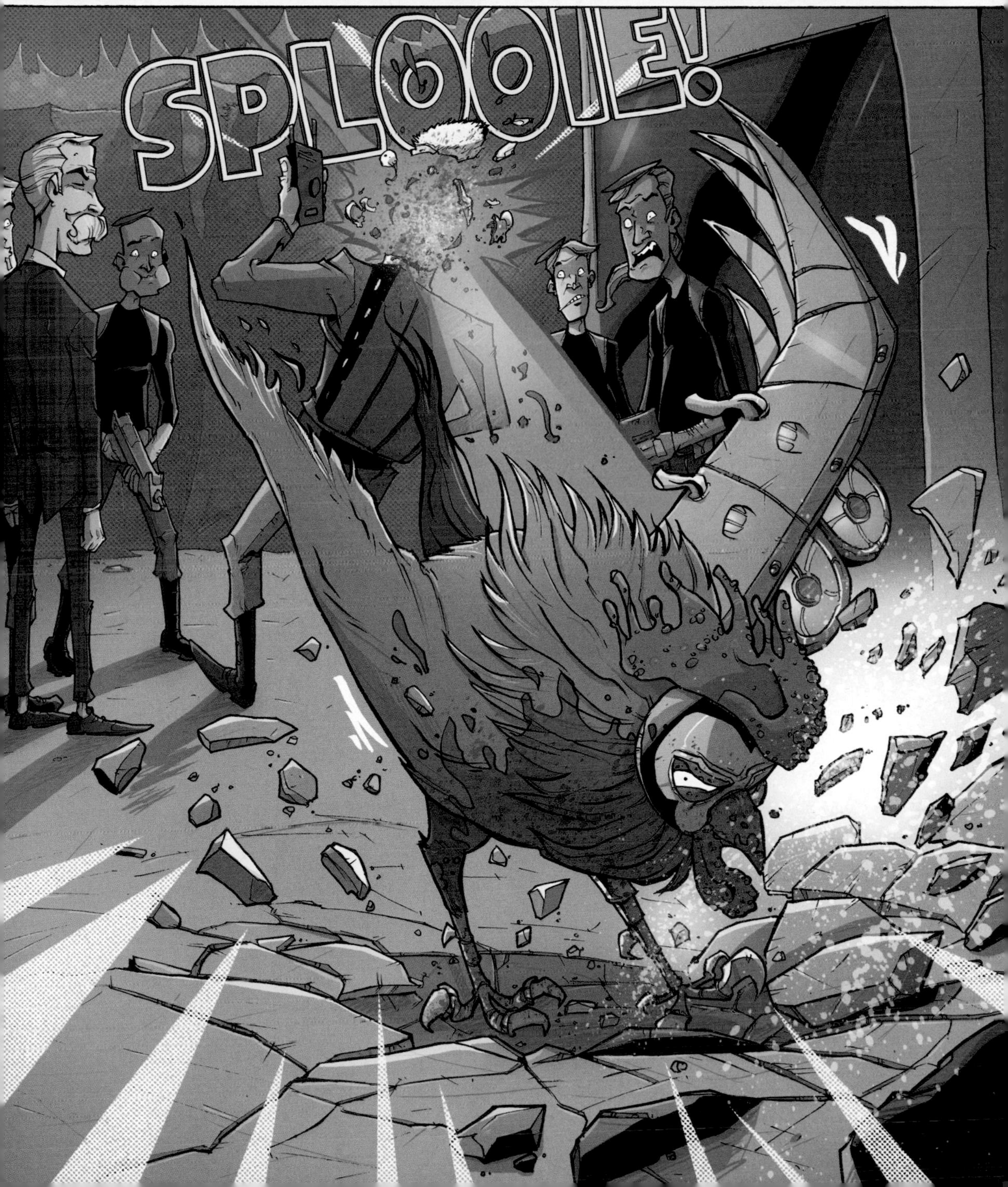
SPLOOIE!

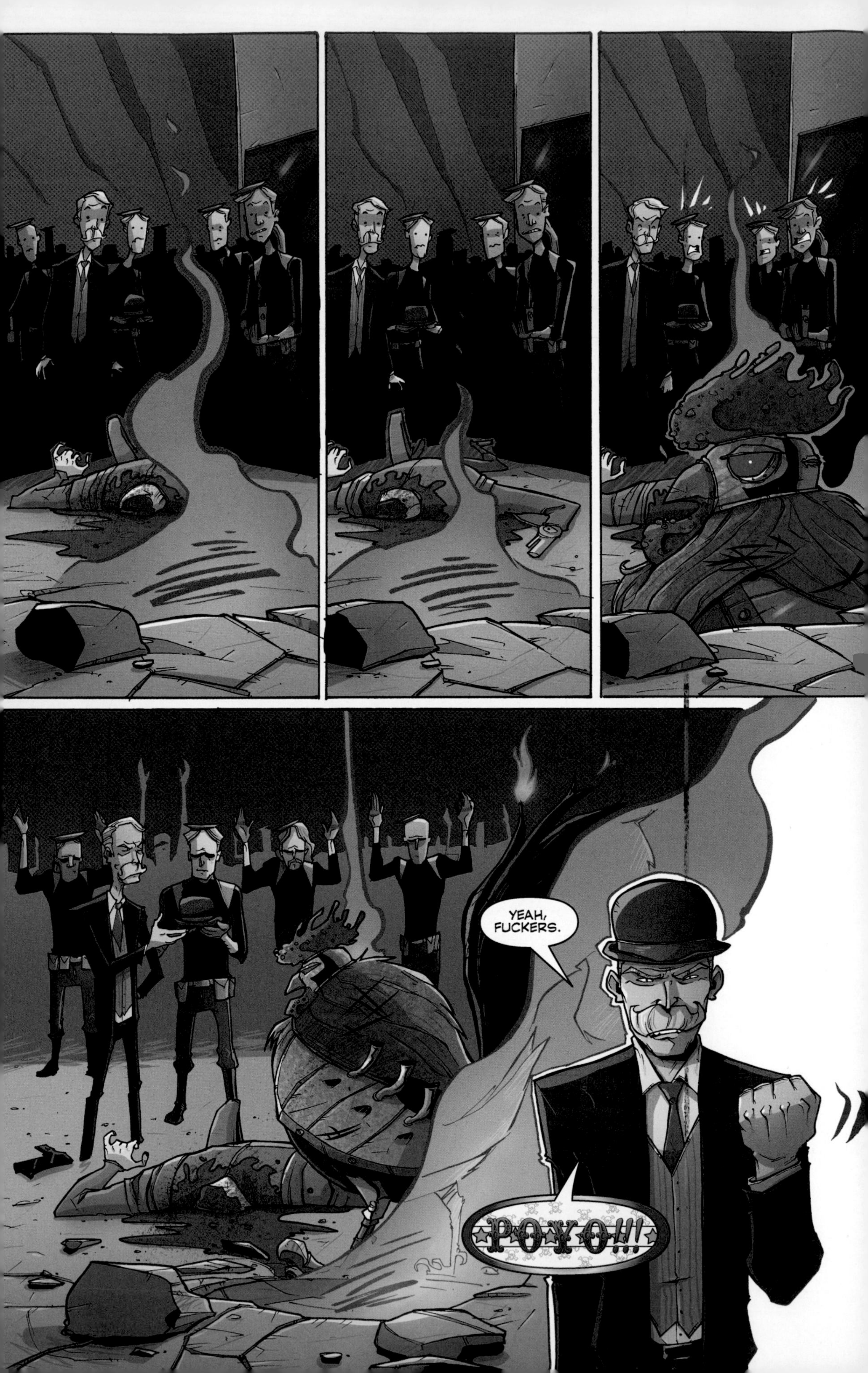
YEAH, FUCKERS.
POYO!!!

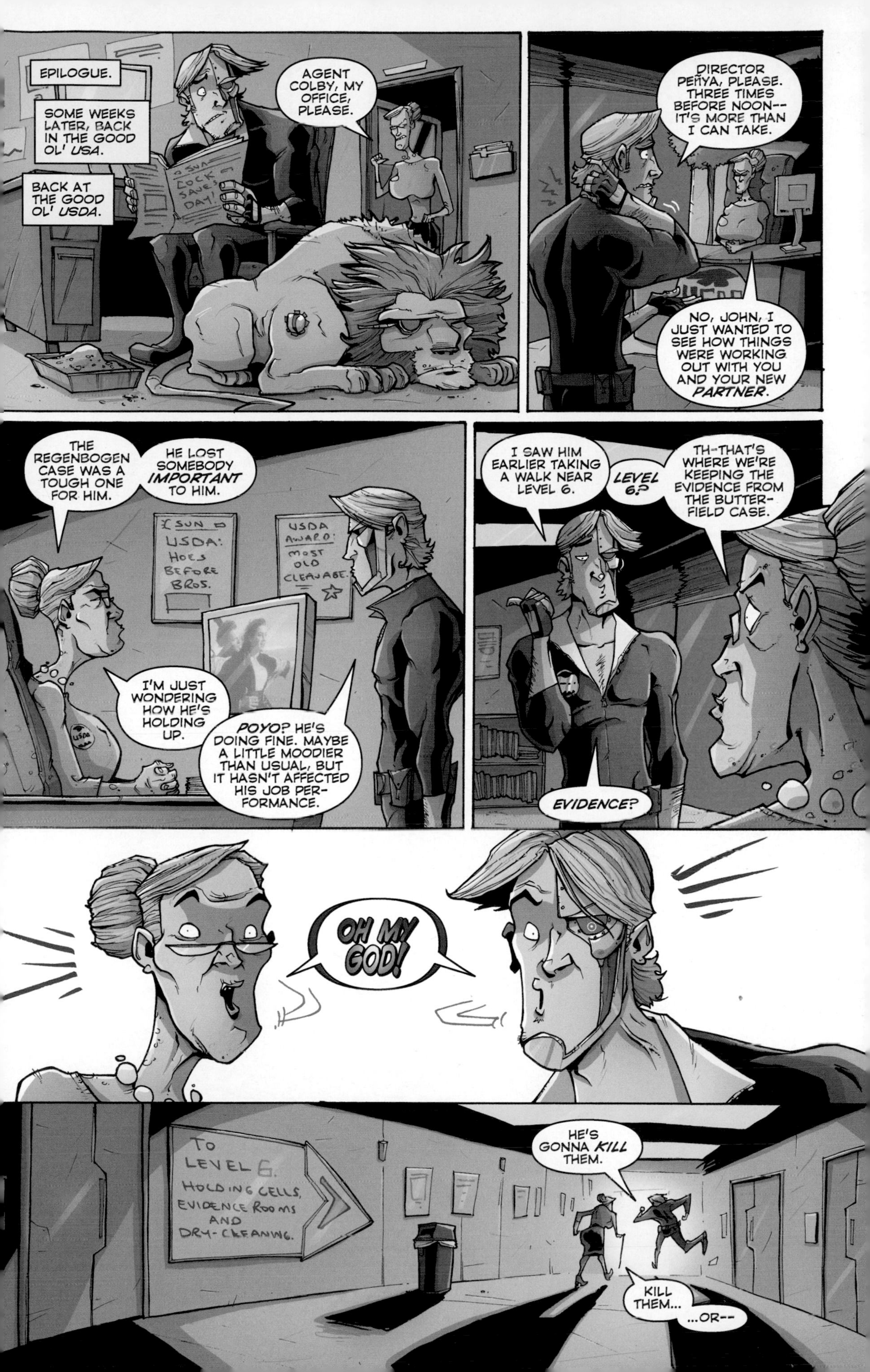

EPILOGUE.
SOME WEEKS LATER, BACK IN THE GOOD OL' *USA*.
BACK AT THE GOOD OL' *USDA*.
SUN
COCK SAVES DAY!
AGENT COLBY, MY OFFICE, PLEASE.
DIRECTOR PEÑYA, PLEASE. THREE TIMES BEFORE NOON-- IT'S MORE THAN I CAN TAKE.
NO, JOHN, I JUST WANTED TO SEE HOW THINGS WERE WORKING OUT WITH YOU AND YOUR NEW *PARTNER*.
THE REGENBOGEN CASE WAS A TOUGH ONE FOR HIM.
HE LOST SOMEBODY *IMPORTANT* TO HIM.
SUN
USDA: HOES BEFORE BROS.
USDA AWARD: MOST OLD CLEAVAGE.
I'M JUST WONDERING HOW HE'S HOLDING UP.
POYO? HE'S DOING FINE. MAYBE A LITTLE MOODIER THAN USUAL, BUT IT HASN'T AFFECTED HIS JOB PERFORMANCE.
I SAW HIM EARLIER TAKING A WALK NEAR LEVEL 6.
LEVEL 6?
TH-THAT'S WHERE WE'RE KEEPING THE EVIDENCE FROM THE BUTTERFIELD CASE.
EVIDENCE?
OH MY GOD!
TO LEVEL 6. HOLDING CELLS, EVIDENCE ROOMS AND DRY-CLEANING.
HE'S GONNA *KILL* THEM.
KILL THEM...
...OR--

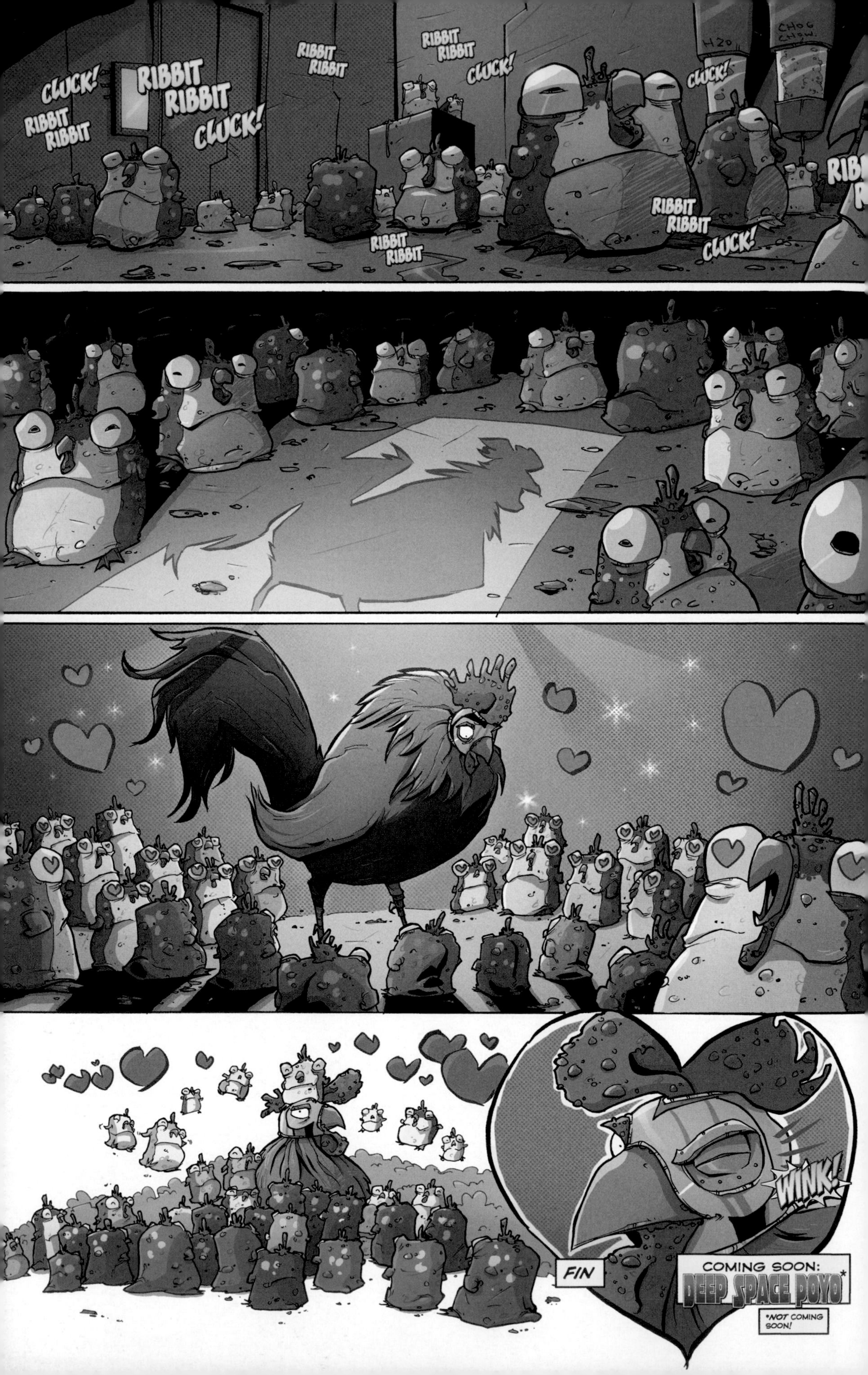

CLUCK!
RIBBIT RIBBIT
RIBBIT RIBBIT
CLUCK!
RIBBIT RIBBIT
RIBBIT RIBBIT
CLUCK!
H2O
CHOG CHOW
CLUCK!
RIBBIT RIBBIT
RIBBIT RIBBIT
CLUCK!
WINK!
FIN
COMING SOON:
DEEP SPACE POYO*
*NOT COMING SOON!

Chapter 3

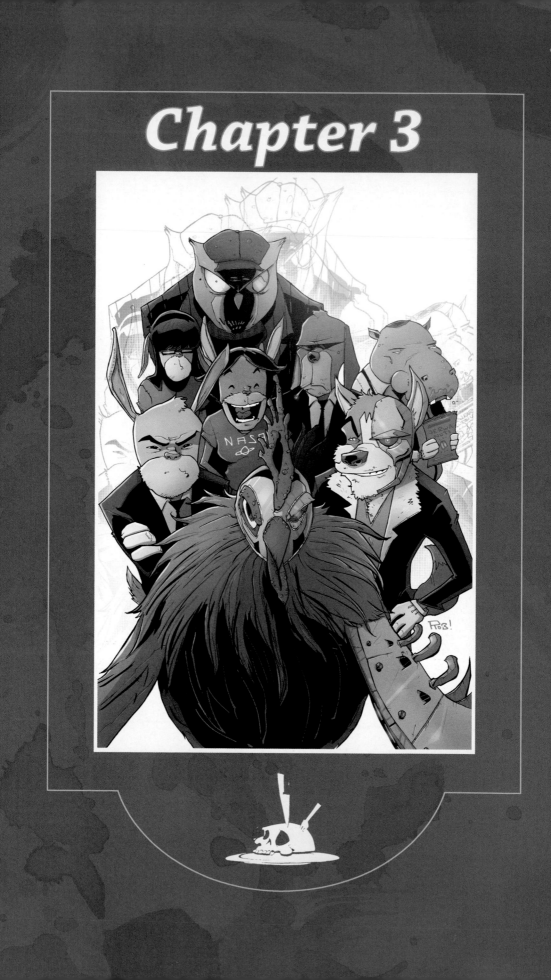

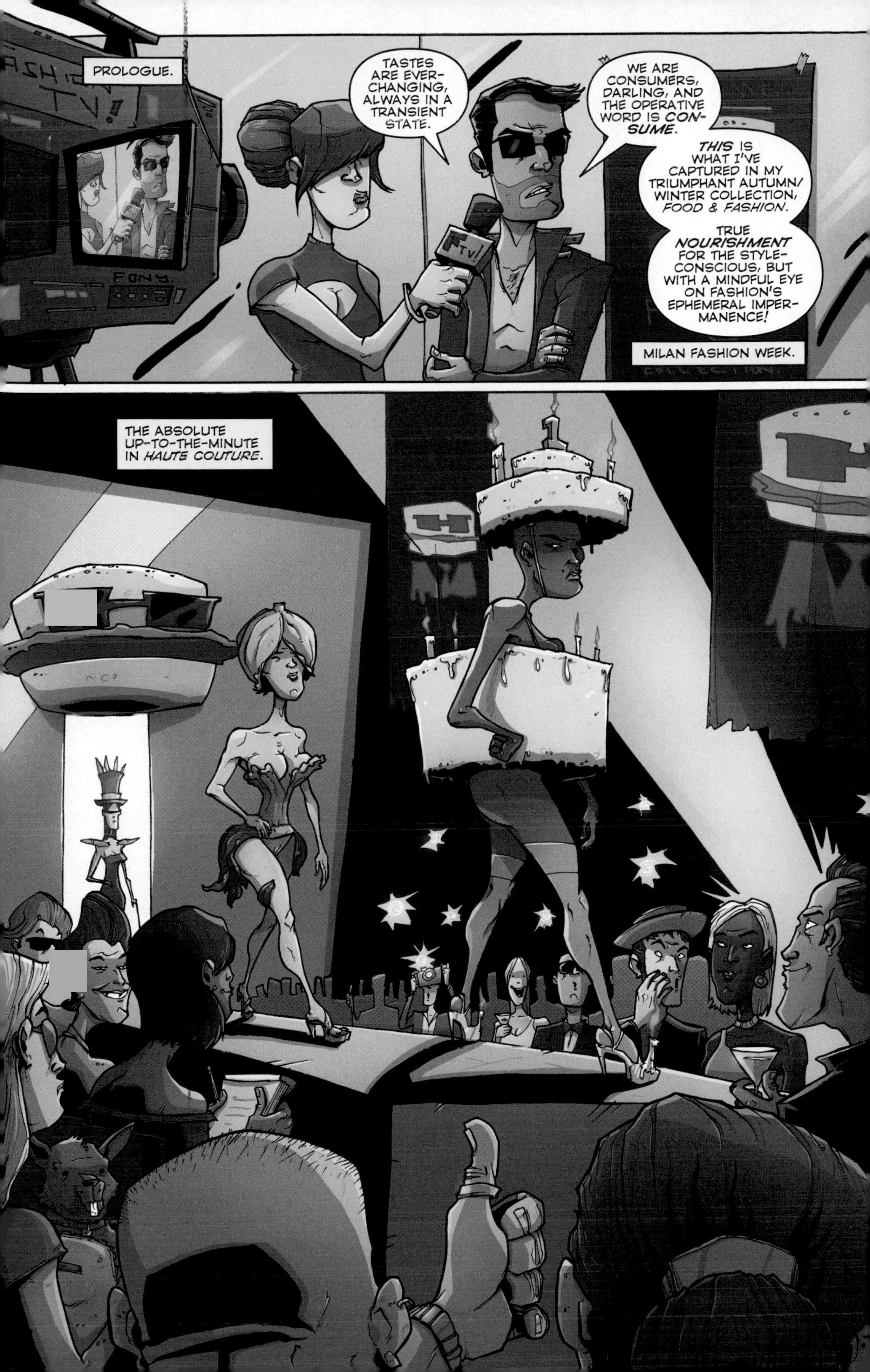
PROLOGUE.
TASTES ARE EVER-CHANGING, ALWAYS IN A TRANSIENT STATE.
WE ARE CONSUMERS, DARLING, AND THE OPERATIVE WORD IS *CON-SUME*.
THIS IS WHAT I'VE CAPTURED IN MY TRIUMPHANT AUTUMN/WINTER COLLECTION, *FOOD & FASHION*.
TRUE *NOURISHMENT* FOR THE STYLE-CONSCIOUS, BUT WITH A MINDFUL EYE ON FASHION'S EPHEMERAL IMPER-MANENCE!
MILAN FASHION WEEK.
THE ABSOLUTE UP-TO-THE-MINUTE IN *HAUTE COUTURE*.

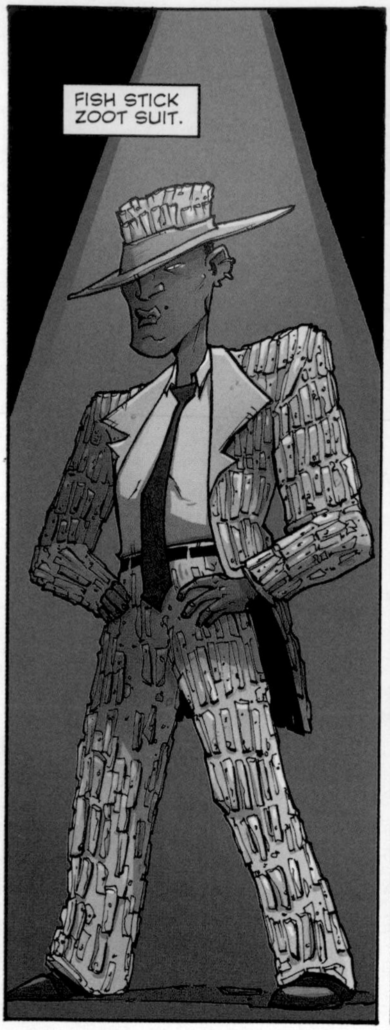
FISH STICK ZOOT SUIT.

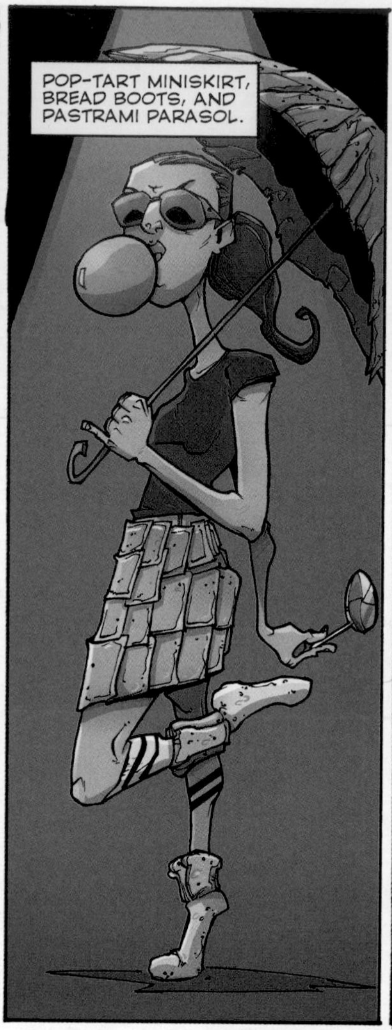
POP-TART MINISKIRT, BREAD BOOTS, AND PASTRAMI PARASOL.

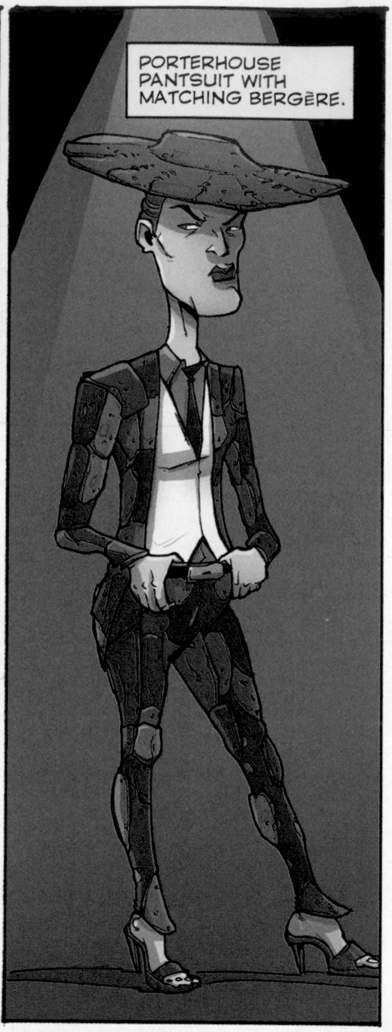
PORTERHOUSE PANTSUIT WITH MATCHING BERGÈRE.

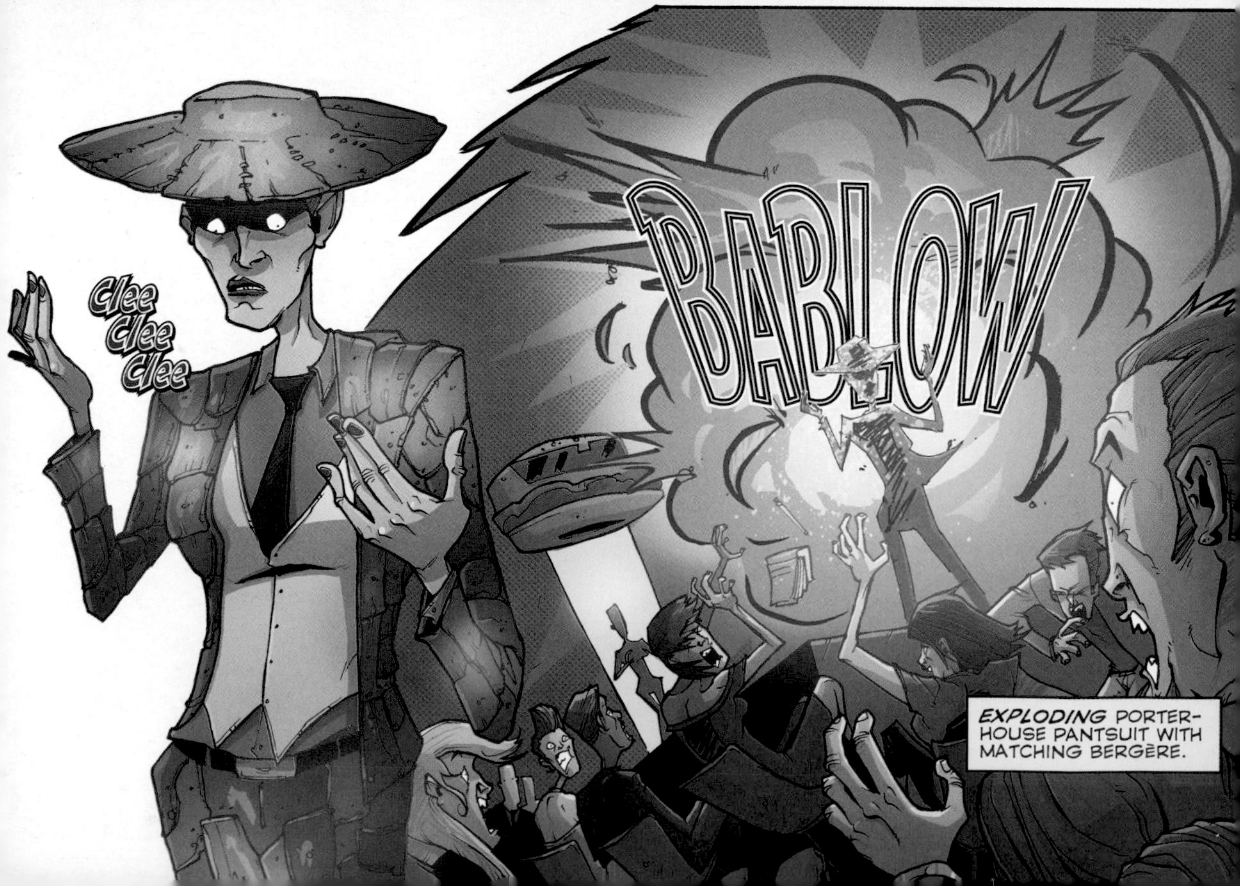
Clee Clee Clee
BABLOW
EXPLODING PORTER-HOUSE PANTSUIT WITH MATCHING BERGÈRE.

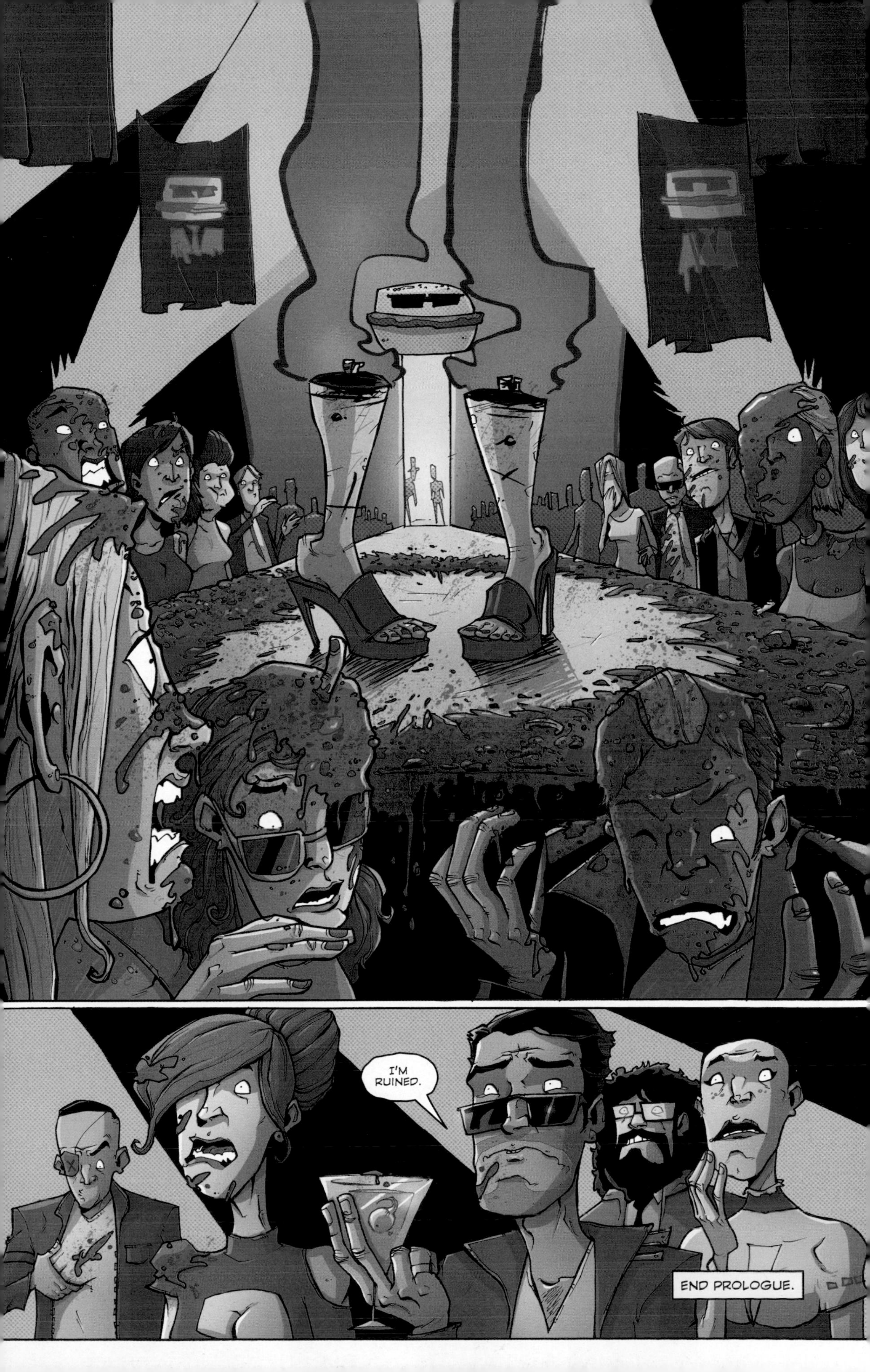
I'M RUINED.
END PROLOGUE.

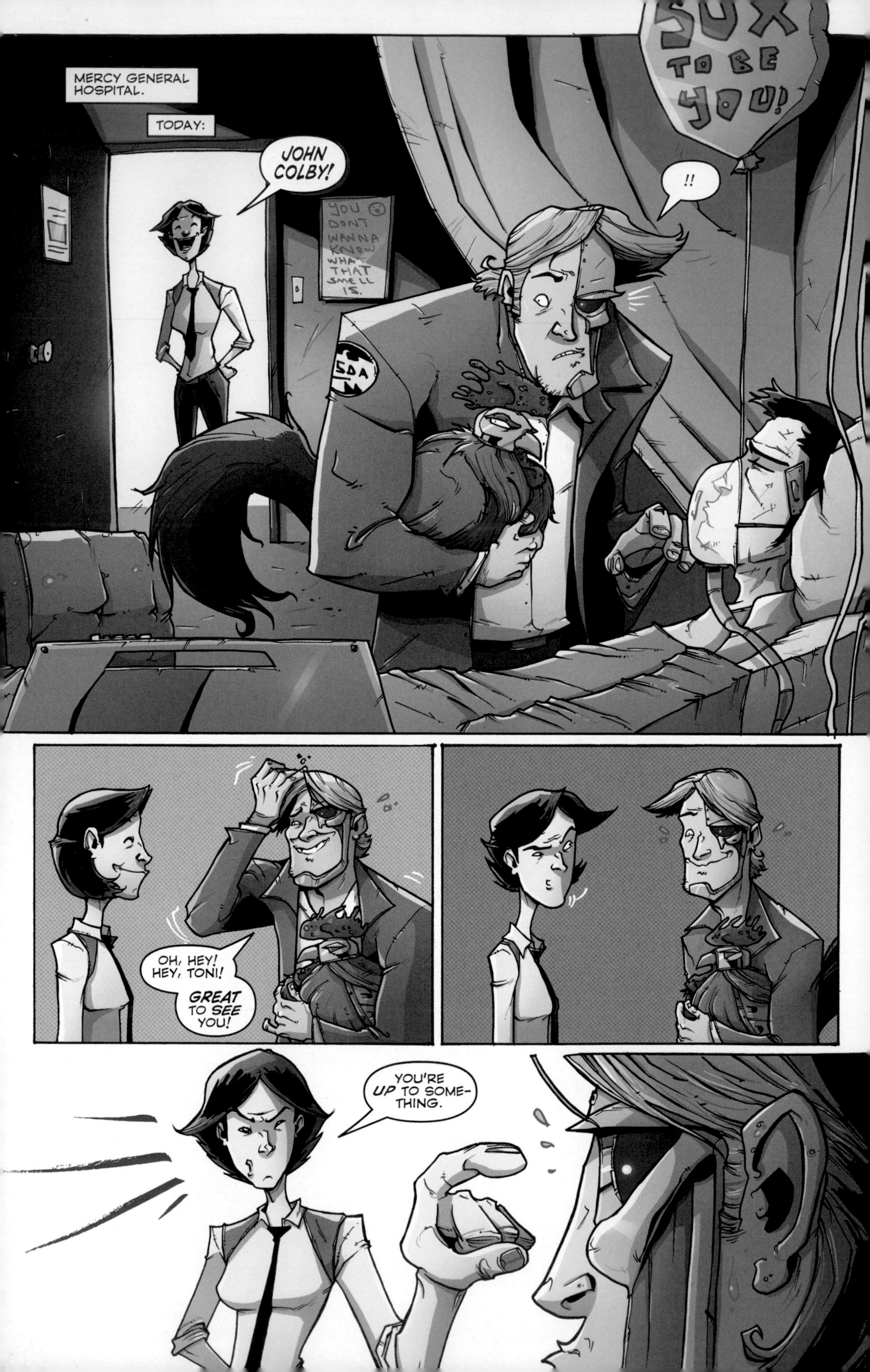
MERCY GENERAL HOSPITAL.
TODAY:
JOHN COLBY!
!!
SUX TO BE YOU!
YOU DONT WANNA KNOW WHAT THAT SMELL IS.
SDA
OH, HEY! HEY, TONI! GREAT TO SEE YOU!
YOU'RE UP TO SOME-THING.

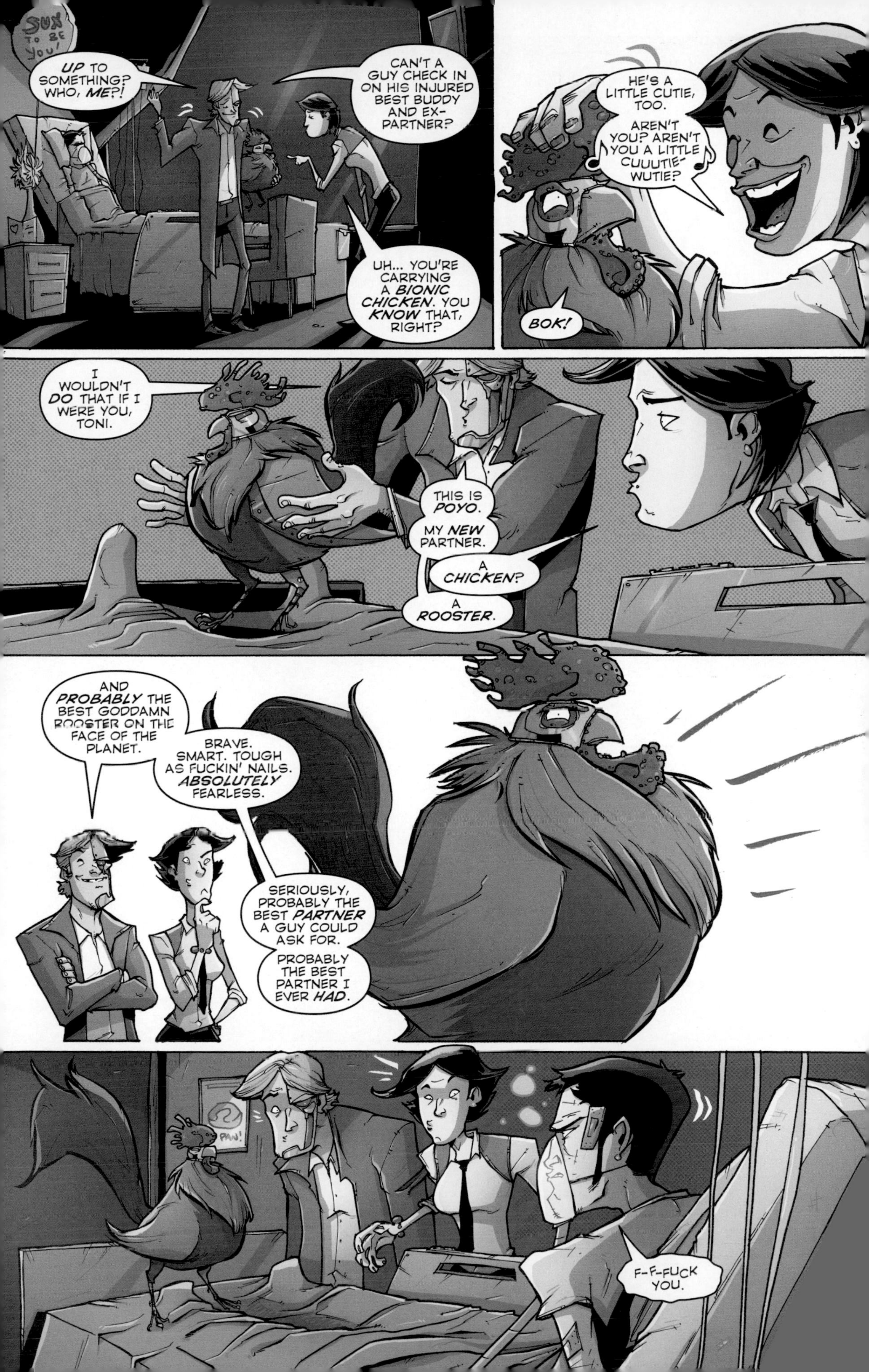
SUN TO BE YOU!
UP TO SOMETHING? WHO, ME?!
CAN'T A GUY CHECK IN ON HIS INJURED BEST BUDDY AND EX-PARTNER?
UH... YOU'RE CARRYING A BIONIC CHICKEN. YOU KNOW THAT, RIGHT?
HE'S A LITTLE CUTIE, TOO.
AREN'T YOU? AREN'T YOU A LITTLE CUUUTIE-WUTIE?
BOK!
I WOULDN'T DO THAT IF I WERE YOU, TONI.
THIS IS POYO.
MY NEW PARTNER.
A CHICKEN?
A ROOSTER.
AND PROBABLY THE BEST GODDAMN ROOSTER ON THE FACE OF THE PLANET.
BRAVE. SMART. TOUGH AS FUCKIN' NAILS. ABSOLUTELY FEARLESS.
SERIOUSLY, PROBABLY THE BEST PARTNER A GUY COULD ASK FOR.
PROBABLY THE BEST PARTNER I EVER HAD.
PAW!
F-F-FUCK YOU.

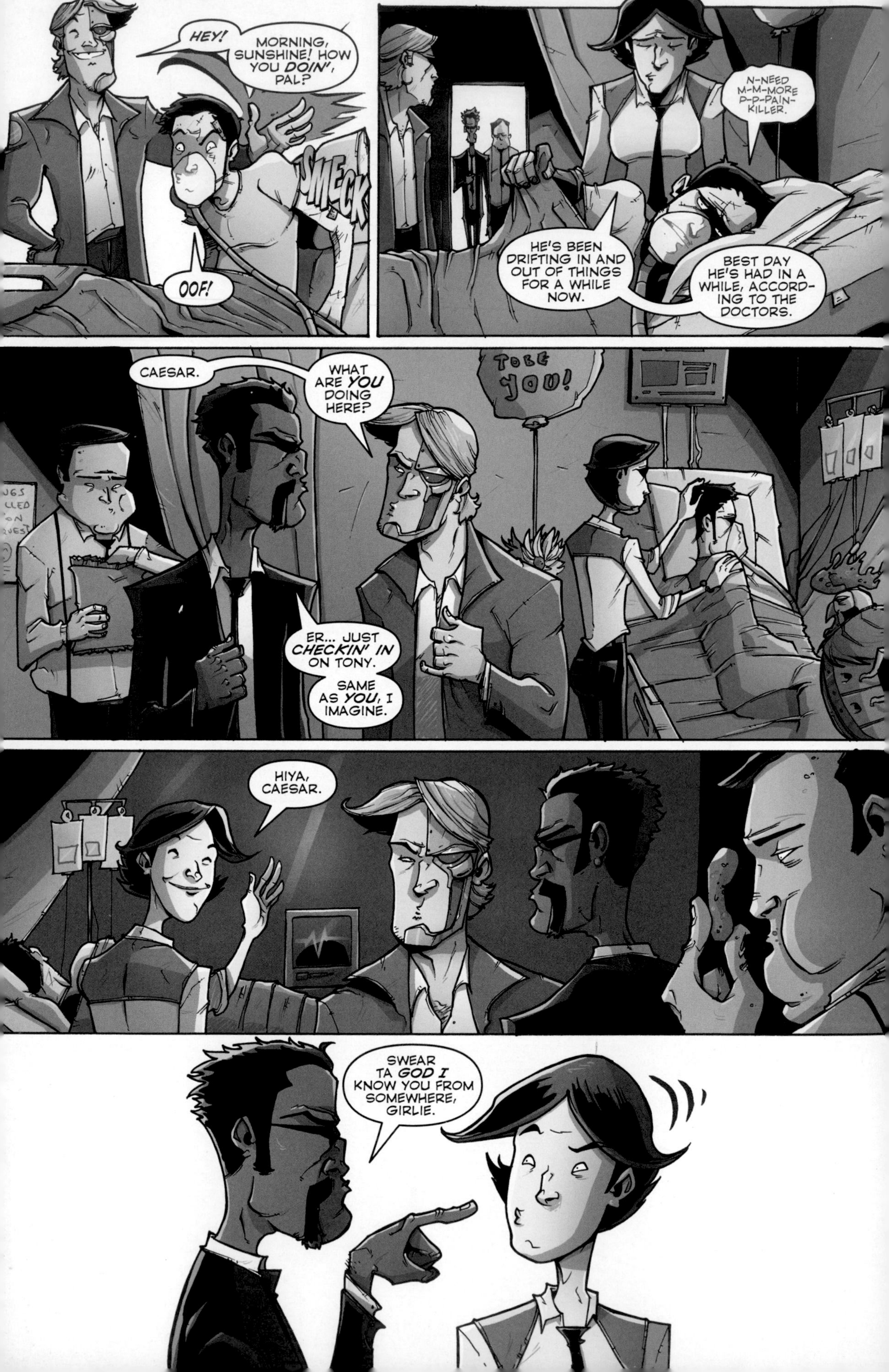
HEY!
MORNING, SUNSHINE! HOW YOU *DOIN'*, PAL?
SMECK
OOF!
N-NEED M-M-MORE P-P-PAIN-KILLER.
HE'S BEEN DRIFTING IN AND OUT OF THINGS FOR A WHILE NOW.
BEST DAY HE'S HAD IN A WHILE, ACCORDING TO THE DOCTORS.
CAESAR.
WHAT ARE *YOU* DOING HERE?
TOBE YOU!
ER... JUST *CHECKIN' IN* ON TONY.
SAME AS *YOU*, I IMAGINE.
HIYA, CAESAR.
SWEAR TA *GOD I* KNOW YOU FROM SOMEWHERE, GIRLIE.

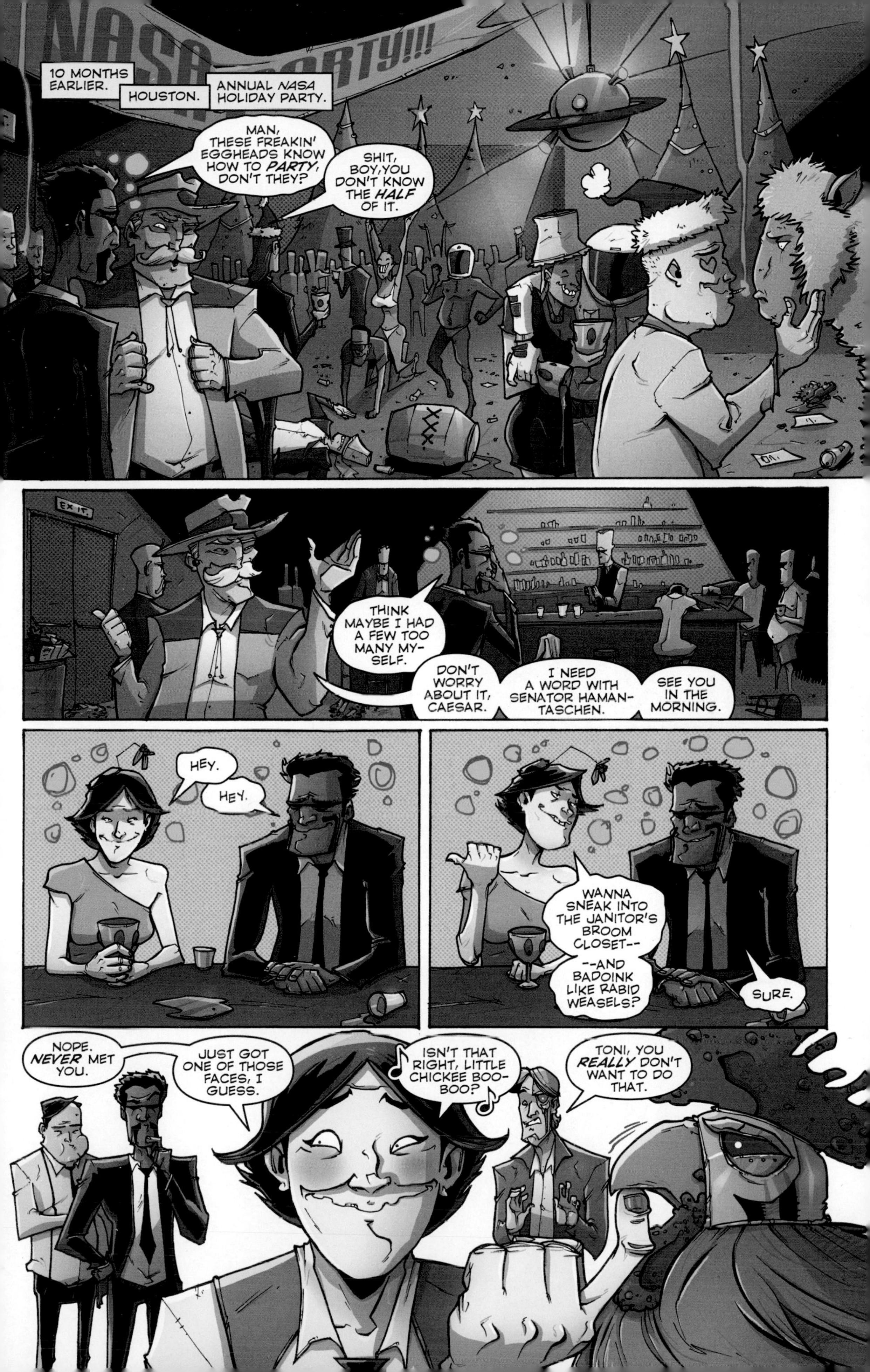
NASA PARTY!!!
10 MONTHS EARLIER.
HOUSTON.
ANNUAL *NASA* HOLIDAY PARTY.
MAN, THESE FREAKIN' EGGHEADS KNOW HOW TO *PARTY*, DON'T THEY?
SHIT, BOY, YOU DON'T KNOW THE *HALF* OF IT.
EXIT
THINK MAYBE I HAD A FEW TOO MANY MY-SELF.
DON'T WORRY ABOUT IT, CAESAR.
I NEED A WORD WITH SENATOR HAMAN-TASCHEN.
SEE YOU IN THE MORNING.
HEY.
HEY.
WANNA SNEAK INTO THE JANITOR'S BROOM CLOSET--
--AND BADOINK LIKE RABID WEASELS?
SURE.
NOPE. *NEVER* MET YOU.
JUST GOT ONE OF THOSE FACES, I GUESS.
ISN'T THAT RIGHT, LITTLE CHICKEE BOO-BOO?
TONI, YOU *REALLY* DON'T WANT TO DO THAT.

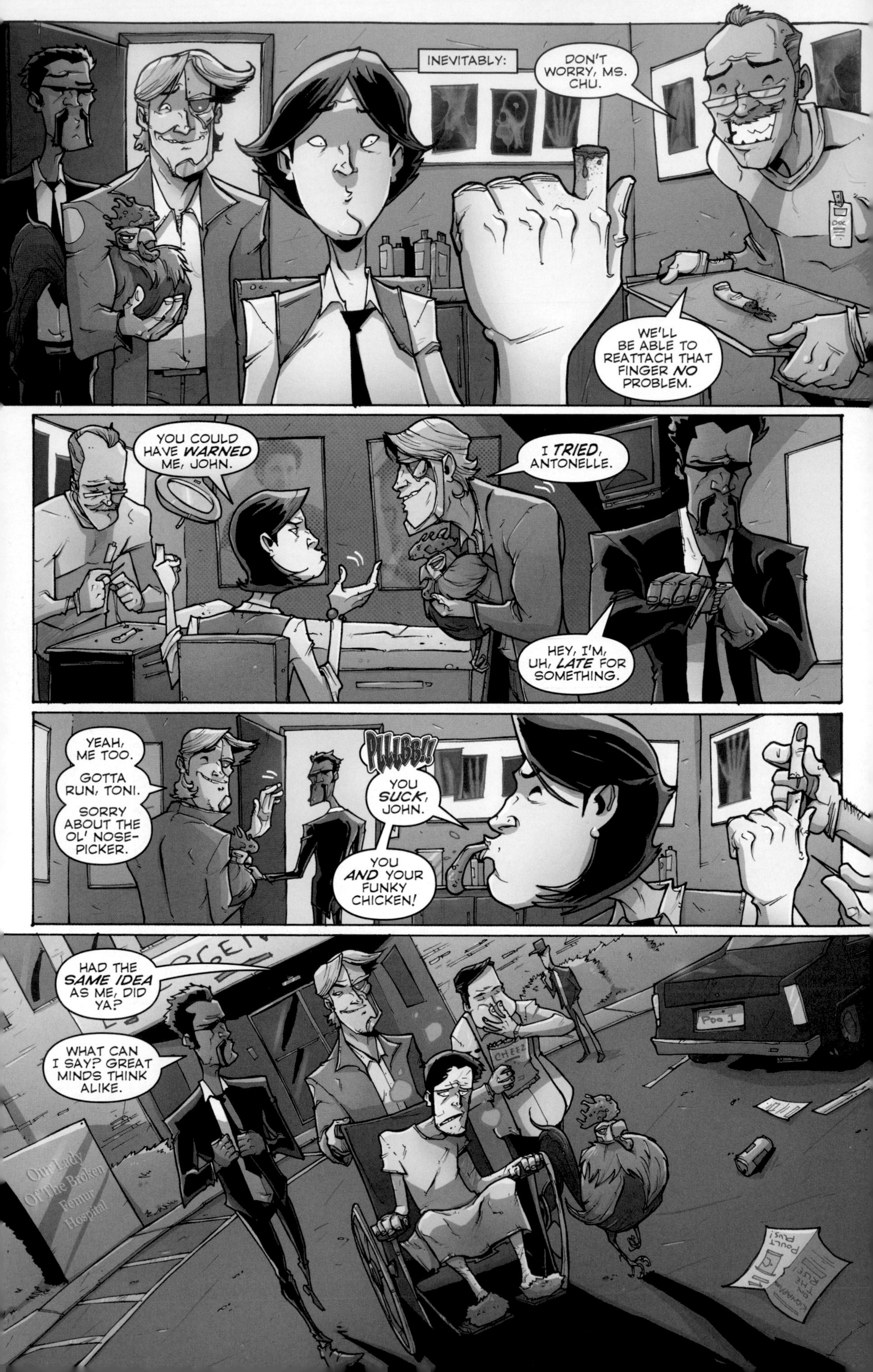
INEVITABLY:
DON'T WORRY, MS. CHU.
WE'LL BE ABLE TO REATTACH THAT FINGER *NO* PROBLEM.
YOU COULD HAVE *WARNED* ME, JOHN.
I *TRIED*, ANTONELLE.
HEY, I'M, UH, *LATE* FOR SOMETHING.
YEAH, ME TOO.
GOTTA RUN, TONI.
SORRY ABOUT THE OL' NOSE-PICKER.
PLLLBB!!
YOU *SUCK*, JOHN.
YOU *AND* YOUR FUNKY CHICKEN!
HAD THE *SAME IDEA* AS ME, DID YA?
WHAT CAN I SAY? GREAT MINDS THINK ALIKE.
POO 1
CHEEZ
Our Lady Of The Broken Femur Hospital

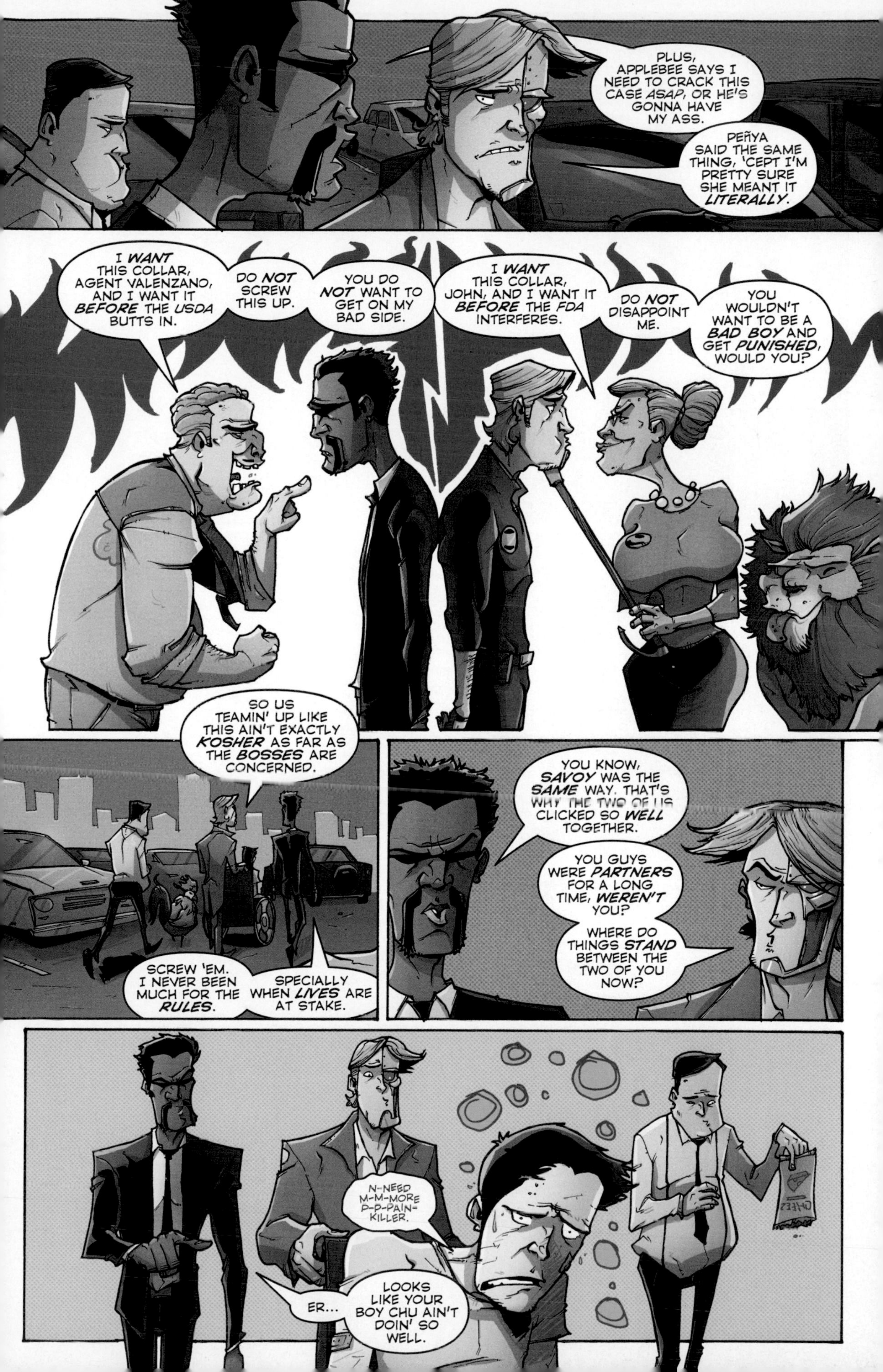
PLUS, APPLEBEE SAYS I NEED TO CRACK THIS CASE *ASAP*, OR HE'S GONNA HAVE MY ASS.
PEÑYA SAID THE SAME THING, 'CEPT I'M PRETTY SURE SHE MEANT IT ***LITERALLY***.
I ***WANT*** THIS COLLAR, AGENT VALENZANO, AND I WANT IT ***BEFORE*** THE *USDA* BUTTS IN.
DO ***NOT*** SCREW THIS UP.
YOU DO ***NOT*** WANT TO GET ON MY BAD SIDE.
I ***WANT*** THIS COLLAR, JOHN, AND I WANT IT ***BEFORE*** THE *FDA* INTERFERES.
DO ***NOT*** DISAPPOINT ME.
YOU WOULDN'T WANT TO BE A ***BAD BOY*** AND GET ***PUNISHED***, WOULD YOU?
SO US TEAMIN' UP LIKE THIS AIN'T EXACTLY ***KOSHER*** AS FAR AS THE ***BOSSES*** ARE CONCERNED.
SCREW 'EM. I NEVER BEEN MUCH FOR THE ***RULES***.
SPECIALLY WHEN ***LIVES*** ARE AT STAKE.
YOU KNOW, ***SAVOY*** WAS THE ***SAME*** WAY. THAT'S WHY THE TWO OF US CLICKED SO ***WELL*** TOGETHER.
YOU GUYS WERE ***PARTNERS*** FOR A LONG TIME, ***WEREN'T*** YOU?
WHERE DO THINGS ***STAND*** BETWEEN THE TWO OF YOU NOW?
N-NEED M-M-MORE P-P-PAIN-KILLER.
ER...
LOOKS LIKE YOUR BOY CHU AIN'T DOIN' SO WELL.

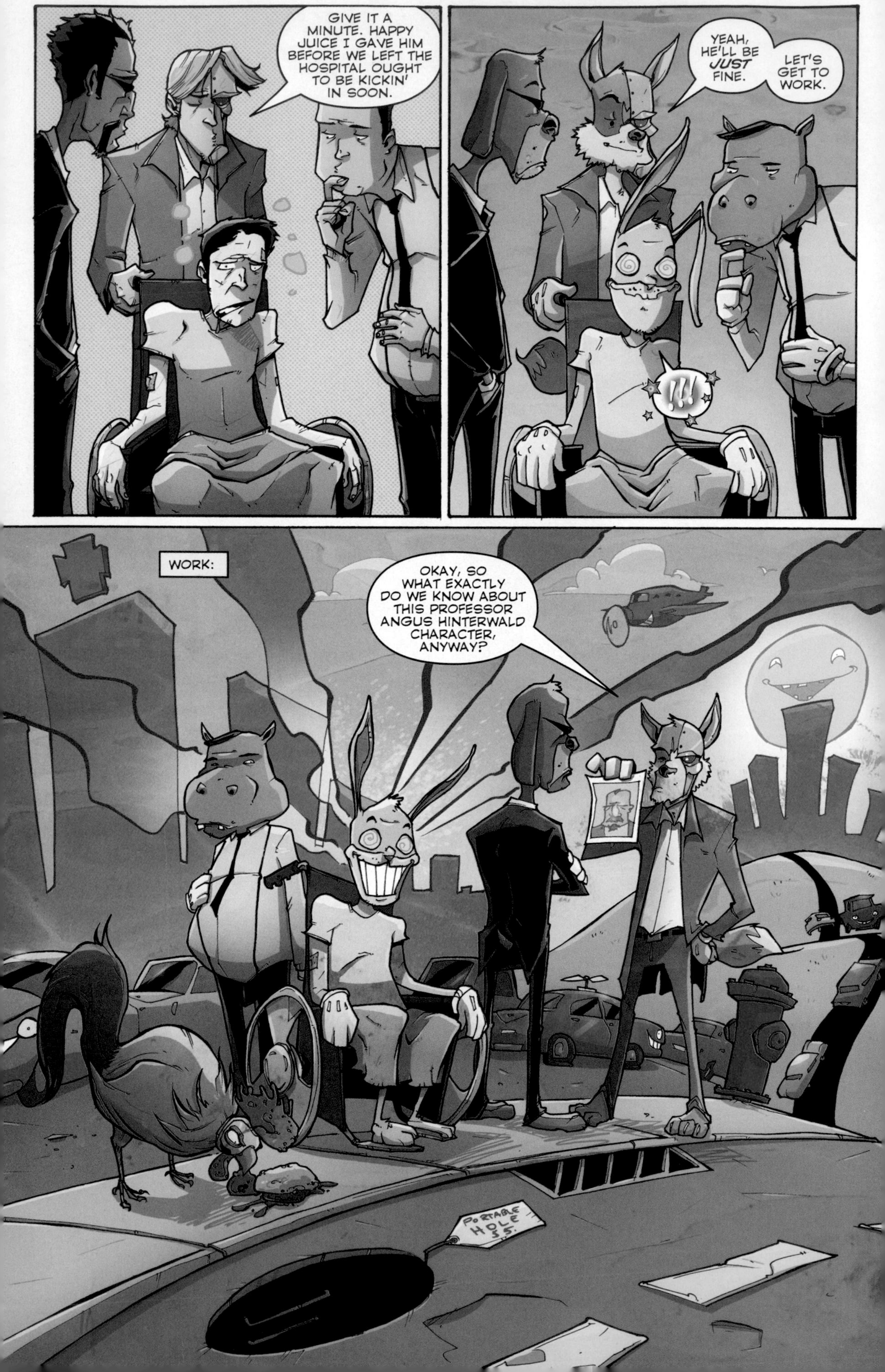
GIVE IT A MINUTE. HAPPY JUICE I GAVE HIM BEFORE WE LEFT THE HOSPITAL OUGHT TO BE KICKIN' IN SOON.
YEAH, HE'LL BE *JUST* FINE.
LET'S GET TO WORK.
!!!
WORK:
OKAY, SO WHAT EXACTLY DO WE KNOW ABOUT THIS PROFESSOR ANGUS HINTERWALD CHARACTER, ANYWAY?
PORTABLE HOLE $5.

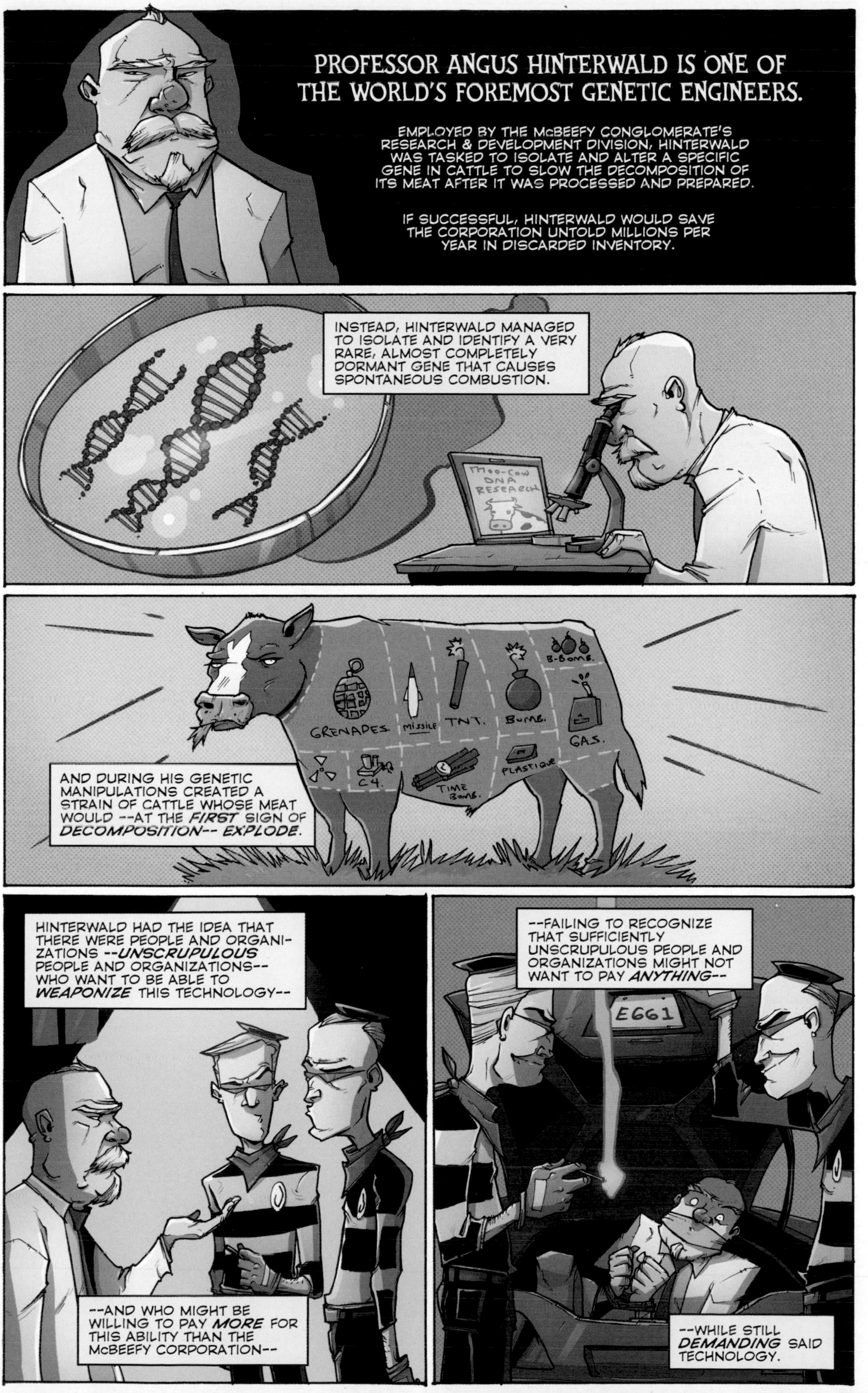
PROFESSOR ANGUS HINTERWALD IS ONE OF THE WORLD'S FOREMOST GENETIC ENGINEERS.
EMPLOYED BY THE McBEEFY CONGLOMERATE'S RESEARCH & DEVELOPMENT DIVISION, HINTERWALD WAS TASKED TO ISOLATE AND ALTER A SPECIFIC GENE IN CATTLE TO SLOW THE DECOMPOSITION OF ITS MEAT AFTER IT WAS PROCESSED AND PREPARED.
IF SUCCESSFUL, HINTERWALD WOULD SAVE THE CORPORATION UNTOLD MILLIONS PER YEAR IN DISCARDED INVENTORY.
INSTEAD, HINTERWALD MANAGED TO ISOLATE AND IDENTIFY A VERY RARE, ALMOST COMPLETELY DORMANT GENE THAT CAUSES SPONTANEOUS COMBUSTION.
MOO-COW DNA RESEARCH
B-BOMB.
GRENADES.
MISSILE
TNT.
BOMB.
GAS.
C4.
PLASTIQUE
TIME BOMB.
AND DURING HIS GENETIC MANIPULATIONS CREATED A STRAIN OF CATTLE WHOSE MEAT WOULD --AT THE *FIRST* SIGN OF *DECOMPOSITION*-- *EXPLODE*.
HINTERWALD HAD THE IDEA THAT THERE WERE PEOPLE AND ORGANIZATIONS --*UNSCRUPULOUS* PEOPLE AND ORGANIZATIONS-- WHO WANT TO BE ABLE TO *WEAPONIZE* THIS TECHNOLOGY--
--AND WHO MIGHT BE WILLING TO PAY *MORE* FOR THIS ABILITY THAN THE McBEEFY CORPORATION--
--FAILING TO RECOGNIZE THAT SUFFICIENTLY UNSCRUPULOUS PEOPLE AND ORGANIZATIONS MIGHT NOT WANT TO PAY *ANYTHING*--
E661
--WHILE STILL *DEMANDING* SAID TECHNOLOGY.

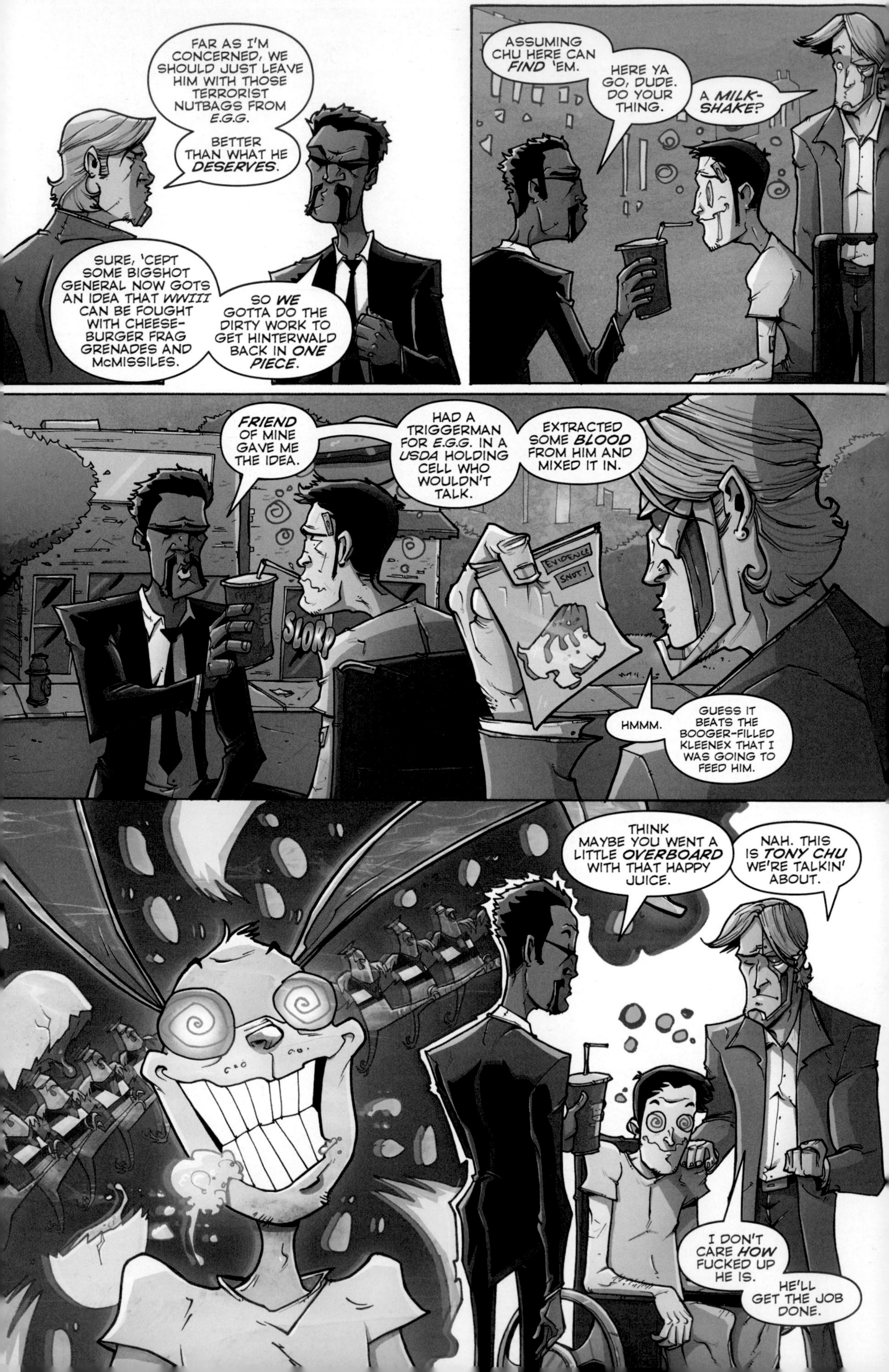
FAR AS I'M CONCERNED, WE SHOULD JUST LEAVE HIM WITH THOSE TERRORIST NUTBAGS FROM E.G.G.
BETTER THAN WHAT HE DESERVES.
SURE, 'CEPT SOME BIGSHOT GENERAL NOW GOTS AN IDEA THAT WWIII CAN BE FOUGHT WITH CHEESE-BURGER FRAG GRENADES AND McMISSILES.
SO WE GOTTA DO THE DIRTY WORK TO GET HINTERWALD BACK IN ONE PIECE.
ASSUMING CHU HERE CAN FIND 'EM.
HERE YA GO, DUDE. DO YOUR THING.
A MILK-SHAKE?
FRIEND OF MINE GAVE ME THE IDEA.
HAD A TRIGGERMAN FOR E.G.G. IN A USDA HOLDING CELL WHO WOULDN'T TALK.
EXTRACTED SOME BLOOD FROM HIM AND MIXED IT IN.
EVIDENCE
SNOT!
SLORP
HMMM.
GUESS IT BEATS THE BOOGER-FILLED KLEENEX THAT I WAS GOING TO FEED HIM.
THINK MAYBE YOU WENT A LITTLE OVERBOARD WITH THAT HAPPY JUICE.
NAH. THIS IS TONY CHU WE'RE TALKIN' ABOUT.
I DON'T CARE HOW FUCKED UP HE IS.
HE'LL GET THE JOB DONE.

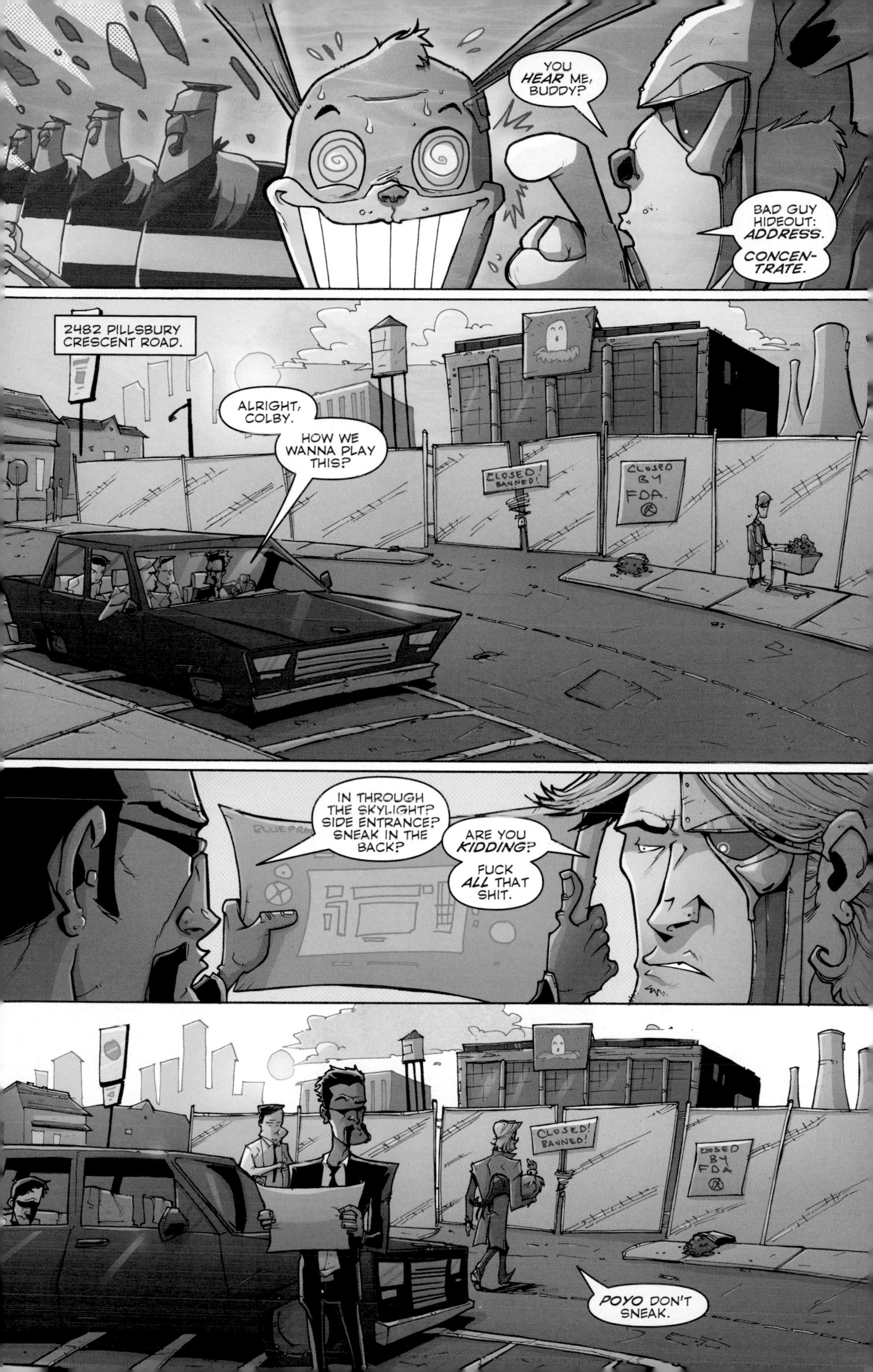

YOU *HEAR* ME, BUDDY?
BAD GUY HIDEOUT: *ADDRESS*.
CONCEN-TRATE.
2482 PILLSBURY CRESCENT ROAD.
ALRIGHT, COLBY.
HOW WE WANNA PLAY THIS?
CLOSED! BANNED!
CLOSED BY FDA.
IN THROUGH THE SKYLIGHT? SIDE ENTRANCE? SNEAK IN THE BACK?
ARE YOU *KIDDING*?
FUCK *ALL* THAT SHIT.
CLOSED! BANNED!
CLOSED BY FDA
POYO DON'T SNEAK.

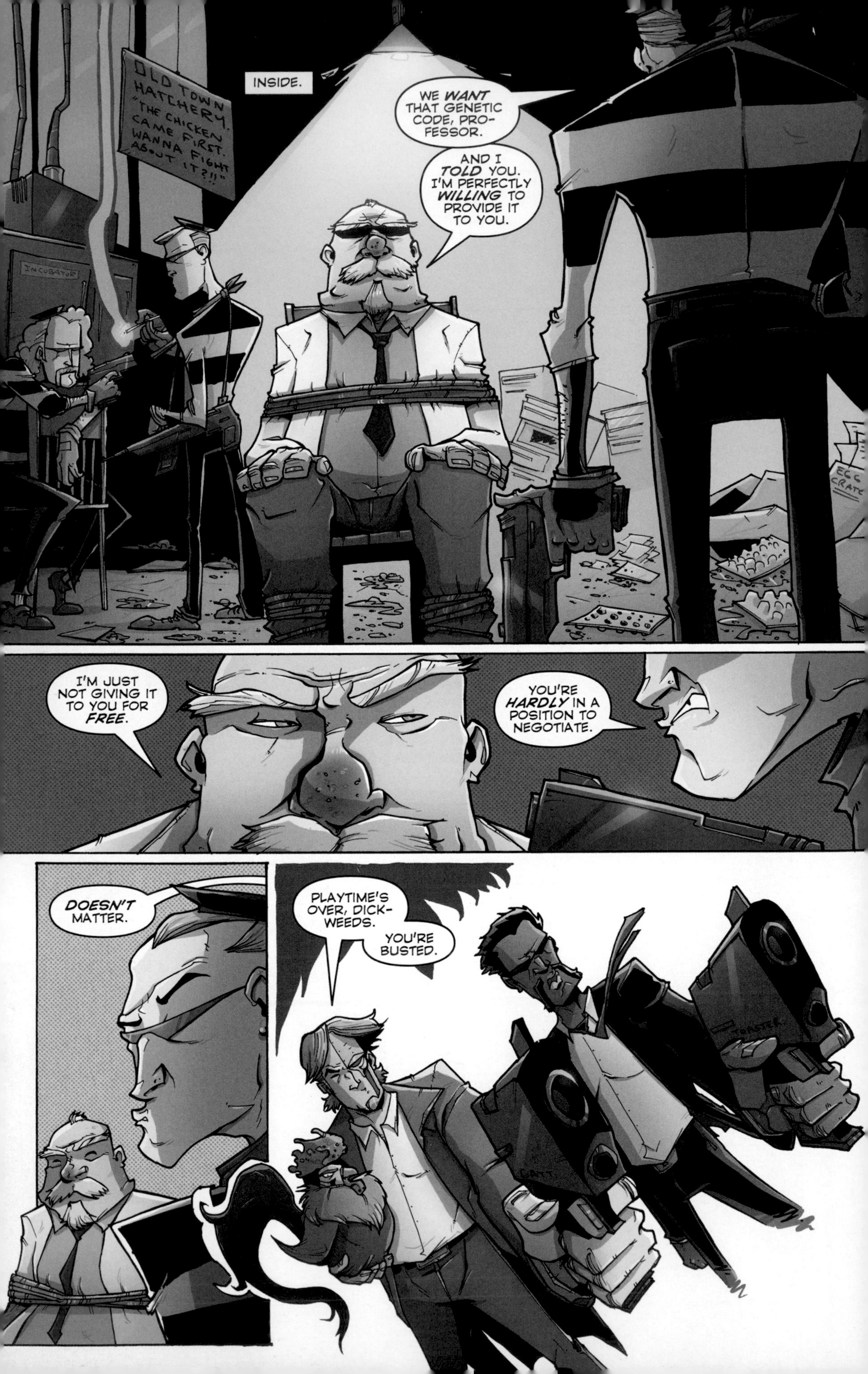

OLD TOWN HATCHERY. "THE CHICKEN CAME FIRST. WANNA FIGHT ABOUT IT?!!"
INCUBATOR
INSIDE.
WE WANT THAT GENETIC CODE, PRO-FESSOR.
AND I TOLD YOU. I'M PERFECTLY WILLING TO PROVIDE IT TO YOU.
EGG CRATE
I'M JUST NOT GIVING IT TO YOU FOR FREE.
YOU'RE HARDLY IN A POSITION TO NEGOTIATE.
DOESN'T MATTER.
PLAYTIME'S OVER, DICK-WEEDS.
YOU'RE BUSTED.

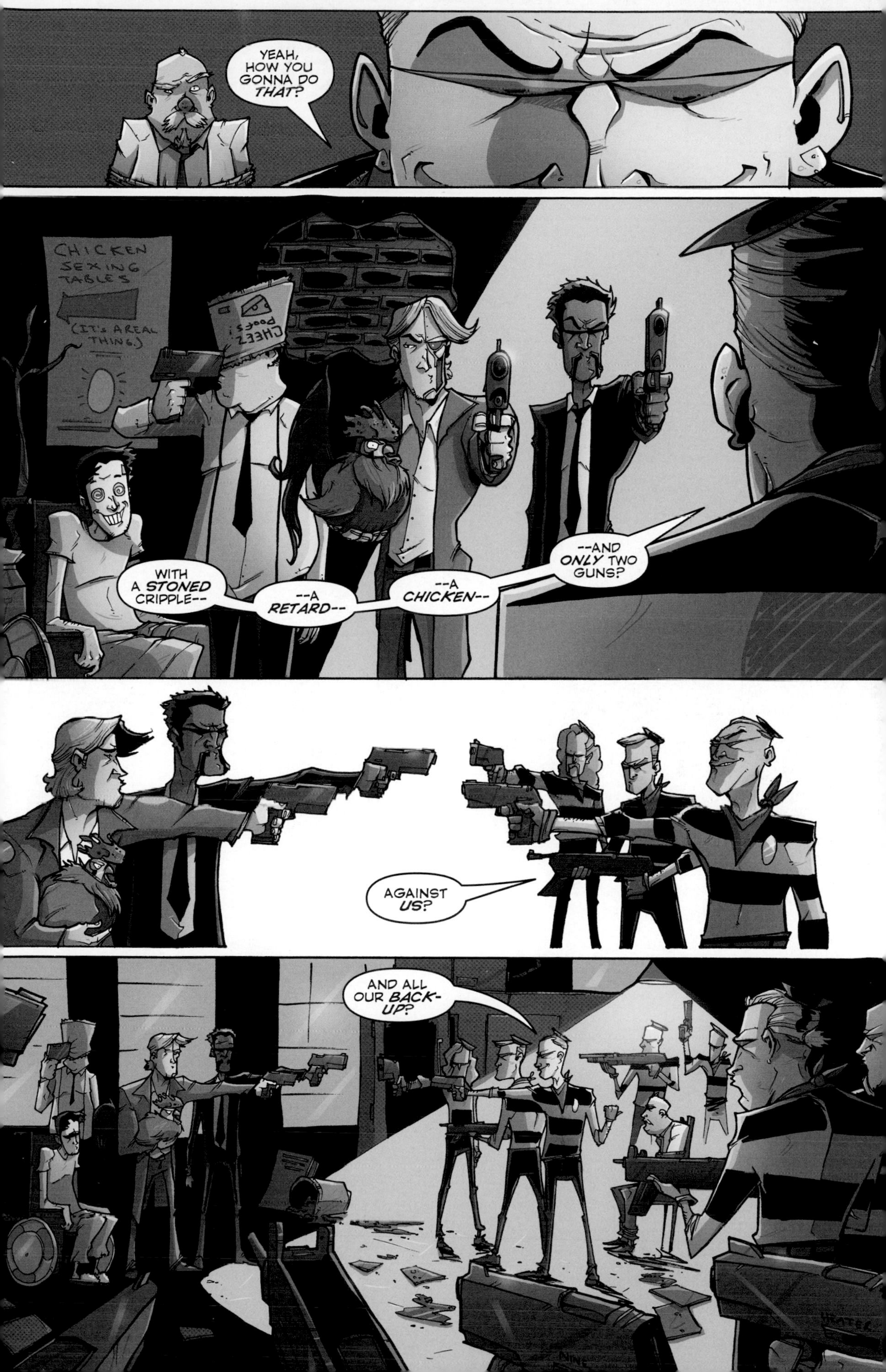

YEAH, HOW YOU GONNA DO *THAT*?
CHICKEN SEXING TABLES
(IT'S A REAL THING.)
WITH A *STONED* CRIPPLE--
--A *RETARD*--
--A *CHICKEN*--
--AND *ONLY* TWO GUNS?
AGAINST *US*?
AND ALL OUR *BACK-UP*?

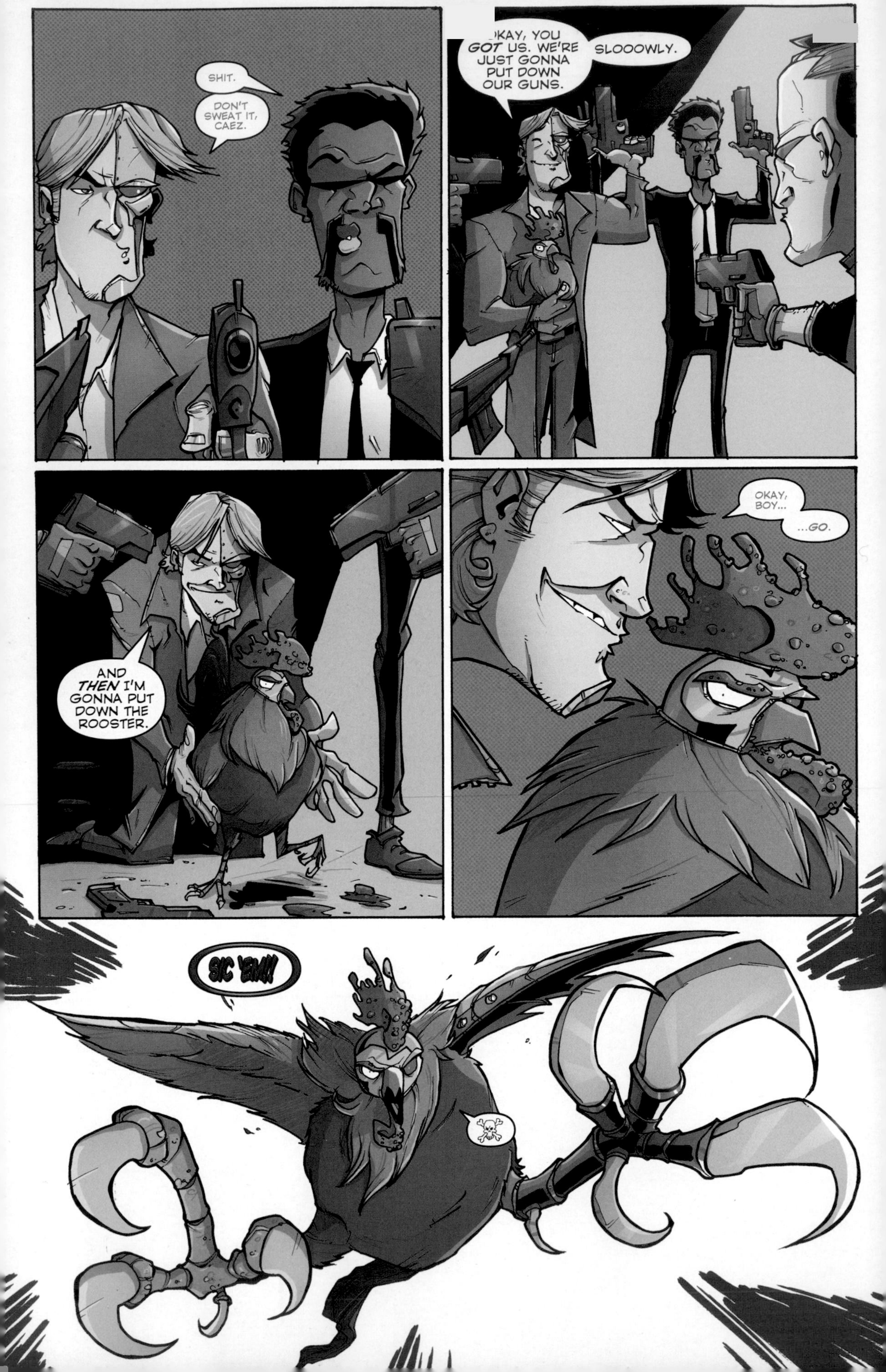
SHIT.
DON'T SWEAT IT, CAEZ.
OKAY, YOU GOT US. WE'RE JUST GONNA PUT DOWN OUR GUNS.
SLOOOWLY.
AND THEN I'M GONNA PUT DOWN THE ROOSTER.
OKAY, BOY...
...GO.
SIC 'EM!!

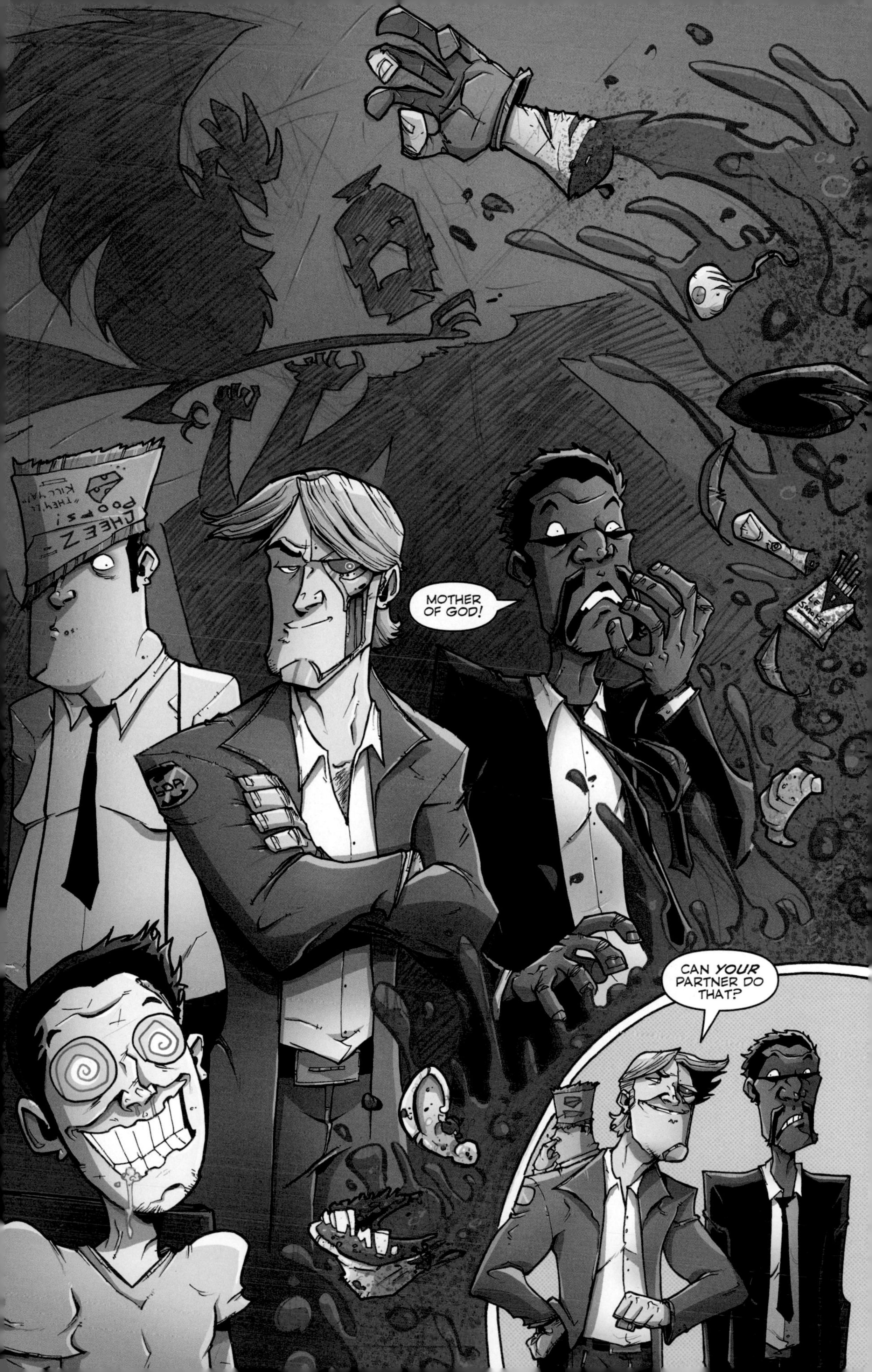

MOTHER OF GOD!
CAN *YOUR* PARTNER DO THAT?

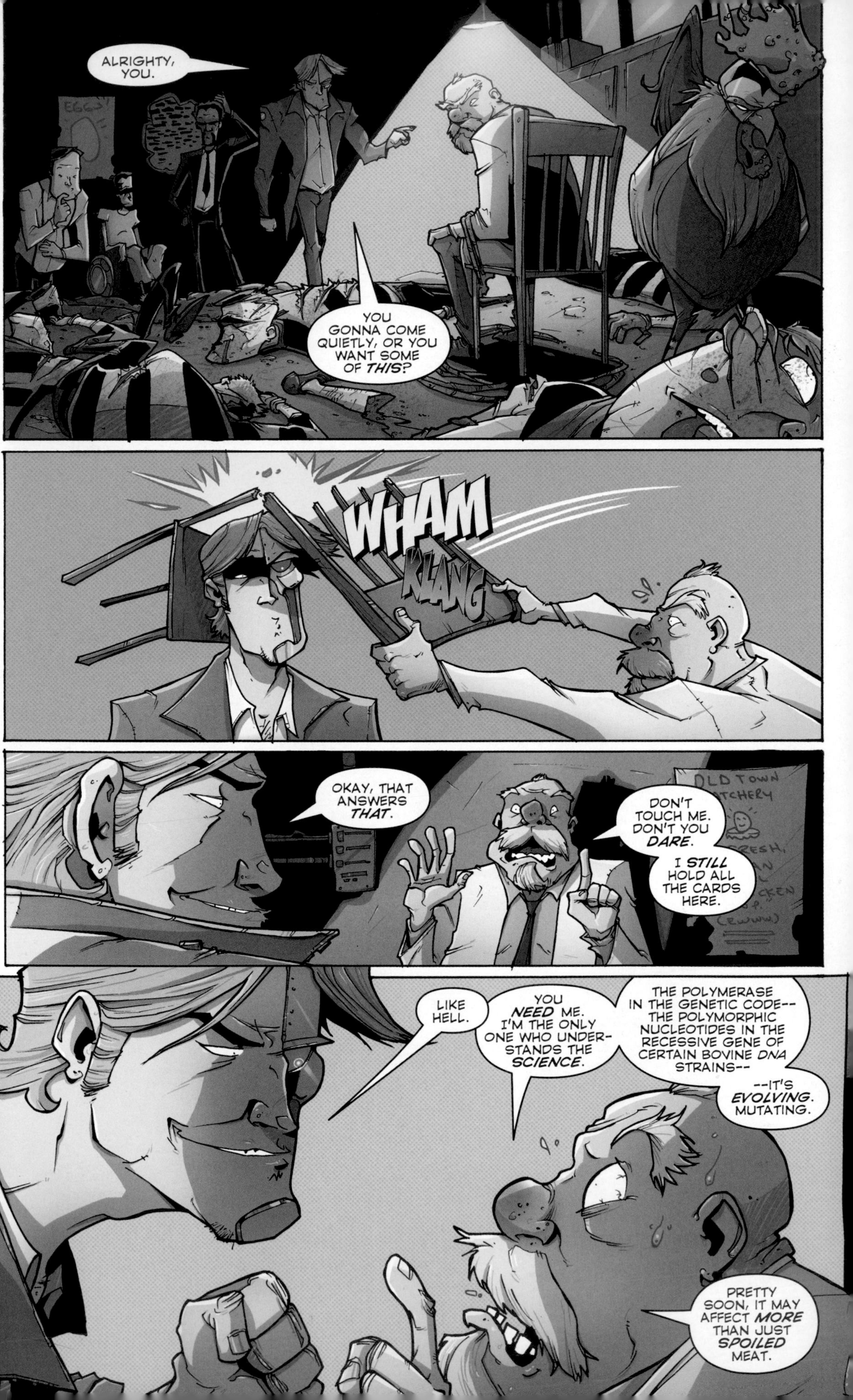
ALRIGHTY, YOU.
EGGS
YOU GONNA COME QUIETLY, OR YOU WANT SOME OF *THIS*?
WHAM
KLANG
OKAY, THAT ANSWERS *THAT*.
DON'T TOUCH ME. DON'T YOU *DARE*.
I *STILL* HOLD ALL THE CARDS HERE.
LIKE HELL.
YOU *NEED* ME. I'M THE ONLY ONE WHO UNDER-STANDS THE *SCIENCE*.
THE POLYMERASE IN THE GENETIC CODE-- THE POLYMORPHIC NUCLEOTIDES IN THE RECESSIVE GENE OF CERTAIN BOVINE *DNA* STRAINS--
--IT'S *EVOLVING*. MUTATING.
PRETTY SOON, IT MAY AFFECT *MORE* THAN JUST *SPOILED* MEAT.

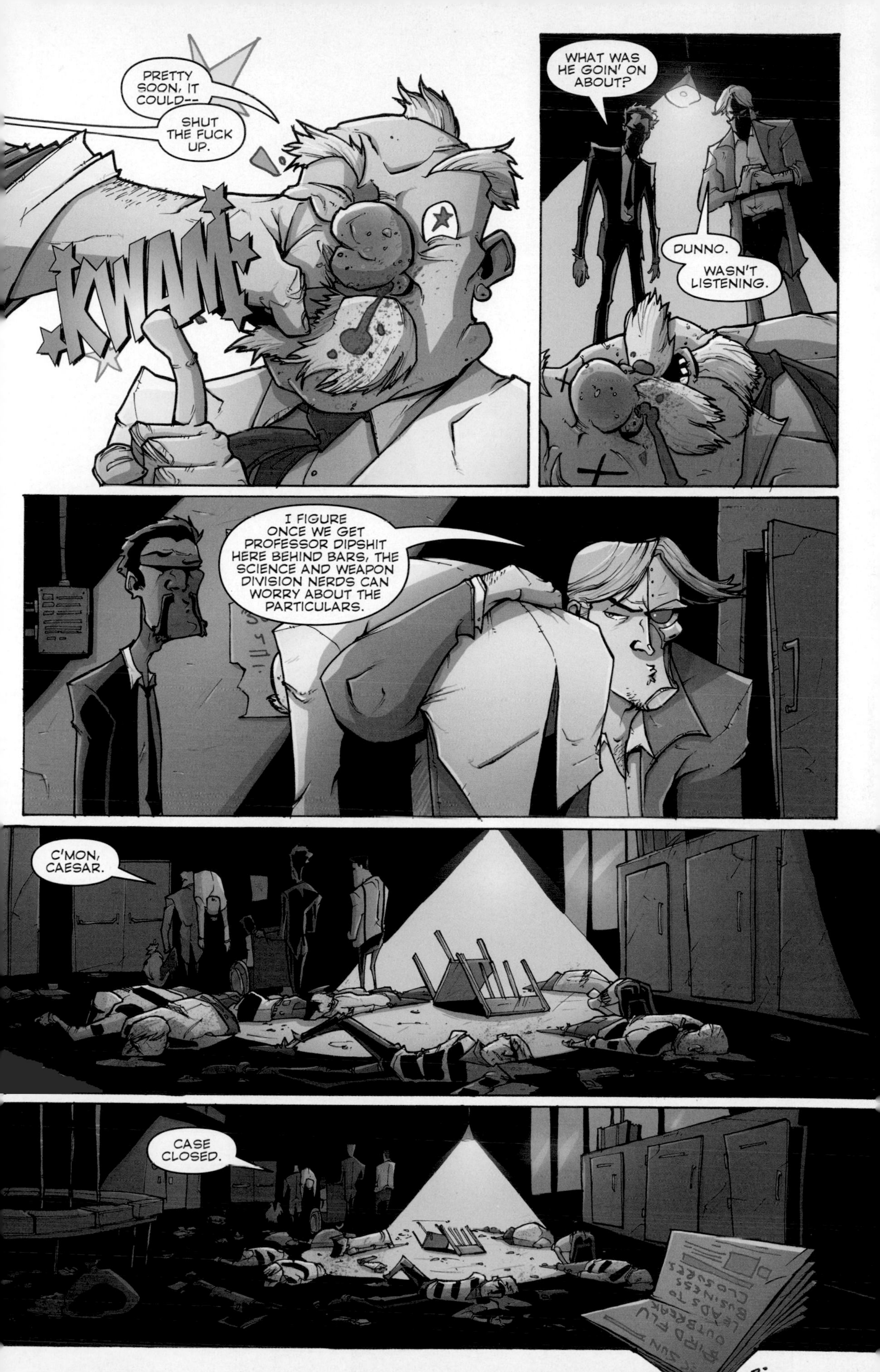
PRETTY SOON, IT COULD--
SHUT THE FUCK UP.
KWAM
WHAT WAS HE GOIN' ON ABOUT?
DUNNO.
WASN'T LISTENING.
I FIGURE ONCE WE GET PROFESSOR DIPSHIT HERE BEHIND BARS, THE SCIENCE AND WEAPON DIVISION NERDS CAN WORRY ABOUT THE PARTICULARS.
C'MON, CAESAR.
CASE CLOSED.

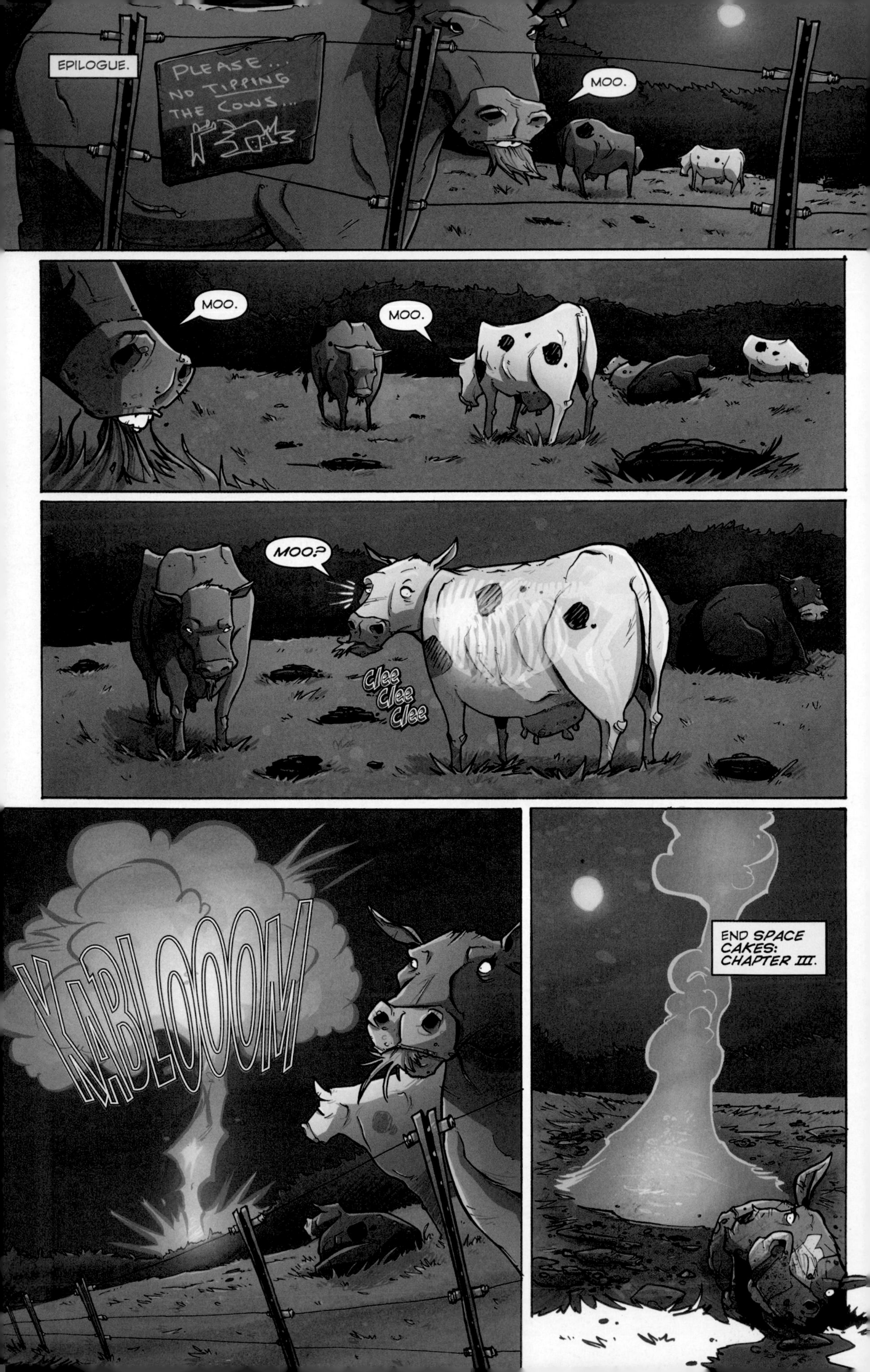
EPILOGUE.
PLEASE... NO TIPPING THE COWS...
MOO.
MOO.
MOO.
MOO?
Clee Clee Clee
KABLOOOM
END SPACE CAKES: CHAPTER III.

Chapter 4

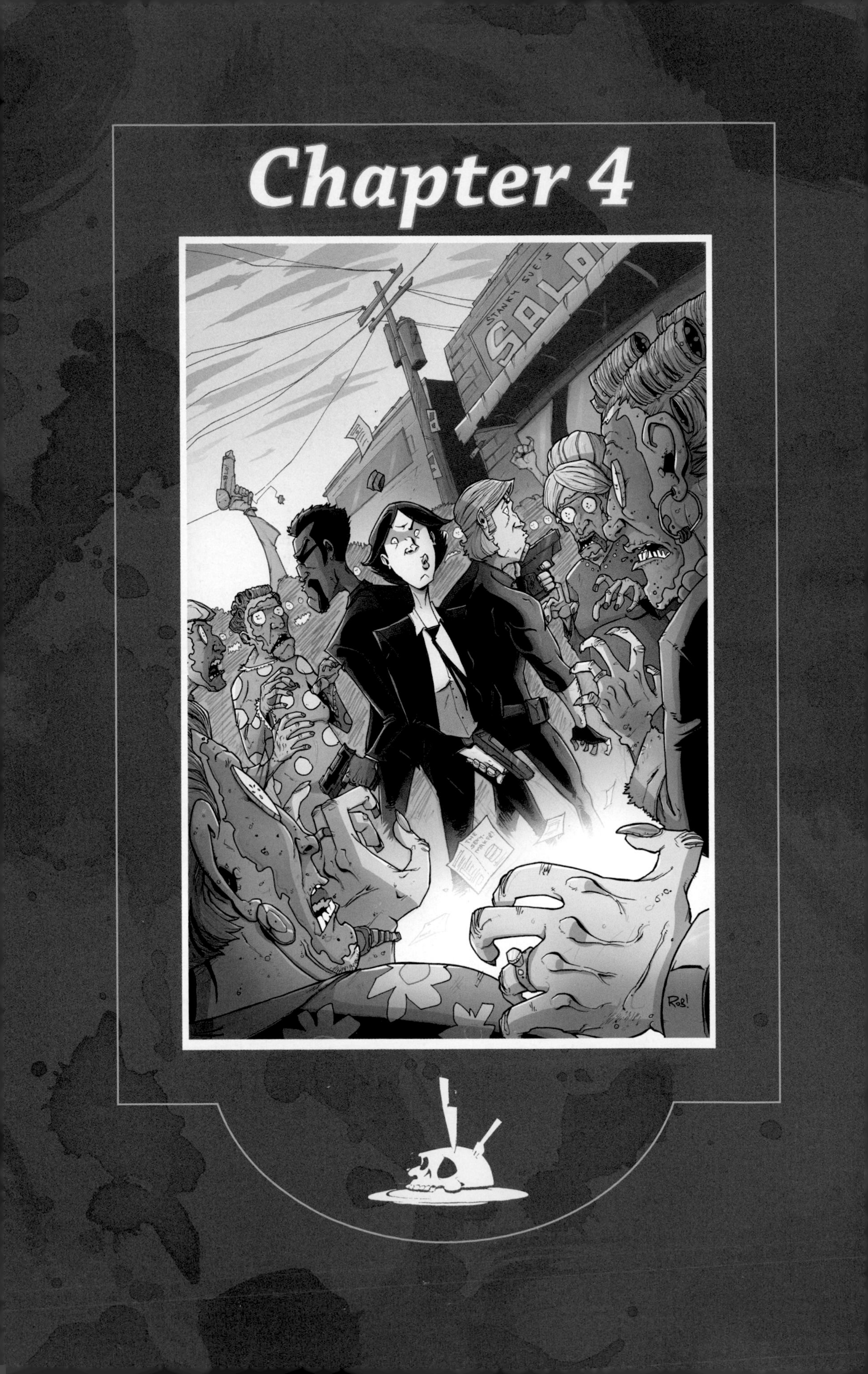
STANKY SUE'S
SALO
ROB!

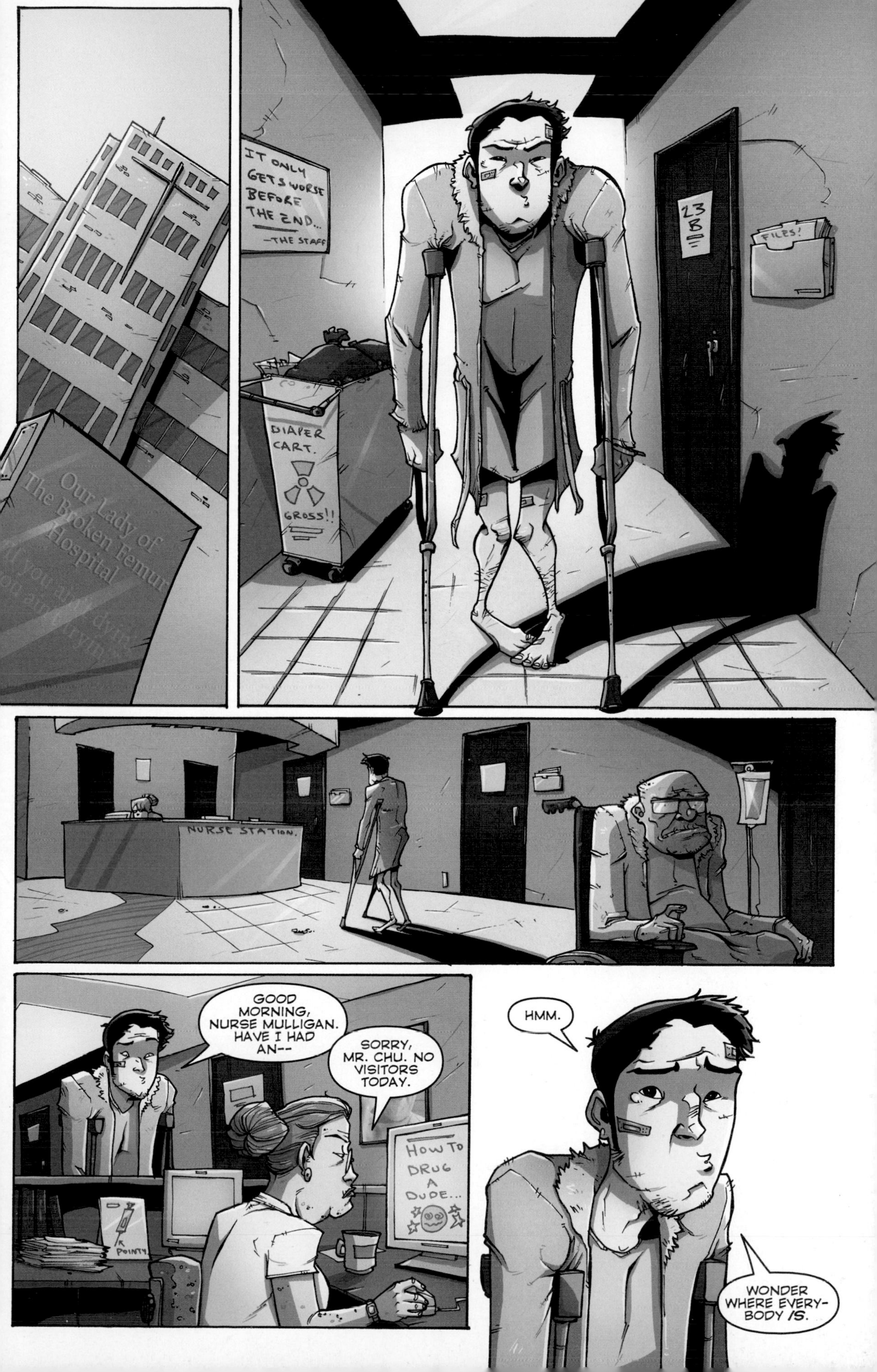
Our Lady of
The Broken Femur
Hospital
IT ONLY GETS WORSE BEFORE THE END... —THE STAFF
DIAPER CART.
GROSS!!
23 B
FILES!
NURSE STATION.
GOOD MORNING, NURSE MULLIGAN. HAVE I HAD AN--
SORRY, MR. CHU. NO VISITORS TODAY.
HOW TO DRUG A DUDE...
POINTY.
HMM.
WONDER WHERE EVERY-BODY *IS*.

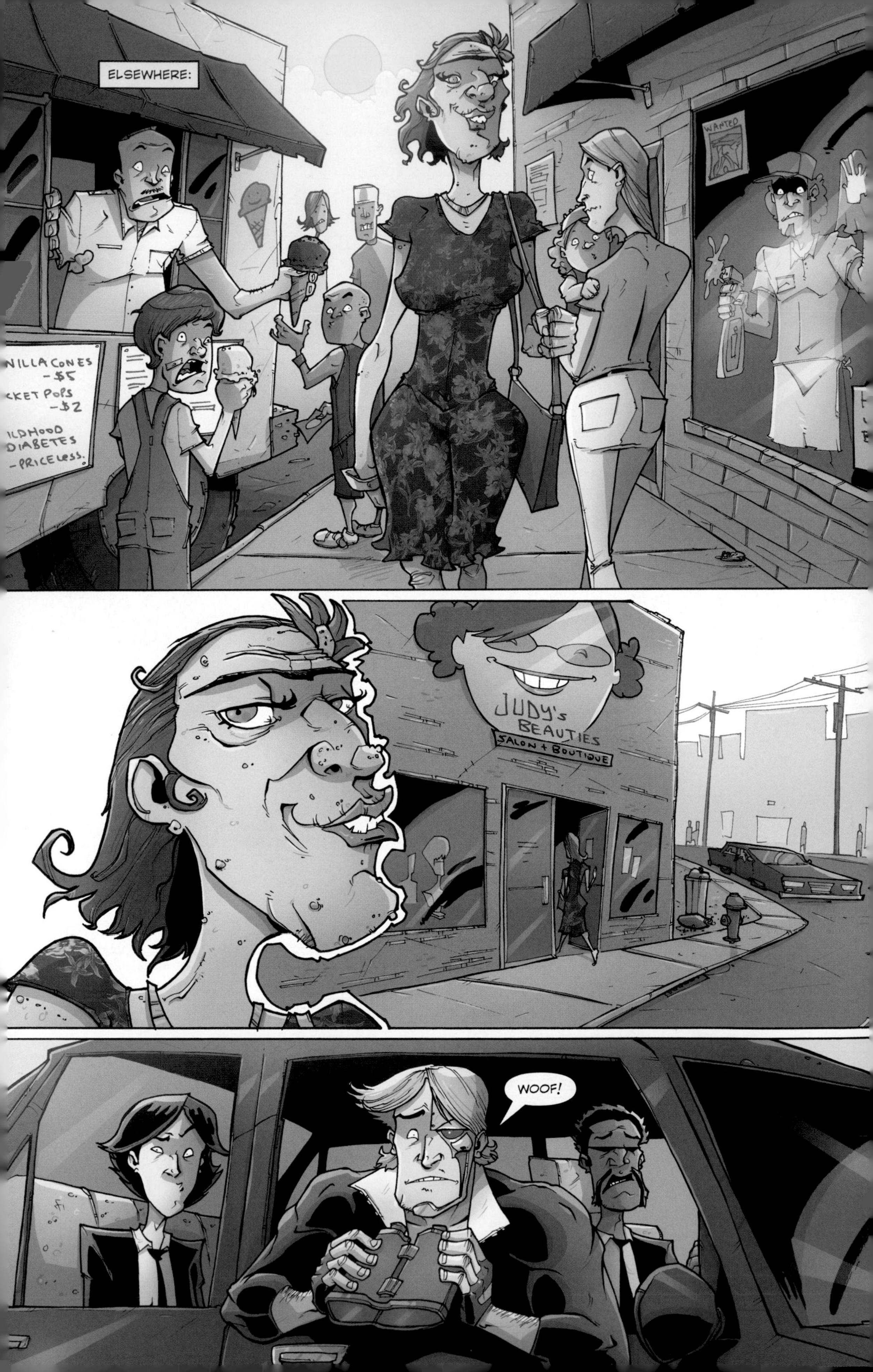
ELSEWHERE:
NILLA CONES -$5
CKET POPS -$2
ILDHOOD DIABETES -PRICELESS.
WANTED
JUDY's BEAUTIES
SALON + BOUTIQUE
WOOF!

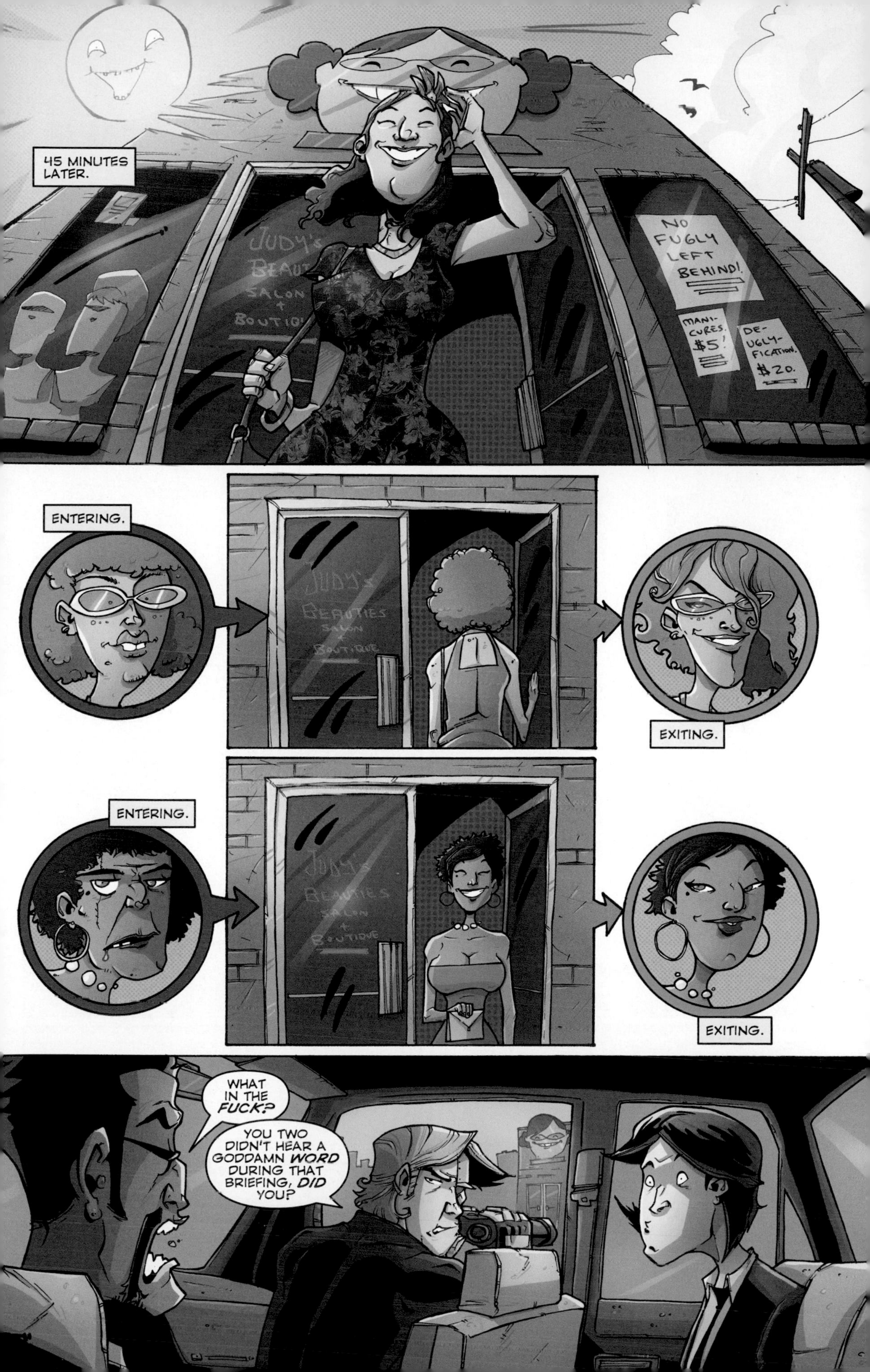
45 MINUTES LATER.
NO FUGLY LEFT BEHIND!
MANI-CURES. $5!
DE-UGLY-FICATION. $20.
ENTERING.
JUDY'S BEAUTIES SALON + BOUTIQUE
EXITING.
ENTERING.
EXITING.
WHAT IN THE *FUCK?*
YOU TWO DIDN'T HEAR A GODDAMN *WORD* DURING THAT BRIEFING, *DID* YOU?

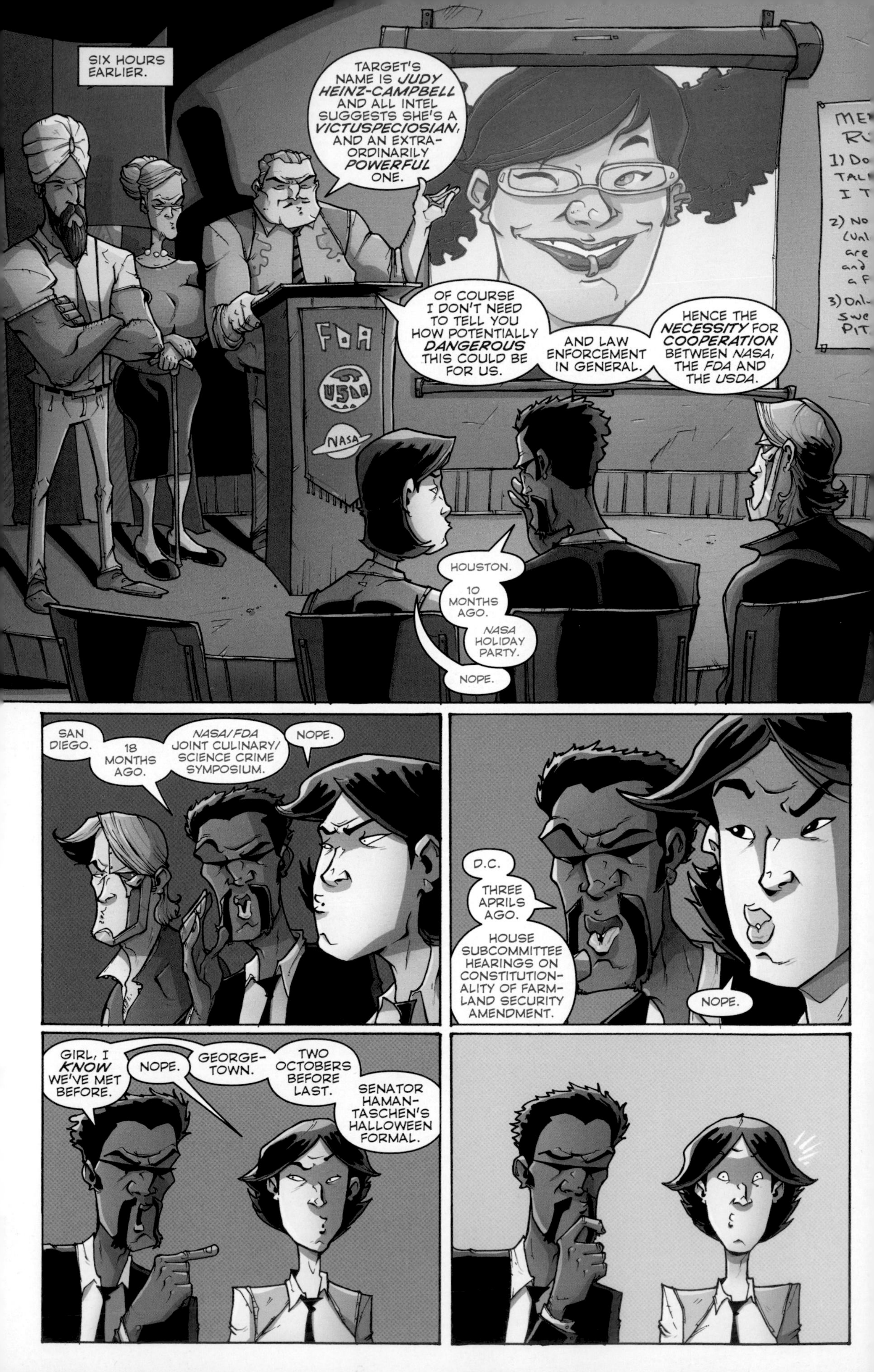
SIX HOURS EARLIER.
TARGET'S NAME IS *JUDY HEINZ-CAMPBELL* AND ALL INTEL SUGGESTS SHE'S A *VICTUSPECIOSIAN*, AND AN EXTRA-ORDINARILY *POWERFUL* ONE.
FDA
USDA
NASA
OF COURSE I DON'T NEED TO TELL YOU HOW POTENTIALLY *DANGEROUS* THIS COULD BE FOR US.
AND LAW ENFORCEMENT IN GENERAL.
HENCE THE *NECESSITY* FOR *COOPERATION* BETWEEN *NASA*, THE *FDA* AND THE *USDA*.
HOUSTON.
10 MONTHS AGO.
NASA HOLIDAY PARTY.
NOPE.
SAN DIEGO.
18 MONTHS AGO.
NASA/FDA JOINT CULINARY/ SCIENCE CRIME SYMPOSIUM.
NOPE.
D.C.
THREE APRILS AGO.
HOUSE SUBCOMMITTEE HEARINGS ON CONSTITUTION-ALITY OF FARM-LAND SECURITY AMENDMENT.
NOPE.
GIRL, I *KNOW* WE'VE MET BEFORE.
NOPE.
GEORGE-TOWN.
TWO OCTOBERS BEFORE LAST.
SENATOR HAMAN-TASCHEN'S HALLOWEEN FORMAL.

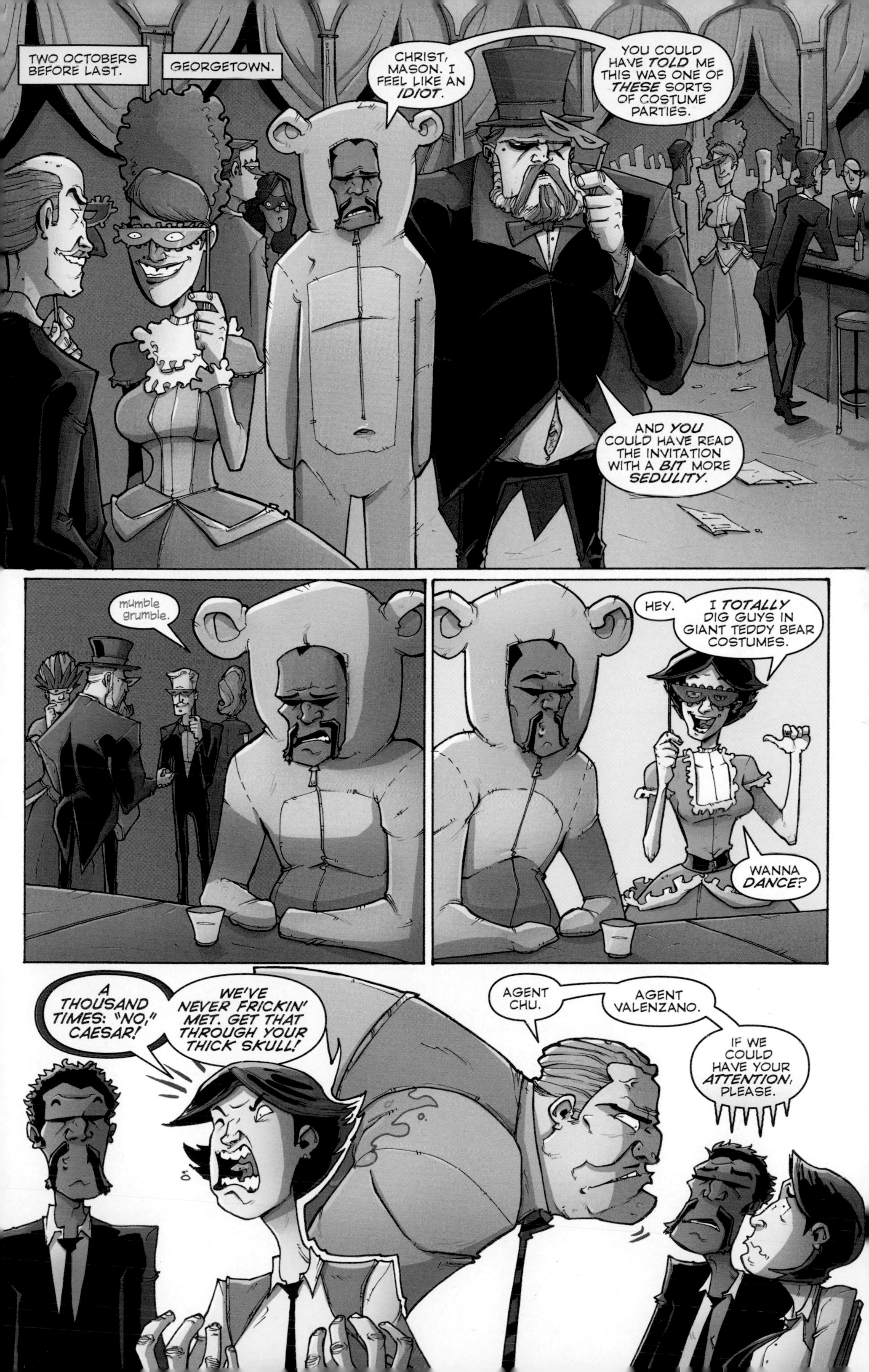
TWO OCTOBERS BEFORE LAST.
GEORGETOWN.
CHRIST, MASON. I FEEL LIKE AN IDIOT.
YOU COULD HAVE TOLD ME THIS WAS ONE OF THESE SORTS OF COSTUME PARTIES.
AND YOU COULD HAVE READ THE INVITATION WITH A BIT MORE SEDULITY.
mumble grumble.
HEY.
I TOTALLY DIG GUYS IN GIANT TEDDY BEAR COSTUMES.
WANNA DANCE?
A THOUSAND TIMES: "NO," CAESAR!
WE'VE NEVER FRICKIN' MET. GET THAT THROUGH YOUR THICK SKULL!
AGENT CHU.
AGENT VALENZANO.
IF WE COULD HAVE YOUR ATTENTION, PLEASE.

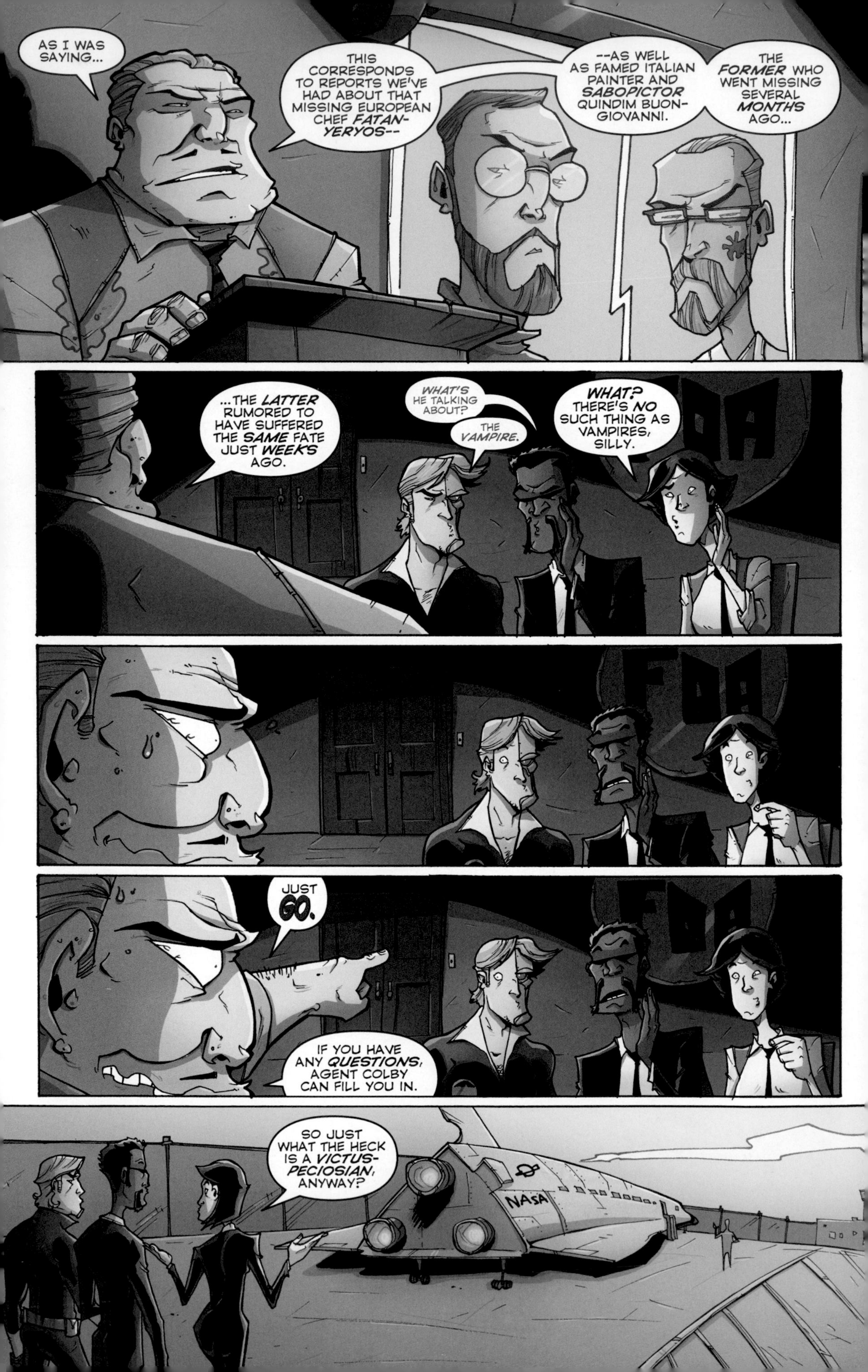
AS I WAS SAYING...
THIS CORRESPONDS TO REPORTS WE'VE HAD ABOUT THAT MISSING EUROPEAN CHEF FATAN-YERYOS--
--AS WELL AS FAMED ITALIAN PAINTER AND SABOPICTOR QUINDIM BUON-GIOVANNI.
THE FORMER WHO WENT MISSING SEVERAL MONTHS AGO...
...THE LATTER RUMORED TO HAVE SUFFERED THE SAME FATE JUST WEEKS AGO.
WHAT'S HE TALKING ABOUT?
THE VAMPIRE.
WHAT? THERE'S NO SUCH THING AS VAMPIRES, SILLY.
JUST GO.
IF YOU HAVE ANY QUESTIONS, AGENT COLBY CAN FILL YOU IN.
SO JUST WHAT THE HECK IS A VICTUS-PECIOSIAN, ANYWAY?
NASA

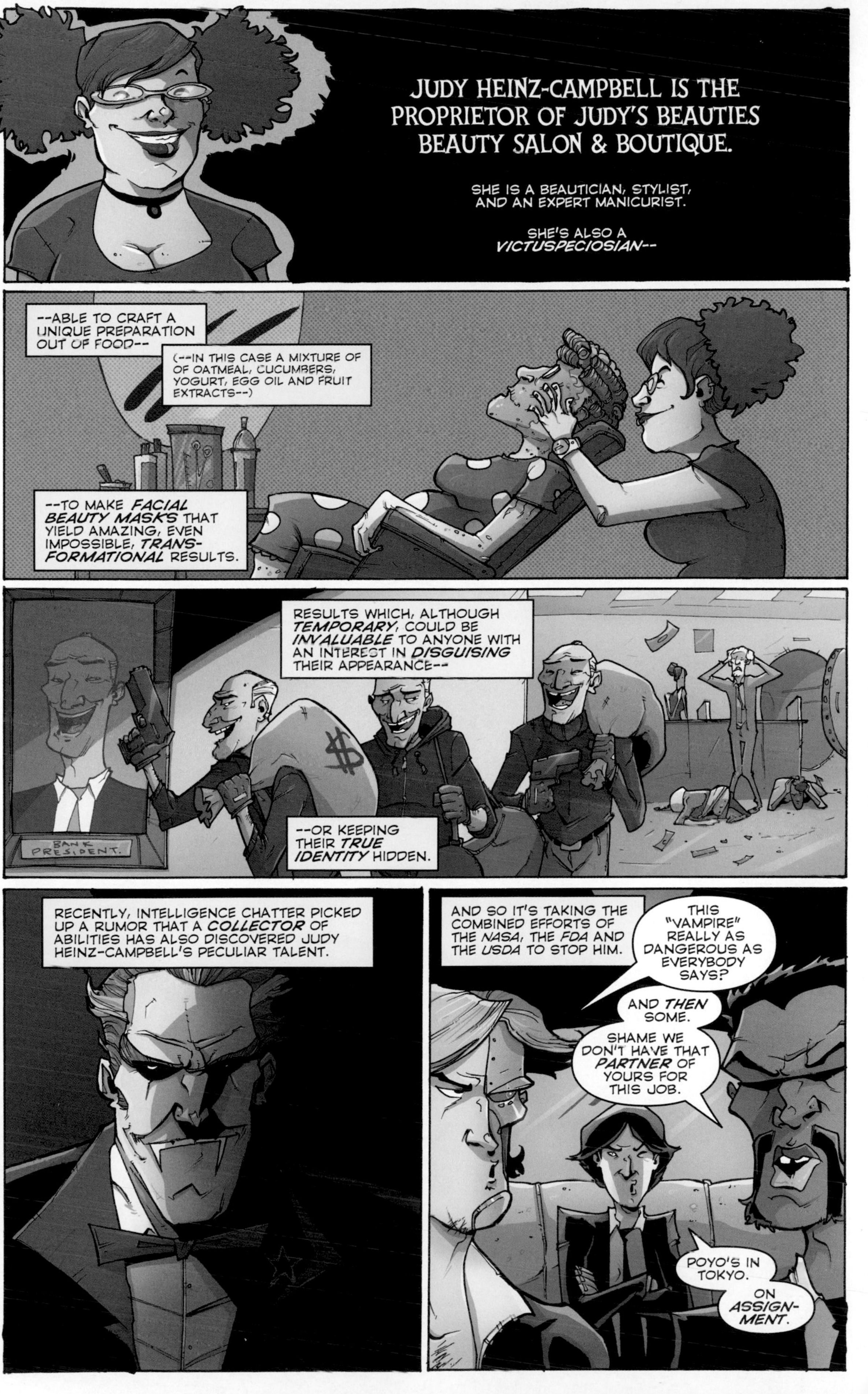
JUDY HEINZ-CAMPBELL IS THE PROPRIETOR OF JUDY'S BEAUTIES BEAUTY SALON & BOUTIQUE.
SHE IS A BEAUTICIAN, STYLIST, AND AN EXPERT MANICURIST.
SHE'S ALSO A VICTUSPECIOSIAN--
--ABLE TO CRAFT A UNIQUE PREPARATION OUT OF FOOD--
(--IN THIS CASE A MIXTURE OF OF OATMEAL, CUCUMBERS, YOGURT, EGG OIL AND FRUIT EXTRACTS--)
--TO MAKE FACIAL BEAUTY MASKS THAT YIELD AMAZING, EVEN IMPOSSIBLE, TRANSFORMATIONAL RESULTS.
RESULTS WHICH, ALTHOUGH TEMPORARY, COULD BE INVALUABLE TO ANYONE WITH AN INTEREST IN DISGUISING THEIR APPEARANCE--
BANK PRESIDENT.
--OR KEEPING THEIR TRUE IDENTITY HIDDEN.
RECENTLY, INTELLIGENCE CHATTER PICKED UP A RUMOR THAT A COLLECTOR OF ABILITIES HAS ALSO DISCOVERED JUDY HEINZ-CAMPBELL'S PECULIAR TALENT.
AND SO IT'S TAKING THE COMBINED EFFORTS OF THE NASA, THE FDA AND THE USDA TO STOP HIM.
THIS "VAMPIRE" REALLY AS DANGEROUS AS EVERYBODY SAYS?
AND THEN SOME.
SHAME WE DON'T HAVE THAT PARTNER OF YOURS FOR THIS JOB.
POYO'S IN TOKYO.
ON ASSIGNMENT.

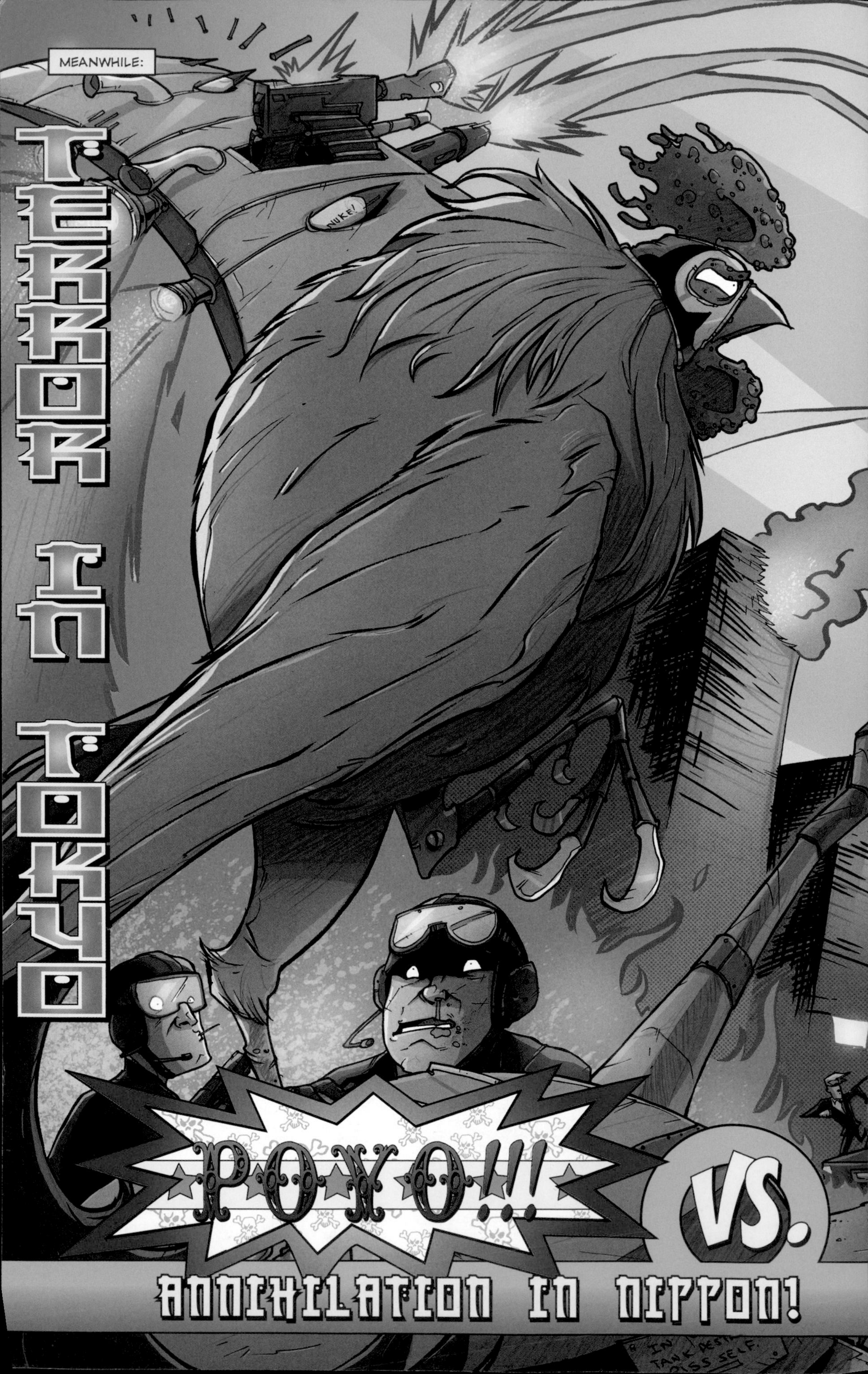

MEANWHILE:
TERROR IN TOKYO
NUKE!
POYO!!!
VS.
ANNIHILATION IN NIPPON!

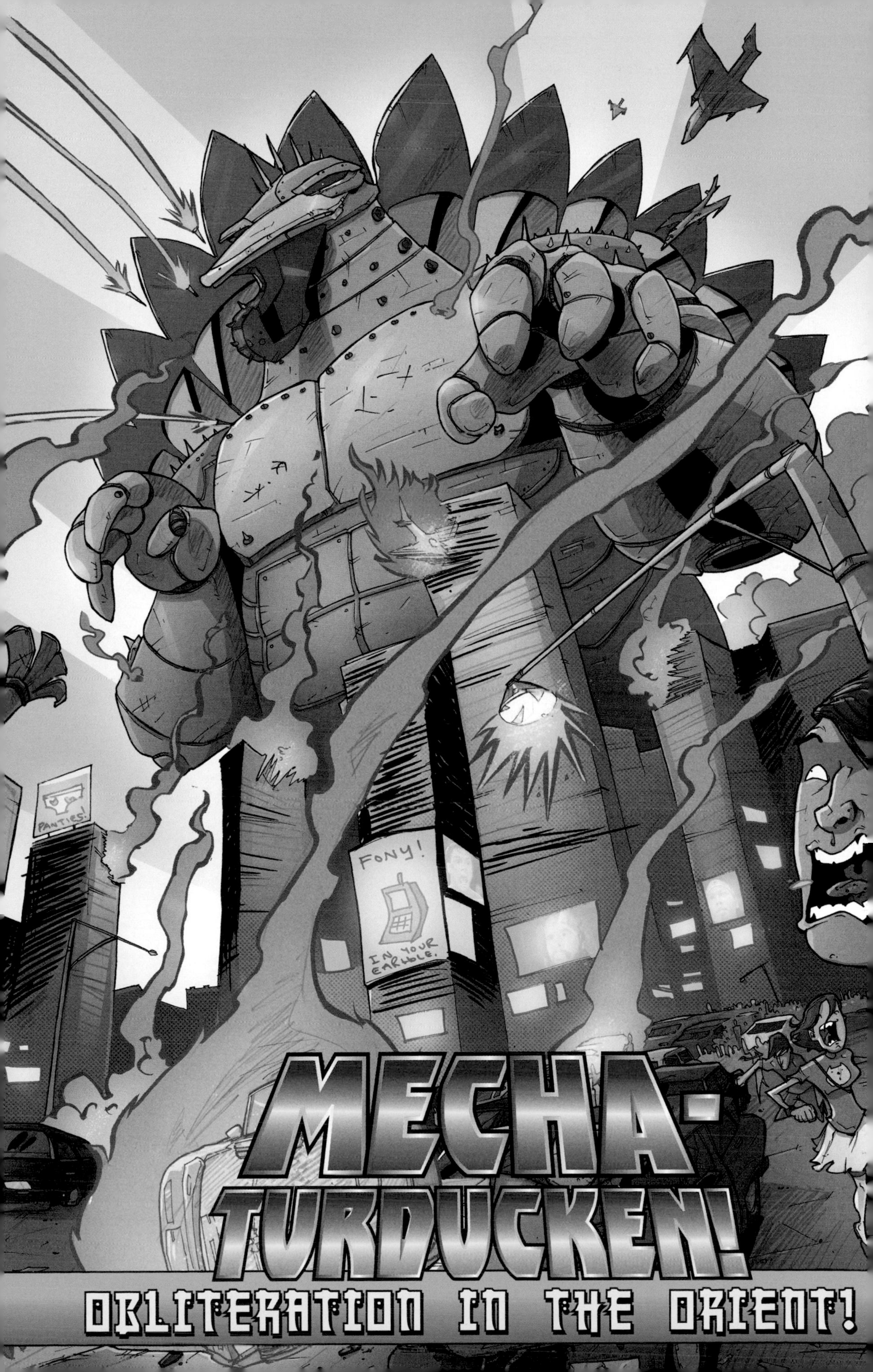
PANTIES!
FONY!
IN YOUR EARHOLE.
MECHA-TURDUCKEN!
OBLITERATION IN THE ORIENT!

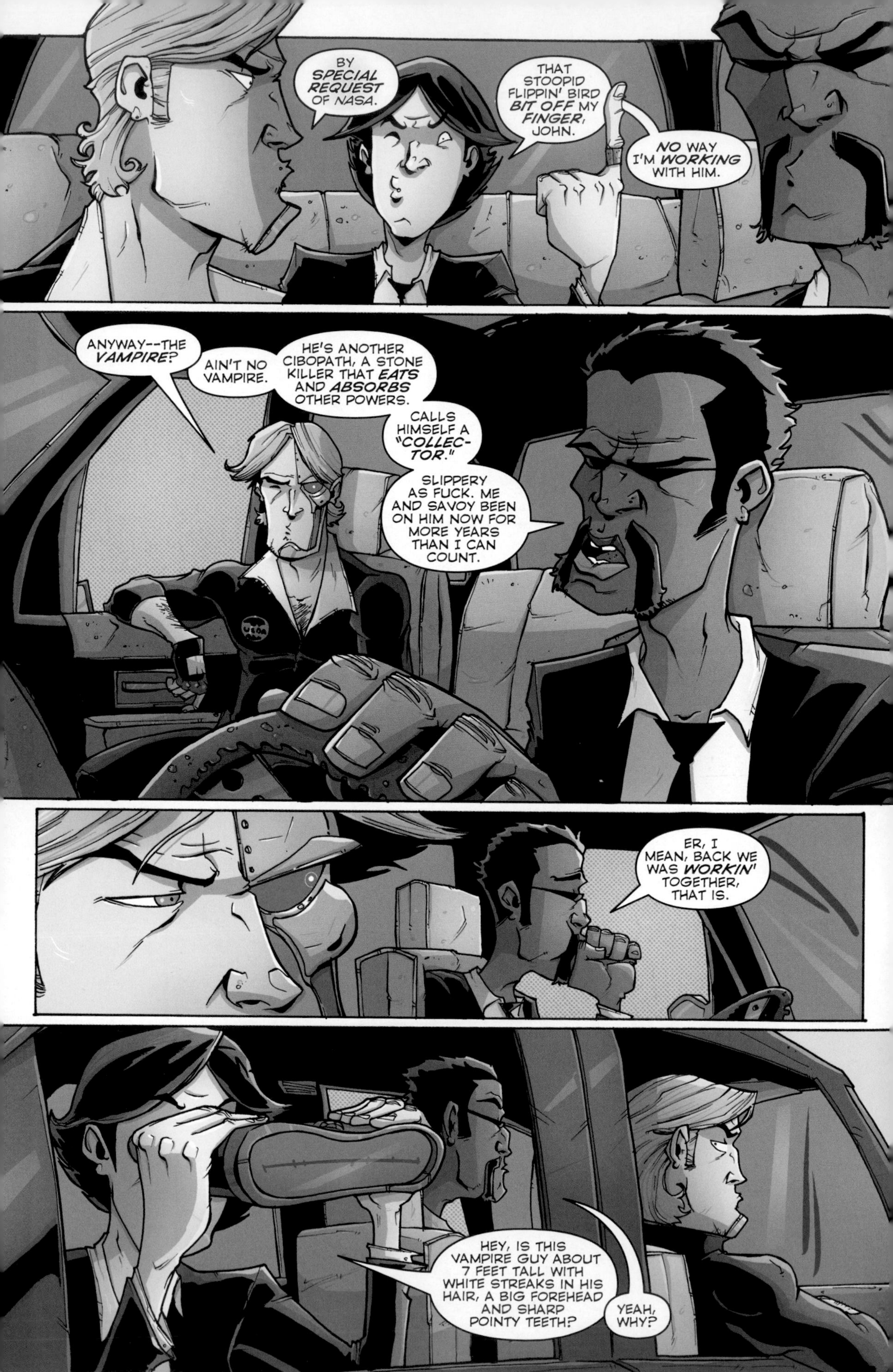
BY SPECIAL REQUEST OF NASA.
THAT STOOPID FLIPPIN' BIRD BIT OFF MY FINGER, JOHN.
NO WAY I'M WORKING WITH HIM.
ANYWAY--THE VAMPIRE?
AIN'T NO VAMPIRE.
HE'S ANOTHER CIBOPATH, A STONE KILLER THAT EATS AND ABSORBS OTHER POWERS.
CALLS HIMSELF A "COLLECTOR."
SLIPPERY AS FUCK. ME AND SAVOY BEEN ON HIM NOW FOR MORE YEARS THAN I CAN COUNT.
ER, I MEAN, BACK WE WAS WORKIN' TOGETHER, THAT IS.
HEY, IS THIS VAMPIRE GUY ABOUT 7 FEET TALL WITH WHITE STREAKS IN HIS HAIR, A BIG FOREHEAD AND SHARP POINTY TEETH?
YEAH, WHY?

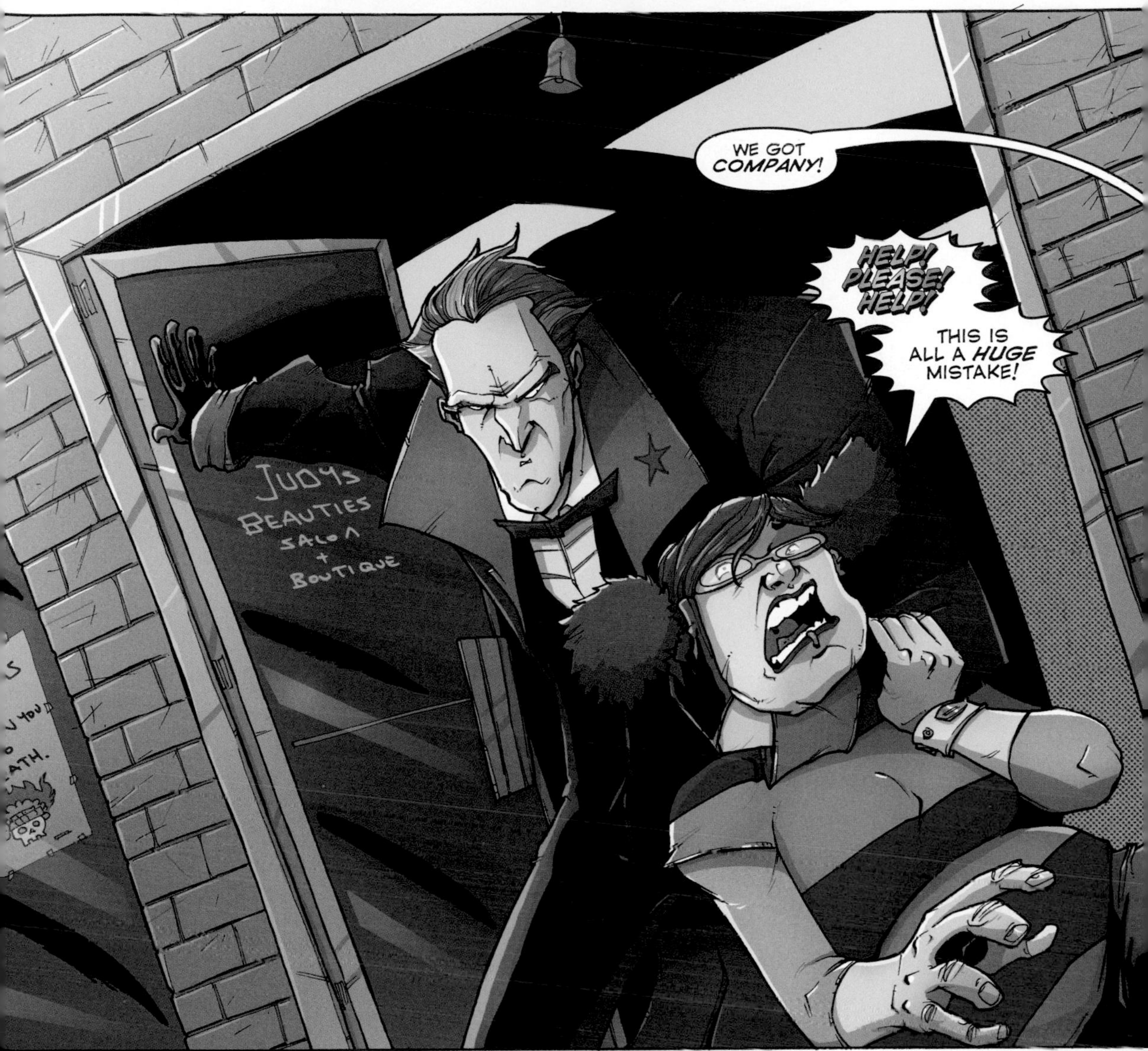
WE GOT COMPANY!
HELP! PLEASE! HELP!
THIS IS ALL A HUGE MISTAKE!
JUDYS BEAUTIES SALON + BOUTIQUE

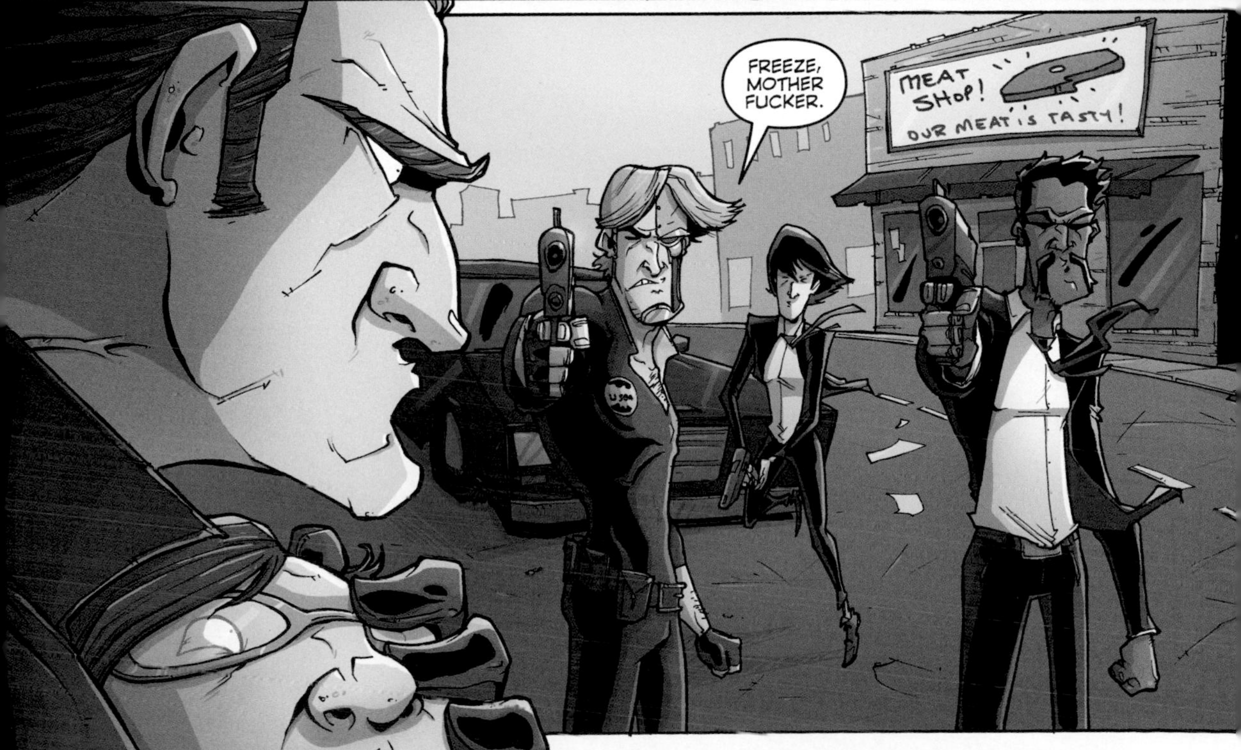
FREEZE, MOTHER FUCKER.
MEAT SHOP! OUR MEAT IS TASTY!

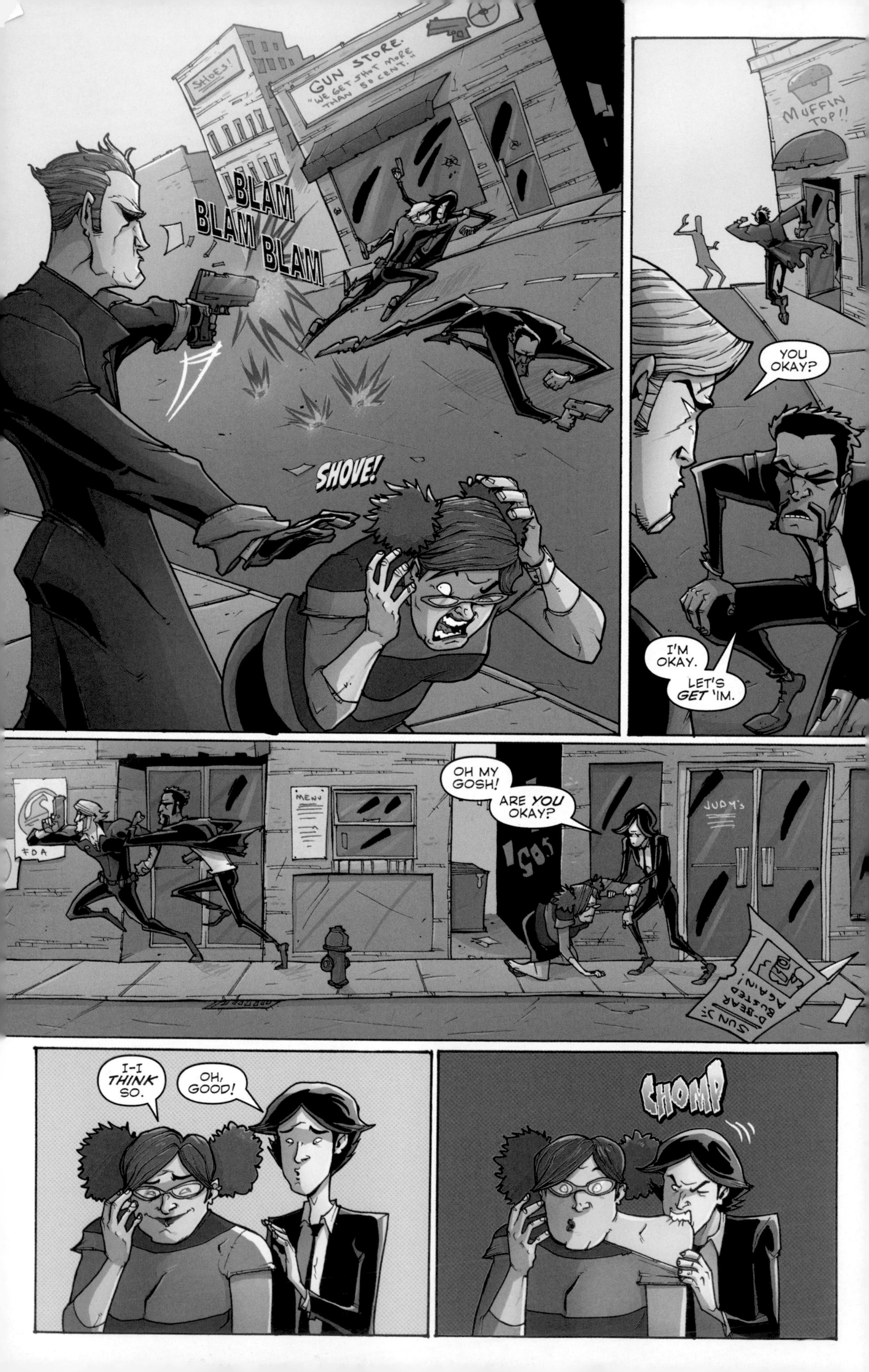
SHOES!
GUN STORE
"WE GET SHOT MORE THAN 50 CENT."
BLAM
BLAM
BLAM
SHOVE!
MUFFIN TOP!!
YOU OKAY?
I'M OKAY.
LET'S *GET* 'IM.
MENU
FDA
OH MY GOSH!
ARE *YOU* OKAY?
JUDY'S
SUN
D-BEAR BUSTED AGAIN!
I-I *THINK* SO.
OH, GOOD!
CHOMP

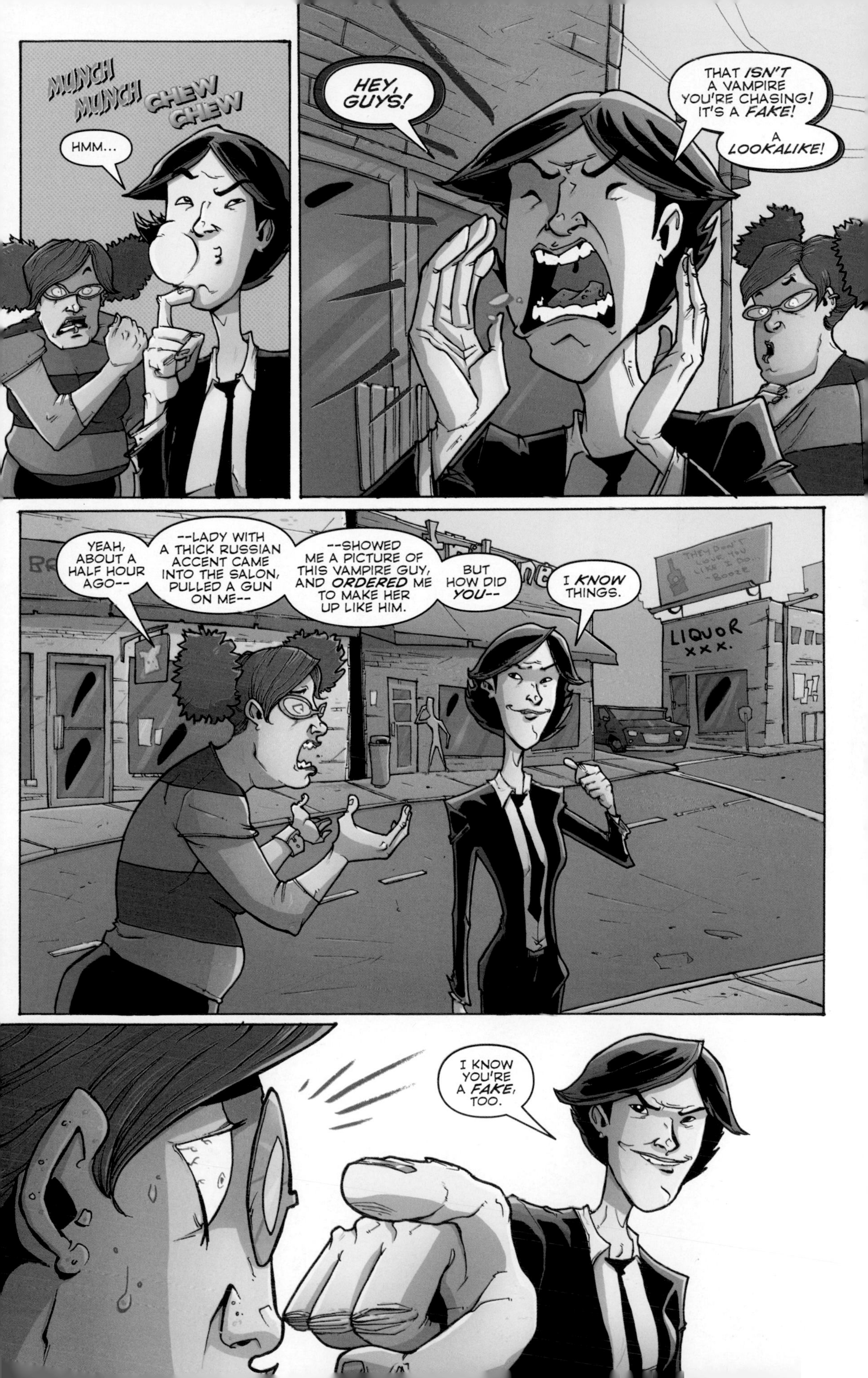
MUNCH MUNCH
CHEW CHEW
HMM...
HEY, GUYS!
THAT ISN'T A VAMPIRE YOU'RE CHASING! IT'S A FAKE!
A LOOKALIKE!
YEAH, ABOUT A HALF HOUR AGO--
--LADY WITH A THICK RUSSIAN ACCENT CAME INTO THE SALON, PULLED A GUN ON ME--
--SHOWED ME A PICTURE OF THIS VAMPIRE GUY, AND ORDERED ME TO MAKE HER UP LIKE HIM.
BUT HOW DID YOU--
I KNOW THINGS.
THEY DON'T LOVE YOU LIKE I DO... -BOOZE
LIQUOR XXX.
I KNOW YOU'RE A FAKE, TOO.

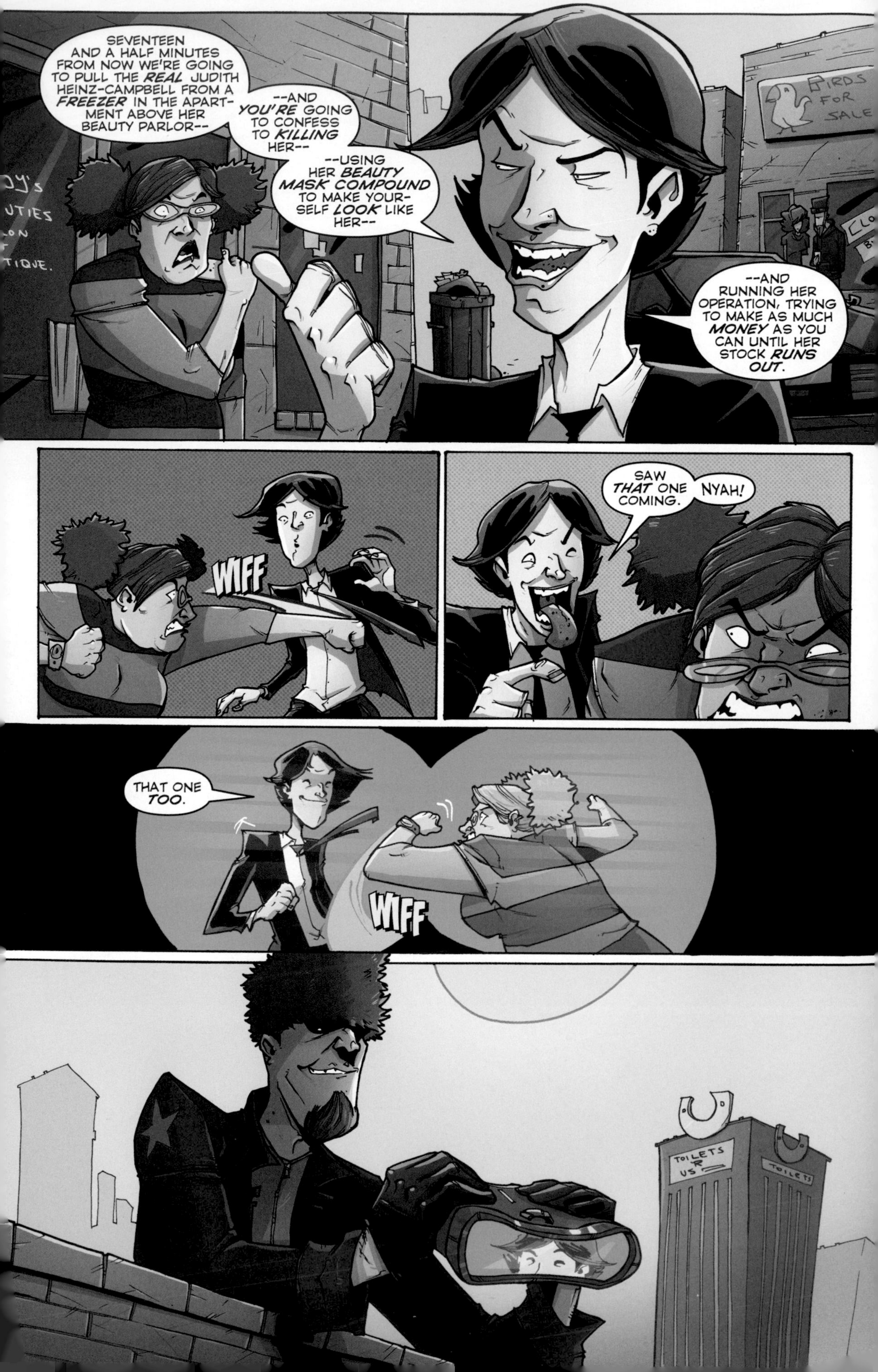
SEVENTEEN AND A HALF MINUTES FROM NOW WE'RE GOING TO PULL THE REAL JUDITH HEINZ-CAMPBELL FROM A FREEZER IN THE APARTMENT ABOVE HER BEAUTY PARLOR--
--AND YOU'RE GOING TO CONFESS TO KILLING HER--
--USING HER BEAUTY MASK COMPOUND TO MAKE YOURSELF LOOK LIKE HER--
--AND RUNNING HER OPERATION, TRYING TO MAKE AS MUCH MONEY AS YOU CAN UNTIL HER STOCK RUNS OUT.
BIRDS FOR SALE
WIFF
SAW THAT ONE COMING.
NYAH!
THAT ONE TOO.
WIFF
TOILETS R US
TOILETS

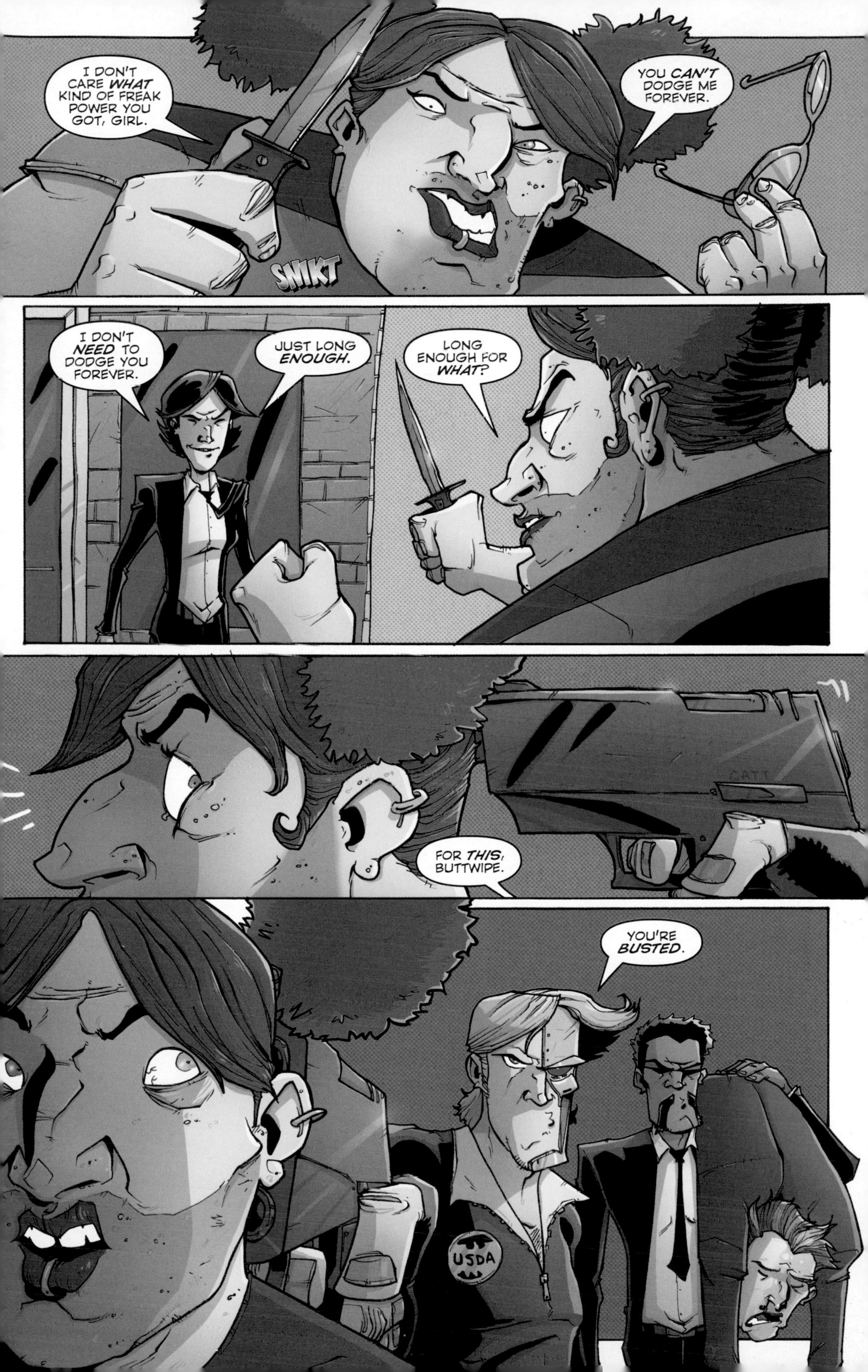
I DON'T CARE WHAT KIND OF FREAK POWER YOU GOT, GIRL.
YOU CAN'T DODGE ME FOREVER.
SNIKT
I DON'T NEED TO DODGE YOU FOREVER.
JUST LONG ENOUGH.
LONG ENOUGH FOR WHAT?
FOR THIS, BUTTWIPE.
YOU'RE BUSTED.
USDA

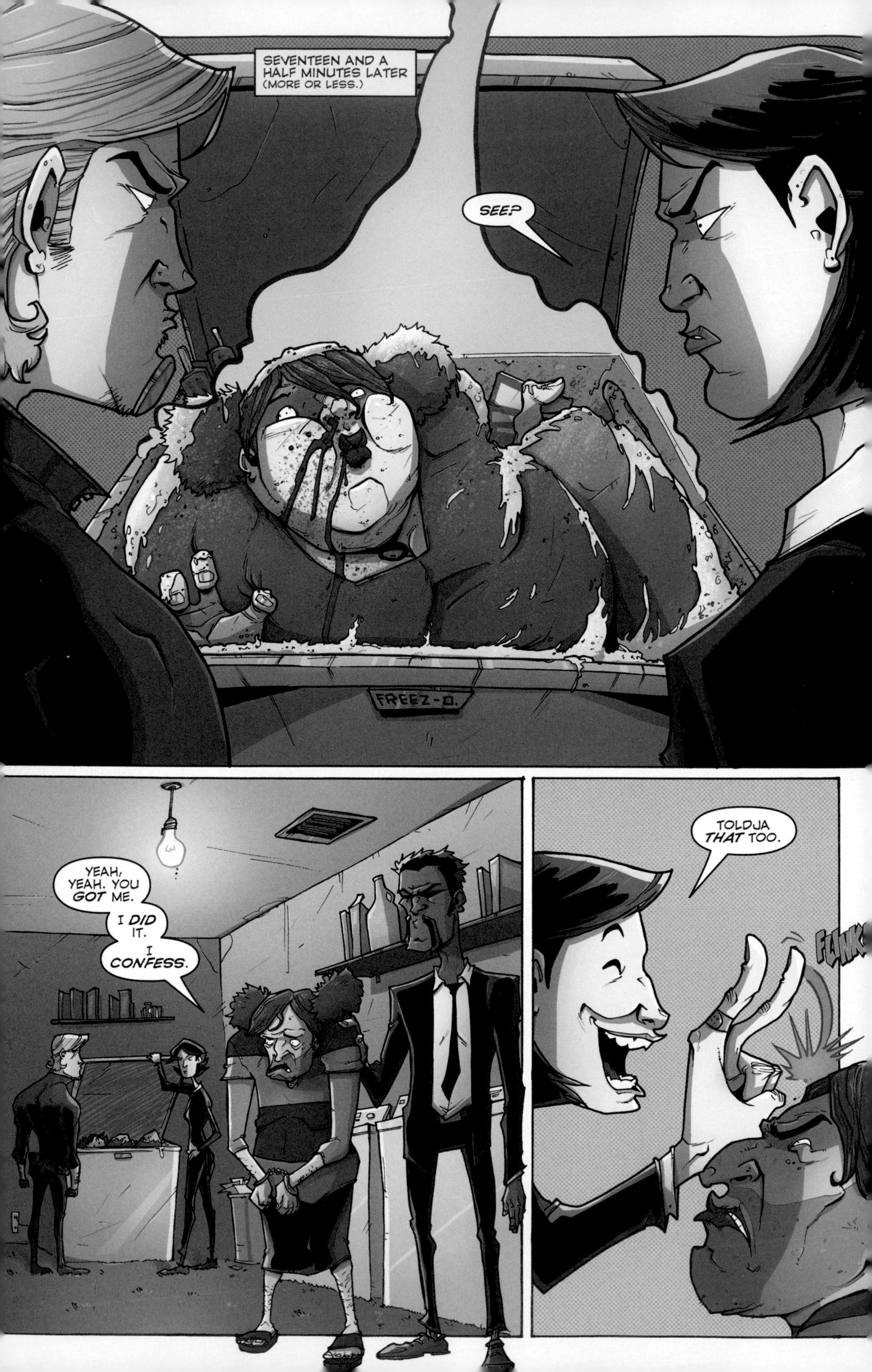

SEVENTEEN AND A HALF MINUTES LATER (MORE OR LESS.)
SEE?
FREEZ-O.
YEAH, YEAH. YOU *GOT* ME.
I *DID* IT.
I *CONFESS*.
TOLDJA *THAT* TOO.

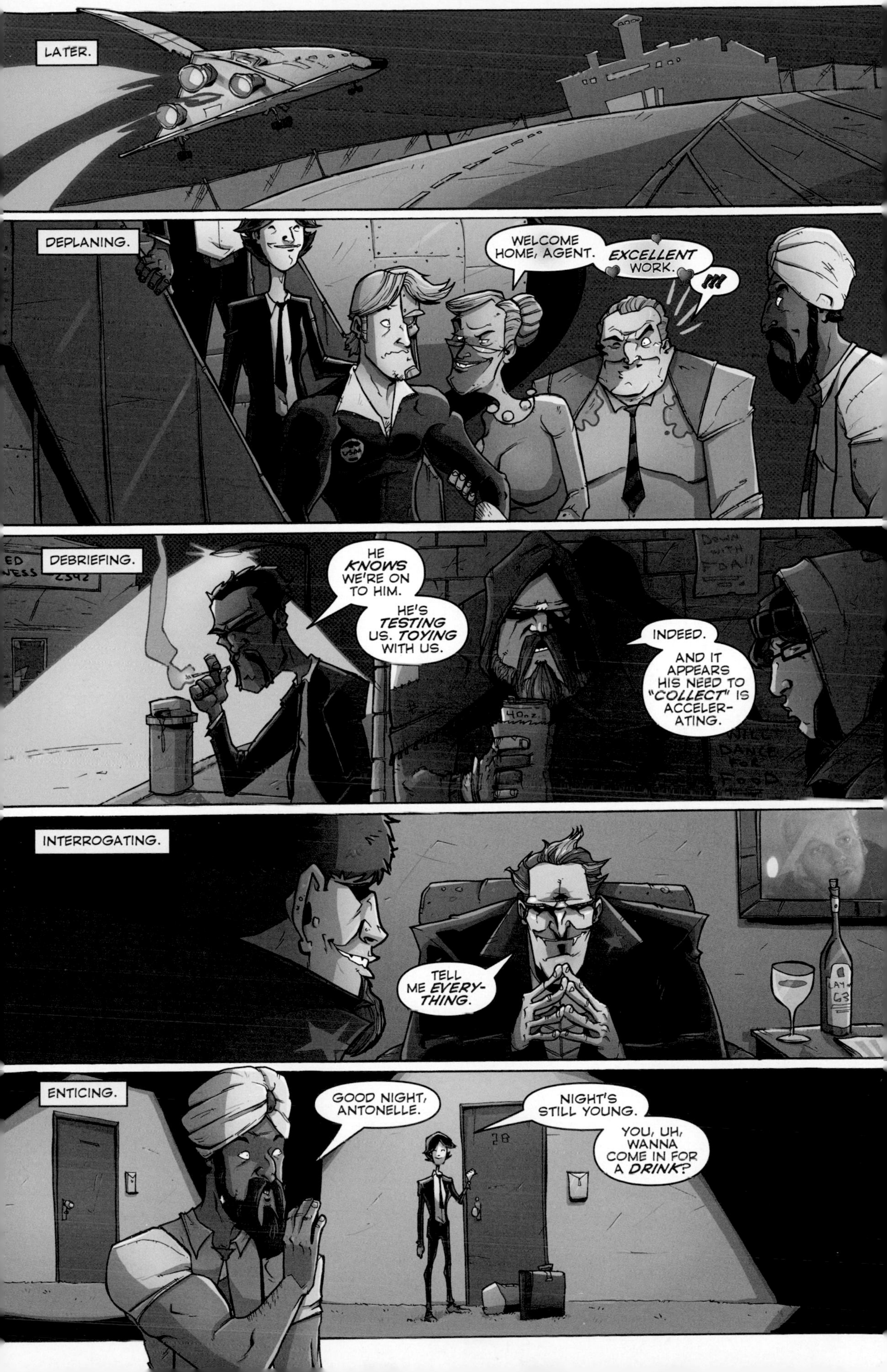
LATER.
DEPLANING.
WELCOME HOME, AGENT.
EXCELLENT WORK.
!!!
DEBRIEFING.
HE KNOWS WE'RE ON TO HIM.
HE'S TESTING US. TOYING WITH US.
INDEED.
AND IT APPEARS HIS NEED TO "COLLECT" IS ACCELER-ATING.
DOWN WITH FDA!!
WILL DANCE FOR FOOD
40oz
INTERROGATING.
TELL ME EVERY-THING.
ENTICING.
GOOD NIGHT, ANTONELLE.
NIGHT'S STILL YOUNG.
YOU, UH, WANNA COME IN FOR A DRINK?

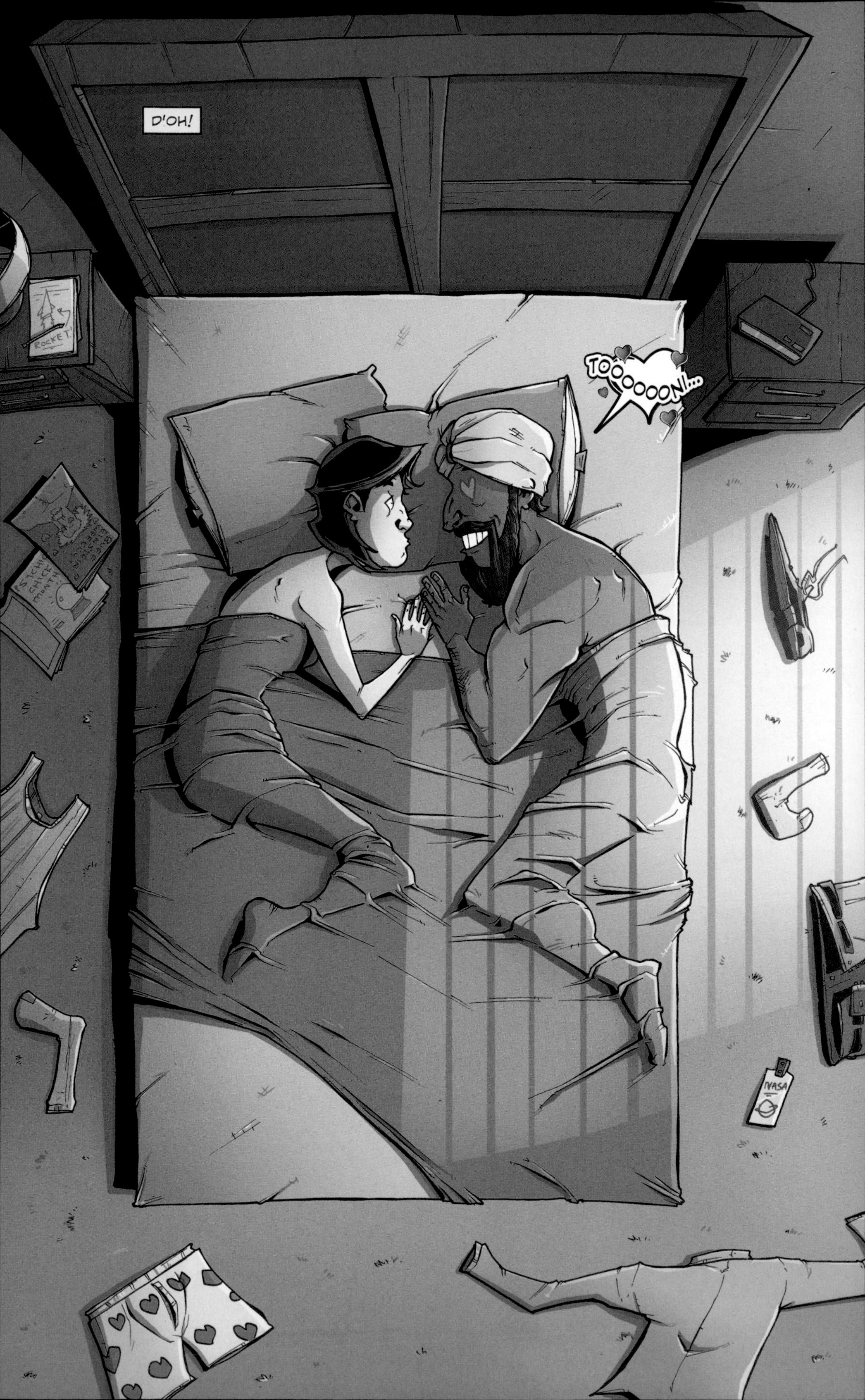
D'OH!
TOOOOOON!...
ROCKET!
PSYCHIC CHICK MONTHLY
NASA

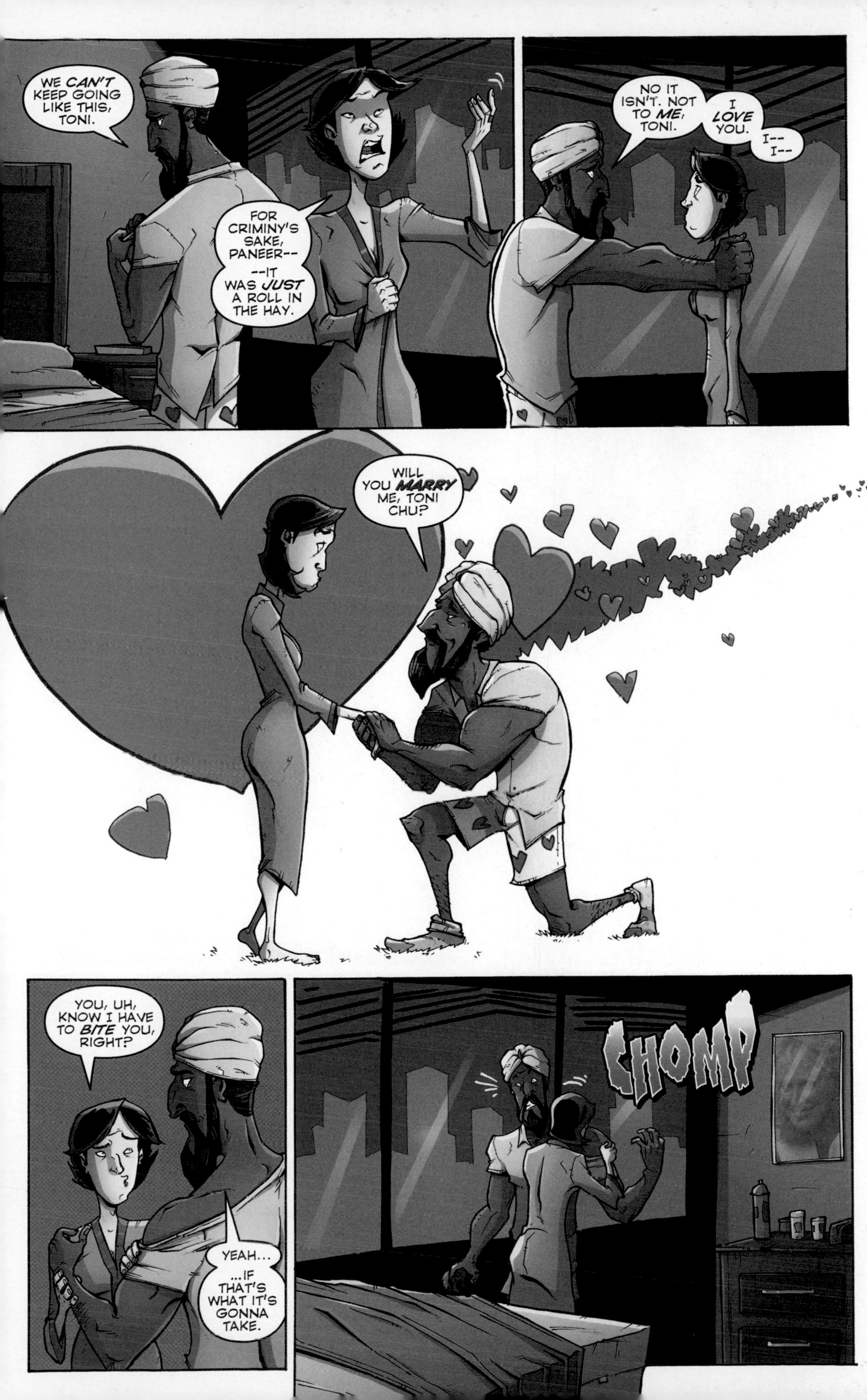
WE *CAN'T* KEEP GOING LIKE THIS, TONI.
FOR CRIMINY'S SAKE, PANEER--
--IT WAS *JUST* A ROLL IN THE HAY.
NO IT ISN'T. NOT TO *ME*, TONI.
I *LOVE* YOU.
I-- I--
WILL YOU *MARRY* ME, TONI CHU?
YOU, UH, KNOW I HAVE TO *BITE* YOU, RIGHT?
YEAH...
...IF THAT'S WHAT IT'S GONNA TAKE.
CHOMP

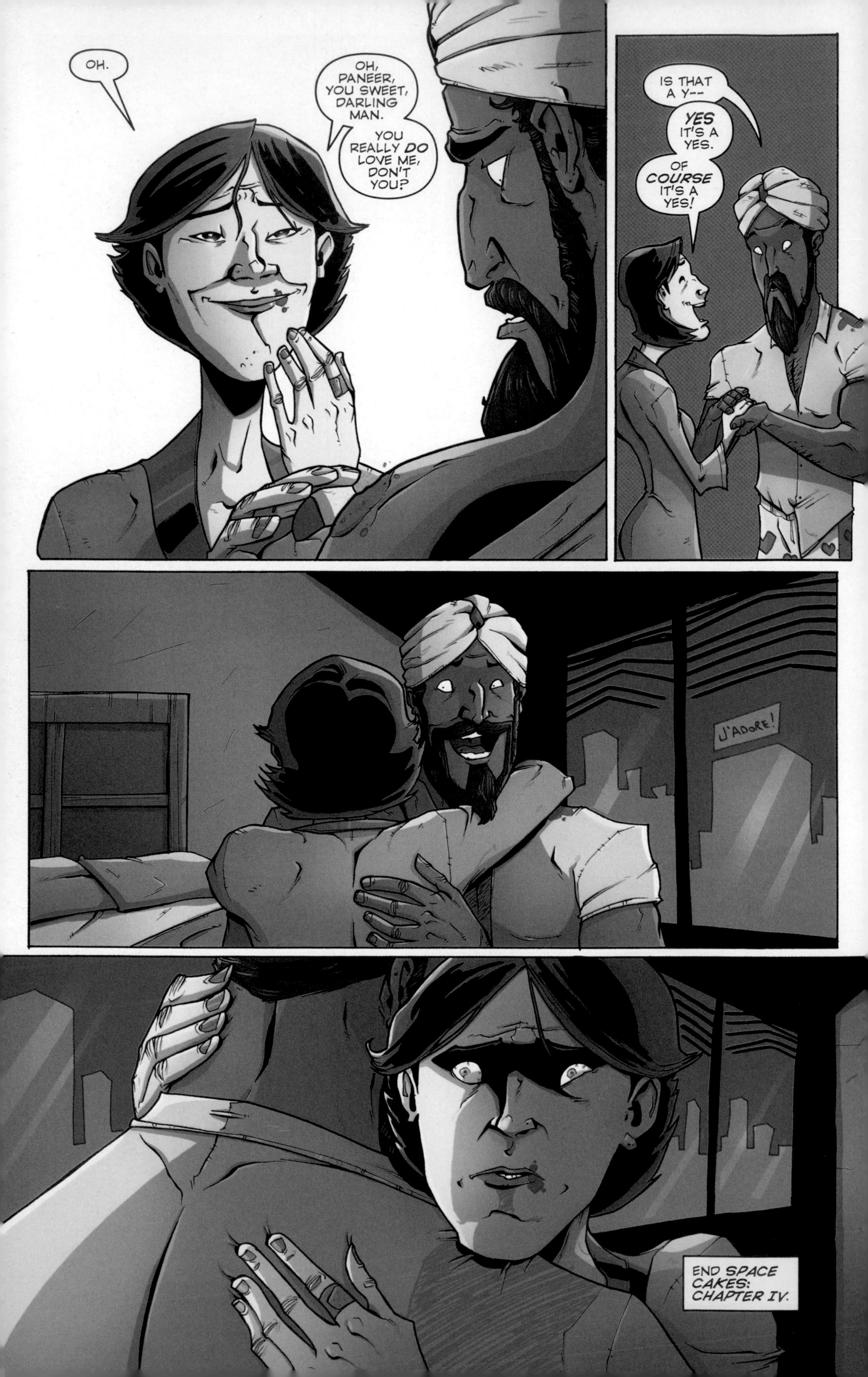
OH.
OH, PANEER, YOU SWEET, DARLING MAN.
YOU REALLY *DO* LOVE ME, DON'T YOU?
IS THAT A Y--
YES IT'S A YES.
OF *COURSE* IT'S A YES!
J'ADORE!
END *SPACE CAKES: CHAPTER IV.*

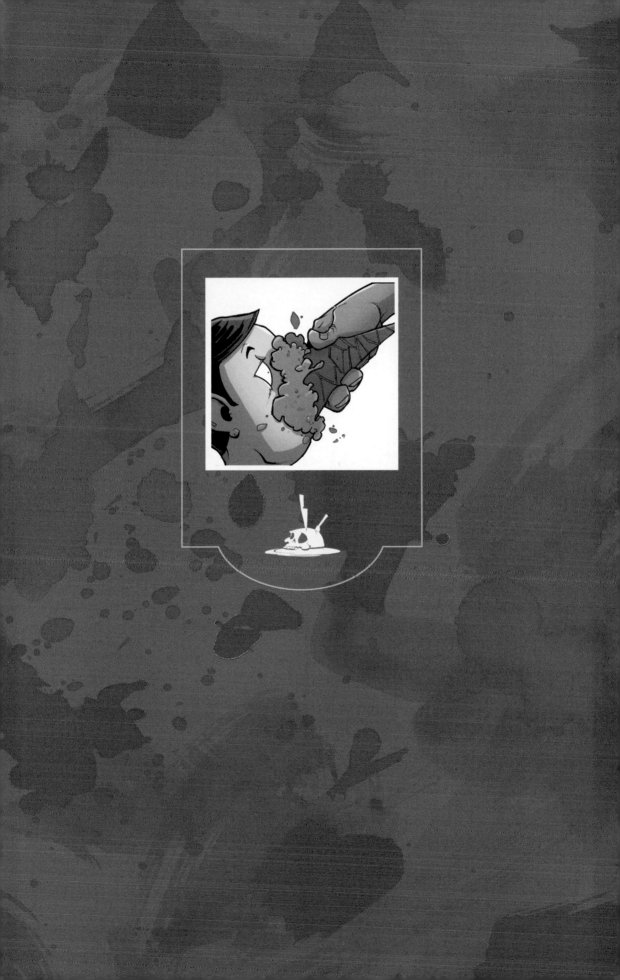

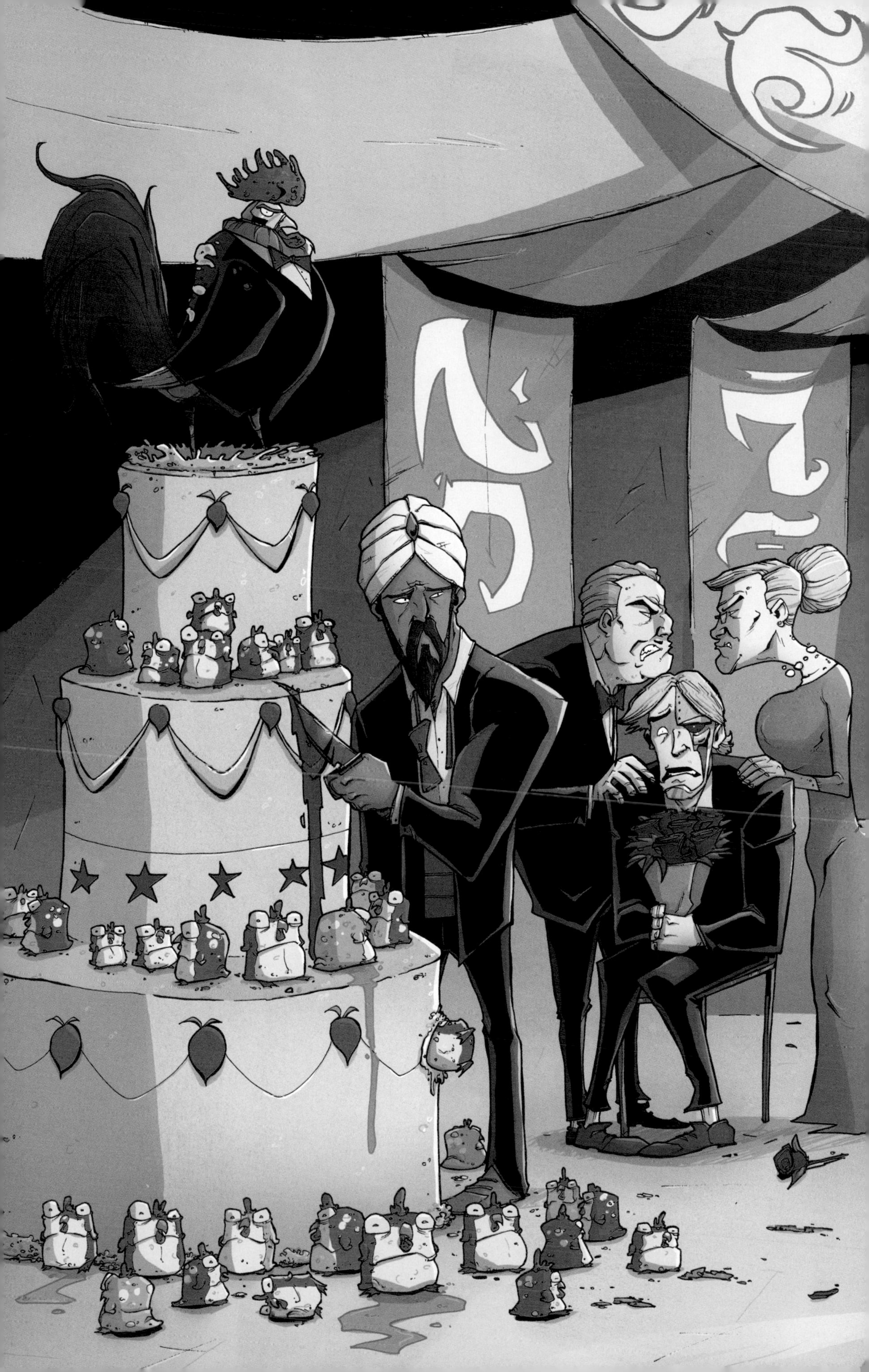

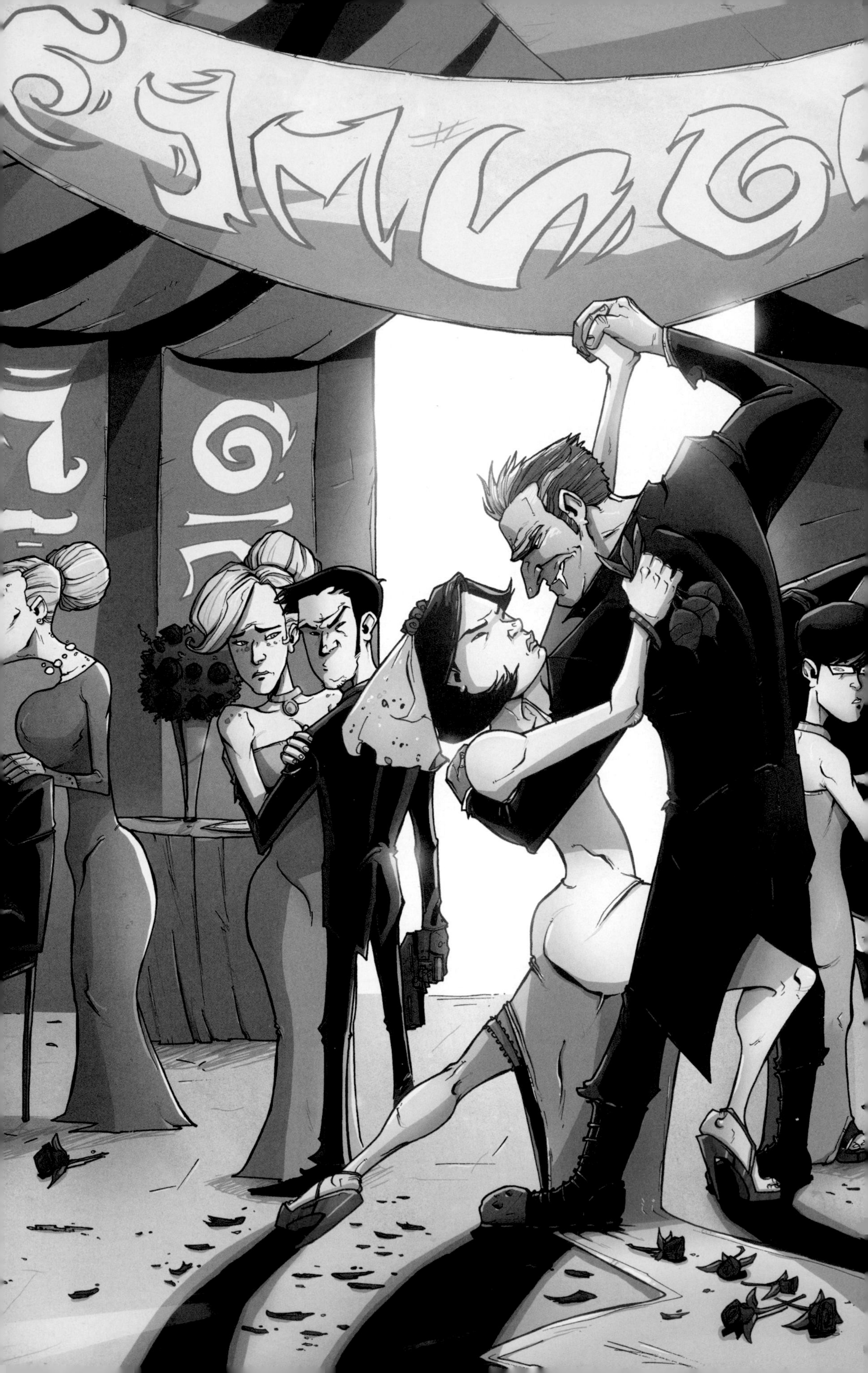

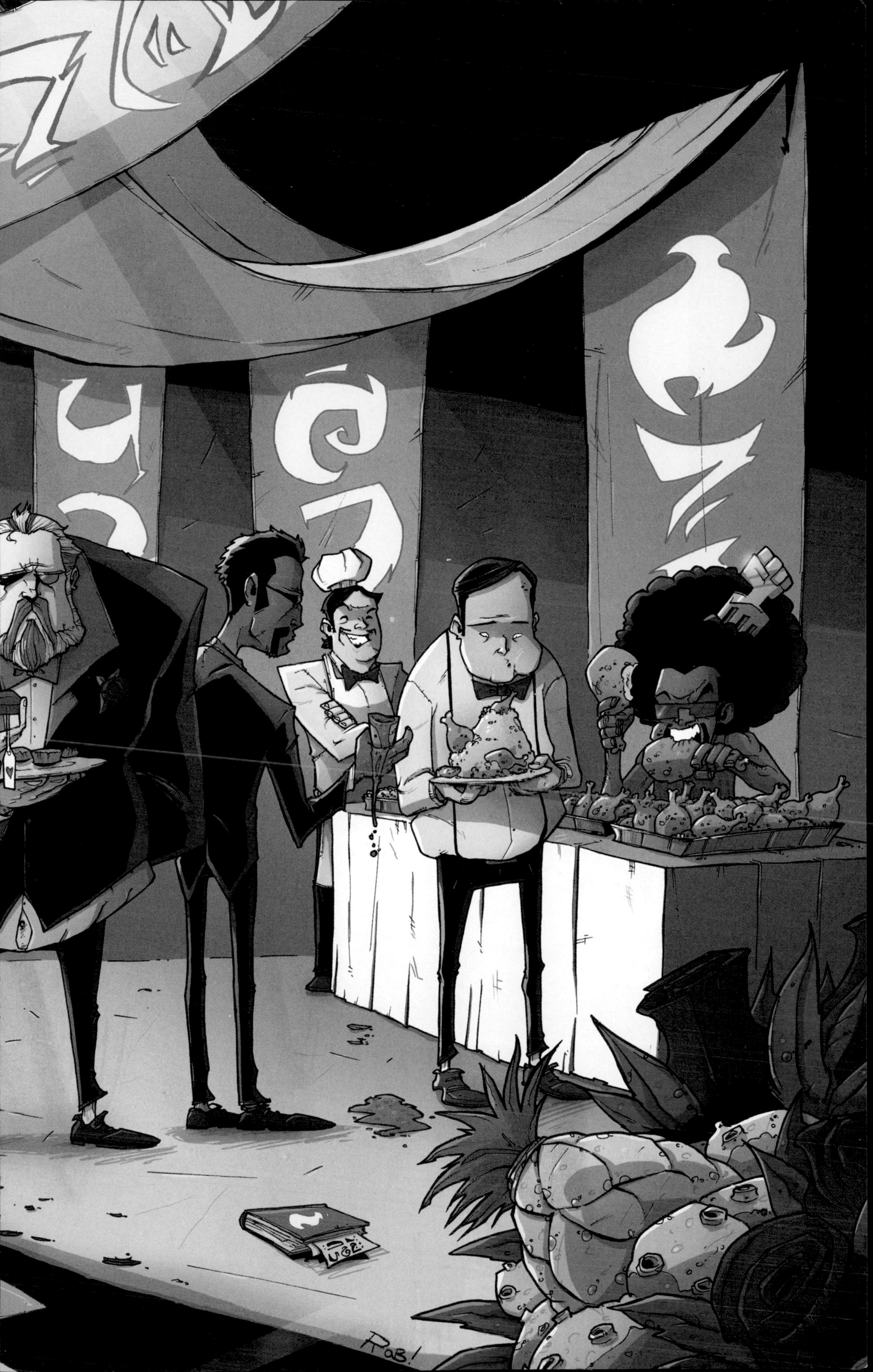

Chapter 5

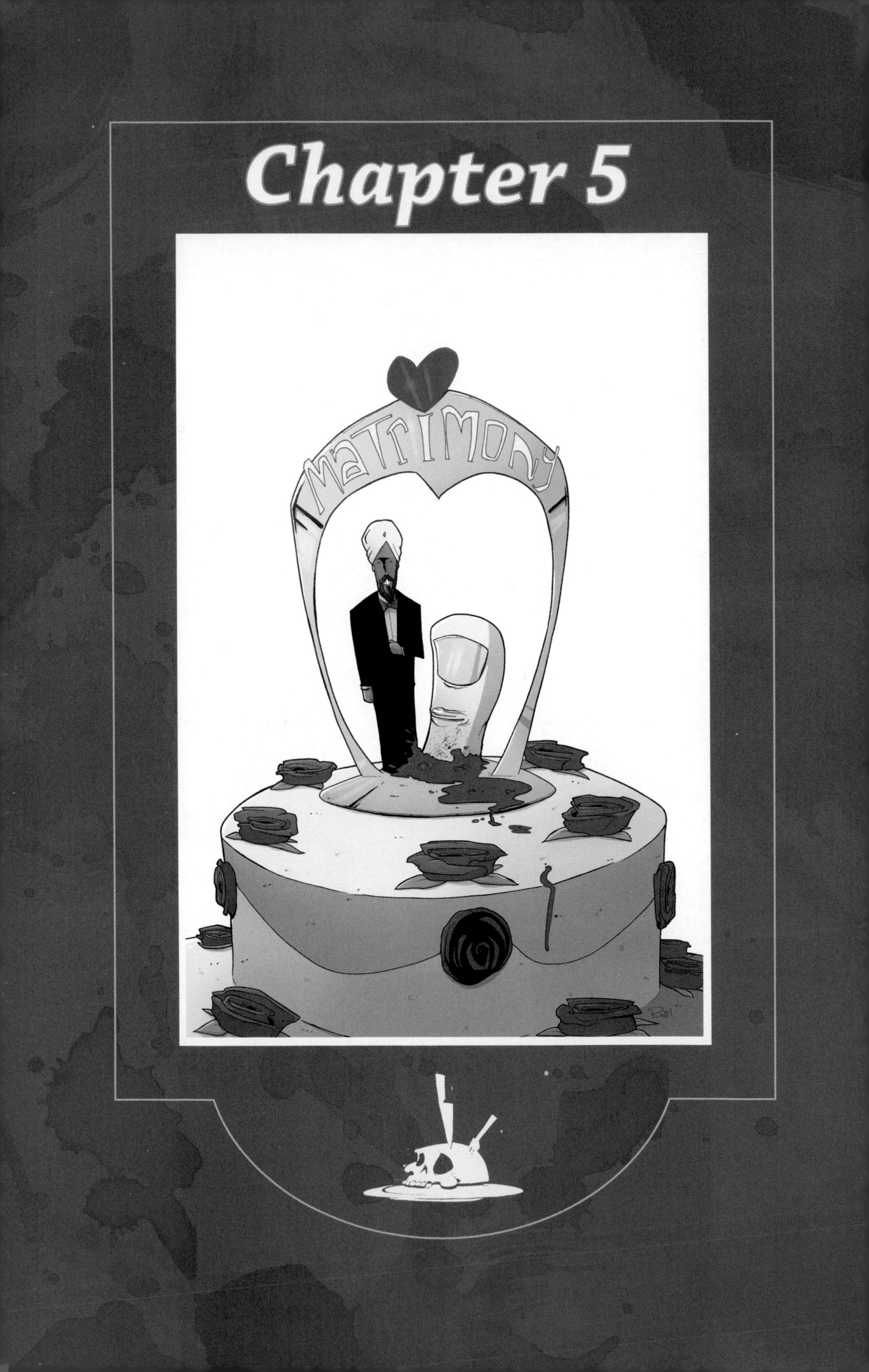
MATRIMONY

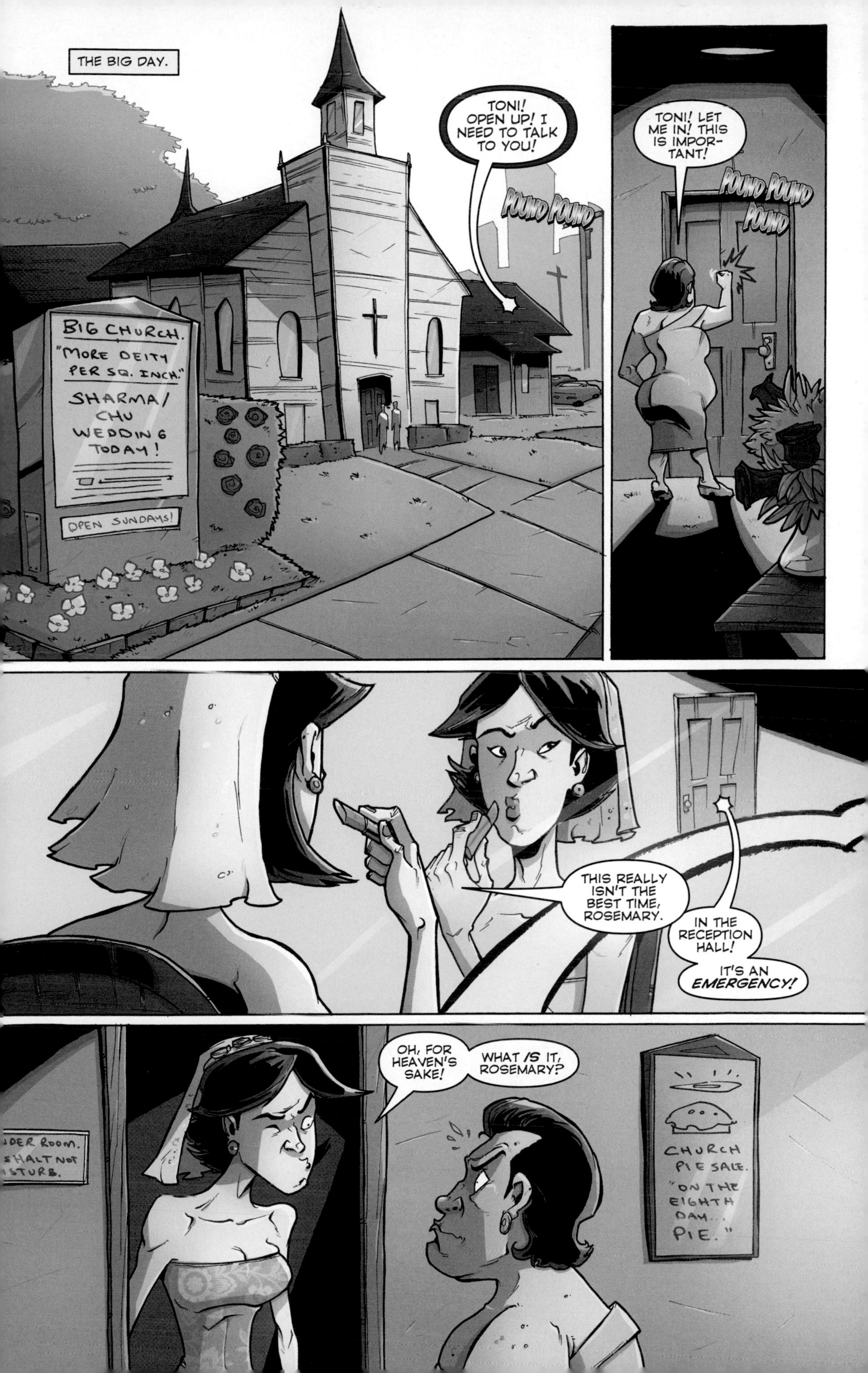
THE BIG DAY.
BIG CHURCH.
"MORE DEITY PER SQ. INCH."
SHARMA/ CHU WEDDING TODAY!
OPEN SUNDAYS!
TONI! OPEN UP! I NEED TO TALK TO YOU!
POUND POUND
TONI! LET ME IN! THIS IS IMPORTANT!
POUND POUND POUND
THIS REALLY ISN'T THE BEST TIME, ROSEMARY.
IN THE RECEPTION HALL!
IT'S AN EMERGENCY!
OH, FOR HEAVEN'S SAKE!
WHAT IS IT, ROSEMARY?
DER ROOM.
SHALT NOT
STURB.
CHURCH PIE SALE.
"ON THE EIGHTH DAY... PIE."

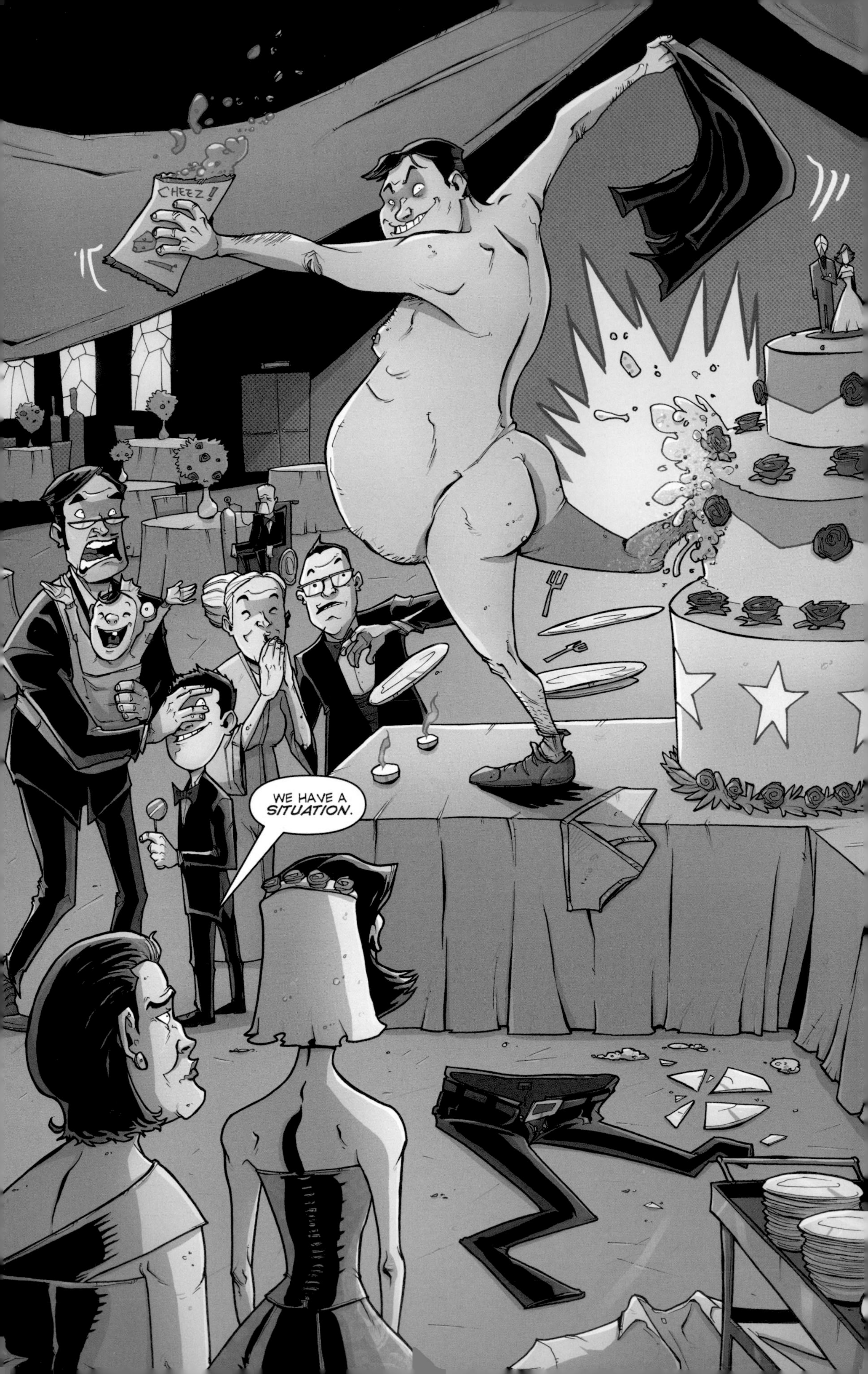
CHEEZ!
WE HAVE A SITUATION.

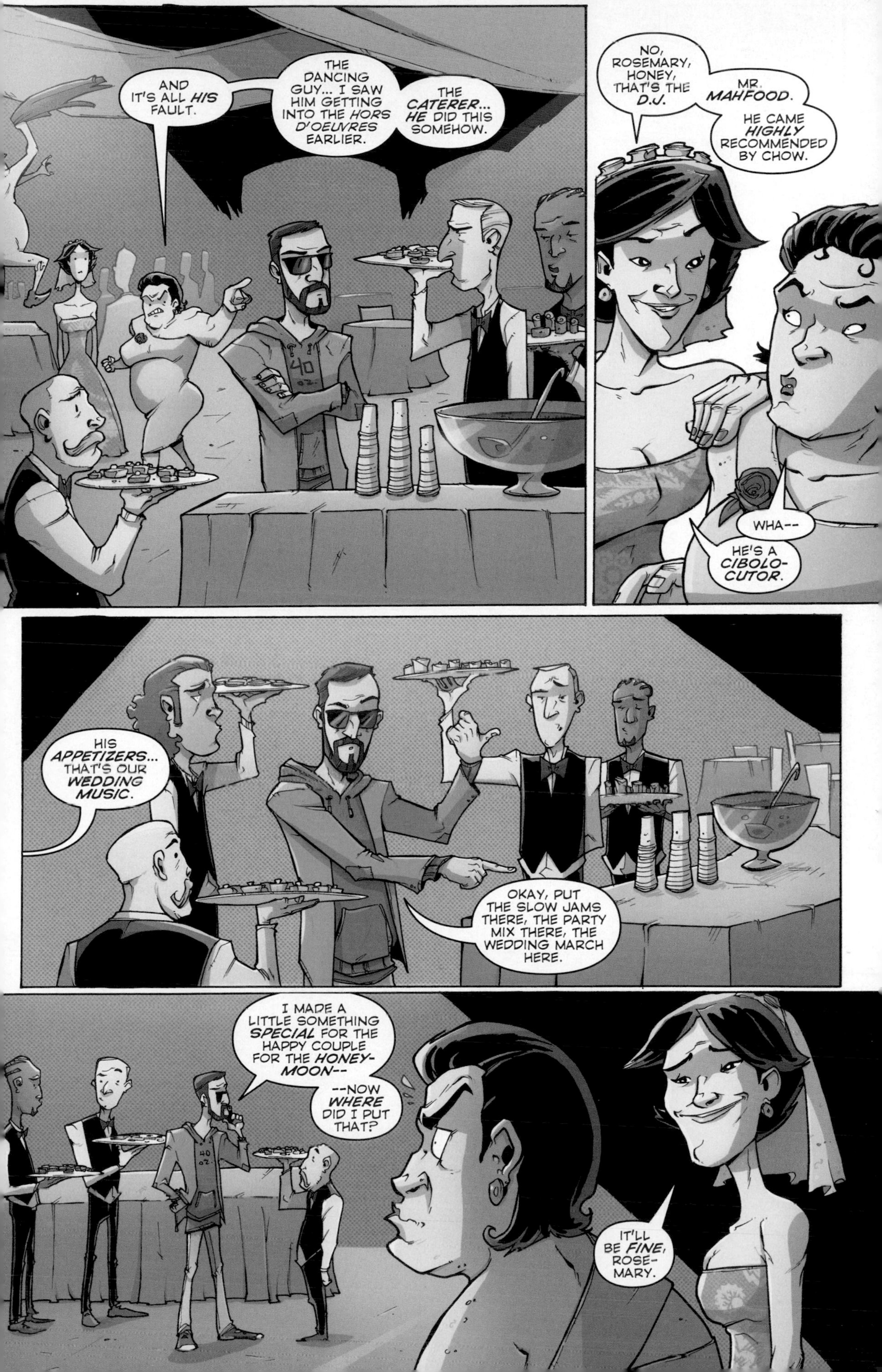
AND IT'S ALL *HIS* FAULT.
THE DANCING GUY... I SAW HIM GETTING INTO THE *HORS D'OEUVRES* EARLIER.
THE *CATERER*... *HE* DID THIS SOMEHOW.
NO, ROSEMARY, HONEY, THAT'S THE *D.J.*
MR. *MAHFOOD*.
HE CAME *HIGHLY* RECOMMENDED BY CHOW.
WHA--
HE'S A *CIBOLOCUTOR*.
HIS *APPETIZERS*... THAT'S OUR *WEDDING MUSIC*.
OKAY, PUT THE SLOW JAMS THERE, THE PARTY MIX THERE, THE WEDDING MARCH HERE.
I MADE A LITTLE SOMETHING *SPECIAL* FOR THE HAPPY COUPLE FOR THE *HONEY-MOON*--
--NOW *WHERE* DID I PUT THAT?
IT'LL BE *FINE*, ROSEMARY.

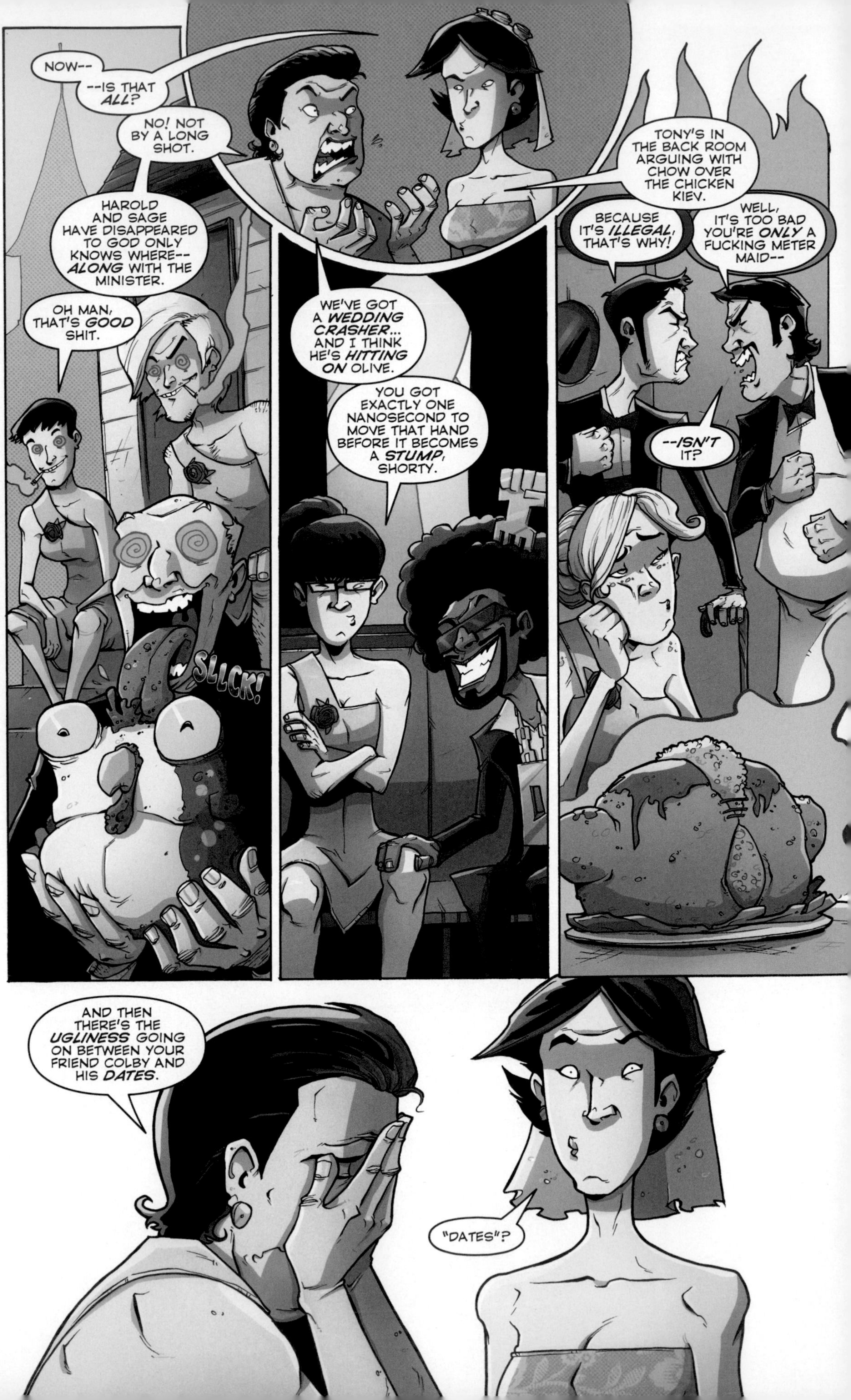
NOW--
--IS THAT ALL?
NO! NOT BY A LONG SHOT.
HAROLD AND SAGE HAVE DISAPPEARED TO GOD ONLY KNOWS WHERE-- ALONG WITH THE MINISTER.
OH MAN, THAT'S GOOD SHIT.
SLLCK!
WE'VE GOT A WEDDING CRASHER... AND I THINK HE'S HITTING ON OLIVE.
YOU GOT EXACTLY ONE NANOSECOND TO MOVE THAT HAND BEFORE IT BECOMES A STUMP, SHORTY.
TONY'S IN THE BACK ROOM ARGUING WITH CHOW OVER THE CHICKEN KIEV.
BECAUSE IT'S ILLEGAL, THAT'S WHY!
WELL, IT'S TOO BAD YOU'RE ONLY A FUCKING METER MAID--
--ISN'T IT?
AND THEN THERE'S THE UGLINESS GOING ON BETWEEN YOUR FRIEND COLBY AND HIS DATES.
"DATES"?

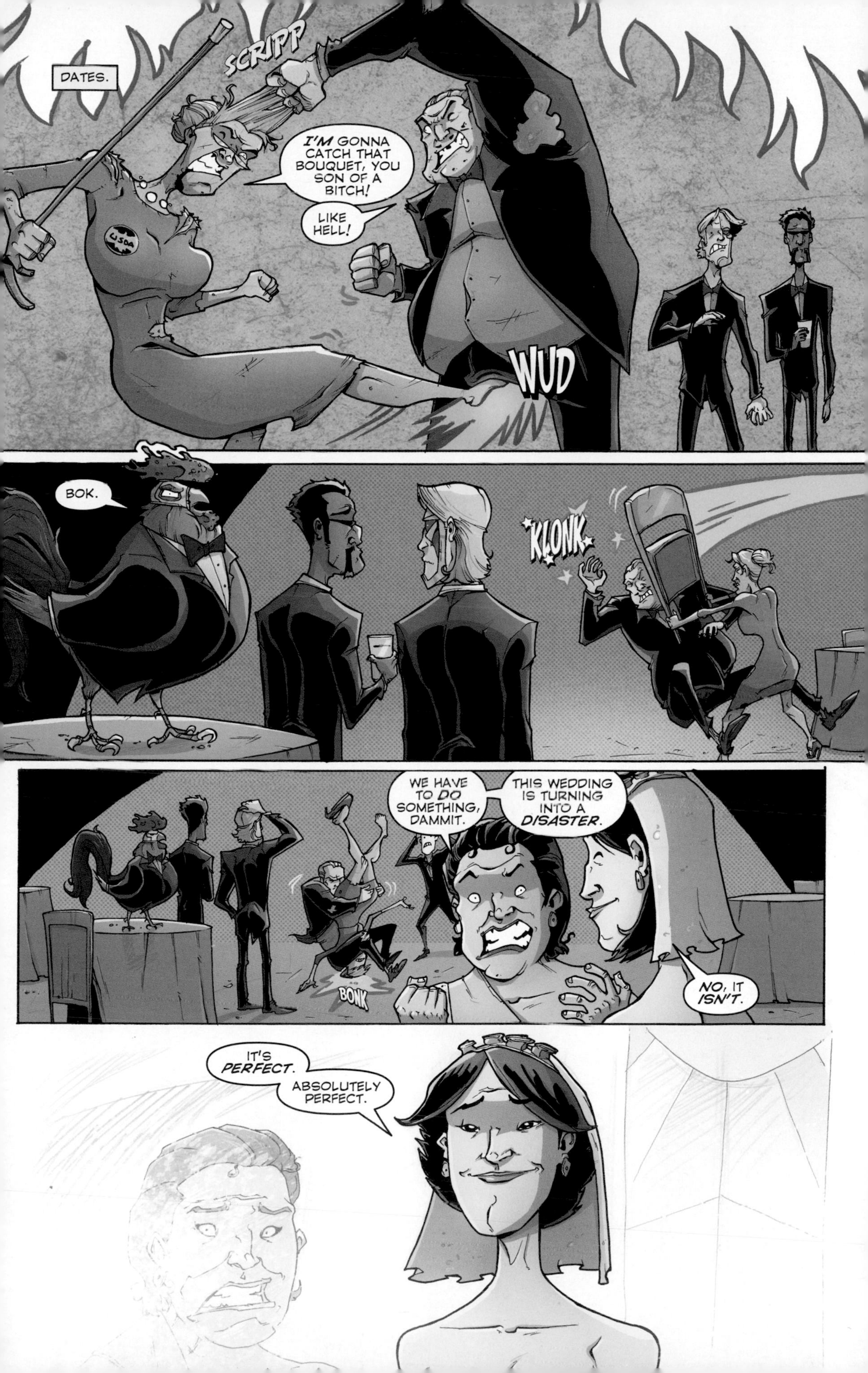
DATES.
SCRIPP
I'M GONNA CATCH THAT BOUQUET, YOU SON OF A BITCH!
LIKE HELL!
WUD
BOK.
KLONK
WE HAVE TO DO SOMETHING, DAMMIT.
THIS WEDDING IS TURNING INTO A DISASTER.
BONK
NO, IT ISN'T.
IT'S PERFECT.
ABSOLUTELY PERFECT.

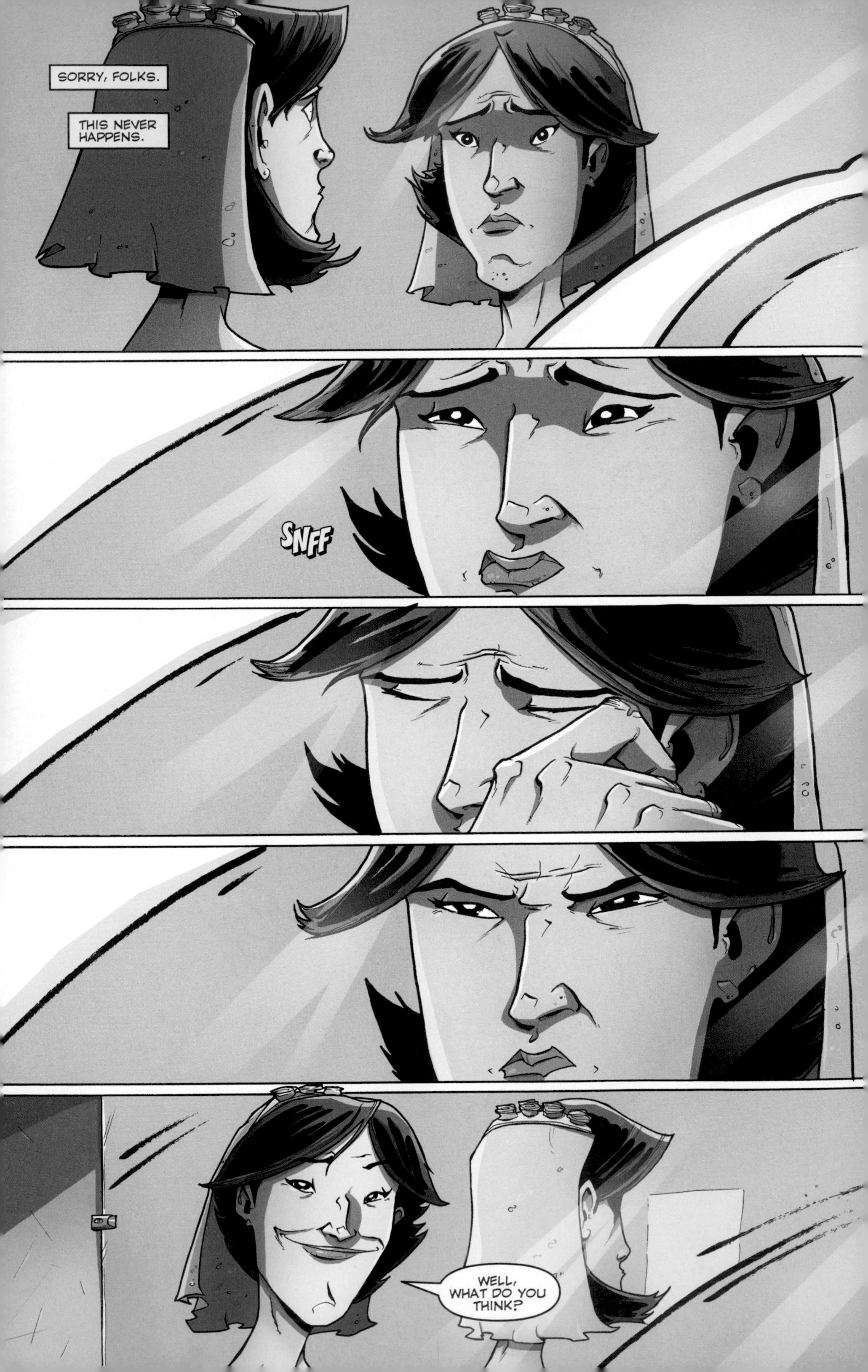
SORRY, FOLKS.
THIS NEVER HAPPENS.
SNFF
WELL, WHAT DO YOU THINK?

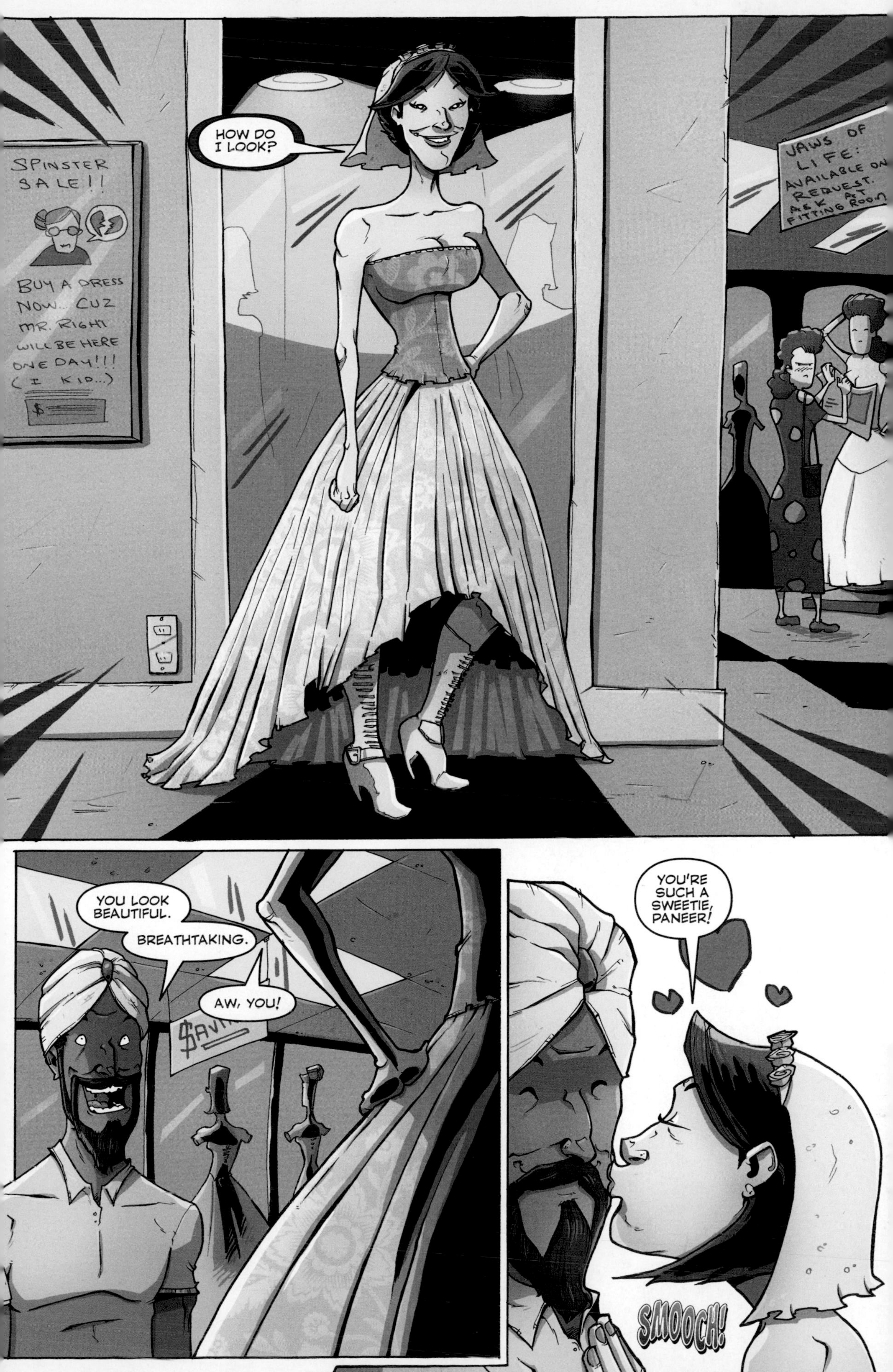
SPINSTER SALE!!
BUY A DRESS NOW... CUZ MR. RIGHT WILL BE HERE ONE DAY!!! (I KID...)
HOW DO I LOOK?
JAWS OF LIFE: AVAILABLE ON REQUEST. ASK AT FITTING ROOM
YOU LOOK BEAUTIFUL.
BREATHTAKING.
AW, YOU!
YOU'RE SUCH A SWEETIE, PANEER!
SMOOCH!

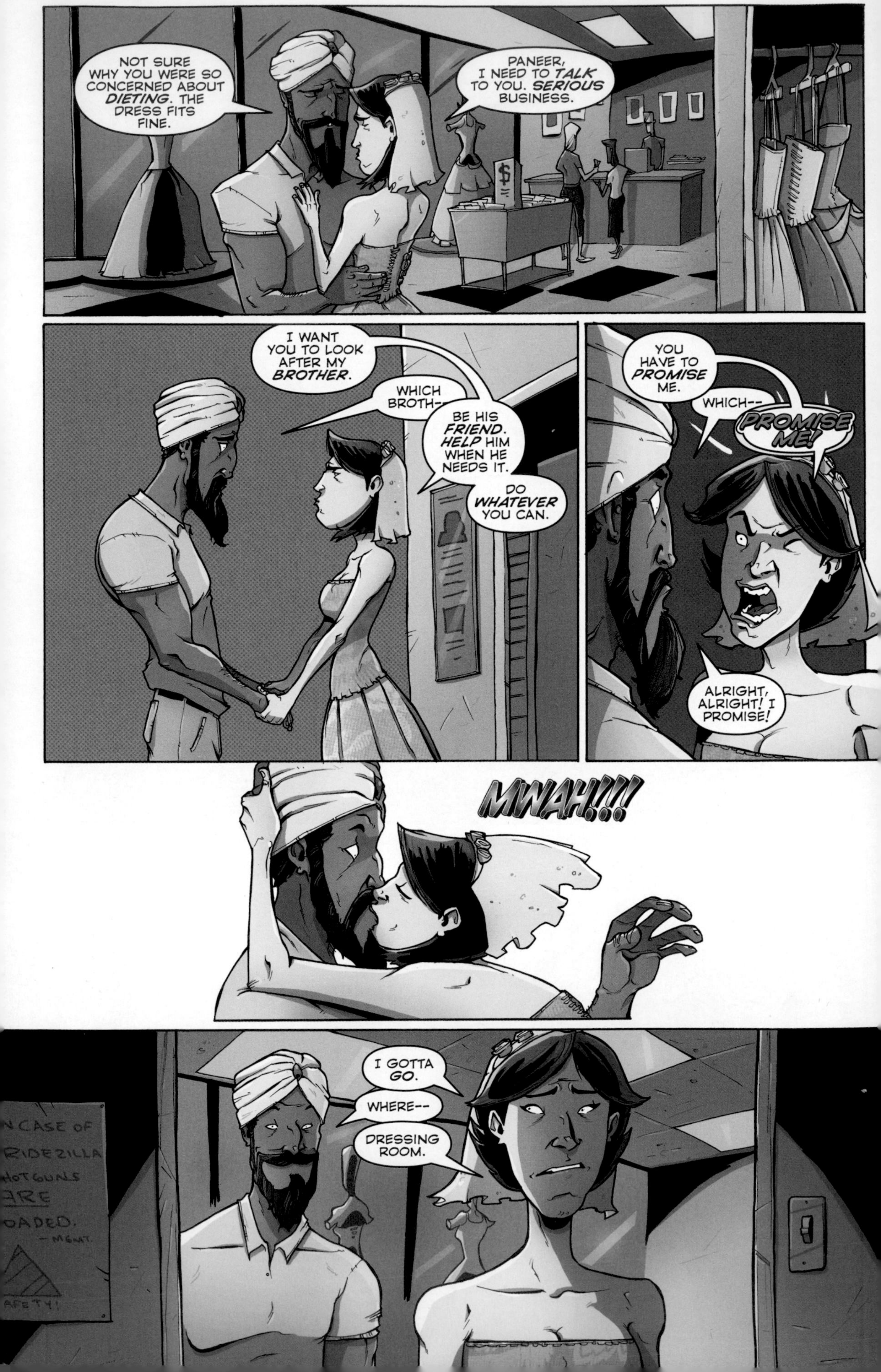
NOT SURE WHY YOU WERE SO CONCERNED ABOUT *DIETING*. THE DRESS FITS FINE.
PANEER, I NEED TO *TALK* TO YOU. *SERIOUS* BUSINESS.
I WANT YOU TO LOOK AFTER MY *BROTHER*.
WHICH BROTH--
BE HIS *FRIEND*. *HELP* HIM WHEN HE NEEDS IT.
DO *WHATEVER* YOU CAN.
YOU HAVE TO *PROMISE* ME.
WHICH--
PROMISE ME!
ALRIGHT, ALRIGHT! I PROMISE!
MWAH!!!
I GOTTA *GO*.
WHERE--
DRESSING ROOM.
N CASE OF RIDEZILLA HOTGUNS ARE OADED.
-MGMT.

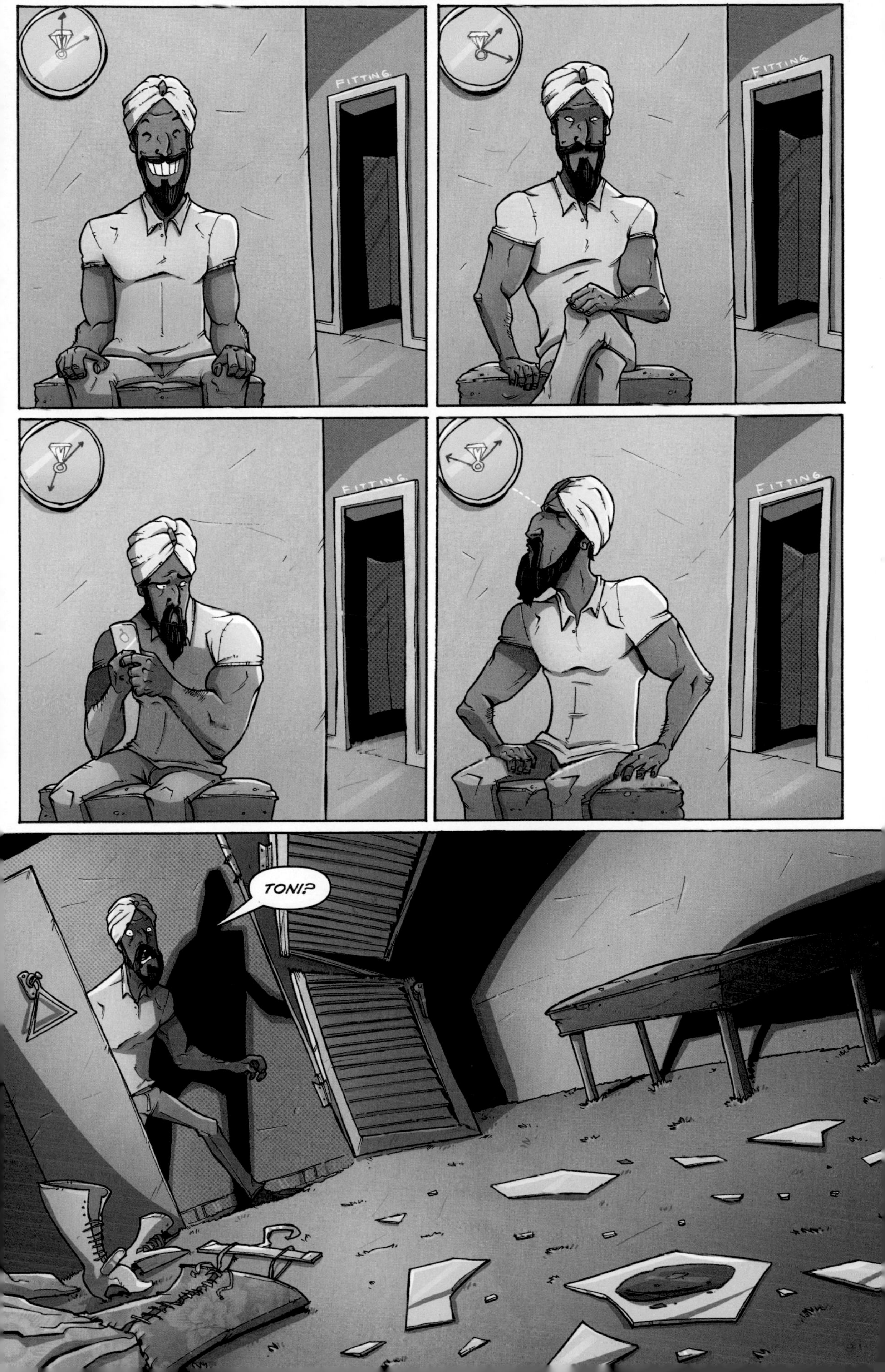
FITTING.
FITTING.
FITTING.
FITTING.
TONI?

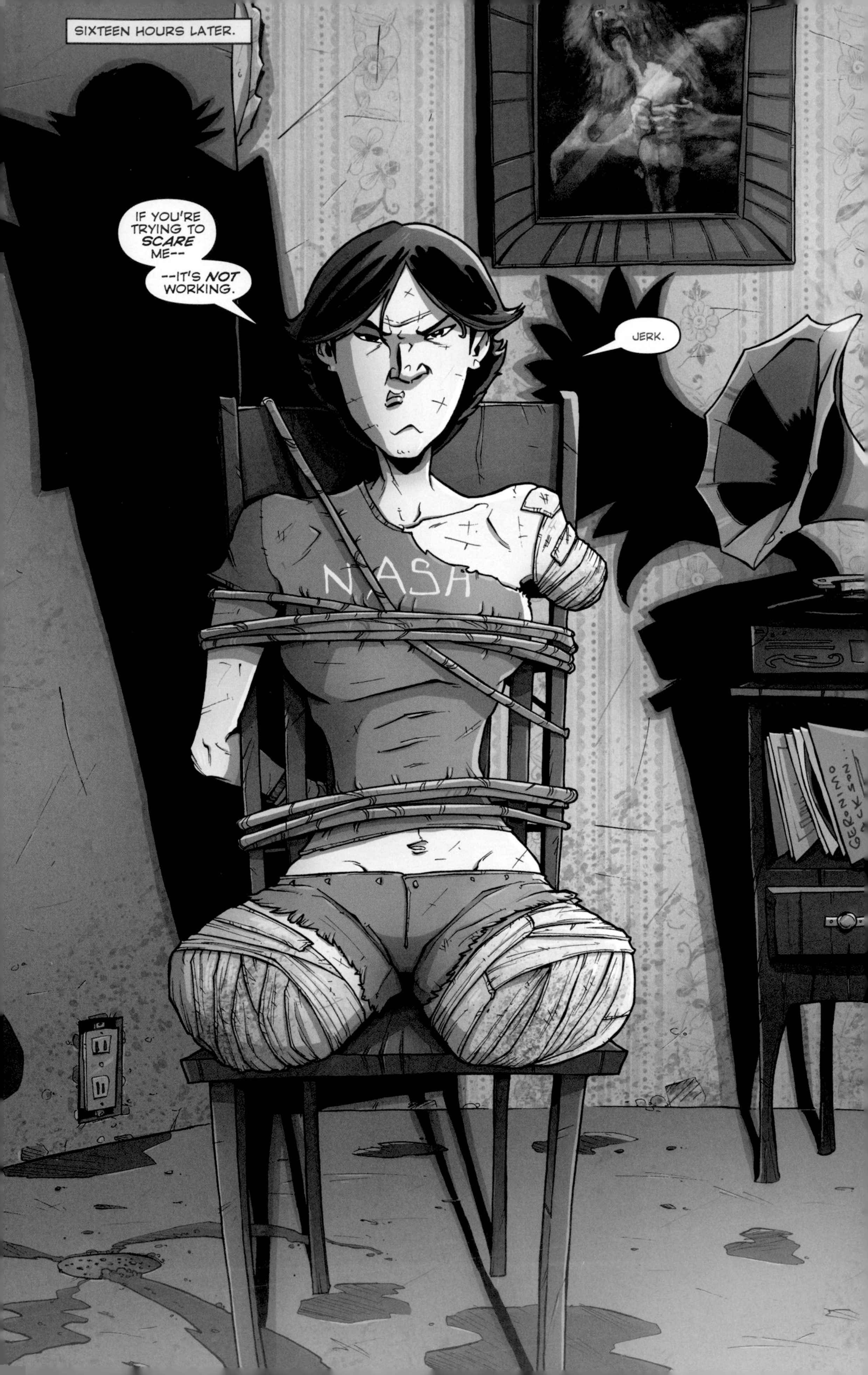
SIXTEEN HOURS LATER.
IF YOU'RE TRYING TO SCARE ME--
--IT'S NOT WORKING.
JERK.
NASA
GERONIMO JACKSON

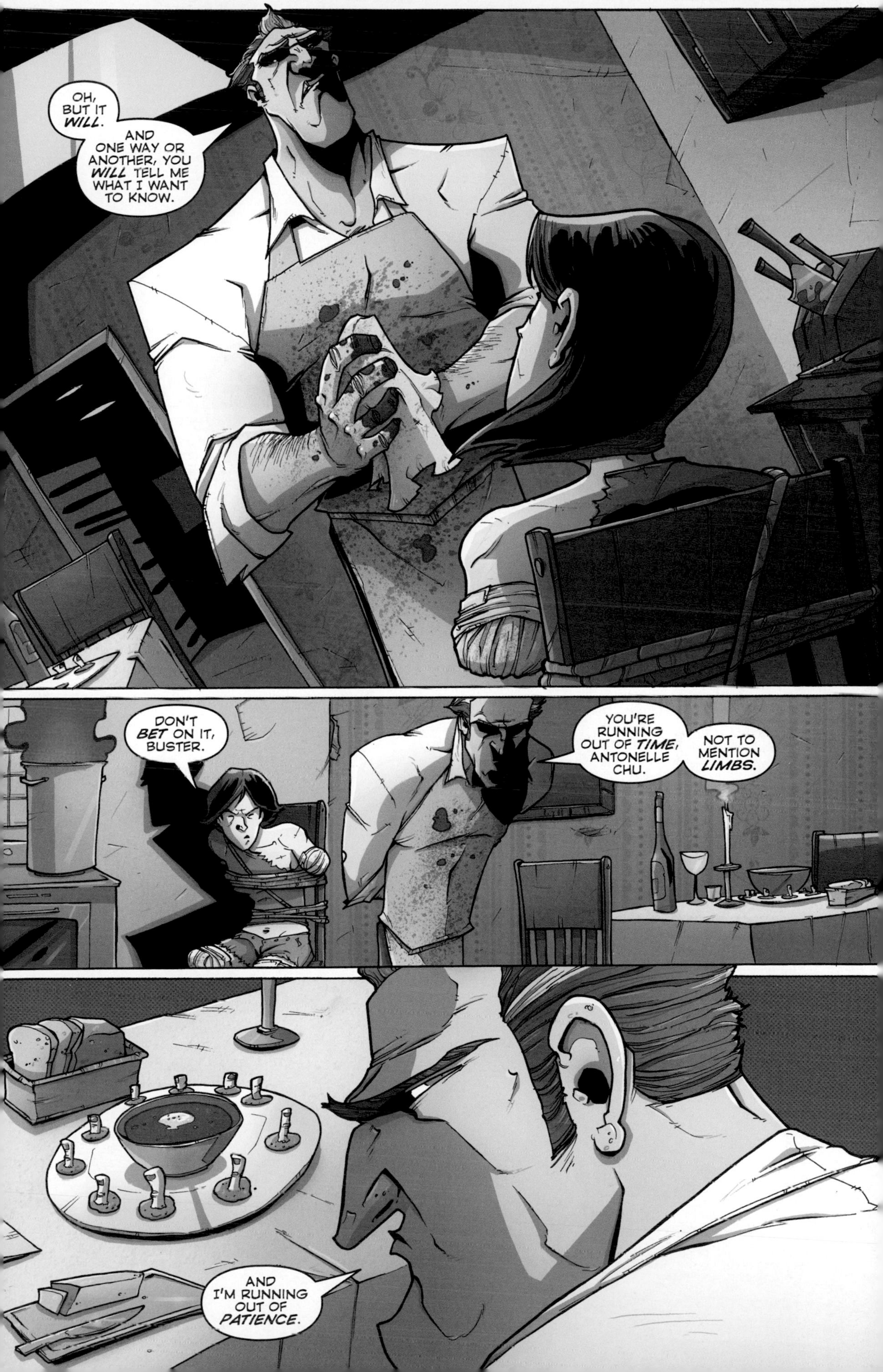
OH, BUT IT WILL.
AND ONE WAY OR ANOTHER, YOU WILL TELL ME WHAT I WANT TO KNOW.
DON'T BET ON IT, BUSTER.
YOU'RE RUNNING OUT OF TIME, ANTONELLE CHU.
NOT TO MENTION LIMBS.
AND I'M RUNNING OUT OF PATIENCE.

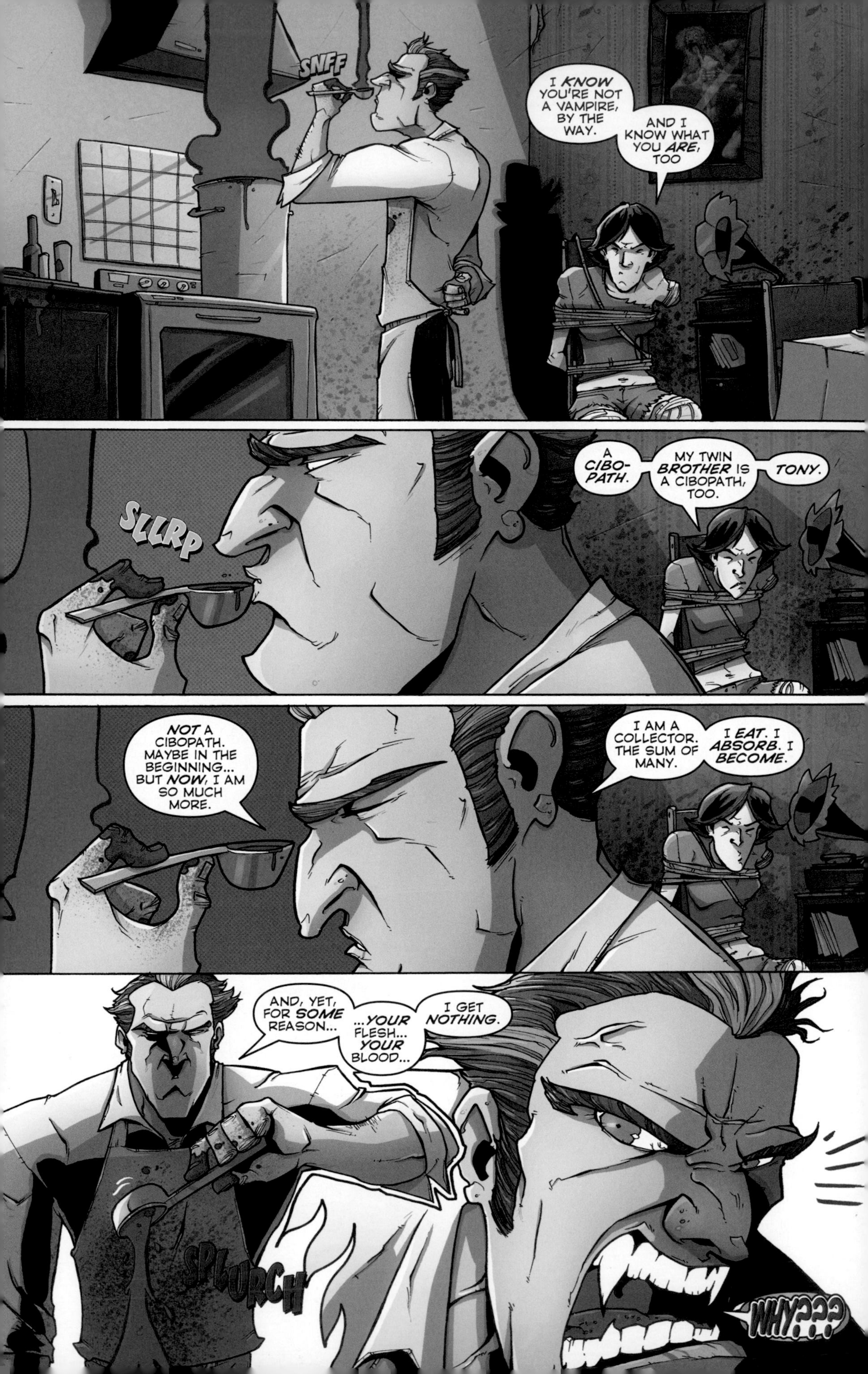
SNFF
I KNOW YOU'RE NOT A VAMPIRE, BY THE WAY.
AND I KNOW WHAT YOU ARE, TOO
SLLRP
A CIBOPATH.
MY TWIN BROTHER IS A CIBOPATH, TOO.
TONY.
NOT A CIBOPATH. MAYBE IN THE BEGINNING... BUT NOW, I AM SO MUCH MORE.
I AM A COLLECTOR. THE SUM OF MANY.
I EAT. I ABSORB. I BECOME.
AND, YET, FOR SOME REASON...
...YOUR FLESH... YOUR BLOOD...
I GET NOTHING.
SPLURCH
WHY???

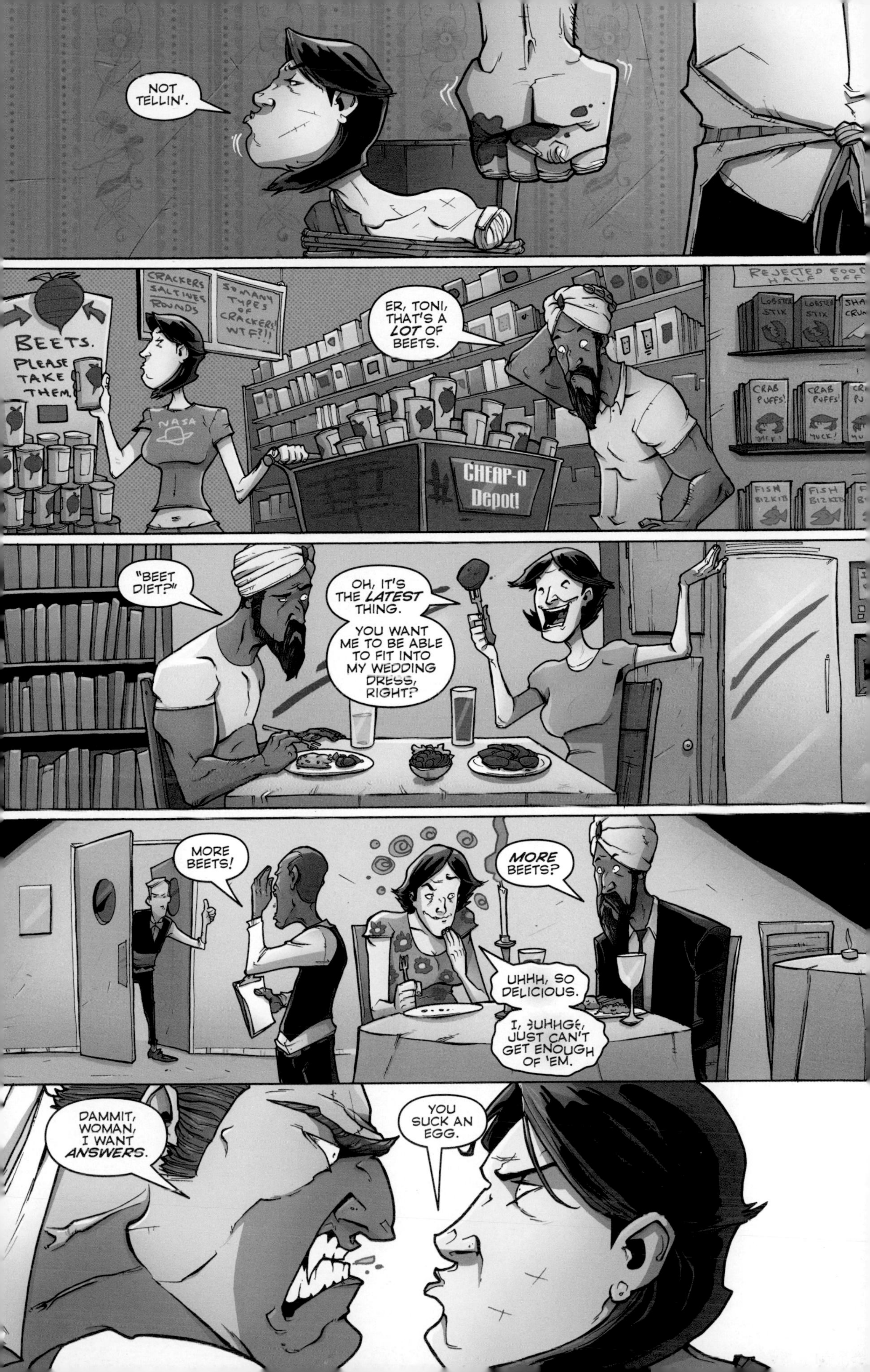
NOT TELLIN'.
CRACKERS
SALTINES
ROUNDS
SO MANY TYPES OF CRACKERS! WTF?!!
BEETS. PLEASE TAKE THEM.
NASA
ER, TONI, THAT'S A *LOT* OF BEETS.
CHEAP-O Depot!
LOBSTER STIX
CRAB PUFFS!
"BEET DIET?"
OH, IT'S THE *LATEST* THING.
YOU WANT ME TO BE ABLE TO FIT INTO MY WEDDING DRESS, RIGHT?
MORE BEETS!
MORE BEETS?
UHHH, SO DELICIOUS.
I, BUHHGE, JUST CAN'T GET ENOUGH OF 'EM.
DAMMIT, WOMAN, I WANT *ANSWERS*.
YOU SUCK AN EGG.

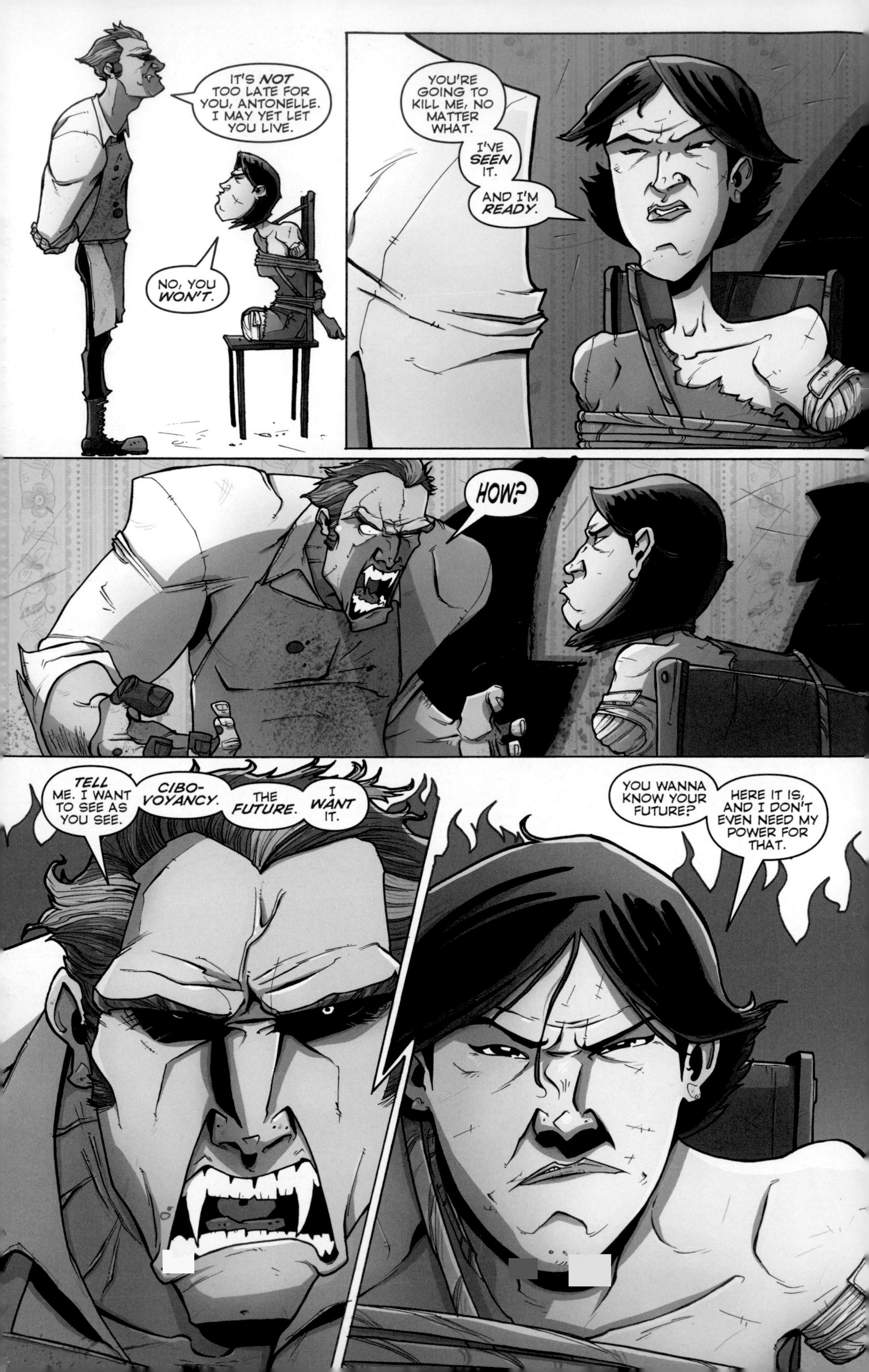

IT'S NOT TOO LATE FOR YOU, ANTONELLE. I MAY YET LET YOU LIVE.
NO, YOU WON'T.
YOU'RE GOING TO KILL ME, NO MATTER WHAT.
I'VE SEEN IT.
AND I'M READY.
HOW?
TELL ME. I WANT TO SEE AS YOU SEE.
CIBO-VOYANCY.
THE FUTURE.
I WANT IT.
YOU WANNA KNOW YOUR FUTURE?
HERE IT IS, AND I DON'T EVEN NEED MY POWER FOR THAT.

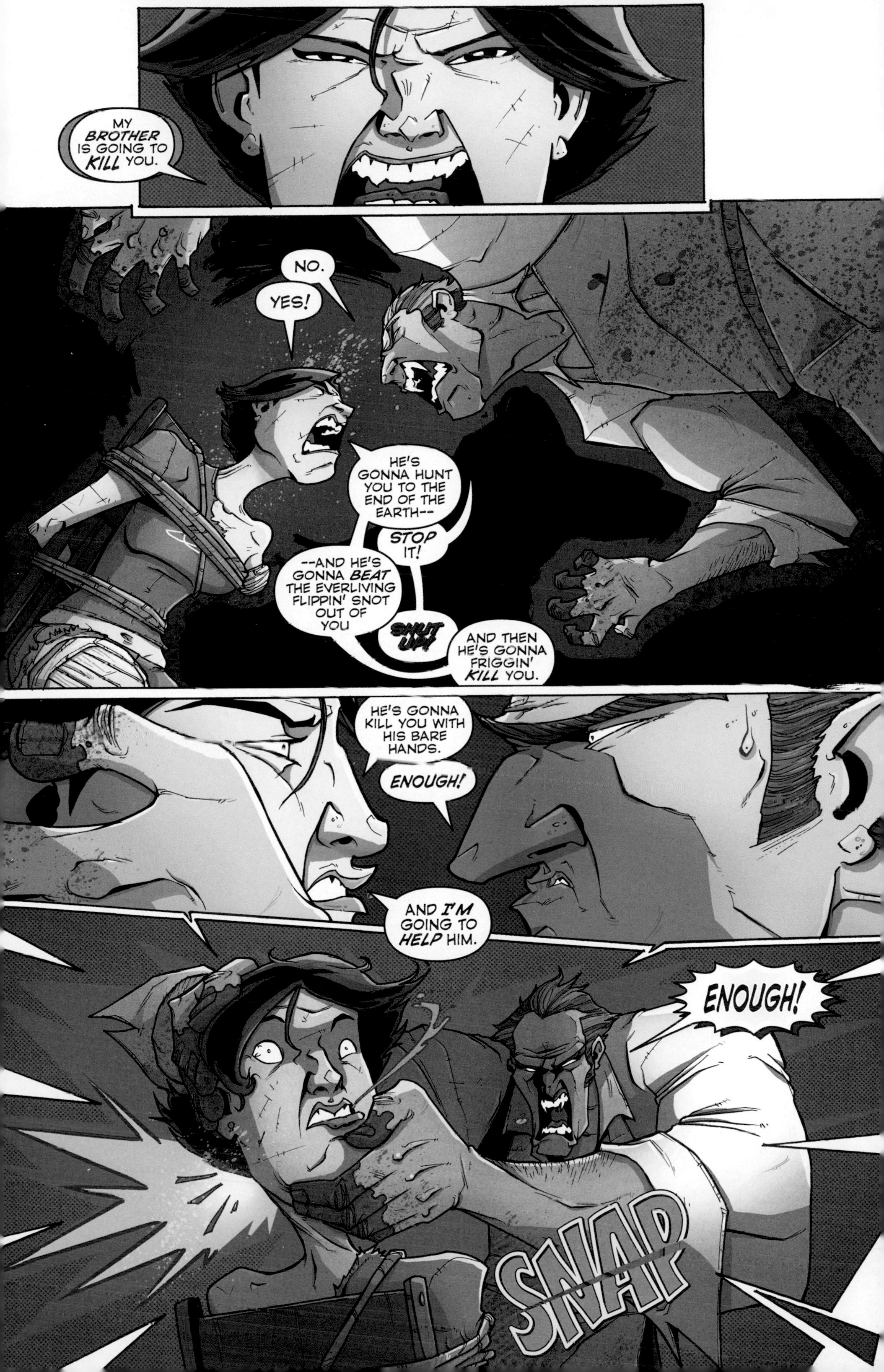
MY BROTHER IS GOING TO KILL YOU.
NO.
YES!
HE'S GONNA HUNT YOU TO THE END OF THE EARTH--
STOP IT!
--AND HE'S GONNA BEAT THE EVERLIVING FLIPPIN' SNOT OUT OF YOU
SHUT UP!
AND THEN HE'S GONNA FRIGGIN' KILL YOU.
HE'S GONNA KILL YOU WITH HIS BARE HANDS.
ENOUGH!
AND I'M GOING TO HELP HIM.
ENOUGH!
SNAP

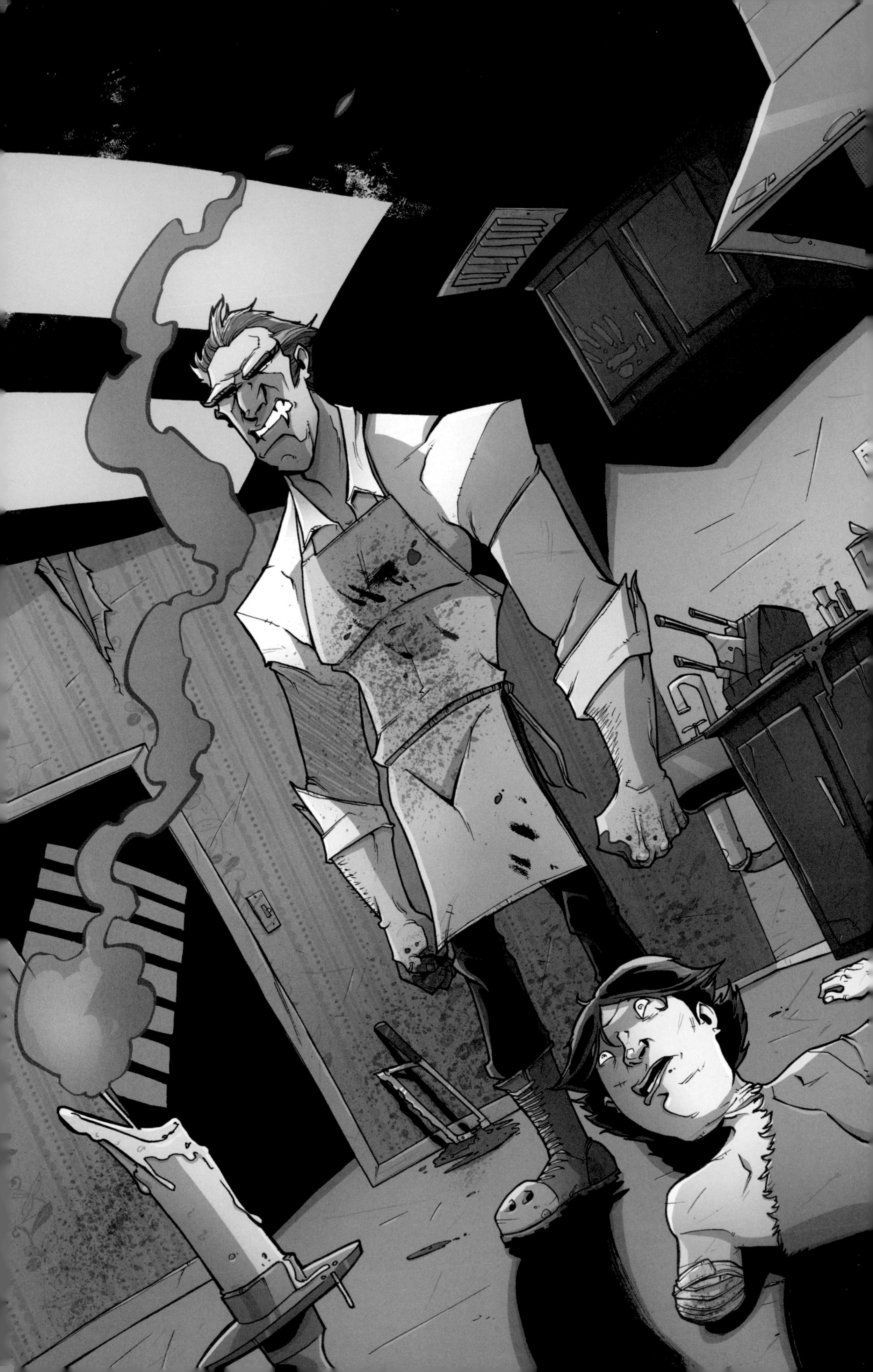

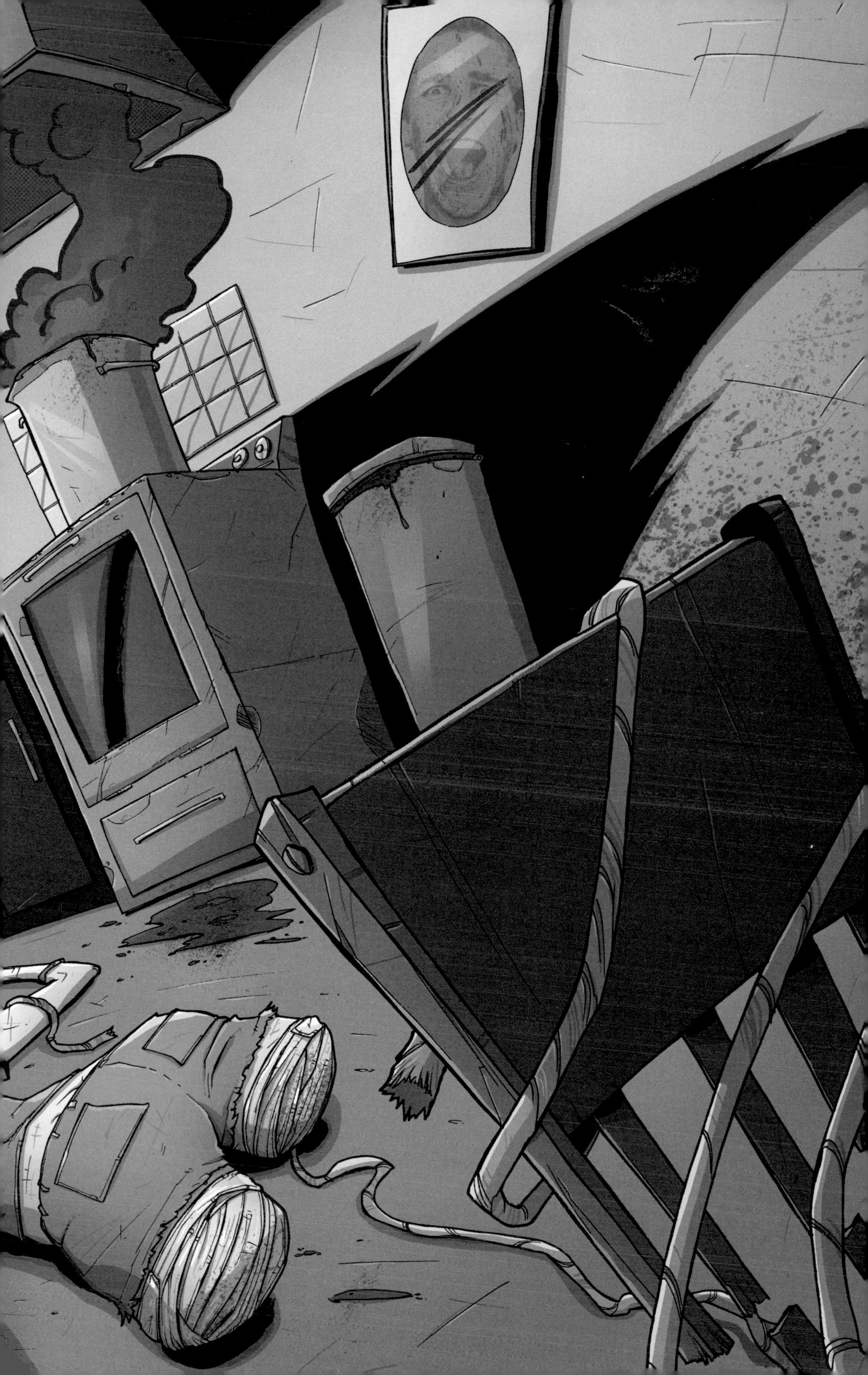

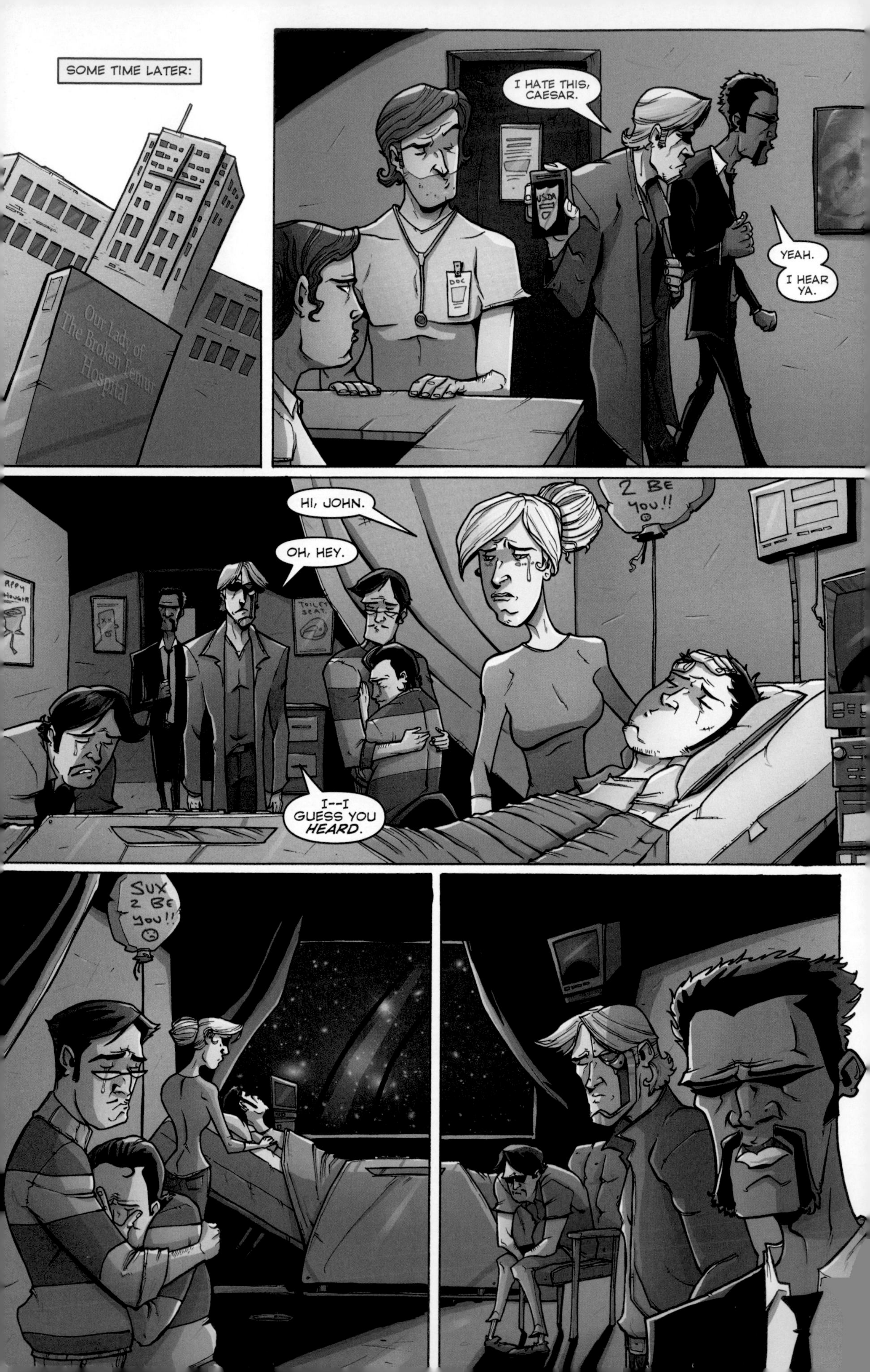
SOME TIME LATER:
Our Lady of The Broken Femur Hospital
I HATE THIS, CAESAR.
USDA
DOC
YEAH.
I HEAR YA.
2 BE YOU!!
HI, JOHN.
OH, HEY.
TOILET SEAT.
I--I GUESS YOU *HEARD*.
SUX 2 BE YOU!!

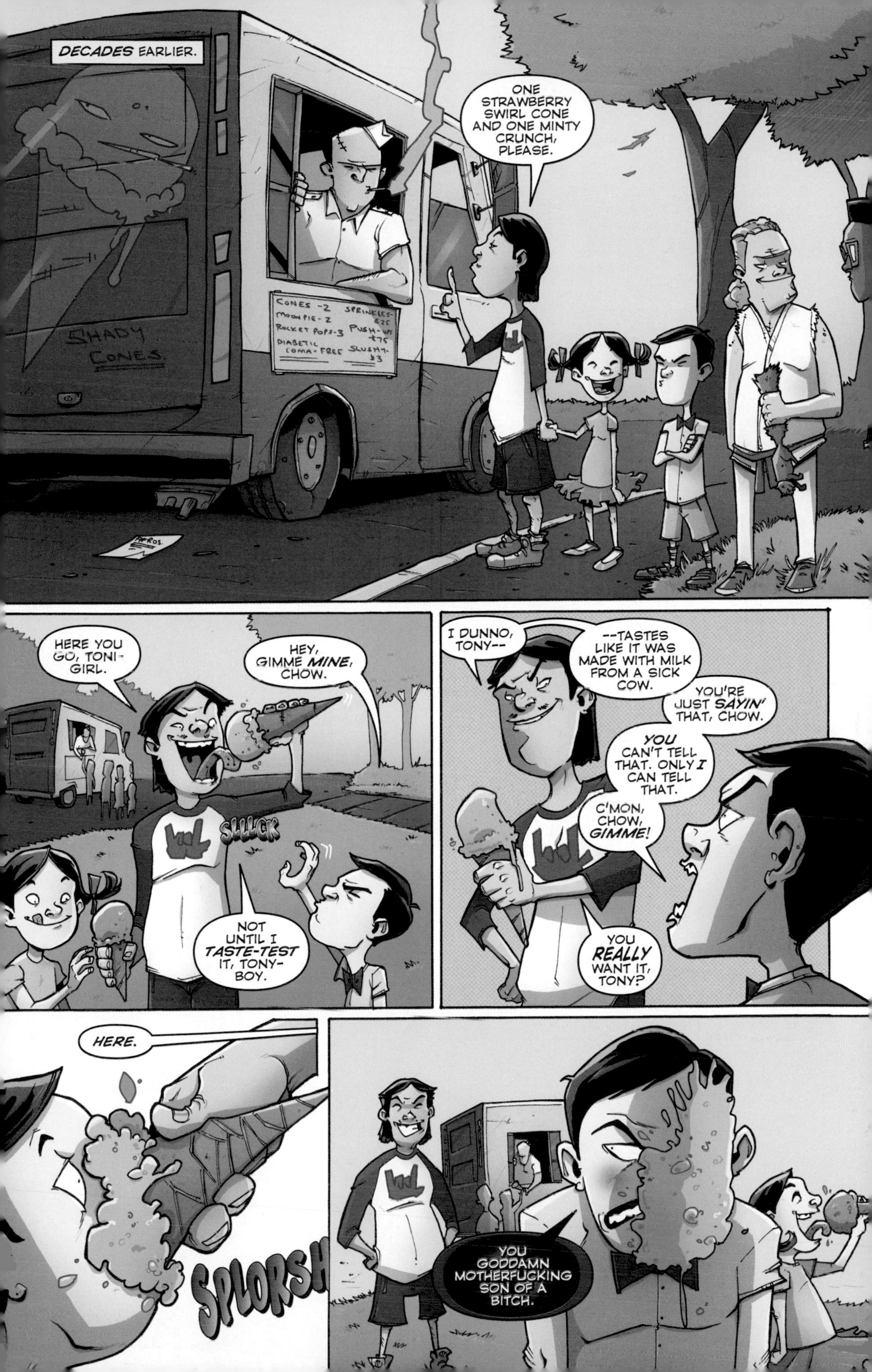
DECADES EARLIER.
ONE STRAWBERRY SWIRL CONE AND ONE MINTY CRUNCH, PLEASE.
SHADY CONES
CONES - 2
MOON PIE - 2
ROCKET POPS - 3
DIABETIC COMA - FREE
SPRINKLES - .25
PUSH-UPS .75
SLUSHY - $3
HERE YOU GO, TONI-GIRL.
HEY, GIMME MINE, CHOW.
SLLLCK
NOT UNTIL I TASTE-TEST IT, TONY-BOY.
I DUNNO, TONY--
--TASTES LIKE IT WAS MADE WITH MILK FROM A SICK COW.
YOU'RE JUST SAYIN' THAT, CHOW.
YOU CAN'T TELL THAT. ONLY I CAN TELL THAT.
C'MON, CHOW, GIMME!
YOU REALLY WANT IT, TONY?
HERE.
SPLORSH
YOU GODDAMN MOTHERFUCKING SON OF A BITCH.

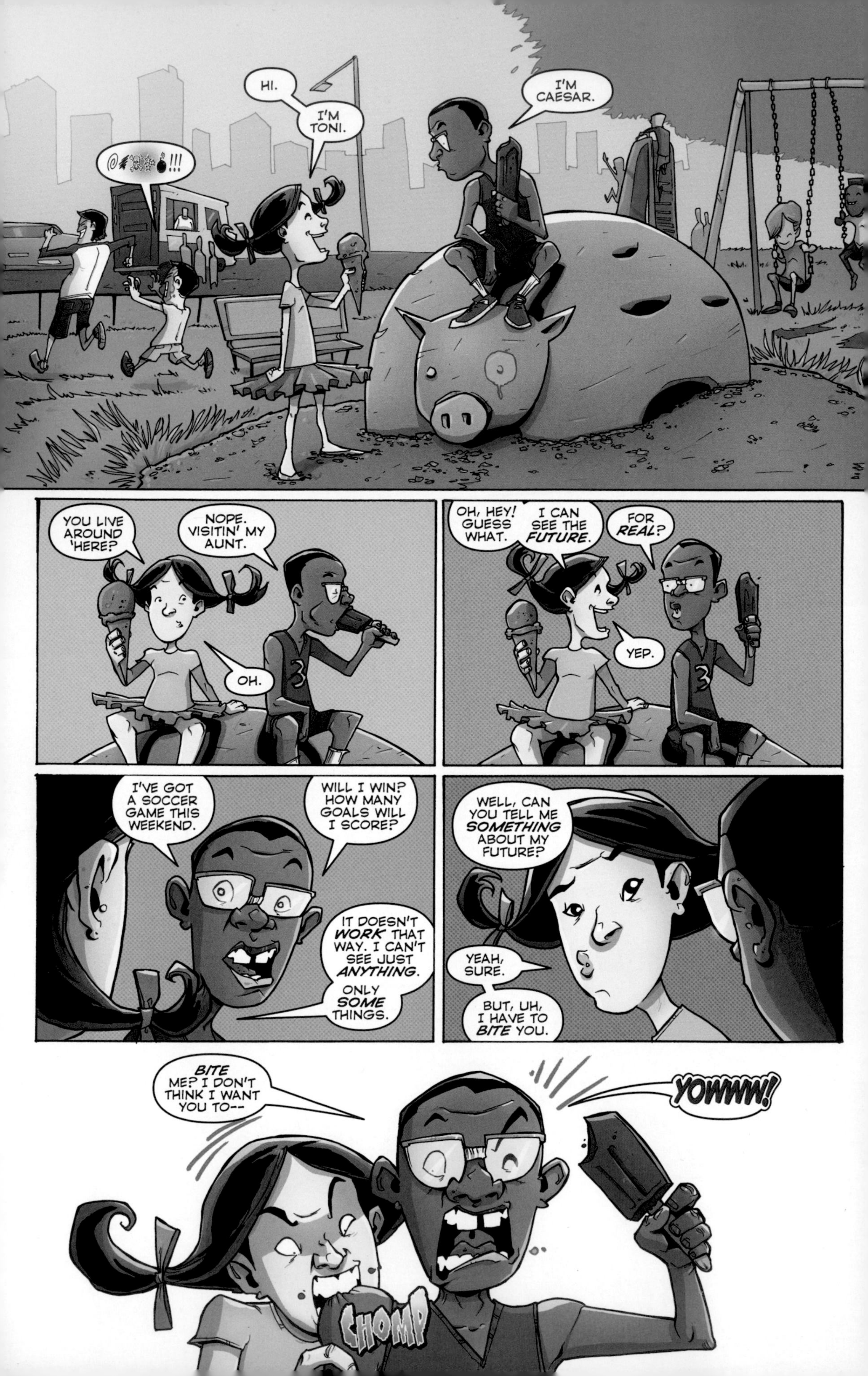
@✶☠✩💣!!!
HI.
I'M TONI.
I'M CAESAR.
YOU LIVE AROUND 'HERE?
NOPE. VISITIN' MY AUNT.
OH.
OH, HEY! GUESS WHAT.
I CAN SEE THE FUTURE.
FOR REAL?
YEP.
I'VE GOT A SOCCER GAME THIS WEEKEND.
WILL I WIN? HOW MANY GOALS WILL I SCORE?
IT DOESN'T WORK THAT WAY. I CAN'T SEE JUST ANYTHING.
ONLY SOME THINGS.
WELL, CAN YOU TELL ME SOMETHING ABOUT MY FUTURE?
YEAH, SURE.
BUT, UH, I HAVE TO BITE YOU.
BITE ME? I DON'T THINK I WANT YOU TO--
YOWWW!
CHOMP

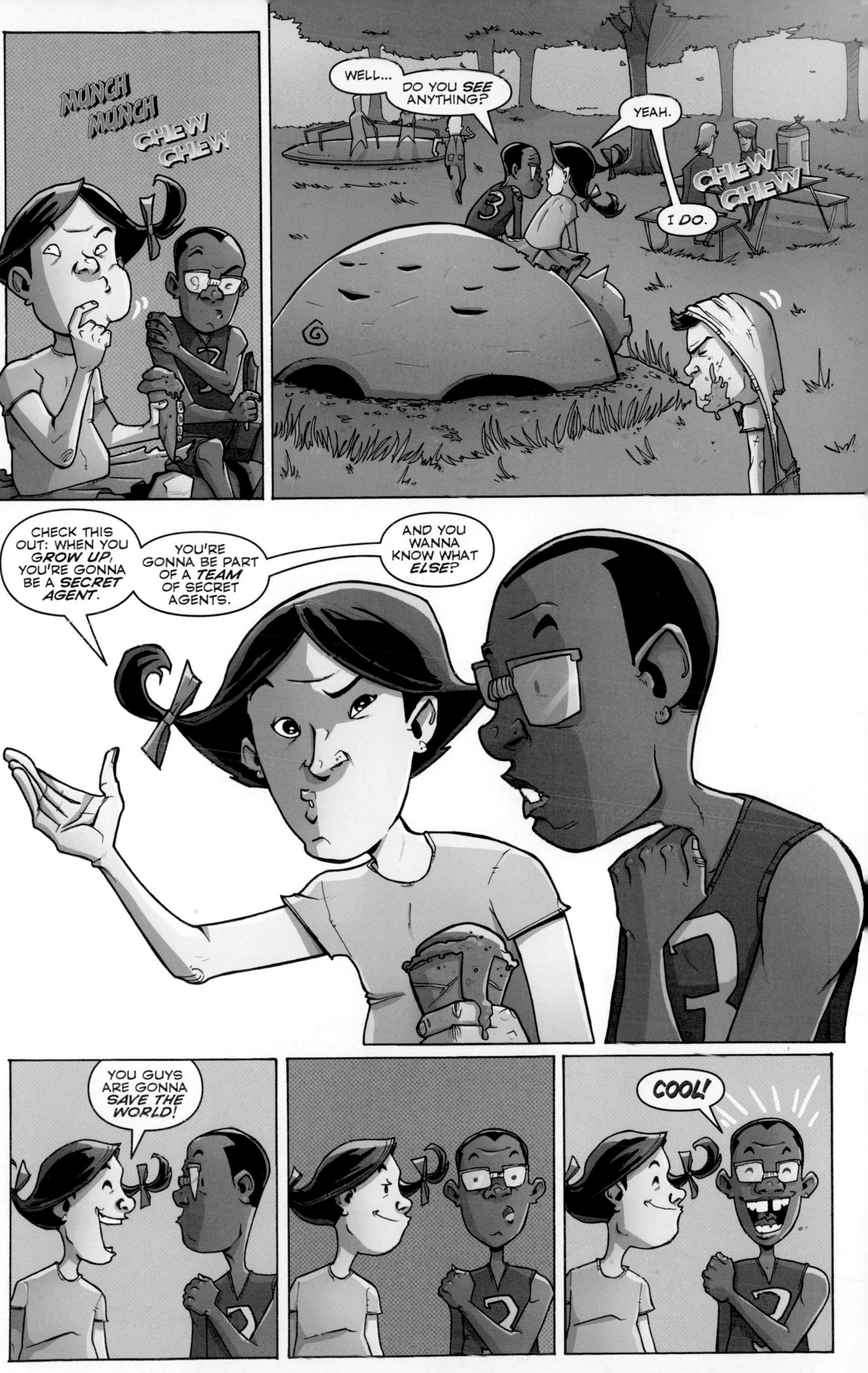
MUNCH MUNCH
CHEW CHEW
WELL...
DO YOU SEE ANYTHING?
YEAH.
I DO.
CHEW CHEW
CHECK THIS OUT: WHEN YOU GROW UP, YOU'RE GONNA BE A SECRET AGENT.
YOU'RE GONNA BE PART OF A TEAM OF SECRET AGENTS.
AND YOU WANNA KNOW WHAT ELSE?
YOU GUYS ARE GONNA SAVE THE WORLD!
COOL!

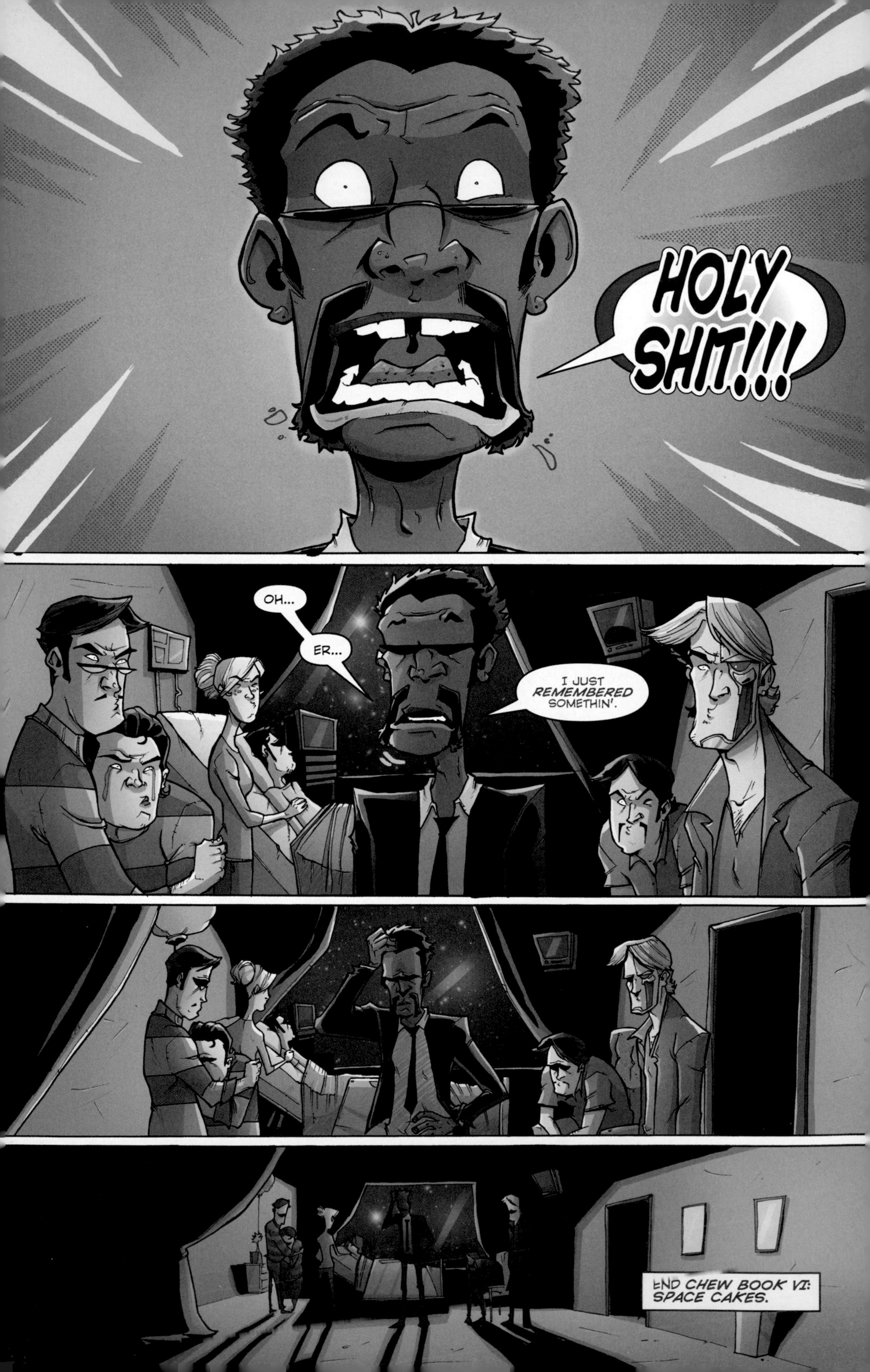
HOLY SHIT!!!
OH...
ER...
I JUST REMEMBERED SOMETHIN'.
END CHEW BOOK VI: SPACE CAKES.

GALLERY

JOE EISMA
supajoe.deviantart.com
AND
ALEX SOLLAZZO
alexsollazzo.deviantart.com

TONY FLEECS
fleecsdesign.com

GABO
@galvosaur

ZACH HOWARD

EMI LENOX
@emibot
emilenox.tumblr
EmiTown.com

JIM MAHFOOD
jimmahfood.com

JOHN McCREA
@mccreaman
AND
ANDREW ELDER

TONY PARKER
tonyparkerart.com
AND
ALLEN PASSALAQUA

NICK PITARRA
AND
FELIPE SOBREIRO

BEN TEMPLESMITH
templesmith.com

CHRIS GIARRUSSO

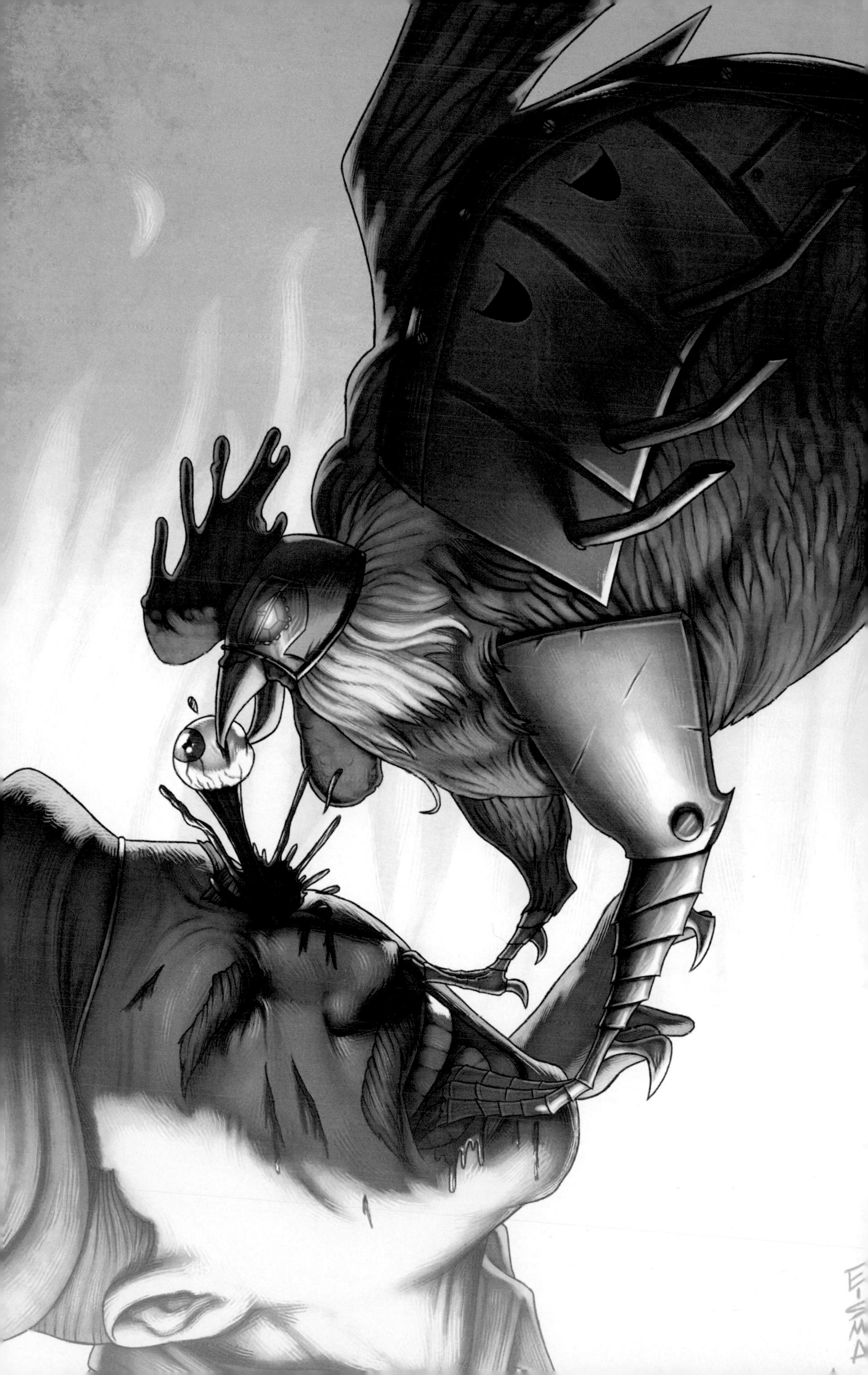

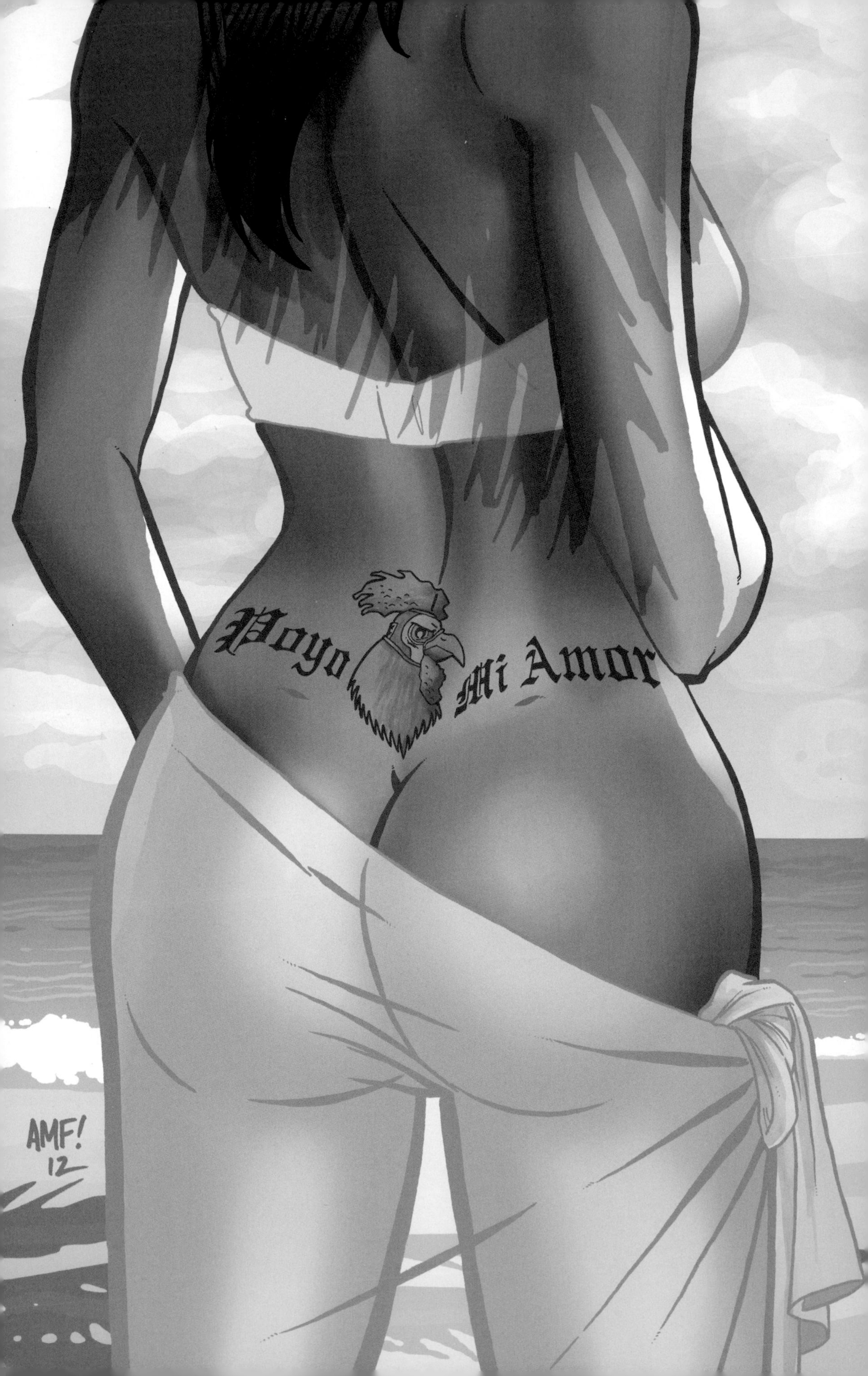
Poyo Mi Amor
AMF!
12

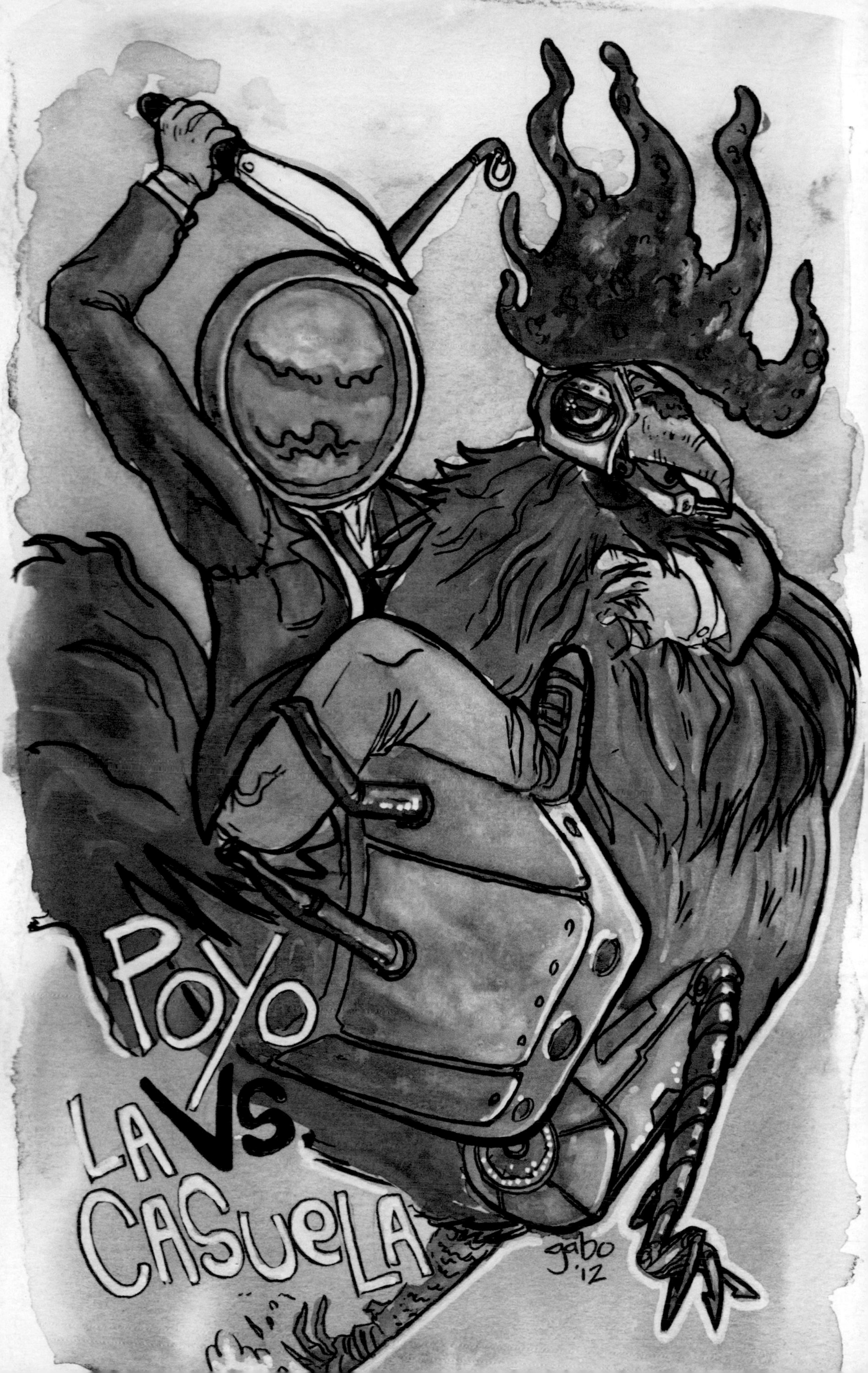
Poyo
vs.
LA
CASUELA
gabo '12

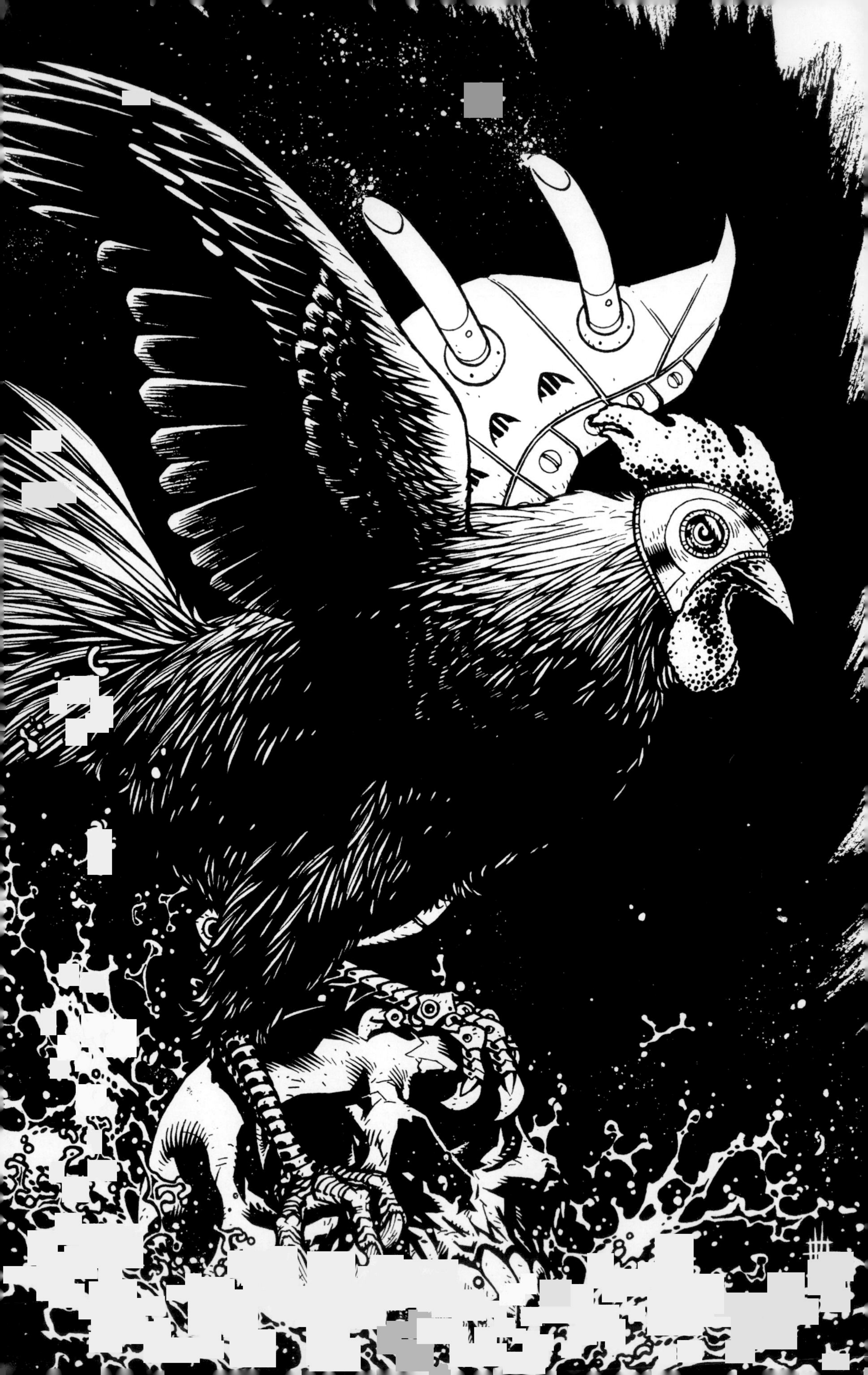

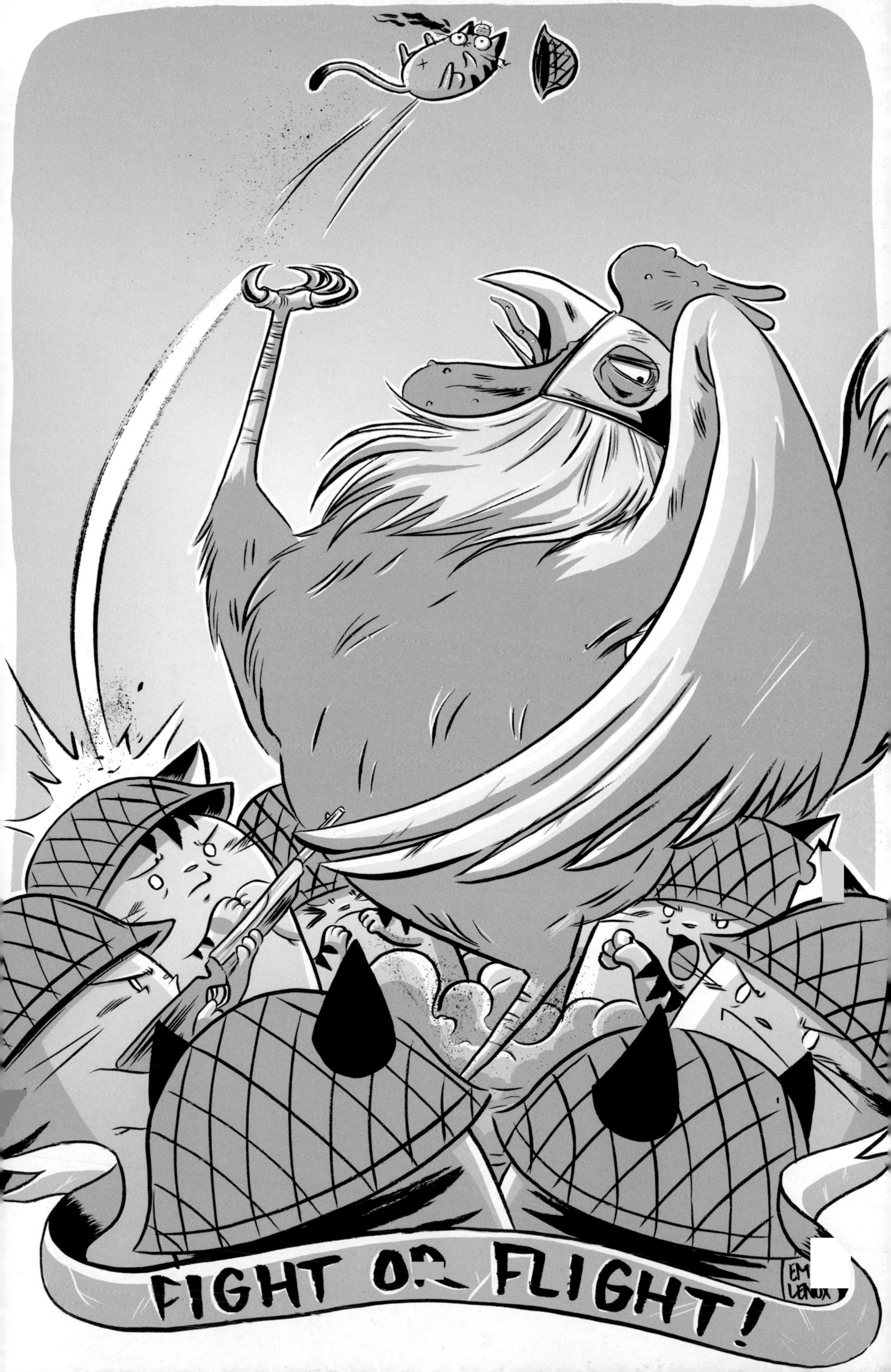
FIGHT OR FLIGHT!

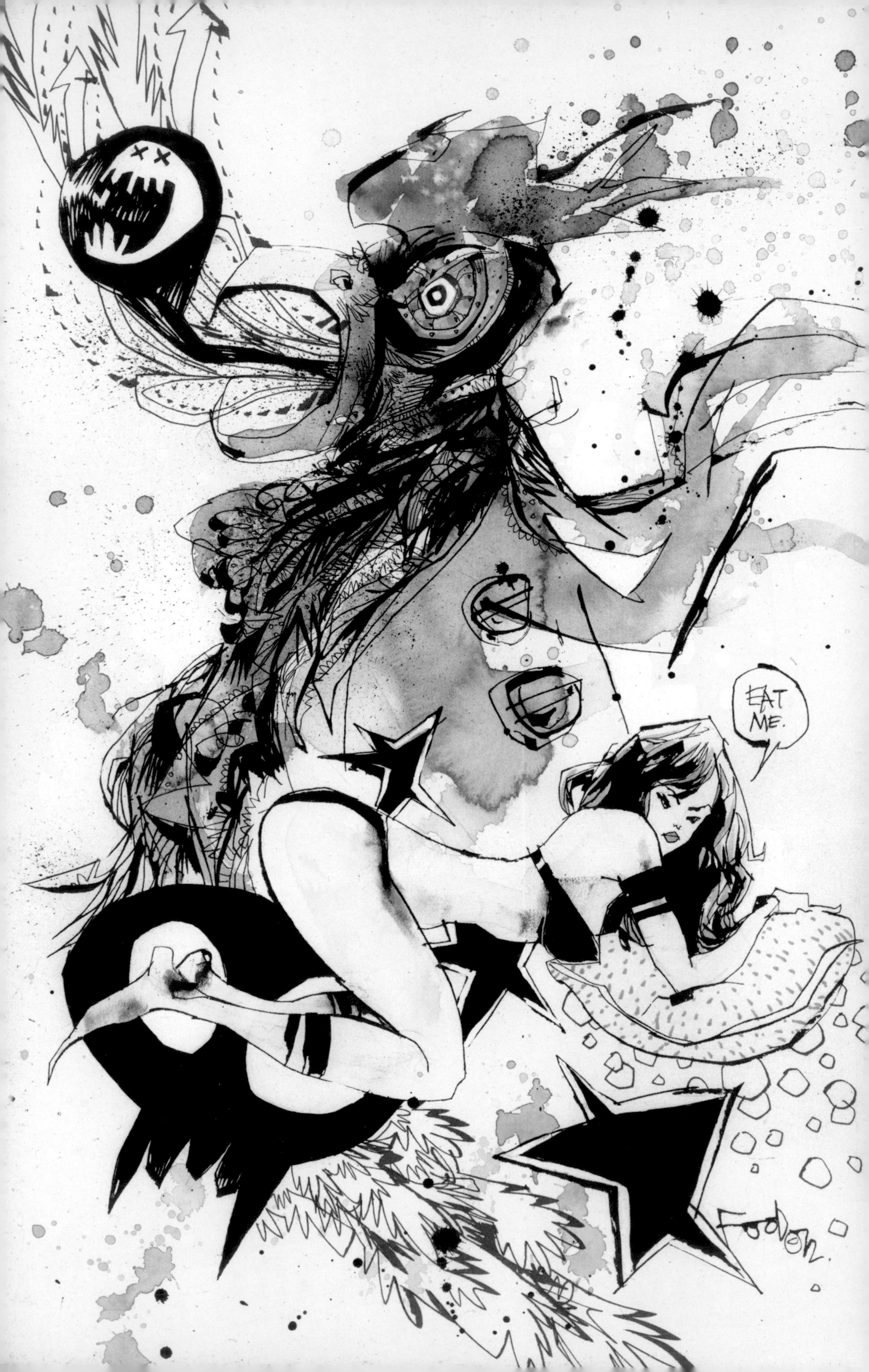
EAT ME.

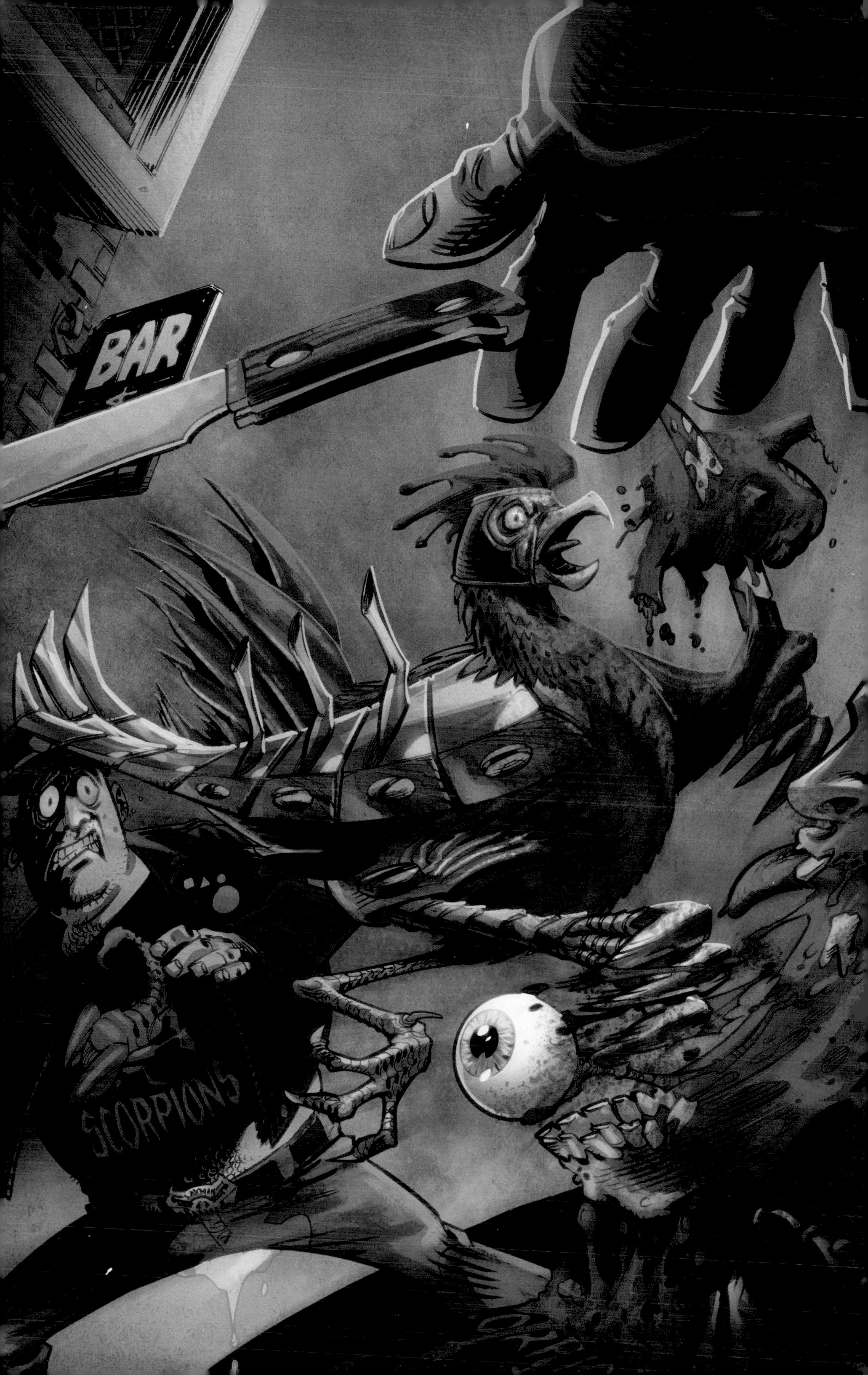
BAR
SCORPIONS

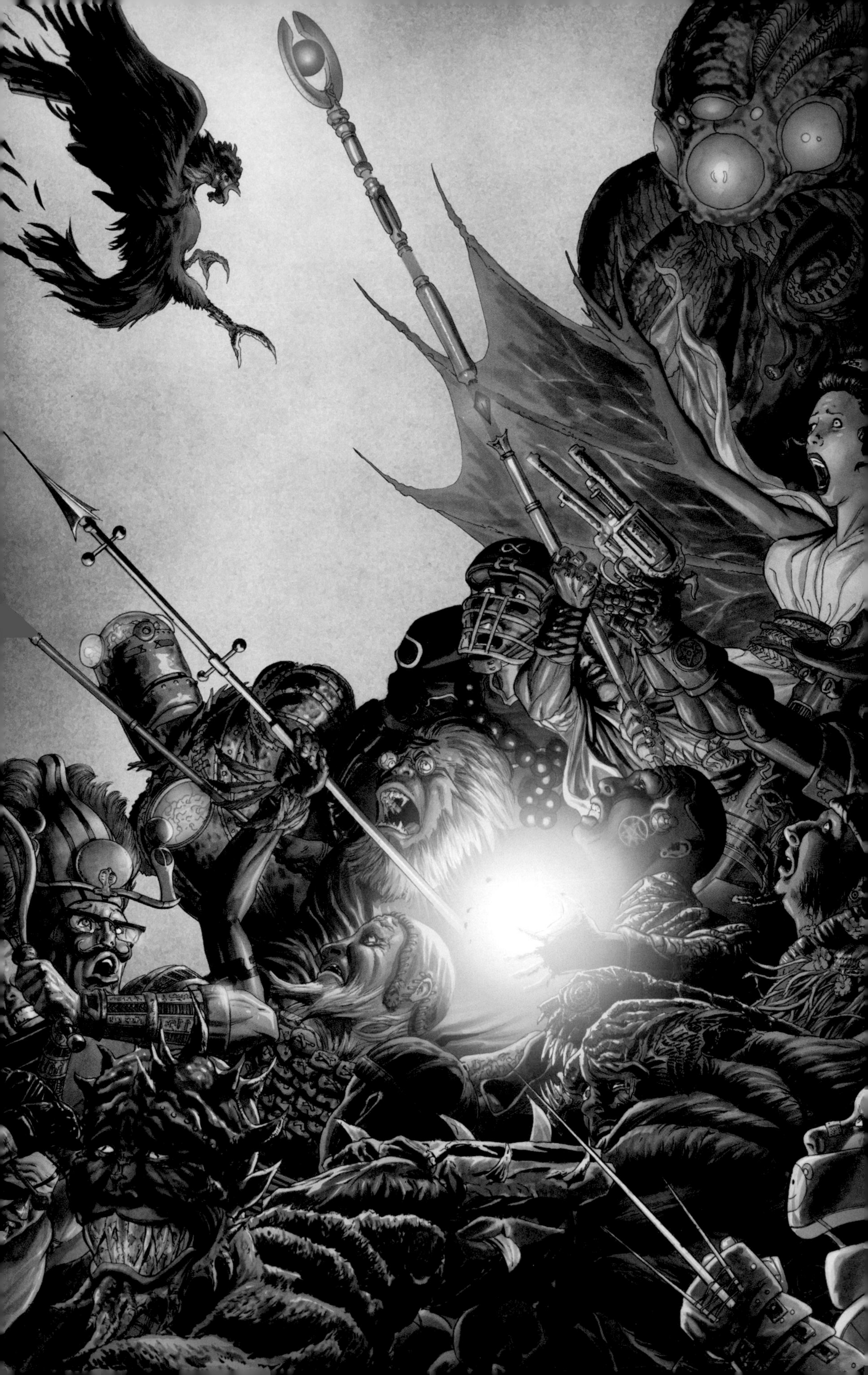

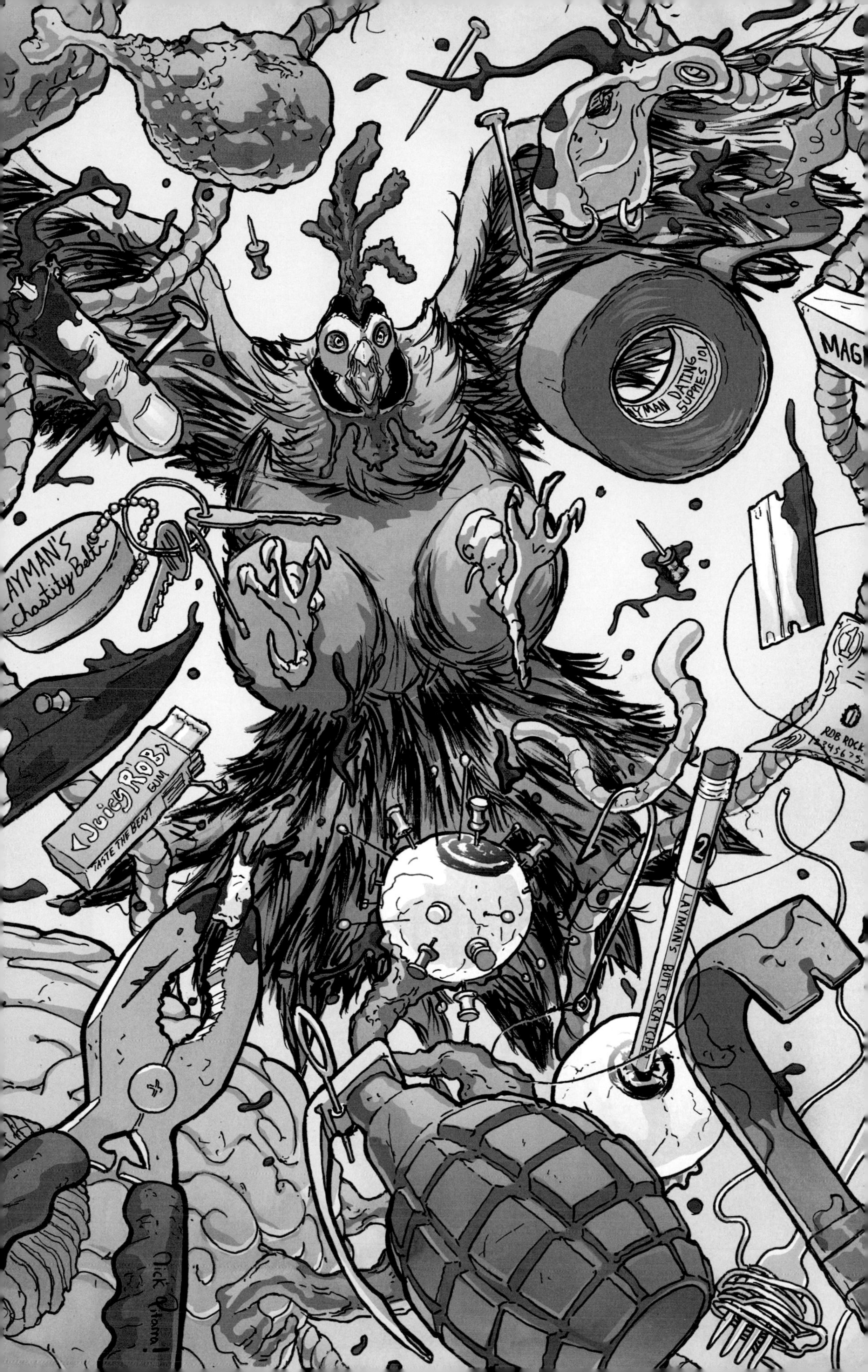
LAYMAN'S chastity Belt
Juicy ROB GUM
TASTE THE BEAST
LAYMAN'S BUTT SCRATCHER
ROB ROCK

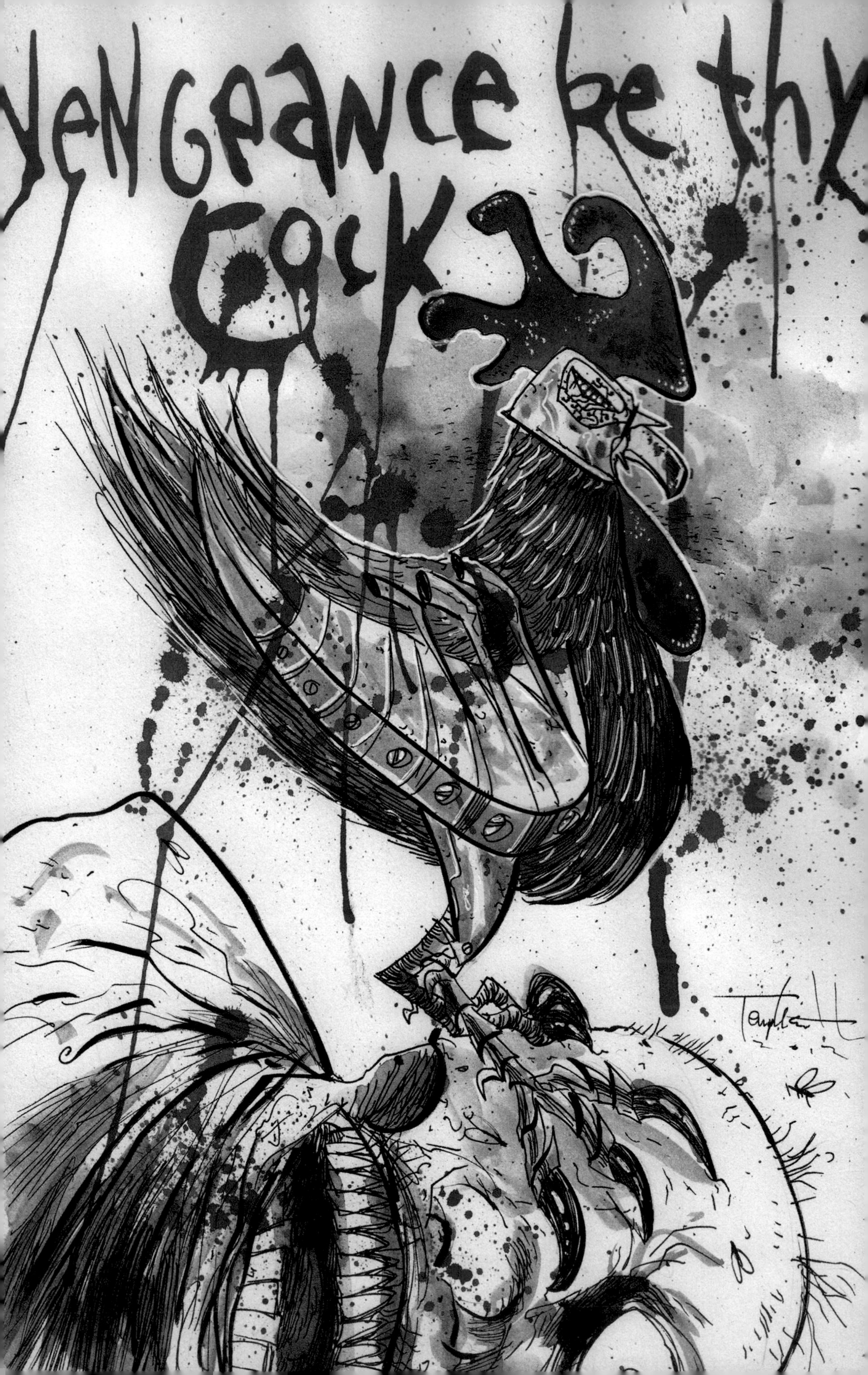
vengeance be thy
cock

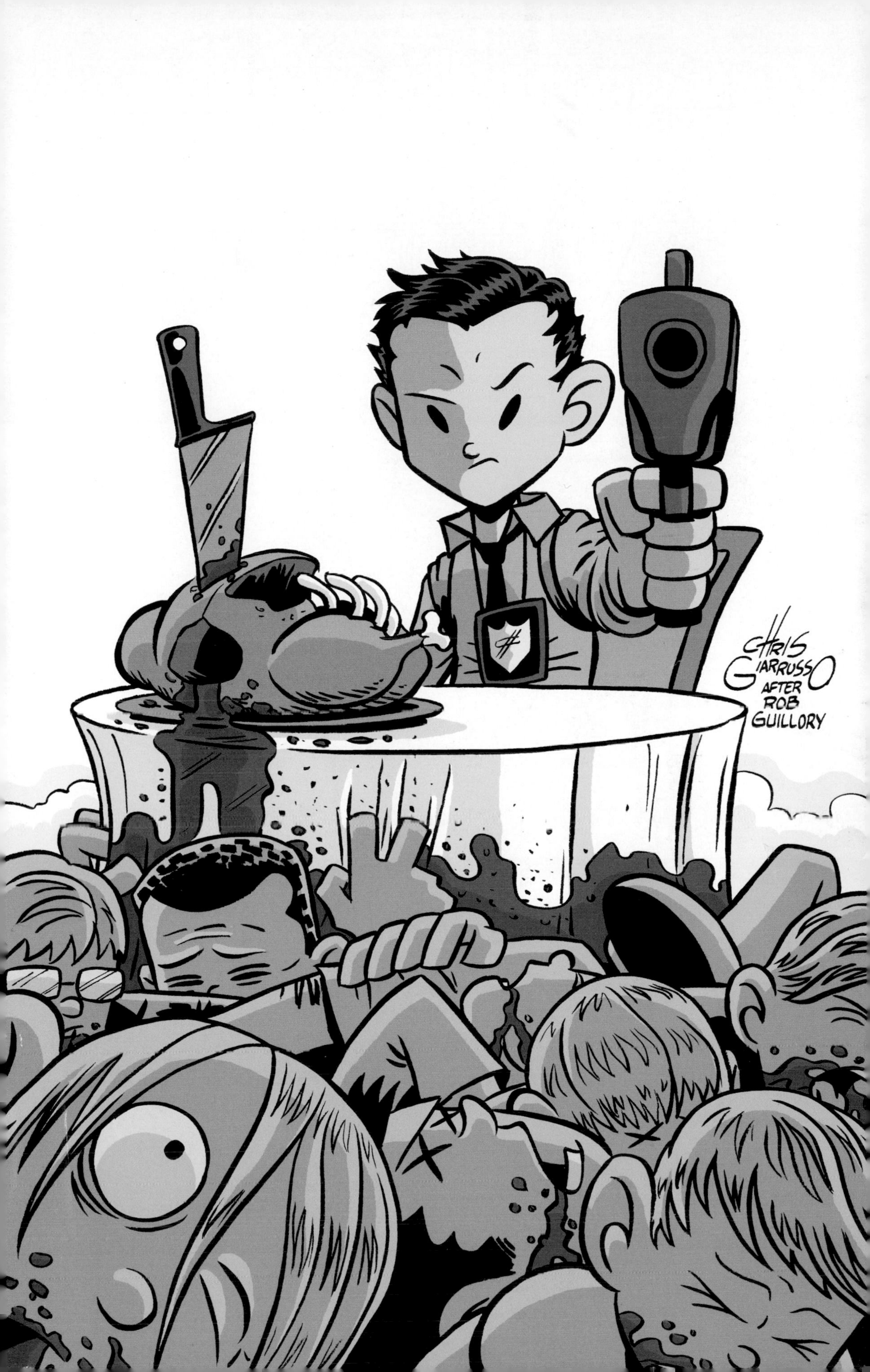
CHRIS GIARRUSSO
AFTER
ROB
GUILLORY

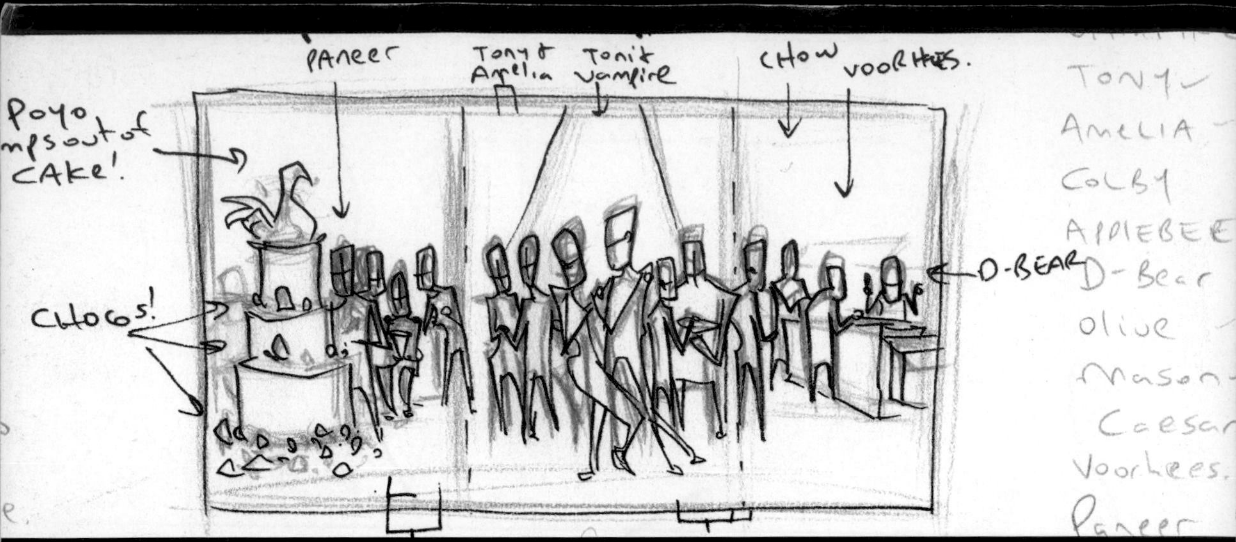
PANEER
Tony & Amelia
Tony & Vampire
CHOW
VOORHEES.
Poyo
mps out of
CAKE!
CHOCOS!
D-BEAR
TONY
AMELIA
COLBY
APPLEBEE
D-Bear
olive
Mason
Caesar
Voorhees.
Paneer

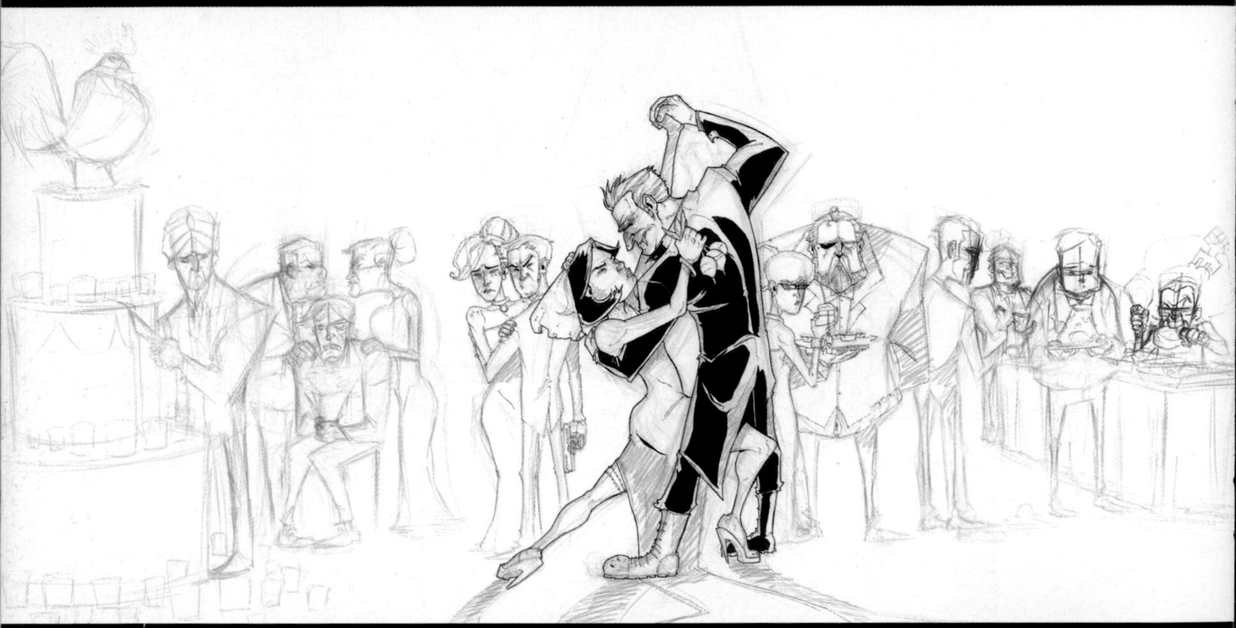

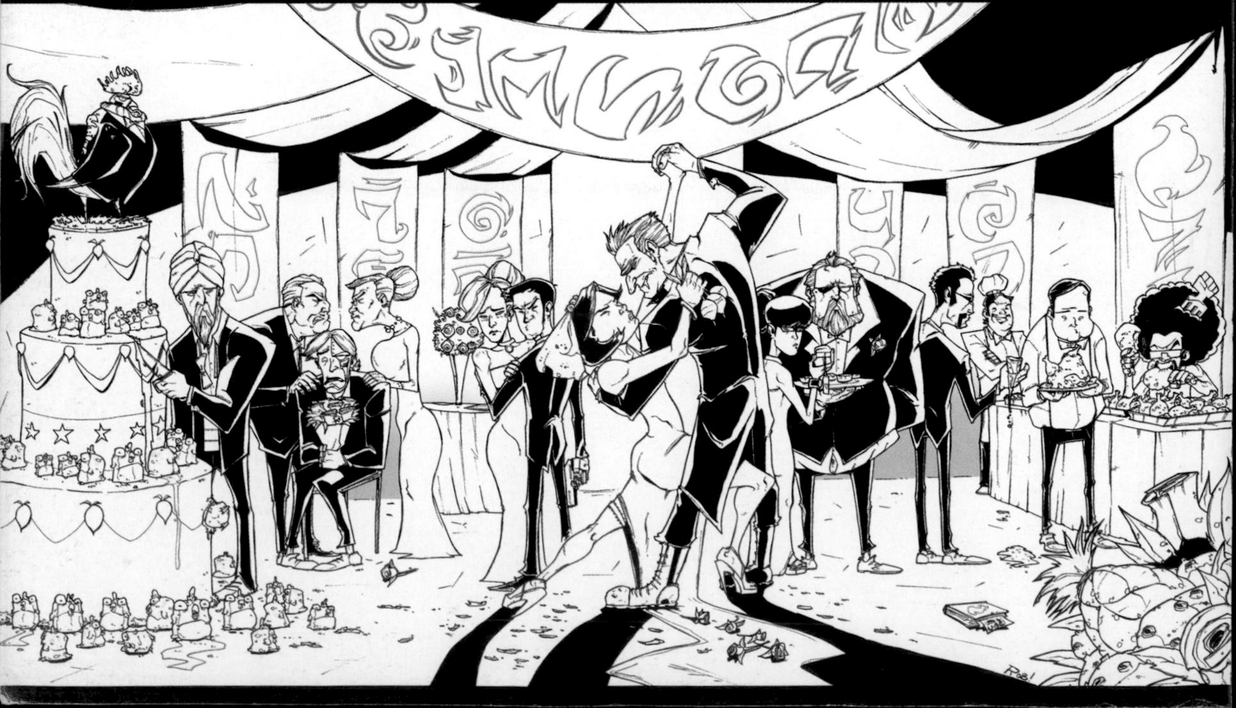

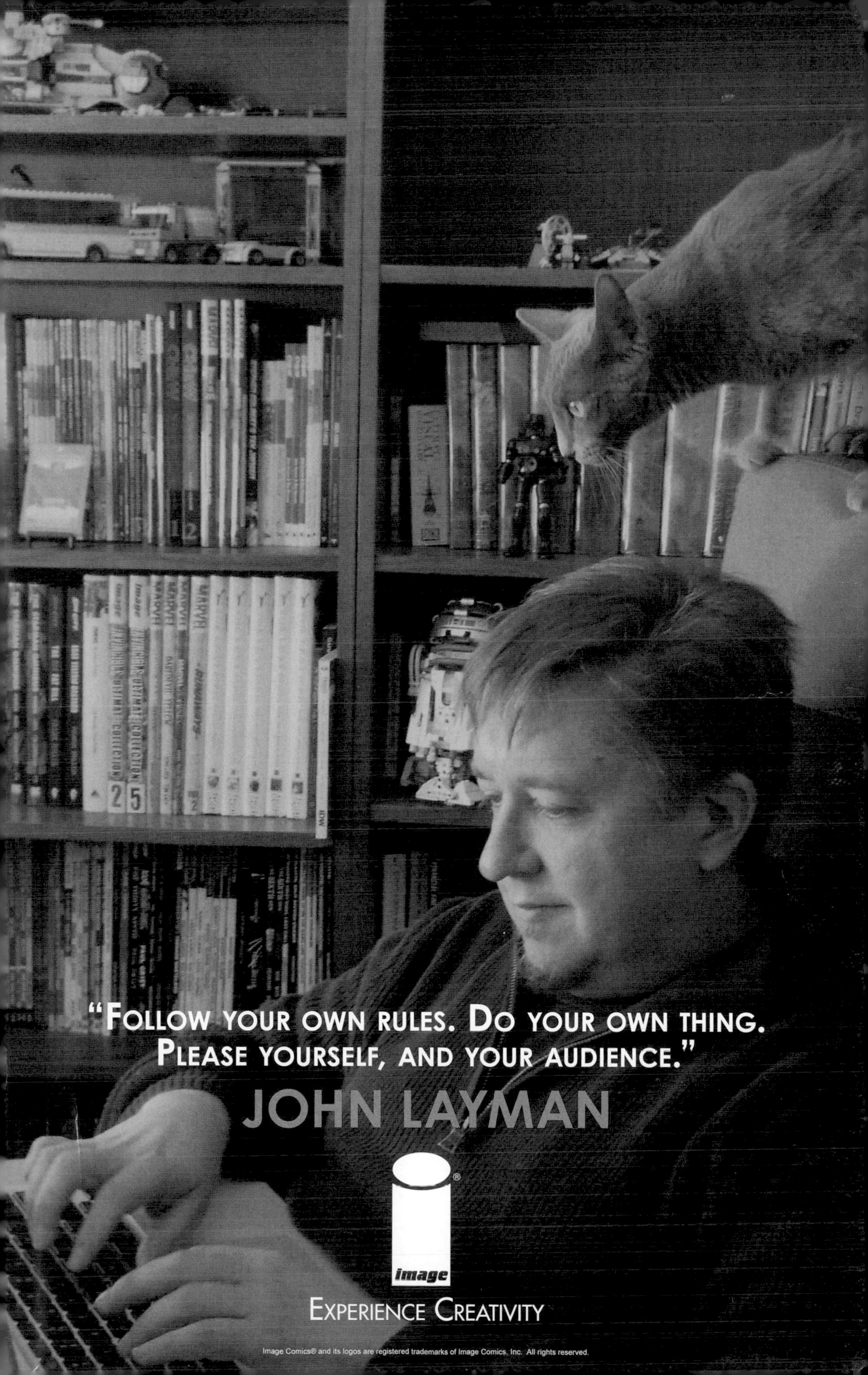
"Follow your own rules. Do your own thing. Please yourself, and your audience."
JOHN LAYMAN
image
Experience Creativity
Image Comics® and its logos are registered trademarks of Image Comics, Inc. All rights reserved.

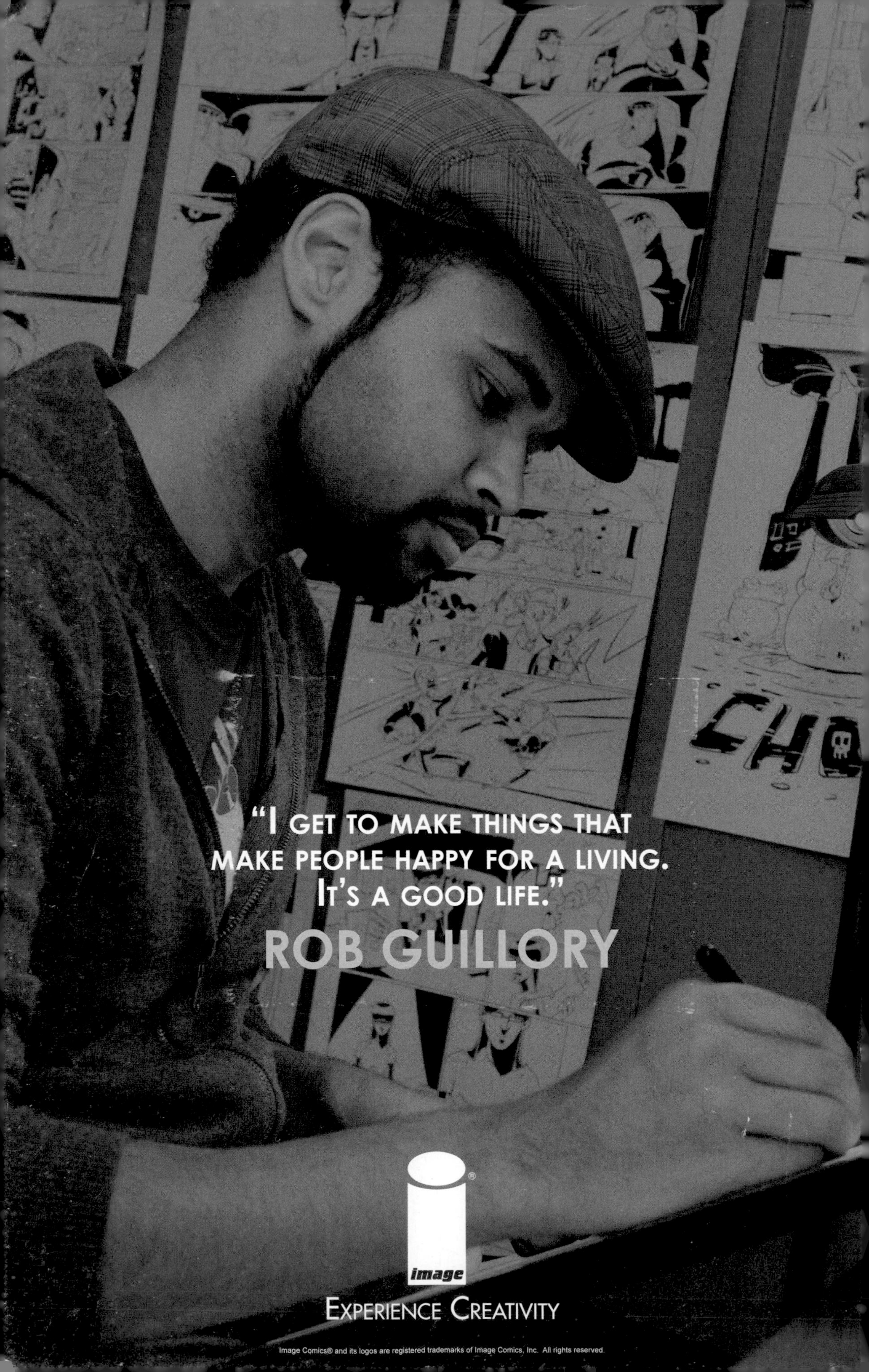
"I GET TO MAKE THINGS THAT
MAKE PEOPLE HAPPY FOR A LIVING.
IT'S A GOOD LIFE."
ROB GUILLORY
image
EXPERIENCE CREATIVITY